A
MATTER
of
GRAVE
CONCERN

ALSO BY BRENDA NOVAK

HISTORICAL ROMANCE

Of Noble Birth
Honor Bound (originally available as *The Bastard*)
Through the Smoke

CONTEMPORARY ROMANCE

Whiskey Creek Series: The Heart of Gold Country
When We Touch (prequel novella)
When Lightning Strikes
When Snow Falls
When Summer Comes
Home to Whiskey Creek
Take Me Home for Christmas
Come Home to Me
The Heart of Christmas

Dundee, Idaho Series
A Baby of Her Own
A Husband of Her Own
A Family of Her Own
A Home of Her Own
Stranger in Town
Big Girls Don't Cry
The Other Woman
Coulda Been a Cowboy

Sanctuary
Shooting the Moon
We Saw Mommy Kissing Santa Claus
Dear Maggie
Baby Business
Snow Baby
Expectations

A Matter

of

Grave
Concern

A NOVEL

BRENDA
NOVAK

NEW YORK TIMES BESTSELLING AUTHOR

Montlake
Romance

Text copyright © 2014 Brenda Novak

Published by Montlake Romance, Seattle

www.apub.com

Amazon, the Amazon logo, and Montlake Romance are trademarks of Amazon.com, Inc., or its affiliates.

ISBN-13: 9781477824528
ISBN-10: 1477824529

Cover design by Laura Klynstra

Library of Congress Control Number: 2014903995

Printed in the United States of America

To Kelli, my editor for this novel. When you told me that editing is one of the great loves of your life, it pulled me out of the "business as usual" mode (easy to fall into after 50 books) and reminded me of how passionately I feel about writing. What a gift that we both get to do what we love for a living. Thank you for that reminder and for all the hard work you put in on this story. Your unbridled enthusiasm made the process such a pleasure.

Chapter 1

It was a perfect specimen. Almost.

Abigail Hale took a steadying breath and stooped into the cool, dark alley to examine the bloodless gash on the cadaver's high forehead. The injury was a minor flaw, really. Nothing to worry about, although she intended to use that imperfection to best advantage when haggling over price.

Straightening, she opened the door wide and motioned the five figures surrounding the body inside. "Quickly!"

Three men followed as two, their features distorted by the flickering light of her lamp, hefted the sack containing the corpse into her father's office and dropped it with a thud as solid as though it contained nothing more than so many rocks.

Nervous about what she was going to do, and the risk she was taking in order to do it, Abigail squared her shoulders and crossed to the desk adjacent to her father's. Although she had dealt with resurrection men during the last school year, thrice, she had never done business with this particular gang. The sheer number of them took her off guard. Usually a couple of gravediggers or sextons showed up, regular men who didn't look nearly so unsavory.

Hoping to keep the "sack 'em up" men from seeing how badly her hands were shaking, she clasped them behind her back.

A behemoth of a man, marked with the smallpox and dressed all in black, stepped forward. "When I saw the name on your letter, I assumed we were dealin' with the good surgeon himself," he said with a thick Cockney accent. "So who the bloody hell are you?"

"*Who* I am doesn't matter so long as you get paid. Am I correct, Mr. . . . Hurtsill?" She was guessing at his name. This was the first time she had ever met him, but he had to be the man she had written. He seemed in charge and had referenced her letter.

"This is some risky business we've got going here, little lady. I have to trust you and you have to trust me. And that means who you are matters more than you might think."

Since he didn't correct her, she assumed she had accurately identified him. "Fine." She gestured as if to say she would agree to almost anything if it would expedite their meeting. "I am steward of the household accounts here, if you must know." She was also a would-be student and would one day become a great anatomist, like her father—if only she could overcome the bias against her gender. Her father kept telling her she should marry instead. But she could never be content to live the mundane life other women did.

He picked a piece of food out of his teeth. "The surgeon's daughter, eh?"

Apparently, he knew more about the school than she had expected. "Does your father know you're doin' this?" he asked.

If they didn't get on with it, he would find out. And she couldn't have that. "Time is money, Mr. Hurtsill. How—"

"Big Jack," he interrupted. "But you can call my brother, here, Mr. Hurtsill, if you like. I wager it'll make him feel quite important."

She didn't care to meet his brother or any of the other men who were lounging around her father's office. "I'm sorry?"

"Call me Big Jack."

Eager to get down to business, she focused strictly on him. He was intimidating enough. "Fine. Mr. . . . er . . . Jack, then. How much do you want for . . . um . . . ?" Abigail nodded toward the sack.

"The stiff?" A low, guttural laugh shook his belly, which rolled well over his belt. "No more'n our due, that's for sure. It ain't easy workin' the supply end these days, what with the number of friends and family posting watchmen to guard the graves of their dearly departed."

She grimaced at the sad picture *that* created. Just last January those appointed to protect the corpse of a man interred in a churchyard in Ireland were fired upon by the resurrection men they had been trying to ward off. "It's a miracle you manage it."

They had to be doing more than loitering about a likely graveyard. The resurrection men she had previously dealt with hadn't been able to get near a corpse in weeks. For the first time in its twenty-five-year history, the school had been forced to open without an anatomy specimen and enrollment was suffering because of it. Every student needed two full courses of anatomy, with dissection, to apply for a license from the Royal College of Surgeons.

Big Jack grinned, seemingly indifferent to her sarcasm. "We have our ways. And this is a damn fine stiff. Big, too. Ain't that so, boys?"

His men—some folding their arms as they looked on, others leaning against the furniture—grunted in agreement, but Abigail continued to anchor her attention on their leader. She didn't want to see the others standing around with dirt from their recent dig still clinging to their shoes and pant legs, didn't want to acknowledge how easily she could be overpowered. She had paid the other resurrection men nine or ten guineas, a few shillings more if the corpse was large and in good condition. Then she'd had them carry the deceased to the cellar on their way out, and that was that.

She hoped this transaction would go as smoothly, but . . . something didn't feel quite so routine. Thank heavens she'd had the good sense to secure Bransby, the college porter, behind the door with a firearm. She had taken the same precaution before, of course. Resurrection men were, generally speaking, a rather desperate and unpleasant lot—but, fortunately, she had never had to call out to Bran.

She prayed she would be able to say the same about tonight . . .

"Your price, sir?" She lifted her chin to suggest they get on with their business.

"Don't you want to see the rest of 'im before we start talkin' money?" he asked.

See the rest of the corpse? Absolutely not! It had been difficult enough peeking at the head. Viewing cadavers when they were properly laid out in a clinical atmosphere was somehow different. She could tolerate that. Anyone who wanted to be an anatomist couldn't faint at the sight of a dead body. But she couldn't face that sight now. What the sack contained was far too fresh. Someone's son, uncle or brother had died, and these men had stolen his corpse from what should have been its final resting place . . .

A necessary evil, she reminded herself, one of those rare instances where the end justified the means. The bodies of those condemned to execution and dissection, which was about the only legal way for a college to gain a specimen, could no longer fill the burgeoning demand, not with only fifty or so hanged in a year. The medical profession required several thousand.

"A more experienced buyer would want to see what he's gettin' for his money." Big Jack spread his hands. "But it's up to you, of course. I'm merely tryin' to be helpful."

Whatever he was doing, trying to be helpful played no part in it. Of that Abigail felt sure. She suspected he was having a bit of fun at her expense, taunting her in front of his men.

But he was right. She *should* take a closer look at what she was buying. Although she'd had great success with the three corpses she had purchased in the past, she'd heard stories about resurrection men selling bodies not quite dead or delivering cadavers too decomposed to do a college any good. She would be a fool to let Big Jack and his "London Supply Company" cheat her so easily.

Clearing her throat, she said, "All right. Show it to me."

He motioned to two others, who opened the sack. Then a swath of pale, white chest covered with dark hair caught the lamplight and

Abigail's eye at the same time, and she couldn't go through with it. She didn't want to see the shriveled private parts of the deceased with an all-male audience eagerly awaiting her reaction. Having never been with a man, she generally tried to look away from that area as it was.

"Wait!" She shouldn't have let Jack goad her into this. She knew the body would be naked. Stealing a corpse was a misdemeanor for which a resurrectionist might receive a public whipping. Technically, a corpse didn't belong to anyone. But taking so much as a sock defrauded the deceased's heirs, and *that* was punishable by hanging.

"I . . . er . . . on second thought, never mind. That won't be necessary." She pulled the mouth of the sack closed lest they ignore her. "You already informed me that it's a fine specimen, did you not? Is there any reason I should doubt your word?"

Big Jack nudged his neighbor, and they both chortled. "A might squeamish to be dealin' in such commodities, wouldn't you say, Miss Hale? But I'm good as my word. This bugger's got all his parts, even those what might interest a young woman like yourself."

"He's got his bloody roger, all right," one of the others called out with an appalling, hoot-like laugh. "You could fondle that if you want. But if it's a kiss you're after, you should know he's not got his teeth!"

Abigail's face burned with embarrassment as Jack winked at her. "Aye. My brother's right. He has everythin' 'cept his teeth. We sold those to a dentist not far away."

This was getting out of control. Abigail couldn't let it continue. "Fine, that's fine."

She didn't want to think about the forceful removal of the cadaver's teeth, the shroud that had been stripped from the body and shoved back into the grave, or her role in supporting a business that filled so many with anger and disgust. She wasn't any more pleased with the way the system worked than anyone else. They needed reform. Despite the public's abhorrence of the idea of allowing surgeons access to all the bodies that went unclaimed from the prisons and the workhouses, the government needed to make these bodies available. That would provide the specimens necessary to advance medical science and do away with this nasty black market. But even with Henry Warburton's Select Committee on Anatomy, formed in parliament two years ago to study the problem and suggest oversight and other regulation, change didn't seem to be coming—at least not very fast.

"Enough games," she said. "I am not amused. And my father won't be gone much longer."

Jack sobered but his expression grew smug. "So he doesn't know what you're up to, eh? I thought that might be the way of it." He dropped his voice, obviously intrigued. "Why are you meddlin' in his affairs?"

"This college cannot go on without subjects. I won't have my father's career ruined, the school closed simply because England cannot keep up with France and Italy and provide a proper supply of bodies for dissection. In case you haven't heard, my father is currently collaborating with Sir Astley Cooper!"

At this, Jack whistled. "He is, is he?"

She wasn't sure he was properly impressed, but she knew he should be. "Yes. They are writing a treatise on the thymus gland."

He scraped dirt out from under one of his fingernails. "Your father runs in high circles, all right. Must feel good, given that surgeons aren't considered much better than resurrection men."

"Not everyone feels that way," she snapped.

"Plenty of those who matter. It's not like you'd ever be considered on par with the bloody aristocracy. Anyway, hobnobbin' with the likes of Astley also makes it a bit messy to run afoul of the law. Is that why you're doin' your father's dirty work for him?"

Of course. Although her father wouldn't want *her* to be the one arranging for the specimens he so desperately needed, *someone* had to do it. So far, no one else had stepped up.

"The dead are dead, sir. Why let their bodies rot, to the betterment of no one?" She came off much stronger than she felt in her heart. She was as sensitive to the humanity of the dead as anyone, but it wasn't as if her father could continue to learn by dissecting dogs and other animals, as anatomists of centuries past had. He'd said himself that doing so was almost useless. And if she wanted to follow in his footsteps, she needed to push for progress, overcome the obstacles in her path.

"Well, your secret's safe with us, luv." Jack advanced on her. "A pretty thing like you could ask just about anythin' from Old Jack. For a quarter hour of your time, I'd even be willin' to give you a deep discount on our latest prize here." He reached out to finger the fabric of her sleeve while indicating the cadaver with a jerk of his head. "We could make it a weekly trade, if you like."

When Abigail stepped away, his companions snickered. These men were definitely worse than any resurrectionists she'd met before. Although none of those previous examples had been exemplary citizens, they hadn't dared show her such disrespect.

"What's wrong?" Big Jack's meaty face creased into a dark scowl. "You too high and mighty for the likes of a workin' man like me? And you, nothing better than a surgeon's daughter?"

Maybe she was only a surgeon's daughter, and therefore denigrated along with the rest of the medical community. But her father was head surgeon here at the college and had prospects many of the others didn't.

Regardless, she wasn't willing to let Big Jack paw her in order to get the college the specimens it needed. Cooking the books would be bad enough.

Eager to consummate the deal and dispense with the whole distasteful transaction, she didn't bother responding to the question. "I will give you six guineas."

The mention of money seemed to mollify him, at least a little. "We'll not settle for less than ten—"

"Make that fifteen." A deep voice interrupted, and for the first time, Abigail looked directly at the man standing to the side and slightly behind Big Jack. His clothes bore as much dirt and his face as much beard growth as the rest of the group, but he was different. Not only was he significantly taller, he carried himself with a certain . . . authority.

How had she not noticed him before?

She'd been doing her best to block him and the others from her consciousness, she reminded herself.

Her gaze locked with an intense pair of sea-green eyes. "Why, that's highway robbery! My father has never paid a resurrectionist more than nine guineas, six shillings. I've got it all in a book, right here." She tapped the top of the desk to convince him.

When he smiled, his teeth looked clean and mostly straight, another detail that set him apart from his companions. "Evidently, you're not a pupil of economics, or not a very good one, Miss Hale. Short supply, high demand, prices go up. Sometimes significantly. Fifteen guineas. No less."

Those short, clipped sentences bore no Cockney accent and revealed a definite culture to his voice, causing Abigail to wonder if she had been dealing with the wrong man all along. She couldn't imagine this stranger taking orders from anyone, much less the likes of Jack Hurtsill.

"Blimey, Max," one of the other men muttered.

Drawing herself up to her fullest height, which was at least ten inches shy of this Max's six feet something, Abigail clung tenaciously to her composure. "At this point, I would rather you take your 'large' and go." Surely, there had to be other resurrection men she could contact; she hadn't gone through *all* the names she heard muttered about the halls of the college and St. Bart's Hospital next door. "I have seen naught but the head, and that small sample revealed a nasty wound."

"There's not a mark on the rest of him," Max responded coolly. "We offered to show you, but you refused."

Abigail had no intention of letting this body snatcher tempt her into dumping the body out onto the rug as she had almost let them do before. "Mr. Hurtsill—I mean, Big Jack, here, was about to say ten guineas. I will go that high."

"I'm afraid it's not high enough," Max countered.

"You're a fast study, mate." Jack slapped him on the back but didn't interfere. Instead, he turned a challenging smile on Abigail and waited for her response.

"Then go," she said, shooing them away. "Take Mr. Whoever He Is and leave. I will not let you rob me. Not if I can help it."

"And what if you can't?" Insolence lit the eyes of the man identified as Max. "Perhaps we should wait here for your father. No doubt he will have better sense of what a corpse is worth at the present time, although I doubt he would want us loitering about the place. What's it been . . . eighteen months or so since those two surgeons were prosecuted for receiving and dissecting stolen bodies? With a possible knighthood on the horizon, and such a close tie to Sir Astley Cooper—the sergeant-surgeon of the late king himself, no less—it would be quite unfortunate if your father were to be found dealing with the likes of us, wouldn't you say?"

Abigail's jaw dropped at the not-so-subtle threat. These were not learned men but, evidently, they had heard of her father's many accomplishments even before she had mentioned his involvement with Cooper. She hadn't said a thing about the crown's probable recognition.

Perhaps she had underestimated these sack 'em up men. *This* man, anyway. "If what you have brought is worth so much Mr. . . . Max, is it?"

He gave her a mocking bow and added his last name, as if to prove he feared nothing from her. "Wilder. Maximillian Wilder, at your service, Miss."

"Mr. Wilder, then. Take it elsewhere to claim your fifteen guineas. Take it to Guy's or . . . or the Webb Street School!"

His chin rasped as he rubbed it. "We could do that, Miss Hale. But you said yourself that time is money, and we don't have all night. You wrote us to request an adult specimen and we brought a large. Now it's time to pay up."

"And if I send someone for the police instead?"

He clucked his tongue. "You don't want to do that."

"Why not?"

Three long strides brought him to the edge of her desk, where he toyed with the ivory elephant her mother had bestowed on her following their last trip to India, only two months before she died. "It's too risky," he said.

Abigail plucked the elephant from his grasp. She wasn't sure she could rely on the new police, anyway. Sir Robert Peel had only recently established the metropolitan force. Like many others, she regarded it with a certain amount of skepticism. "It's the sensible thing to do," she said. "After how you have behaved, I am not opposed to seeing the five of you spend considerable time in gaol." Hoping the weight of her own threat would give him and his companions reason to squirm, she smiled, but Maximillian Wilder merely shrugged.

"You do what you feel you must, Miss Hale, but you should be aware that Bill over there has a wife and children. You will not want his dependents looking to the college for support while he is imprisoned, now would you?"

"Looking to the college for support?" she echoed. "Why, you have some nerve, sir. Perhaps there have been faculty members blackmailed into such an arrangement in the past, but don't expect *me* to be so accommodating. I wouldn't allow you to—"

"I recently heard of an anatomy teacher at Great Marlborough Street School of Anatomy who refused to pay a fair price to men such as ourselves," he interrupted, turning casually to one of his cohorts. "Did you hear about that, Emmett?"

A man with shaggy blond hair, who looked more like a boy, nodded. "Aye. He found a stinkin' corpse at each end of his street every day for more'n a week as retribution. 'Twas a shame, really. Terribly bad for business. That's what I heard."

Impotent rage warmed Abigail's blood as the import of their words struck her. For a brief moment, she flirted with the temptation of calling Bransby in to force them out at gunpoint. She even imagined handling the pistol herself, pressing the barrel of it into the solid chest of the man named Wilder and watching his arrogance crumble into fear.

But Bransby couldn't shoot them all. Truth be told, he would be hard-pressed to shoot *one*. And she sensed this Max made no idle threat when he hinted at how the gang would respond should she put up a fight. She couldn't risk the public uproar of having some stranger stumble upon a rotting carcass outside the college doors. Not only would her father lose any chance of a knighthood, he would be prosecuted like those other poor surgeons.

Clenching her teeth, she reined in her temper. "I see your point." She retrieved a purple pouch from her desk and began counting out the necessary remuneration. "Eleven, twelve, thirteen . . . Here we have it. Fifteen guineas. Take it and go."

Max looked at the money but made no move to accept it. "Actually, your haughty attitude should cost you a little more. That was entirely too easy."

"*Easy?*" She would have had to alter the books just to hide the loss of the eight or nine guineas she had been planning to pay. She had no idea how she would cover any more.

"I think perhaps . . . twenty guineas should relieve your debt," he said.

Someone coughed and the men began to murmur amongst themselves.

Abigail curled the nails of her free hand into her palm. "Twenty, indeed! You great lout—"

The rest of her words stuck in her throat as Maximillian's dirty hand shot across the desk and caught her own, sandwiching the money in her fist.

"You have already run up a *sizable* bill, Miss Hale. Are you sure you can afford to make me angry?" He quirked an eyebrow at her, and Abigail once again noticed his striking, blue-green eyes. An aquiline nose, high cheekbones and a strong jaw combined to create an arresting face, not quite handsome but striking. His features were too stark to be handsome in the conventional sense, although they were certainly . . . memorable.

"Come on, fifteen's well an' good, Max." The way Jack shifted on his feet made him appear anxious. "She is the surgeon's daughter, after all. And he bein' a friend of Cooper's, a fair deal's good for business, eh?"

Much to Abigail's dismay, Max ignored his leader, if Jack really was the leader, and continued to glare at her. "You have gotten involved in something you are incapable of navigating," he continued, his voice softening just enough to make him sound as if he might be addressing a child. "I suggest you let this go, and take it as a well-deserved lesson."

His fingers tightened, but Abigail refused to admit that his grip was beginning to hurt. "You are every bit a louse," she said, "and I think we both know I could call you much worse."

His laugh, deep and rich, seemed to flow out of his mouth as naturally as his threats. "Perhaps," he agreed, and wrested the money from her grasp.

Without those funds, Abigail couldn't continue to stock the kitchen with foodstuffs, purchase candles and coal, or pay the help. Desperate to salvage what she could, she grabbed for the pouch, but Max used his height to keep it well out of reach.

"There is far more in there than what you have demanded!" she cried.

Jack was no longer laughing. "How much more?"

"Two or three times as much!" She didn't know, exactly. She hadn't bothered to count it. She had been too confident that she had all contingencies covered, with Bran and that firearm in the hallway. She had also been preoccupied with making sure her actions went beneath the notice of the college housekeeper, who would tell her father exactly what was going on if she found out.

"I'm depending on it," Wilder said.

"But—"

"I doubt you can spare any more coin," he broke in, "so I suggest you cease flinging insults, while you still have the dress on your back." His meaningful grin sent fear of another kind coursing through her. It was that look, and the sure knowledge that she could never overpower him, that stopped her from rounding her desk.

She glanced at the door that hid Bransby, even opened her mouth to call out to him. But Wilder silenced her with a quick shake of his head.

"I wouldn't, Miss Hale," he said. "Whoever you have tucked in that hall probably doesn't have the nerve he would need, and your pride is hardly worth his life."

"My *pride*? That money belongs to the school—"

"Also far less of a consideration, I'm sure."

Never had Abigail wanted to strike a leveling blow at anyone more. The arrogance of this body snatcher! His blatant greed! Since his intervention, she had lost the small amount of power she had initially possessed, and he had laughed in her face while stripping it from her. None of last year's encounters had prepared her for this. She had felt so confident coming into this deal—confident enough to carry her entire purse.

She sorely regretted that now. "You know me well enough that you can predict my next move, Mr. Wilder?"

"I could always know you better."

A half smile curved lips that looked soft and foreign to the hard planes and angles of his face. His eyes darkened to a glittering blue and appraised her with such boldness that Abigail folded her arms across her breasts in a rather primitive move to defend herself against his piercing gaze. Dear God . . . what had she done?

"Please, don't go!" she whispered. "Let's . . . let's work out some sort of . . . arrangement." Her father was due to arrive home at any moment, but she had to detain these men, regardless. "You will get no more business from me if you do this. Wouldn't it be . . . wouldn't it be preferable to . . . to agree to an ongoing contract? Other gangs have offered to do that with my father, with . . . with start-up money for . . . for all the bribes you must pay and . . . and finishing money when the school year is over. If you give me back my purse, I could possibly . . . get more for you later."

"You mean you will turn us in," Wilder said. "But remember, we have your letter, which we can show, if necessary. And now, we really should be going."

"No!" She grabbed hold of him, but he easily shook her off and followed the others outside.

Tears burned the backs of her eyes. "That's it?" she cried. "That's all?"

"That's all," Wilder repeated.

Abigail gripped the doorframe so she wouldn't launch herself at him in a fit of temper. "I hope one day you and I will meet again, Mr. Wilder, under very different circumstances."

His smile broadened as his gaze settled on her mouth. "Is that an invitation, Miss Hale? Because meeting you, under any circumstances, would be my pleasure. There is much I would like to teach you yet."

"You have already taught me a great deal, sir. Rest assured, I will never call upon you again."

Max threw the pouch in the air and caught it with a jingle. "More's the pity, pretty lady. More's the pity." He tilted his head toward the sack they had left in the middle of the floor. "Enjoy your time alone together, and give my regards to your father," he said. Then he followed Jack and the others down the alley, but his voice, raised in recital, carried back to her:

"Bury me in my brother's church,
For that will safer be,
And I implore, lock the church door,
And pray take care of the key."

Chapter 2

When silence descended, Abigail locked the door, stumbled to her chair and, completely shaken, sank into its firm, tufted leather. What was she going to do? All the scenarios she had played out in her mind, for days, had done nothing to prepare her for the London Supply Company. Maybe Jack and the others were men she could have negotiated with. They would have taken her for nine or ten guineas. But Maximillian Wilder was something else entirely. He had managed to bilk her out of a fortune! And it wasn't her money, which made it that much worse.

Not only would she have to figure out a way to hide the loss, she would have to come up with what the college needed as far as supplies—

"Miss Hale?" Bransby poked his head inside the room. "Are you all right, Miss?"

Flushing at the reminder that she'd had a witness to her humiliation, Abigail shoved back the stray wisps of hair that had fallen from her practical topknot. It had been a long, difficult day; even her hair wouldn't cooperate. "I'm fine," she said, struggling to keep her voice from cracking.

He eyed the sack with the body but kept his distance. "Will there be anything else you'll be needing?"

Abigail shook her head, as eager to release him from further duty as he was to go. "Seek your bed, Bran. I am sorry I kept you up so late."

"Yes, Miss. And where would you like me to put this?" He held the pistol she had given him pinched between two fingers, like a baby's soiled wrappings. The metal barrel glinted in the lamplight below his aging, narrow face.

How she wished she'd had the nerve to call him in! But as impulsive as she could be—always her father's greatest lament—Wilder had been right. She and Bran would have been too easily overpowered. A woman and an old man taking on five body snatchers was not an option.

"Hand it to me," she said. "It goes in the bottom drawer of my father's desk."

The taciturn servant gave the corpse a wide berth, and came to set the pistol in front of her. "Good night, Miss," he said with a slight bow.

"Good night, Bransby."

He shuffled across the carpet to double-check that she had locked the door leading to the alley. Then he made another big arc around the body, and soon she was alone. Or almost alone. She stared, heartsick, at the sack the resurrection men had brought. She had acquired a damned expensive cadaver. How would she ever cover the expense?

She had no answers. Nor did she have time to sit around, stewing over the problem. She had to do something with her prize, or her father would arrive and the corpse would still be in his office.

After putting the pistol back in his drawer, she hurried to the door through which Bransby had left and called after him. At first, she wasn't sure her whisper had carried as far as his stooped, retreating figure. But then he stopped and turned.

"Yes, Miss?"

She waved him back, waiting to speak until they were safely ensconced in the office once again. The housekeeper, Mrs. Fitzgerald, had a light burning down the hall. The last thing Abigail needed was to rouse her. "I don't know what I was thinking, Bran. I need your help to move the body."

His eyebrows shot up. "Around to the *cellar*, Miss? I don't think you and I could carry it so far."

He was right. That was why she usually had the resurrectionists do it; most arrived with a cart. And this was a particularly big corpse, which meant it would be heavier than usual.

"Just into the operating theatre, then," she said. "We will let Mr. Holthouse or whoever is lecturing tomorrow discover it in the morning."

The porter's already ashen face turned a shade paler than moonlight. "You're going to . . . to *leave* it there, Miss?"

"Why not?"

"The maids will discover it first. You will frighten them to death!"

"Fine, we will put it in the large hamper I have been using to save cast-off clothing for the rag-and-bone man. Run and grab it from the attic."

"Yes, mum."

She frowned at the filthy sack while she waited and was relieved when he returned right away. "You didn't see Mrs. Fitzgerald?"

"She is snoring with her chin on her chest and her needlework in her lap."

"Good." Their work was almost done. Once one of the faculty took charge of the cadaver, he would pack it in salt to preserve it for as long as possible. Even with salt, most of its parts wouldn't last more than a couple of months. And then she would be faced with the daunting task of purchasing *another* cadaver.

But not from the London Supply Company. She would steer clear of them at all costs.

"Won't your father and the others wonder how a body got in the rag hamper?" Bransby asked.

"They might wonder, but I doubt they will seek the answer with any diligence. They never said a word about the three I put in the cellar last year, did they?"

"I wouldn't know, miss."

"I'm telling you they didn't. There are four anatomists at this school, every one of them in desperate need of a specimen. They will each assume it was one of the others and be grateful. In any case, being a woman and my father's daughter, I am the last person anyone would suspect."

"Evidently they don't know you the way I do."

Hearing his sarcasm, Abigail nudged him. "Few people know me as well as you do," she said. "So come on. This should only take a minute, but it will be heavy."

Reluctantly, Bransby situated himself beside her and they each took hold of the sack.

"On the count of three," Abigail said, ignoring his pained expression. "One, two, *three*." By some miracle, they managed to heave the corpse into the hamper, but just as they lifted that, her father's voice sounded outside in the corridor.

"How nice of you to wait up for me, Mrs. Fitzgerald."

With a worried mewl, Bransby nearly let go. Only a fierce scowl from Abigail kept him on task. "Steady," she advised as they staggered toward their goal.

"I wait up for you every time you go out, Mr. Hale." Mrs. Fitzgerald seemed to be following him down the hall. "You should be used to it by now. I can't sleep till you're safe in bed; that's a fact. Shall I make some tea?"

"Take the tea," Abigail muttered. Exhausted, she and Bransby were forced to lower the hamper. They could no longer carry it, but they couldn't leave it where it was, either. So they started bumping it and scooting it across the floor.

"No, no, it's much too late for that," her father said. "I'll just retrieve the journal I was reading and take it with me to my chambers."

"I noticed the latest issue of *The Lancet* has arrived."

"I will have a look tomorrow. Is Abby asleep?"

"Aye. She went up over two hours ago."

Bransby stiffened as her father's footsteps drew near. Abigail nearly had to drag the corpse herself. "Don't give up on me," she whispered harshly. "When I open the door, you swing your end around and pull while I push. Got it? We're almost there—"

"Thank you, Mrs. Fitzgerald." Her father's voice filtered into the room again. "I don't know what Abby and I would do without you. Please, get some rest."

Bransby jerked the hamper around as her father, presumably, turned the knob. Strengthened by her alarm, Abigail gave her new acquisition a final shove, unwittingly causing the porter to fall and the hamper to go down with him. The sack containing the corpse must have caught on the wicker sides when the body tumbled out because Abigail caught sight of a man's hairy arse as the corpse landed on top of the poor servant. She knew Bran had to be horrified, but there was no time to help him.

She closed the theatre door as her father walked into the office.

"Abby, my love." He blinked at her in surprise. "What are you doing here? Mrs. Fitzgerald said you went to bed hours ago."

Abigail leaned against the door that hid Bransby and the cadaver and tried to speak above the pounding of her heart. "I couldn't sleep, so I came down to . . . to get a book."

Her voice sounded too high-pitched, even to her own ears. But, by some miracle, Edwin Hale didn't seem to notice.

"What am I going to do with you, my girl?" He crossed to his desk and began thumbing through papers. Although he was nearing sixty, he had aged well. Thanks to a full head of white hair, a tall physique and a rather austere presence, he looked every bit the distinguished surgeon. He could easily have remarried had he wished to do so, but ever since they lost her mother, medicine had become the sole love of his life. He didn't even socialize much. The opera, where he had spent the evening, remained one of his few indulgences.

"Why do you need to do anything with me?" Abigail asked.

His attention fixed on some medical document, he said, "You have studied almost every anatomy book I possess. You pore over the latest *Lancet* before I can even get to it. And you beg me constantly to admit you to the college. Your Aunt Emily says it's not natural."

"What's so unnatural about an interest in medicine?" Abigail took up their old argument with enough passion to justify raising her voice. Thanks to some shuffling and a few groans emanating from the operating theatre, she feared Bransby would get them caught.

Fortunately, Edwin Hale remained preoccupied with whatever he was reading. "What? Oh yes, well, you know how I feel about that. There is nothing more intriguing than medicine. But you are a woman, after all, and Aunt Emily insists I have ruined you. I received a letter from her just today, scolding me for not sending you to her last summer as I promised. She says you will never marry unless you learn your rightful place in the world."

Abigail made a face. "And where is that, pray tell? Darning socks in some parlor? Too bad Aunt Emily has nothing better to do than spend her time worrying about me and heckling you."

"Ah, but I fear she may have a point."

"What do I care about catching a husband?" She tapped her foot, allowing her pout to linger in case he looked up to see it, which he didn't. "A man would only try to force me into a similarly dull life. I could never bear it. I don't wish to leave you—or the college."

"As much as I would miss you, my dear—"

A loud crash caused Abigail to jump and her father to look up.

"What was that?" he asked with a perplexed frown.

Abigail leaned against the door and thumped the wooden panel with her elbow to warn Bransby to silence. The terror of his situation seemed to be sending the man mad, but Abigail needed a few moments more. "What? Oh, that was me, bumping into the door."

A gasp, a rattle and another thud called her a liar.

"By Jove, I believe someone's in the theatre!" After retrieving the pistol she had returned only moments before, he took the lamp from the desk and headed toward her.

Abigail's hopes of escaping this night without further incidence disappeared. Her prospects would be ruined—and all because of *Wilder*.

"Perhaps I should go stay with Aunt Emily for a brief time, just to appease her," she said, blocking her father's path. He wouldn't hesitate to cart her off to her aunt's small estate in Herefordshire if he discovered she had involved herself in the purchase of a cadaver. No matter how lofty her intentions, such evidence of unladylike conduct would, no doubt, convince him that his sister had been right all along.

Her capitulation didn't seem to faze him. The same razor-sharp focus he used in his work was now trained on solving the mystery of what he had heard.

"See that you stay behind me. I will not have you harmed."

Abigail tried to think of an excuse for what her father was about to see, but her mind went blank. She had gotten herself into scrapes before, many that required quick thinking and a glib tongue, but never had she been caught so red-handed.

Holding his candle aloft, he motioned for her to step aside. The dissection room was quiet, but the silence came far too late to stop him from venturing within.

Resigned to her fate, Abigail finally did as she was told.

Her father cracked open the door and held the lamp high. "Who's there?"

Her heart heavy in her chest, Abigail followed him inside. He rarely grew angry enough to berate her with any real conviction, but the few times he had lost his temper had left an indelible impression on her mind. She feared this would be one of those occasions.

"I'm sorry, Father. I know I was wrong to—" Her words fell off as she saw that the room was empty. The hamper and Bransby were both gone. So were the cadaver and its sack. Only some dirt remained.

Her father didn't seem to have heard her. Intent on his purpose, he crossed to a door that stood open on the opposite side and called back. "Look at this! It appears someone tried to break in, although what they would want to steal from in here is a mystery to me."

Abigail rushed over to see what he had found. The window in the office opposite her father's was open, letting in a cold breeze—and, sure enough, several marks on the sill indicated a tool had been used to force it open.

"Whoever it was is gone now," he added.

Abigail didn't respond. She didn't know what to think. Where was Bransby? What the devil had happened?

She was contemplating telling her father the truth, in case Bransby needed help, when her father gave a short cry of alarm and stuck his head out the window. "What are you doing in the alley, poor man? Come back inside. Here, I will let you in."

Abigail's chest constricted. That had to be Bran. Was the body out there with him?

Hurrying to beat her father to the door, she opened it for their porter. Bran was rumpled and slightly battered, but he didn't appear seriously injured. Neither did he have her cadaver with him. At least, she saw no hint of it. No hamper. No sack. Nothing. "Are you hurt?"

"What happened?" Her father skirted past her.

The servant sent an accusing glare at Abigail. "I tried to stop them, sir."

"*Who?*"

"The thieves, of course." Abigail ushered the porter inside, giving his arm a meaningful pinch in the process. "Bran was probably banking all the fires when he heard the same noise we did and came to investigate. Isn't that right, Bran?"

Judging by the porter's sullen expression, he was tempted to reveal her duplicity. But she implored him not to with her eyes. Surely, she could count on Bran's loyalty. He had worked at the college for as long as she could remember. For all his reluctance to participate in her most recent scheme, he knew she had her father's best interest at heart.

Thankfully, he didn't disappoint her. "Yes, Miss. I-I believe I scared them away."

"*Whom?*" her father demanded again.

"Several men of the lowest character, that is for certain, sir."

"You have no idea who they were or what they wanted?"

"Until tonight, I had never seen them before in my life." Bransby gave Abigail another purposeful glance. "But I did hear one of them called *Max*."

Max? That didn't make sense. She had assumed Bran had tried to hide the body. But this . . . Why would the sack 'em up men return when they had already gotten away with so much?

Her gaze shifted to the window, which was exactly like the window in her father's office. They had been watching her, she realized, assuming she might take the cadaver to the cellar. That was where it would likely be stored, and they could break in with ease. When she didn't . . . they broke in, anyway.

Only a man like Wilder would be so bold . . .

Leaving her father to fuss over Bransby, she went to stand in the doorway that separated her father's office from the dissection theatre. "Damn him," she cursed under her breath. He had stolen her specimen—after taking her entire purse as payment! The miserable wretch probably carried it straight to St. Thomas's or another college, where he had gleaned an additional nine or ten guineas. *We haven't got all night*, he'd said when she suggested they sell the body elsewhere.

She was willing to bet they had found the time.

"Did you say something, dear?" her father called. He had just seated Bransby on Mr. Holthouse's sofa but, hearing her say something, had come to see what she was doing.

"No, nothing." Abigail pasted a smile on her face to hide the panic rising inside her, and he returned to their porter. But that was when she saw it. The elephant her mother had given her. It was gone from her desk. They had stolen it, too, right out from under her nose, and she had been too caught up to notice.

The anger she felt in that moment instantly built into a fury the likes of which she had never experienced before. And that was when she made herself a promise. Come what may, Maximillian Wilder hadn't seen the end of her yet.

Chapter 3

"Thirsty work, that." Jack Hurtsill tossed the elephant he had taken from Miss Hale's desk into the air and caught it as they hurried through the dark, barren streets. "What do you say, lads? Shall we stop for a pint or two?"

Max resisted the familiar impulse to land a fist in Jack's face. The man was greedy enough to sell his own mother for a farthing. But now, more than ever, Max needed to exercise patience. He had spent too much time gaining the trust of the sack 'em up men to give himself away too soon.

Hunched against raindrops that rang like coins against the pavement, he continued to stride a pace or two behind the gang's leader.

"What about you?"

When Jack twisted around to face him, Max managed a pleasant nod. "A pint would suit me fine," he said, echoing the sentiment of the others.

"Then we are in luck." Jack turned in at the Lion's Paw, a redbrick building with long dripping eaves. Inside, a lone barmaid sat at a table, studying her nails. She glanced up when they entered but made no welcoming sign. Instead, she yawned, adjusted her stained frock and shook a man snoring next to her into wakefulness.

"I've had just about enough o' that racket," she told him.

The stench of sweat and gin pervaded the small, dingy tavern, competing with the tobacco smoke coming from a group of men lingering over cards in the corner. Low, slurred voices hummed on air warmed to a stifling degree by a fire that looked far livelier than any of the Paw's patrons.

Jack pulled in his stomach, swelled his chest and slapped the bar to gain the serving girl's attention. "Bring us each a glass of gin, lassie, will you?"

With a sigh, she moved to do his bidding, and they found a table next to the far wall.

"Tonight was bloody beautiful!" Emmett exclaimed as they took their seats. The youngest member of the gang at barely sixteen, he had narrow shoulders, no facial hair and fine-boned hands. His childlike face looked as innocent as an angel's, but he had grown up on the streets of London and could pick any pocket or lock he came across. "What luck! What timing!" he marveled. "I *still* can't believe we snatched that stiff right out of the dissection room. That poor porter didn't know what to do when we came through that window."

"He wasn't hard to hold down, but the poor bugger did what he could. I was surprised by that. He even tried to come after us." Jack's brother Bill, who was as wide as Jack only shorter, shook his head for the porter's pluck, then clapped Jack on the back. "But we did well for ourselves, all right. One body, two sales and no one but Hale's lass the wiser. Like you said, she can't even tell her father without givin' herself away."

Max wasn't excited, just relieved. As attractive as the doctor's daughter was—with her large brown eyes and raven-colored hair—she was too willful and impulsive for her own good. And he had no kinder thoughts for her father. Why wasn't Edwin Hale more aware of Abigail's actions? She had no business instigating any kind of trade with Jack Hurtsill. He was as unpredictable as a man could be. Had Max been forced to protect her when Jack demanded they go back to take the body, it would have destroyed everything he had worked so hard to establish over the past several weeks.

Jack was beginning to suspect his story as it was.

"I'm in favor of anythin' that saves our backs from diggin' another hole." This came from Tom Westbrook, a weasel of a man born with a cleft in his palate that made his speech difficult to understand. He hadn't had an easy childhood, and it showed in his behavior as an adult. "I would have liked to see her pretty face when she found it gone," he added, pulling his chair closer.

"Oh yeah? Well, I doubt she'd like to see *your* bloody face again. What woman would?" Jack placed the elephant he had taken on the table in front of him and slapped the serving wench on the behind as she delivered their drinks.

"Keep your hands to yourself or leave," she told him, but she spoke in a bored monotone. She was too used to such behavior to get angry about it.

"Come on, Missy." Jack pointed at Tom. "Least I don't look like him, eh?"

Unwilling to be drawn into the conversation, she scowled and moved away. The others chortled, and Tom fell into the same morose silence he usually hugged about him like a cloak.

When Tom didn't provide Jack with the fight he had been angling for, Jack forgot about baiting him and changed the subject. "Maybe we should go back and visit Miss Hale again next time her father's out. I have half a mind to know her better." He chuckled as he slid his thick, filthy finger over the smooth finish of her elephant.

Barely able to stop himself from snatching the figurine away, Max hooded his eyes. "Selling cadavers makes us money. Wasting time with the surgeon's daughter does not." Neither did stealing essentially worthless objects, but Max let his opinion on the elephant go unstated.

Jack's smile slid from his face. "You won us a mighty fat purse with that play at Aldersgate College. And the lass was ripe for the pickin'; I'll not argue with you there. But you weren't really thinkin', Max, not of the future." He forgot the elephant and took a swill of his drink, cradling it fondly in one hand while the others watched. "The bitch offered us a contract and you turned your nose up at it. Now she'll never do business with us again. She even said as much."

That was precisely the point. Max had done his damnedest to guarantee it. "There are plenty of other colleges. St. Joseph's was eager enough to see us tonight. When they heard Hale was dealing with us again, they agreed to a contract. So we got a sizeable purse from Abigail *and* her competitor's business. You also got your elephant." He shrugged out of his coat. Fresh gusts of rain-laden air flooded the room with each opening of the pub door, but as the clock approached midnight, the portal remained closed for longer and longer periods of time.

Jack smiled fondly at what he had stolen. "Right, my elephant. A pretty bauble, eh? And one she seemed to fancy. But you need to understand somethin', Max. You're feelin' like a bloody hero, what with all the boys clappin' you on the back. An' I'm not displeased myself, overall. Tonight's was a fancy piece of work." He set his mug down with a *thunk* and leaned halfway across the table, nearly knocking everyone's gin into their laps. "I'm willin' to forgive a mistake or two because you're new and you're clever and you don't understand how everything works just yet. But if you think I don't got eyes nor ears in my head, you're wrong. I hear the purrin' of your voice an' see the pretty-boy face beneath that black stubble. I see the way the ladies gaze after you."

He broke off to study Max for an interminable moment, causing the others to shift uncomfortably at this unexpected chastening. "You think you got me fooled. But I know you're different from the rest of us. I just haven't figured out how different yet, or what it is you want."

"I have a degree from Cambridge. I come from the other side of town. And I have been cut off from my family. What's not to understand about that? In any case, what I want is not very complicated." Max took a drink of his gin, sorely missing the fine brandy he was more accustomed to drinking. "I want some brass in my pocket like the rest of you."

"An' we got plenty of that tonight." Bill spoke up, obviously hoping to diffuse the situation.

Jack glowered at his brother before returning his gaze to Max. "I know. You told me all about those gamblin' debts and how they're catchin' up with you. And like I said before, you're welcome to run with us as long as you remember one thing: *I* am the leader of this here gang and always will be. You forget yourself again, like you did at Aldersgate with that little lass, and you'll find yourself the next bloody corpse we sell for ten guineas. We'll see what the ladies think of you then."

With a wink, he sat back to drain his mug. "And as for the Hale bitch"—he punctuated his words with a hearty belch—"don't be tellin' me what makes us money."

Afraid of drawing Jack's ire, the others buried their noses in their cups.

Max shrugged. "Just trying to make sure you're not letting your willy do your thinking. Because I don't want to follow any man who does."

Alcohol affected Hurtsill in one of two ways: he became either the most generous drunk alive or the meanest. And from one evening to the next, there was no telling which way he would go.

Max tensed, in case his words met with a violent reaction, but relaxed—marginally—when Jack's face split into an appreciative smile.

"There is more to life than money, Max."

The man was a pig. Shoving his chair back, Max stood. He knew his limitations, and Jack was pressing him dangerously close to them.

"Where you goin'?" Bill asked.

"Back to the house," he replied. "My bed awaits and I am eager for it." Grabbing his coat, he raised his mug in a final salute and hoped the others wouldn't soon follow. He needed a break from them. He also needed some time to search the ramshackle house he shared with Jack and Tom before they returned.

"Stay for another drink." Jack motioned to his brother and the boy Emmett, who bawled out an old sailor's ballad as if to convince him. "Another few minutes and we'll be singin' along with 'em."

Max curved his lips into his best approximation of a smile. Singing he could do without, but the thought of a good brawl once Jack sank a little deeper into his cups proved tempting. He wanted nothing more than to break the man's jaw and be done with him. But that would have to wait. He wouldn't jeopardize his search for Madeline.

"Another time perhaps," he said and slipped into the dark night.

Long after her father and Bransby retired, Abigail paced in her bedroom, thinking about Max Wilder and the other sack 'em up men. She had originally planned to conceal what she spent on the cadaver by padding the cost of beeswax and tinder and everything else she bought over the next couple of months. But the members of the London Supply Company had taken *all* of her operating capital. The college could never get by. And trying to hide such an amount put her at risk of being accused of thievery even if they could manage without more supplies.

Then there was her elephant. Her *mother's* elephant. It was the only thing Abigail possessed that held any sentimental value.

Pressing her fists into her eyes, she fought hard to keep tears from slipping down her cheeks. Although they still got the best of her now and then, she had learned at a young age that crying didn't help. There was never anyone she could confide in, no one to comfort her. Providing her father deigned to notice her distress, he would shake his head in disapproval and grimace as he told her that he hated a woman's tears. He didn't know how to cope with them, didn't know how to cope with a woman's *anything*. If he found out what she had done and how badly she had botched it, she would be shipped off to Aunt Emily for good.

So he wouldn't find out, she decided. She would make it right.

If only Wilder hadn't taken so much. And the elephant . . . that meant even more.

When she was a child and missed her mother so badly she could hardly stand the ache in her chest, she would slip into her father's office while he was teaching in the anatomical theatre or handling patients at St. Bartholomew's Hospital and crawl into the footwell beneath his desk. There, the smell of ink, leather and musty old books would surround her, helping her feel close to him. She would hold her elephant in her lap and let her fingers glide over the smooth ivory planes while the memory of her mother's voice echoed through her mind.

I love you, my beautiful girl. Why, you are no bigger than a faery sprite! . . . So you think you look like me, do you? Ah, you are far prettier than I, and so beautiful on the inside, where it really counts . . .

Sometimes Abigail would stay under that desk for hours. No one ever came looking for her, other than Bran. And when he eventually dragged her out, she always remembered to put the elephant in its rightful place. Otherwise, her father would know she couldn't simply lift her chin and carry on without Elizabeth as he seemed to have done.

She wanted that elephant back! She *needed* that elephant back.

But if she involved the police and accused the resurrection men of robbing her, Big Jack would retaliate by producing the letter she had sent requesting a cadaver, and her father could spend the rest of his days in gaol as an example to the whole medical community. If that happened, the college and its professors would suffer, too, not to mention its students.

Abigail pivoted at the window. She could take someone to strong-arm Jack Hurtsill and Maximillian Wilder into returning her property . . .

But who? According to the address she had used for that letter, Hurtsill lived in Wapping. Since the docks at St. Catherine's had been built, the area had fallen to ruffians and the like, especially at night.

What if she waited until the gang separated for the night and Jack Hurtsill was at home, asleep in his bed? If she had the pistol, she could coerce *one* man if necessary, couldn't she?

The odds were certainly better than when she had been staring at *five* . . .

Or maybe she wouldn't have to confront anyone. Maybe she could simply slip into his house and steal back her property . . .

She sent a worried glance toward the clock ticking on the mantel. It was just after midnight. As fraught with risk as her plan was, she had no time to come up with a safer alternative. She couldn't put off recovering the money; it would be spent if she did. She had to act right away, while under the cover of darkness.

Suddenly firm in her convictions, Abigail riffled through her writing desk to locate Hurtsill's address. He lived at No. 8 Farmer's Landing. If she hired a hackney, she could find it. She just hoped Hurtsill would keep the money and the elephant with him when the gang split up for the night.

Catching sight of her drawn face in the mirror on one wall, she paused. Was she really going to do this?

She swallowed hard. As far as she was concerned, she had no choice. If she didn't recover the money, she would be sent away.

She had already lost her mother. She would not lose her father, too.

Chapter 4

As Abigail descended from the cab she had hired to take her from the college in Smithfield to Wapping, her heart pounded, but she drew courage from the awkward bulk of the pistol stuffed in the deep pocket of her cloak. Her father had taught her how to use a gun when she was barely fourteen, so she could protect herself should the need arise. It was one of the few times she remembered having his full attention. A woman living in a man's world could never be too careful, he'd explained.

But if everything went as planned, she wouldn't have to fire a single shot.

"Thank you, mum." The cab driver told his horses to "get on up" as soon as Abigail dropped the fare in his palm. He was obviously nervous about having traveled so far into this quarter after dark, and for good reason. Everyone knew a cabby carried a certain amount of coin, which made him vulnerable.

Abigail, on the other hand, had gone to great pains to appear as downtrodden as possible. Dressed in worn-out clothes that looked about to be torn into rags—a tattered skirt, a cotton smock she had hurriedly mended to make it serviceable and a threadbare cloak that hid her face and hair inside the cowl of its deep hood—she'd had a devil of a time convincing the cab driver to bring her to this location in the first place. He had demanded to see the color of her money before he would venture past Gray's Inn Road. But at least his reluctance to trust her had given her some confidence in her beggar's disguise.

A fresh trickle of unease slid down her spine as the grind of the hackney's wheels receded. But she took a deep breath and began to walk. If she wanted to go unnoticed, she had to travel on foot the rest of the way.

She came upon three men, deep in conversation, outside a dilapidated house on Wapping High Street. Other than that, the neighborhood was deserted. Although a gas lamp burned at one corner, it provided only a dim circle of light that cast everything outside it in deep shadow.

At least the rain had stopped.

Wrinkling her nose at the terrible stench, she skirted several piles of manure that had been left in the street and began to follow the directions the cabby had given her.

Farmer's is one of the many alleys that run off this street here, second turn on your left.

Careful to walk without too much of a sense of purpose so she wouldn't draw attention, Abigail kept her head bowed and her eyes on the uneven cobblestones in front of her. As she passed the men, she could hear snippets of their conversation.

"You can get hundreds from Billington for three- or fourpence a piece . . ."

"I've got my own ratter. Maybe he's not quite up to Billington's standards, but he supplies me well enough . . . and you should see my new dog. He can kill twenty in four minutes, he can."

Much to her relief, they paid her little mind. She thought they would ignore her completely, until one tossed her a halfpenny. A shot of alarm went through her as the coin hit the street. She didn't want to be addressed. But she shouldn't have worried. When she played her part by scrambling to pick it up, the giver turned back to his friends.

"What are you going to name this one?"

"Billy, of course, after the best bull and terrier in the business . . ."

Once Abigail rounded the corner, she saw the unusual crooked-looking house the cabby had told her to look for. This muddy court, lit by a single gas lamp, was, apparently, Farmer's Landing. There was the typical water tap that served the whole street, the privies that did the same and the miskin—the part of the court where everyone piled their garbage. Neglected laundry hung, dripping from the recent rain, on lines strung from roof to roof, and moonlight glinted off the shards of glass from a neighbor's broken window, which had been covered on the inside with an old blanket.

Behind the standpipe, in the darkest recesses of the court, sat No. 8.

Hurtsill's house was quiet. It was also dark, which gave her a modicum of hope that he was asleep after a hard night's work.

She would slip in, take a quick look around and, with any luck, recover her property. If he wasn't home, she would hide and wait until he was. She just had to remember to steal more than her money and the elephant. It had to look like a regular burglary, or she would leave her father and the college open to retaliation.

She could manage that, couldn't she?

Of course. Soon, she would be able to go home, peel off her costume and be no worse for having met the men behind the London Supply Company.

But approaching the house was the most difficult thing Abigail had ever done. Palms sweating, she circled wide, hoping to find a door or a window unlocked in back. It wasn't as if they had butlers or housekeepers in this part of town keeping an all-night vigil over the silver and plate.

What Hurtsill did have, however, was a big dog. The beast took Abigail by surprise, lunging at her out of nowhere. A rope attached to the animal's collar was the only thing that saved her from those snapping jaws.

Thanking the Lord the tree he was tied to had caught him up short, she hurried around the corner and pressed her back against the house just in time to avoid being seen by a neighbor, who lifted a window and shouted for the dog to shut its bloody muzzle. When the animal continued to bark and strain at its leash, the neighbor muttered something she couldn't make out and slammed the window. Then, except for the dog, there was a long silence.

No one came to the door of No. 8.

Jack had to be passed out, drunk. Or he wasn't home. That dog had been loud enough to wake the dead. If such a racket wasn't enough to produce Hurtsill, she should be safe to venture within.

But what if he hadn't returned? What if he was still gone and had her money and her elephant with him?

She was at his house. She had to at least check.

Pulse racing, she crept up to the back door and put her ear to the panel. All was quiet.

Hopefully he was inside; hopefully he was sleeping and couldn't wake up even if he wanted to.

He and his companions had made a fortune tonight. Any man of Jack Hurtsill's character would probably celebrate with a few pints. But it was late. They should be home by now.

Despite all her self-talk, her hand shook as she tested the knob.

The door was unlocked. As warped as it was, she could probably have broken it, anyway. It wasn't much of a barrier. But she preferred not to do that.

The hinges creaked loudly as she let herself into a single room that was obviously used as kitchen, dining room and parlor. Moonlight streamed through the front window.

He won't be wary; he has no reason to expect me.

She chanted those words over and over to herself, focusing on the positive. She definitely didn't want to think about the thick, greasy hair and ogling grin of Big Jack. Or the incredible power in Wilder's every move. Jack's friend was more frightening than Jack, in some ways. But he had to be wherever he lived by now.

Even if he wasn't, she had a gun and, unlike Bran, she knew how to use it.

She felt around for a lamp and the supplies to light it. Then she paused, listening again just to be sure. When she didn't hear any sounds of movement, she proceeded to check the coat rack. She had seen Wilder put her money in his pocket. Since she had no idea where Max lived, she could only pray that Jack had demanded it as soon as they left and brought it here . . .

There *was* a greatcoat hanging on the rack inside the living room. But that greatcoat didn't belong to Big Jack. *Wilder* had been wearing it.

Did they live together? If so, she would be outnumbered again. But that could be fortunate, considering she had no idea which one of them had her elephant. She guessed it was Wilder. He had been closest to her desk at the end. But it could also have been Jack. He had shown more interest in it.

The dog outside quieted as Abigail set the lamp on the floor. *Please let the money be here, and my elephant, too.*

She didn't want to come into contact with Wilder's coat. Jack and the others rarely bathed. Chances were they bought their clothes from a pawnbroker and never washed them—and Lord knew what they touched on a daily basis. But, to her surprise, Wilder's coat was heavy and well made and smelled more like rain than body odor.

She delved into his pockets, searching for the ivory elephant and the purple pouch—but came up empty.

God's teeth! What now? She could scarcely breathe for the fear charging through her.

But all remained quiet. There was no need to panic. She had free rein of the place, could keep looking.

She turned to survey the rest of the room, which contained so much stuff there was hardly any space to walk: a sofa, several tables, a broken chair, a large steamer trunk, a washbasin she guessed was rarely used and a bin of coal against the far wall. The drapes hung at an odd angle above the window, but Abigail did her best to get close enough to pull them shut. She didn't want the neighbors to see her light—if, indeed, anyone other than the man who had yelled at the dog was up.

Once she got the drapes closed, she slipped off her hood so she could see better and began to search in earnest. Her elephant and money had to be in the house somewhere. *Please* . . .

But that prayer wasn't answered. She couldn't find either. Could Wilder or Jack have taken them upstairs?

She didn't have the courage to look there—not under any circumstances. If she drew too close to the resurrection men, she wouldn't be able to use her gun. They would wrest it away before she could fire. And there was no way out from the second floor except the stairs, which would make it far too easy for them to trap her.

She couldn't let that happen. So . . . had she come all this way for nothing?

Tears of frustration and discouragement welled up as she stood in indecision. Briefly, she contemplated pulling out her firearm and charging upstairs despite all reservations. She craved nothing more than to wave it in front of Wilder's face and watch his arrogance turn to fear.

But she wasn't *that* reckless. She couldn't confront him. She didn't know how many were there or which rooms they occupied. No way could she risk having one of them come up behind her.

A tear rolled down her cheek as she realized that all was lost. She had failed—there was nothing more she could do.

Filled with a sudden and overwhelming despair, she choked back a sob as she started for the door. She had tried so hard and risked so much, and for what? What would she tell her father? How would she come up with the money? And, if she couldn't, how would the college get by?

She didn't see how they could . . .

She got only halfway across the room before she heard a man's voice coming from outside: "Keep that damn dog quiet, you hear?"

Hurtsill! He wasn't *in* the house; he was just coming home. She heard another voice, too. Someone was with him, someone who, when he muttered an answer, sounded *very* close to the back door.

Abigail whirled around to head out the front. But there was too much furniture and clutter blocking the door. She would never be able to move it in time.

All she could do was hide herself—and hope they went to bed soon.

She blew out the lamp and set it down, but before she could decide where to hide, a man's hand clamped over her mouth, making it impossible for her to scream.

Chapter 5

"What are you doing here, you little fool?" Max breathed in her ear. But Abigail couldn't answer, and he knew it. He had his hand over her mouth. He couldn't risk that she might yell or make some other noise that would alert Jack to her presence.

Yanking her back against him, he kept her silent while hauling her up the stairs.

"You've done it now," he told her as he dragged her into his room. "What the hell were you thinking?"

When he closed the door and pinned her against it, she squirmed to get loose. She seemed to be heading into a full-blown panic. He warned her to be absolutely still—unless she wanted Jack to charge up the stairs—and, only when she complied, did he test her by taking his hand from her mouth.

She didn't scream. Instead, chest heaving as she filled her lungs with air, she glared her hatred at him. He could see the gleam in her eyes despite the darkness. "Were you trying to suffocate me?" she whispered.

"I am trying to save your willful hide," he told her. "But I have to be honest with you, unless you cooperate, the odds aren't in our favor."

There was a ruckus going on downstairs. Max could hear Jack slinging commands, and wondered why he sounded sober. What could he be going on about at this hour?

Miss Hale seemed too concerned with him to pay much attention to what was happening below. "Let me go," she insisted.

"Where?" He pressed against her that much tighter to make sure she wouldn't attempt to run. "Where would you go?"

She fumbled in her cloak. Then he felt the barrel of a gun jab his ribs.

"Anywhere away from you. Take your filthy hands off me." Her tone was unyielding, her body rigid enough to make him believe she would pull the trigger.

Evidently, she was crazier than he had thought.

Hurtsill and someone else were clomping up the stairs. Whoever was with Jack was laughing and stumbling ahead of him, by the sounds of it. But Hurtsill seemed tense, angry. "Get out of my way, you blimey bastard. You think we got all night?"

Max felt fairly confident he could strip Hale's daughter of her firearm before she did him any harm. But he feared she would fire in the process and alert the others to her presence. Then she would really be in trouble.

"Think about what you're doing," he cautioned, his words barely audible. "You have one ball. You shoot me, Big Jack will be on you in minutes."

She started sliding away from him, presumably so she could get out the door when it was clear. "Where is my elephant?" she whispered back. "I won't leave without it."

Incredulous, Max laughed and shook his head. "You risked your hide for a bauble worth less than two pounds?"

"Not just the bauble. I need the money, too!"

He scowled, keeping his eye on the pistol. "I don't have your elephant, Miss Hale. But I will gladly return your money. I was just trying to figure out a way to leave it out for you. I heard the dog, saw you searching my coat and knew what you were after."

She seemed justifiably confused. "I-I don't believe you. Why would you give up forty guineas after . . . after how you treated me?"

"Because it seemed like the quickest way to be rid of you. But I didn't manage it soon enough, and now Jack is home, which changes everything."

"It doesn't change how badly I want my elephant!" The tremor in her whisper belied her calm bravado.

How would he get her out of the house? He was afraid, even if he could devise a plan, she would refuse to go without that damn carving. Could he get it for her?

"Do you have any idea what Big Jack would like to do to you?" he asked, angry that a cheap ivory elephant threatened everything he hoped to accomplish.

Jack and Tom were in the hall, snapping at each other.

Eyebrows drawn, Miss Hale nibbled on her bottom lip. "I know he is not an honorable man."

"No, he is not." He kept his voice as low as hers; he had to. "If you have half a brain, you will do exactly as I tell you."

"Which is?"

"Hand me the gun."

She shook her head.

"Give me the blasted gun!"

"Why should I trust you?"

"Because, the way I see it, you have no choice—"

"Max, open up! We 'ave business," Jack bellowed, banging on the door.

Max froze. *Business?* What could Jack possibly need now?

Miss Hale's eyes went wide and riveted on his face. She might be impetuous and stubborn, and unlike any lady he had ever met, but she was definitely beautiful . . .

"It's me or him," he said, scarcely making a sound. "You will never get past Jack even if you shoot me."

She hesitated, but another insistent knock helped her decide. After relinquishing her weapon, she scuttled across the room and hid on the far side of the bed. She also said something but spoke so low he couldn't make out the words. He understood the gist, however: *Get rid of Jack.*

"Max! Wake up!" Jack shouted.

"Comin'." Max muffled his voice so that Jack would believe he was climbing out of bed. "What do you want?" he demanded when he cracked open the door.

"We got work to do."

Max had Abigail's gun hidden on his person, just in case. "Have someone else do it. I'm tired as hell—"

"Bill had to go home to his wife before she leaves him for good. Emmett's keepin' the dog quiet." He jerked his head toward Tom, who was staggering drunk. "An' you can see the state he's in. Come on, it'll just take a minute."

"To do what?"

"You'll see."

"We got us a bonus tonight," Tom piped up from his room across the hall.

Jack told him to shut the hole in his face and go to bed, and Tom laughed as though it was the finest joke in the world.

"Fine. But give me a minute." Max closed the door and leaned against it, listening to Jack's heavy tread recede. He hated to leave Abigail alone, but if he satisfied whatever it was Jack wanted, Hurtsill might go to bed. Then maybe Max could grab the damn elephant and the money and send Miss Hale on her way.

"Stay here."

"No—"

He cut her off before she could say more. "Your life may depend on it. Do you understand? *Stay here!*"

When she nodded, her eyes wide as saucers, he donned a shirt and shoved her pistol back in the waistband of his trousers. He hoped, without the gun, she would be less likely to try something that could get one of them killed.

Jack was waiting downstairs, in the dark.

Max's gaze circled the familiar sitting room. "Why not light a lamp?"

"There's no need. Come on." He motioned for Max to follow him to the back door. Outside, Emmett was kneeling next to Borax, petting and crooning to the dog to keep him calm.

"Hello, Max," he called as loudly as though it were midday.

"Shut up, you idiot," Jack hissed. "Do you want to wake the whole neighborhood?"

A wheelbarrow sat in the weeds to Max's right, hidden in the deeper shadows of the house. When he saw what it held, he understood. It was another corpse.

"Help me get her inside," Jack said. "This old gal is bloody heavy."

Max sucked in a bolstering breath. "I thought we were done for the night. Where did you get this one?"

Jack considered him for a moment, almost said something, then changed his mind. "Let's call it a . . . lucky turn of fate."

Steeling himself against the distaste he felt—the same distaste he always felt at the prospect of disturbing the dead—Max put his hands under the arms of the corpse while Jack took the feet. But the moment he touched the body, he knew something was terribly wrong. This woman was still *warm*!

He drew back as though stung. "She's not dead."

Jack laughed at his reaction, revealing the fact that he *was* at least partially drunk. "She's dead all right. She's just a mite fresher than those we pull from the ground. Come on, Emmett can't keep Borax quiet forever."

Anger and accusation churned through Max like acid. Was it as he had suspected all along? Were Jack and the others following in the steps of Burke and Hare and killing people for the money their corpses could bring? Had this woman been murdered for ten bloody guineas?

He didn't want to believe it, mostly because he couldn't bear the thought that Madeline might have come to such an end. Although he suspected just that, it was his worst fear.

"Tell me what you did," he demanded.

Jack motioned to the house with a jerk of his head. "Inside."

When Max didn't move, Jack scowled. "What? Would you have the neighbors comin' out to meet our new guest?"

The powerful emotions assaulting Max threatened to expose him. *Madeline* . . . Her name was a silent wail in his head and his heart.

But he had to go on, had to continue with the charade. His younger half sister had disappeared after being seen in the company of Jack Hurtsill. Jack was his best bet of finding her—or finding out what happened to her.

"Let's go." Max helped lift the woman through the back door and into the sitting room, where they dumped her on the sofa.

Sweating from the exertion, Jack wiped his brow with one hand and sank into the chair next to her.

Too keyed up to sit, Max remained standing. He was completely unnerved. To make the moment that much worse, the woman had one eye open and seemed to be staring at him. When he looked closer, however, he realized that eye was made of enamel. "What happened to her eye?"

"How the hell should I know?" Jack replied. "I didn't ask, and I don't care. She has enough real parts to serve my purpose."

Max felt ill at the memory of her disconcerting warmth. "Did you kill her?"

"What are you talking about?"

"You heard me."

"I heard you, but I don't like the tone of your voice. I thought you were one of us. If you are, you need to mind your own business and don't ask questions."

Max schooled his face into the emotionless mask he needed it to be and considered his response. He was nothing like Jack Hurtsill, prayed to God he never would be. "No one said anything about murder."

"That's because *we* didn't murder anyone."

"Then who did?"

"I didn't ask."

"What's that supposed to mean?"

"Some bloke supplies me with a body here and there. I don't harass him about where they come from. I don't think he'd take kindly to it. I give him twenty-five bob, sell the body to one of the schools at a hefty profit and everyone goes away happy."

Except for the victim, and the victim's friends and loved ones. "They didn't get this woman from a grave. There isn't a speck of dirt on her. She's not even cold."

"So maybe they have a connection with an almshouse. Maybe they pay a stipend or two for those who die with no kin. Or they pose as kin to claim the dead. Why not save England the price of another pauper's burial? It ain't none of our business either way. She'll be cold enough when we take her to Webb Street School tomorrow night."

Max wanted to accuse Jack of more than stealing corpses. A crime against public mores didn't bring the same punishment as a crime against a person. But he had to hold off until he had proof. It was possible this woman hadn't been murdered. Besides taking advantage of the poor, some resurrection men snatched dead bodies right out of private homes while they were being watched over until they could be buried.

A creak on the stair drew Jack's attention. When he looked up, Max did, too—just in time to see Abigail dart around the corner and run for the back door.

"What the hell?" Jack bellowed.

Max couldn't believe it. He should have locked her in. But he was afraid she would panic and start to scream.

Weaving around the furniture, he lunged for the fabric of the cloak fluttering behind her, but there was too much in his way and it slipped through his fingers. She charged outside ahead of him, a half step out of reach—until she ran headlong into Emmett. They both grunted and fell when they collided, and the dog went wild, but Max grabbed Miss Hale by the collar and hauled her inside.

She couldn't leave now. From the look on her face, she had heard too much. She would go to the police—anyone would. But Max couldn't let that happen. Not yet. He needed to hold out long enough to discover who was supplying Jack.

That was the only way to put a stop to the London Supply Company, whether they were murderers or not, and find out what happened to Madeline.

"What's *this*?"

Tentacles of fear squeezed Abigail's heart as Jack Hurtsill gaped at her. The third man—more of a boy, really—who had hung her up long enough for Wilder to grab her, got up to look on, too. Clearly, she had made a mistake. But she'd had to make a run for it while she had the chance. She couldn't wait for Max Wilder to return, hoping he would let her out, nice as can be. Look what he had done at the college!

Besides, he had just proved he was unreliable. Without him, she would have evaded the boy and escaped.

"I have a visitor," Wilder explained. "Evidently, she didn't like my room as much as I thought."

Abigail tried to free herself of Wilder's hold. *Something* had to go her way tonight. But struggling proved futile. His grip was as unyielding as his chest, which formed a wall at her back.

Big Jack pulled off Abigail's hood, exposing her face and making her feel more vulnerable than she had at any other time in her life. "The surgeon's daughter? You had the surgeon's daughter in your room? I'll be damned," he said. "She didn't get enough of us at the college, eh?"

"She came for the money." Max dipped his free hand in her cloak pocket and recovered the money he had left on the dressing table upstairs, which he tossed to Jack.

Because her attempts to wrench away did nothing, Abigail reached for her pistol. She had seen where he put it, but Max shifted enough to retain possession.

"Let me go!" she cried. "I should have shot you while I had the chance. You deceitful pig! You said you would help me!"

Max gave her a polite half bow while maintaining his hold on her cloak. "I *will* help you, Miss Hale—right back to my bed." He dragged her to the stairs, the noise of which roused the body snatcher with the cleft palate. He came out to see what was going on, but it was Big Jack who stopped their progression.

"Wait a bloody minute. Is this why you left us at the Lion's Paw? You had other plans?"

"No! I came home, like I said."

"You also said you had no interest in her at the tavern."

"So?"

"What makes you think she's yours for the taking?"

"I had no interest in risking my hide," Max clarified. "But Miss Hale came to me, which changes everything. At this point, why would I refuse her?"

"You can't do this," Abigail warned. "My father will come after me, and you will all hang like you deserve."

Max shrugged. "Then I guess we will have to make sure your father doesn't find you here when he arrives."

She had heard them talking. With a woman most likely murdered lying on the sofa not five feet away, Abigail thought she knew how they planned to get rid of her. By the time Bransby went to her father and told him about her involvement with the resurrection men, and Edwin managed to track down Jack Hurtsill and his gang, she would be a cadaver at Great Marlborough Street School.

Suddenly, her elephant didn't seem like such a great loss. Making do without specimens at the college didn't sound so bad, either. She just wanted to go home, where she was safe. "Keep the money," she said. "I won't tell anyone you took it. I won't tell anyone anything. I'm very good at keeping secrets."

"Forgive me if I can no longer take you at your word," Max said.

Jack guffawed, but Abigail noticed that he was watching Max carefully, and marked the subtle tension between them. "You'll pass her on to me when you're finished with her, then?"

His words were more of a command than a question.

"Aye! Pass her on!" The man at the top of the stairs licked his split upper lip.

"What would she want with ye, Tom?" Jack made a grotesque face. "You'd only scare the bloody life out of her. But Emmett here. He's young and fresh. She might not mind having him 'tween her legs."

Emmett shook his head. "I like 'em willing. I have to go anyway."

"Then Tom it is. Me and Tom," Jack said.

Max glanced between them as if considering their petition. "Why not?" he said at last. "I'm not a greedy man."

Chapter 6

Abigail hugged the far wall as Maximillian Wilder locked the door of his bedroom and pocketed the key. He had just told the others he would use her first, then pass her around, but she would die before she let him do that.

"I should have locked you in before," he said. "But I never realized you would actually be so foolhardy as to try to escape when your chances were so slim." And he was used to being obeyed . . .

While searching for a possible weapon, her eyes landed on the water pitcher that sat atop a marble-topped washstand. She dumped what remained of its contents into the bowl and clasped it to her bosom. But Wilder didn't advance on her as expected. He leaned against the door, closed his eyes and breathed a sigh that sounded very much like relief.

He stayed where he was until the house fell quiet. Then he seemed to remember she was in the room.

"Shall we get some sleep?" he asked, removing his shirt. "I don't think this has been a particularly good night for either of us."

Abigail didn't move. If he was trying to take her off her guard, it wouldn't work. She would defend herself, or she would die trying. "I won't sleep with you. I won't sleep anywhere *near* you."

Large drops of water splashed onto the table as Wilder buried his head in the bowl and washed his hair and naked torso. Without a fire or a lamp, she could see him only in outline. But his straight back and wide shoulders were impressive all the same. Abigail doubted she had ever met a man so comfortable in his own skin, so well made.

Too bad his character wasn't as flawless.

"I'm not going to hurt you, Miss Hale—Abigail," he said, toweling off. "At least not seriously."

Not *seriously*? He didn't consider forcing a woman to be a serious offense?

"You won't touch me," she gritted out.

"Actually, I have to touch you, but I will be as gentle as possible. Come here." He beckoned to her as though he expected her to place the pitcher meekly on the table and accept his hand.

"You are mad if you think I will do *anything* you say."

He planted his fists on his hips. "Either you will cooperate, or you will spend a long, miserable night on the floor. It's that simple."

"And what of your promise to help me escape?"

"You lost that promise when you crept downstairs and got yourself caught. So don't blame me for your predicament."

"Don't blame you? Maybe it was someone else who chased me down and hauled me back!"

"Emmett had you dead to rights. You wouldn't have gotten far."

She *might* have slipped past him.

Changing tactics, Abigail permitted a note of desperation to leak into her voice. It was an approach that often worked well with her father. "Let me go."

As Wilder studied her, Abigail refused to let her gaze drift any lower than his chin. She found his bare chest rather . . . *disconcerting*.

"I'm afraid I can't do that," he said with a frown.

"Is there no speck of decency in your black heart?"

"If there is, you wouldn't be the first person unable to find it." He shrugged. "I can't let you go. You wouldn't be home a day before your conscience got the better of you and you ran straight to the authorities. It's amazing how one's perspective changes when one is safe."

"If you won't let me go, what do you plan to do with me . . . other than tonight, I mean?" After what he had said to Big Jack, she knew perfectly well what he had planned for tonight and certainly didn't want to hear it reiterated.

"I plan on keeping you with me until it's safe to let you go. That's all."

As simple as his answer was, it told her nothing. Safe? How could she believe that? He could have let her escape. *That* would have kept her safe. But he didn't.

Abigail's eyes flicked to the door. She longed to run again—she had come *so* close—but the key to the lock was buried in Wilder's trousers, her hopes of success buried with it.

Unless the window afforded some small opportunity . . .

While she tried to ascertain her options, her captor cleaned his teeth, rinsed with the water from a cup on the same table as the bowl, ransacked a trunk full of clothes and came up with a shirt he tore into strips.

"What will it be?" he asked as he advanced on her.

Abigail couldn't take her eyes away from his hands. "Ex-excuse me?"

"Do we do this the easy way or the hard way?"

There didn't seem to be an easy way, at least for Abigail. She couldn't imagine him forcing her skirts up under any circumstances, but being tied while he abused her was especially terrifying.

Her throat dry as parchment, she swallowed. She had to think, had to use her head. "Listen, m-maybe we could make a deal."

Her words elicited an expression of surprise on his rakish face. "What kind of deal?" he asked, halting in front of her.

"My father would pay for my safety. He is not a rich man, but . . . but you could earn several pounds by returning me. We could leave now, make the college in an hour's time and—"

"And get a hangman's noose as my reward? If you think your father wouldn't send a constable after me, you're a lunatic. Besides, I don't need your money."

"You seemed to need it badly enough when you stole the college's purse!"

"Such temper, Miss Hale." He tut-tutted softly. "I did only what I had to."

He wasn't making any sense. Abigail had no idea how to reach him, how to bend him to her appeal. But there had to be a way. Every man had his weakness . . . "What then?" she asked. "You must have a price. Maybe I have s-something else you want."

Even in the dark, Abigail could see his eyes slide appraisingly over her body. "That sounds like you would be willing to grant me certain liberties."

He was going to take them anyway. If she allowed him free access to her body, perhaps he would help her, or at least keep her from Jack and the others. The thought of Jack's sweaty body poised above her own was enough to make Abigail ill. In the face of certain compromise, wasn't it smarter to give herself to one man to avoid the degradation and humiliation of being used by many? "Indeed. So . . . so long as you won't tie me up."

"What has you so convinced I would be willing to make this trade? Are you not the same woman who recently called me a lout? A deceitful pig? A louse? And, if I am all the things you say, why would I bargain for something I can simply take? Are you claiming to have such vast experience in these matters that it would be worth my while to enlist your cooperation?"

Abigail took quick stock of what she might use to sweeten her offer. "I haven't had firsthand experience, no," she admitted, "but I have read about human intercourse many times, in . . . in my father's medical journals."

Her father had kept such books on the top shelf of his bookcase. He assumed putting them out of reach would be enough to keep his daughter from spoiling her mind. But his reluctance to share the volumes, and his claims that they were not for a lady's delicate sensibilities, only piqued Abigail's interest. She had poured through them all by the time she was seventeen, many a second time in the four years since. "I may be a virgin, but I am not an uneducated one."

Max paused at this announcement, the makeshift bonds he planned to use dangling from his hands. "A virgin, Miss Hale? How old are you?"

"One and twenty."

"Isn't that a bit old to be so innocent?"

Abigail felt her face grow warm. It wasn't as if she had never had a man show interest. Sometimes the students at the college made overtures, but she was so immersed in her duties . . . "I have been busy."

"Doing what?"

"Working, of course. And . . . and studying. I plan to become an anatomist like my father."

She waited for the snort of derision this announcement normally produced, but Maximillian Wilder merely looked interested. "You have been admitted to the college, then?"

"Well, no. Not yet. But . . . I do work at the college. I am in charge of the household accounts. I see that everything runs smoothly, orchestrate events hosted by the school and help our housekeeper hire and manage the cooking and cleaning staff."

"Evidently you have lived a very secluded life. Your precious college sounds more like a nunnery."

"Perhaps, but the mechanics of mating are very clear to me."

"You have done comprehensive research on the subject, have you?"

"I wouldn't say *comprehensive* . . . but I am not completely unaware of what goes on between a man and a woman."

Due to the darkness, Abigail was having difficulty reading the expressions on Wilder's face. If she wasn't mistaken, he seemed to be struggling against a smile. "And what did your textbooks teach you? Do you think a woman such as yourself would enjoy the experience?"

"*Enjoy* it? How preposterous, Mr. Wilder. Of course not. Sexual congress isn't to be enjoyed, at least by the female. It is supposed to satisfy the male primate's drive to mate, to ensure the longevity of the race. But I would hold still and let you have a go, should you agree to help me escape from Jack and the others when you are . . . er . . . finished. You look healthy enough to me. You wouldn't take long, am I right?"

This time Wilder laughed out loud, a deep, boisterous sound that revealed sincere amusement. "God forbid I ever establish a reputation along those lines. But, feeling as you do, I can understand why you are not married."

"I have no intention of marrying. I told you what I will make of my life. I will be a surgeon."

"But they haven't even admitted you. What makes you think they will?"

"They have to . . . someday." The pitcher was growing heavy in her hands. "What do you say?"

"About your hopes of following in your father's footsteps?"

"About our little . . . deal. I allow you to . . . you know . . . and then, after you are . . . satisfied . . . you let me go."

He gave her a kind smile—something Abigail never dreamed she would see on his face. "As appealing as you make . . . er . . . copulation sound, especially with someone as well versed in matters of the flesh as you are, I will not be requiring such sacrifice at your hands. I cannot let you leave here regardless of what you have to trade, so you are better off letting me relieve my . . . um . . . primal urgings elsewhere."

"Elsewhere?" she echoed. "So you are not going to—"

"No. Although I do believe you deserved the scare. Now, hold out your hands like a good girl."

For once, Abigail found herself at a loss for words. She had never expected him to refuse her. She had thought he might take advantage of her by accepting her offer and passing her off to Jack despite any promise to the contrary. But such an unqualified rejection took her by surprise. Was there something *wrong* with her?

"Miss Hale?" he prompted when she didn't respond.

"I'm thinking." Without Wilder's help, Abigail had no choice but to escape on her own. She had seen it that way earlier, when she had made her first attempt, and she saw it that way now. She couldn't remain a docile captive. She had to fight for her freedom.

But how? She could never get the window open with him in the room. Even if she did, she had no idea whether or not she would be able to survive the two-story drop, not without breaking her legs, or maybe even her back.

Stomach churning with anxiety, she decided she had better do as he bid her, before he grew angry, and he set about tying her hands in front of her. When he was finished, he connected her to the iron bedstead with a short span of knotted fabric.

"That should keep you for a while." He stood back to survey his handiwork. "You can reach the bed, should you decide to join me in it. Otherwise, feel free to sit on the floor and plot your escape."

"I will be gone by morning," she told him.

He unloaded her gun, threw the ball out the window and tossed the pistol onto the bureau. "That brings up a good point," he said. "Should you get loose, the key to the door is in the pocket of my trousers. But now that you can't shoot me, you might have some difficulty getting it. And if you were to try such a thing when I am not fully awake and capable of governing my faculties, you just might learn how far from your expectations sexual congress can be."

Abigail narrowed her eyes. "I thought you weren't tempted."

He stretched out on the bed, yawned and closed his eyes. "I never said that."

Was he teasing her? "Why else would a man of no moral fiber refuse the offer I have made?"

"I will let you figure that one out for yourself."

She inched closer to him. "So that's it? You're going to sleep?"

He cracked one eye open. "Doesn't it look that way to you?"

"Yes."

"Good. Because that's exactly what I'm doing."

"What about . . ." She was afraid to say Jack's name, but she had to. Abigail didn't like surprises. She preferred to know what was coming so she could organize it or prepare for it or, at the very least, *count* on it. ". . . Big Jack?"

"He is not as big as he would like you to believe."

"*What?*"

He chuckled. "Never mind. Emmett went home, and Tom and Jack have both had so much to drink I think we're safe for tonight."

Did he mean it? "But . . . but what will happen in the morning?"

"I don't know," he said. "Which is why I need my rest." Punching his pillow, he rolled over.

She pulled at the bonds on her wrists, hoping to get them to loosen, but succeeded only in making them tighter. "You're just going to . . . to leave me here like this?"

"I am considering a gag. Would that satisfy you?"

She drew herself up straight. "Not at all, sir. But I would like a word or two of assurance."

"Oh, right. I forgot." When he got up and came toward her, Abigail feared she had said something to trigger a backlash. She pressed herself into the corner, then stood, helpless and uncertain, as he cupped her chin and tilted up her face. "This might hurt a bit," he warned, "but you will thank me in the morning."

"Ouch! That does hurt! What are you doing?" she asked, trying to wiggle away from the roughness of his chin as he chafed it against her face and neck.

Max could feel the ridge of Miss Hale's collarbone beneath his cheek, then more smooth skin as he slid his chin up the column of her throat. "I am leaving a few marks on you, for Jack's edification," he said. "He will never believe you were ravished without *something* to show for it." Pausing just below her left earlobe, he began to suck on her neck.

She squirmed some more, resisting, but that soon subsided and she started to giggle. He guessed from her bossiness that she didn't laugh often but, strangely enough considering all the trouble she had caused him, he liked the sound of it.

"Nothing in my father's books said anything about *this*," she said. "What on earth are you doing? Stop! It tickles. What could possibly be the point?"

He lifted his head only when he was satisfied that he had left a deep purple mark. "What your father's books didn't tell you, Miss Hale, is that much of what goes on between a man and a woman, at least in the bedroom, has no point. It is simply for the sake of pleasure, for the pure, heady passion of reveling in the opposite sex, of letting go of all inhibition long enough to enjoy giving everything and receiving everything all at the same time."

He knew his voice sounded slightly hoarse, but she smelled so damn clean and fresh. And her skin—it had to be the softest he had ever touched.

Moonlight lit her face as she cocked a finely arched eyebrow at him. "You seem quite well versed on the subject."

"I have never read any bloody medical journals, that's for damn sure. After hearing what they have to say, I think I'm glad."

"What's wrong with what they say?"

Max ignored her in favor of nipping at her neck again. Why did she have to feel so good? Not five minutes earlier, he had told himself he wouldn't have any difficulty sharing a room, even a bed, with Miss Hale. He could control his "drive to mate," as she put it.

But that was before, when Miss Hale—Abigail—was at an arm's distance. Now that she was so close and not nearly as stiff as he had expected, he found his perspective changing. And he was only rubbing his chin on her cheeks and neck. What would it feel like to part her lips and slip his tongue inside her mouth for that first sweet taste?

Under the guise of more chafing, he let their lips brush once, felt their breath mingle and measured Miss Hale's response. The tension in her shoulders, where he had anchored his hands, relaxed ever so slightly. Her eyelids lowered as her gaze fell to his mouth, and she kept her head tilted at just the right angle for their lips to brush again.

She's curious, he realized. *She has never been kissed.*

Proceeding to rub her cheek with his, only lighter because he hated to hurt her, he let his lips pass over hers a second time. It was all he could do not to linger there, not to pull her against him and answer her curiosity with the demands of his aroused body. But his conscience wouldn't allow it. She might be partly to blame for her predicament, but he owned as much of the responsibility as she did. He had unwittingly pushed her too far at the college. He wouldn't take advantage of her on top of everything else.

"Now what are you doing?" she asked.

Suddenly, Max realized that he was doing nothing, except staring at her face in a kind of hungry stupor.

Clearing his throat, he stepped away. "Just making sure I did a proper job."

"Oh. Did you leave the marks you wanted?"

"Some." He wondered what she would think when she saw them in the mirror come morning. "I should probably tear your dress as well, but I hesitate to reveal anything that might tempt Big Jack and the others any more than your presence already does." He feared what the temptation might do to him, too.

She didn't say anything.

"Did your father's medical journals mention anything about kissing?" he asked.

Her eyes, wide and honest, never wavered from his. "No, they concentrated mostly on the viscid whitish fluid of the male reproductive tract that consists of spermatozoa suspended in secretions of accessory glands and—"

"Spermatozoa?" he repeated, incredulous. "I am sure I have never heard a woman use that word before. Or a man, either, for that matter."

"It's the—"

"I think I can guess what it is." Tempted to kiss her soundly, he framed her face with his hands. "Are those bloody books of your father's the only instruction you have had on human intimacy? What of your mother? Didn't she see that you were properly educated?"

"Six would have been far too young."

"*Six?*"

"She died of consumption when I was just a girl."

"I see." He sat on the bed to put some distance between them. The fact that she had lost her mother at such an early age explained a lot about Miss Hale—why she was so unconventional, for a start. "And your father?"

"My father is a busy man. His work is very important to him."

The way she said it indicated Hale's work was more important to him than she was, and Max feared she was right. That something so integral to his daughter's development could fall so easily beneath his notice didn't speak well of Edwin Hale.

"Was there no one else?" he asked.

"No one else to do what?" She slid down the wall to sit on the floor and rested her head against the bedpost, her interest in kissing seemingly forgotten.

Max wished he could forget it as easily. "No one else to raise you, to befriend you."

She paused as she considered the question. The lateness of the hour seemed to be taking a toll on her, but after what she had been through, she was holding up remarkably well. Miss Hale may not have been the most disciplined or cautious woman he had ever met, but she had plenty of other attributes. Max couldn't fault her courage.

"Well, there was Bransby, of course," she said. "He's the porter at the college—and the poor soul you set upon when you stole back the corpse I purchased!"

"A harmless fellow."

"Getting on in years. How could you have frightened him so?"

"I was more worried about making sure he didn't sustain serious harm. We left him no worse for the wear. I saw to it."

She couldn't argue that. Bran had been flustered, but that was all. "Anyway, he has worked for us as far back as I can remember. And then there's Mrs. Fitzgerald, the housekeeper at the college. She came to us when my mother died."

Servants? Max was beginning to get the idea. Evidently, Abigail had been left on her own to grow up as best she could, with the aid of some house help and a library of medical journals. No wonder she had led such a sheltered life. He was willing to bet she had never circulated enough to attract many beaux. How else could such a beauty have remained untouched?

The image of her as the lonely girl she must have been evoked his protective instincts, but he tamped them down. He had his hands full with his missing sister. And once he'd done right by Madeline, he had to return to his usual life with all the responsibilities that entailed.

Chapter 7

The minutes passed like hours until Abigail thought morning might *never* come. Considering the uncertainty she faced, she wasn't sure she wanted it to. But, if Max Wilder was suffering similar anxiety, it didn't seem to be bothering him. He looked to be sleeping peacefully.

Although she had spent plenty of time scowling at his back, she was too stubborn to climb in with him. What kind of woman would that make her?

Certainly not an *admirable* one . . .

But she had to admit that he wasn't *quite* as bad as Big Jack. Although Max had stopped her from leaving when he might have let her go, which she highly resented and refused to forget, he could have done so much more than scruff her neck with his beard growth.

If he were Big Jack he would have.

And yet . . . Max Wilder couldn't be classified as a saint. There was something *dangerous* about him, something bordering on the uncivilized. From what she had seen so far, he dared more than a man should. He flouted whatever rule he chose to flout, and seemed to have no compunction about asserting his will in any given situation, regardless of how it affected others.

Still, he didn't make her skin crawl as she thought he should. He was a resurrection man, the very dregs of society. Her father—anyone with good sense, really—would be appalled that she could find *anything* redeeming about him.

So why did those few seconds when he touched his lips to hers loom so large in her mind?

Because it hadn't been an entirely unpleasant experience, she realized. Just the memory of it made her body grow warm and weak, as if she would lean into his strength if she could. Although she had never reacted to a man like that before, she was fairly confident those were signs of *attraction*, as shocking and scandalous as it was to acknowledge.

Her poor mother must be rolling over in her grave . . .

"Are you done pouting?"

She stiffened when his voice issued out of the dark. So he wasn't asleep, after all. She was sort of glad about that—it mitigated her jealousy. But she wanted to shush him at the same time, to tell him to be quiet for fear he would wake Jack or that other terrible man. They hadn't come to demand that he hand her over, as she feared they might, but that didn't mean they wouldn't if they had half an inkling Max was finished with her.

"Don't pretend you are asleep," he said when she didn't respond. "I can hear you shifting around, looking for some way to get comfortable. Are you really going to force yourself to remain on the floor all night?"

"As opposed to what?" she snapped.

"As opposed to the more practical solution of coming over and getting some sleep. Tomorrow will arrive before you know it. You would be wise to conserve your strength. Sleep will help you cope—and remain rational, a benefit to both of us, I dare say."

She squinted, trying to see him in greater detail. "Rational? How is this for rational? Let me go. Untie me so I can slip into the night. You can tell Big Jack I managed to free myself while you were sleeping."

He hesitated as though he was tempted but ultimately refused. "I'm sorry. I can't."

"Because . . . "

"I have my reasons."

"There is a dead woman downstairs!" she whispered.

"But Jack would never believe your escape was an accident, even if I tried to convince him otherwise. And I can't arouse more suspicion."

"What about the dead woman?"

"You and I deal in corpses, so don't pretend to have a case of the vapors."

"We don't deal with them in quite the same way."

"What you do is so much better than what I do?"

"Those at the college are gathering knowledge, and that will improve the quality of medical care in England."

"Then so are we. There would be no body snatchers, Little Miss Abigail, if you and others like you hadn't turned the human corpse into a commodity."

She'd had this argument before, with any number of people. "Medical colleges need specimens," she insisted. "We have to get them from somewhere. What good will it do to let every human who dies rot in the ground? When the information to be gleaned from their bodies could save other lives?"

"Aren't you conveniently ignoring the religious implications? It doesn't bother you that so many believe you are hampering the resurrection of their loved ones?"

She didn't want to think of that. Her own father eschewed religion, proclaimed himself an atheist, so she'd had little training. But she liked ducking into a chapel now and then. Something about the reverence and solemnity appealed to her. It also made her feel closer to her mother somehow.

Still, she offered her father's argument instead of revealing her own lack of clarity on the subject. "Religion can be an enemy to progress."

"I won't argue with you there. But that's a case you'll have to make in parliament if you want change—and it'll take more than one or two lords on your side."

"Many anatomists have tried, including my father. If change is coming, it's not coming fast enough."

"Another point on which we can agree."

"But that isn't the issue here," she said. "We aren't talking about body snatching."

"Then what are we talking about, Miss Hale?" He sounded annoyed.

"Murder."

"I should have governed my tongue earlier," he grumbled.

"Perhaps. But you didn't, and I heard what you said. You suspect Big Jack of more than digging up those who have died. You suspect him of Burking!" William Burke, and his partner, William Hare, were so infamous for their crimes that the practice of murder for the sake of anatomy had taken on Burke's name, even though he had been executed eighteen months ago—following which his body was publicly dissected at the College of Surgeons. Hare was released and managed to find work, but once his mates figured out who he was, they tossed him in a pit of lime. If what Abby had heard was correct, he was now a blind beggar.

"The body downstairs was a bit different than our usual, that's all," Max explained. "I had some questions, and I voiced them. Jack's answers were plausible."

"Plausible? Really? Then why don't you believe him?"

The bed creaked as he shifted. "Miss Hale, it is the middle of the night. I think we should both get some sleep, don't you?"

As exhausted as she was, how could she succumb to sleep when she was in such peril? "What will happen to me in the morning?"

"That, I can't tell you."

"What if . . . what if Big Jack and that other man demand"—she drew a deep breath—"demand that I . . ."

"I won't let them force themselves upon you. I will turn you loose first. Satisfied?"

"But it might be too late by the time you intercede. How will you stop them?"

"I will have to act smitten enough to be possessive, I suppose."

"You already promised to pass me off."

"I was holding a weak hand, a hand I wasn't willing to gamble on."

"How will it be any stronger in the future?"

"Last night Jack would not have understood why I would stop him. After several hours spent enjoying your charms, I will be in a much stronger position to claim you as my own. So we will establish new boundaries tomorrow, when Jack can, hopefully, see past the gin pickling his brain."

"Gin or no, if you plan to keep your promise to *me*, you will have to cross *him*. I don't see any other way. And why would you do that?"

"I may be a body snatcher, but that doesn't mean I take pleasure in deflowering innocent women. They are two different things."

"You were happy enough to rob me at the college."

"I was trying to teach you a lesson, if you must know."

"And that was?"

"That you were out of your depth. Had you not ventured into such dangerous territory, none of this would have happened."

She feared her father would see it the same way.

"Sadly, you have compromised us both," he added.

How could he blame *her*? Had they sold her the specimen she needed and gone on their way, like the other resurrectionists she had dealt with before, everything would have been fine.

"You caused this as much as I did," she insisted. "I was merely trying to solve a problem no one else seemed willing or capable of solving."

"Because they knew better than to risk their good name and their safety! And you, a woman! Jack wanted you the second he saw you. I was hoping to insure there would be no more contact between you."

Was that true?

She sighed as she rubbed her forehead. She supposed it was possible. Max Wilder did seem to have *some* scruples. "How was I to know how he would react to me?"

"Look in a mirror, for God's sake," he grumbled.

Did that mean he thought she was pretty? He hardly seemed affected. *She* had been more excited by the prospect of a kiss, or he would have kissed her in earnest. She had wanted him to, wanted to see what it would feel like to taste a man who looked and smelled like Max Wilder did. He was infuriating and stubborn and domineering— but so alive and daring and remarkable in other ways. And he had saved her from a fate worse than death with Jack Hurtsill. There was no reason he'd *had* to do that.

To continue to protect her could cost him a great deal, maybe even his life.

It was all so confusing. She wasn't quite sure *how* to feel about Wilder . . .

"How long do you plan to keep me here?" she asked.

"I hope it won't be more than a few days. I will let you go as soon as I can."

"Why can't you let me go *now*?"

"Miss Hale, we both need to rest." He pulled back the bedding. "Are you coming?"

Her body ached—and sitting there waiting for her hour of doom was taking a heavy toll on her frame of mind. Would it be so terrible to lie next to him? To take what comfort she could in having a mattress beneath her and the warmth of a few blankets on top?

She had seen him wash, knew he was clean, which gave her hope that his bed would be, too.

It had to be cleaner than the floor.

Grudgingly, she got up, but before she climbed in, he stopped her. "Is there any way you might remove those rags first?"

"Absolutely not!"

He let his breath go in an audible sigh. "Fine, if you must," he grumbled and allowed her to lie down.

Sure enough, the linens smelled as if they had been washed almost as recently as he had. No wonder he hadn't wanted her to wear the clothes in which she had been tackled in the dirt. But she didn't trust him enough to remove them; she was already taking a leap of faith.

Fortunately, he didn't touch her. He covered her with a quilt, since her hands were tied and she couldn't easily use them. Then he slid to the far edge to allow her more space.

As the temperature in the room dropped, it was *she* who gravitated toward *him*. She couldn't stop shivering, and his body exuded such tremendous heat. She thought, if only she could get warm, she could fall into unconsciousness and at last escape the fatigue, the pain and the worry.

"That's it. I won't bite," he assured her and pulled her right up against him, once he realized what she was after.

She would have made sure he understood that only practical concerns caused her to seek him out. That almost-kiss had nothing to do with it. But she was suddenly too tired to move her lips. His words were the last thing she remembered until, jostled awake by movement, she opened her eyes to find him staring at her.

"Is it morning?" she asked.

He broke off that steady gaze and raked a hand through his hair. "I'm afraid so."

A crushing depression descended when she realized that her father would soon find her missing, if he hadn't already. Once dawn broke, Aldersgate turned into a beehive of activity, which was partly why she liked working at the college. There was always *something* to do, the doing of which made her feel valued.

"Will you let me go today?"

He wasn't pleased to hear the question; she could tell by his expression. "You already know the answer to that."

She squeezed her eyes closed as she struggled to deal with the disappointment and was surprised that, when he spoke again, she heard real tenderness in his voice.

"Don't be frightened, Abigail. I will take care of you. You just have to trust me—and do everything I say. Do you understand? If you do, we might *both* survive the coming ordeal."

"*Trust* you?" she echoed. "Not only have you kidnapped me, you have bound me and you want me to trust you? I can't even feel my hands!"

Although he winced at the accusation, he seemed no less resolute. "If I could trust *you*, I wouldn't have had to bind you. And as for your charge of kidnapping, it isn't as if I carried you off. You came to me."

"I had no choice."

"You risked your life over money."

"It wasn't my money to lose. *And* you took my elephant!"

"Jack took your elephant."

She shrugged. "Doesn't matter. The moment it went missing, I had no choice."

"*Why?* Why does that damn thing mean so much to you?"

She wasn't going to answer. It would be a sacrilege to speak of Elizabeth to such a man.

But maybe, if he understood, he would be more prone to help her get her figurine back. "It was a gift from my mother."

As she had hoped, he seemed to reconsider his pique. "Then I will try to safeguard that, as well."

When he ran a finger along her cheek, she didn't jerk away as if she found his caress unacceptable. There was a magnetism about this man that made his attention feel like some kind of gift. She feared the charisma he wielded would get the better of her if she wasn't careful, but she couldn't pretend she didn't like his touch. Not while he was being so gentle.

"Will you comply?" He beseeched her with his eyes and the timbre of his voice. "Tell me you will, Abby. Because I won't be able to protect you if you don't."

Did she have any choice? What were her other options? As long as he was with her, she couldn't escape. And she certainly couldn't trust Jack. She didn't want to let Jack or any of the other three members of the London Supply Company, with their filthy clothes, rotting teeth and ogling grins, anywhere near her.

"I took care of you last night, didn't I?" he asked.

It was true that last night would have ended much differently if he hadn't stood by her in the end. And he hadn't ravished her. That had earned him *some* credibility.

"I will do as you say," she conceded, "until you prove to me that my trust has been misplaced."

"As long as you obey, you will come to no harm."

Swallowing hard, she nodded. For better or for worse, they would be joining forces in order to survive the next day, two, maybe more—a frightening prospect, given he was nearly a stranger to her. But having such a capable man as a shield while in Jack's house was also reassuring.

Accepting that nod for the acquiescence it was, Max sat up to untie her. Then he massaged her palms and fingers to help the blood flow back into them. When the tingling grew so painful she could no longer withstand his ministrations, she pulled away.

He slid some of the hair, which had fallen from her topknot while she slept, out of her face. "I wish we could have come to this agreement last night."

She focused on something else, so she could tolerate the terrible throbbing. "My father will be looking for me. You realize that."

"He won't be looking here."

"He will if Bransby tells him about you and the others."

"The porter you told me about last night? What might he say?"

"He was waiting in the hall, as you guessed. No doubt he overheard the whole exchange. I don't remember any of us mentioning the London Supply Company by name, but there can't be too many Big Jacks—not in London and not engaged in the same business."

"Did you tell Bransby you were coming here? Because if you did, I can't believe he wouldn't stop you."

She had just agreed to trust him, but . . . how much? At what point did she begin to do herself a disservice? "I didn't tell him. He would have gone straight to Mrs. Fitzgerald."

"So it should take a day or two for your father to trace Jack to this house. And I will handle the inquiry when it comes."

"You expect me to hold my silence, to sit up here, while my father is at the door?"

"Do you value his life?"

She didn't answer that. There was no need to. She simply watched Max warily.

"If he becomes a threat to Jack," Max went on, "he won't be any safer than you are."

Tears gathered in her eyes. "I couldn't bear it if anything happened to him."

"Then you will not only maintain your silence, you will do everything else I ask, just as you promised."

"What if you are wrong? What if you are unable to protect me?"

"I am your best chance," he said. Then a knock at the door interrupted, and Max pressed a finger over her lips to indicate silence.

Chapter 8

"Blimey, Max. What happened last night? You kept the surgeon's daughter all to yourself, just like I thought you would."

Abby grabbed Max's arm in an act of panic *and* appeal as the young man with the harelip called through the door.

"What I do is none of your business, Tom," he responded. "Go back to bed before you make me angry. 'Tis early yet, and we had a late night."

"Give her to me!" he insisted, ignoring everything except the fact that Max had refused. "I haven't had a woman in so long my bollocks ache. And be quick about it," he added, lowering his voice to a harsh whisper, "before Jack wakes up an' asks for her himself."

Max started to massage her hands again. Abigail guessed it was his way of trying to reassure her, his way of keeping her calm. She couldn't say it was helping, but she was far too anxious to stop him. Pain or no pain, she wasn't about to do anything he could construe as a rejection when she needed him to be her champion as badly as she did.

"You heard what I said!" Max called out.

"Jack won't like it," came Tom's response. "Wait and see. He's gonna put you in your place once and for all."

A muscle flexed in Max's cheek. "That would be my concern, not yours."

"Come on!" His voice changed to a high-pitched whine. "Why do you have to be so niggardly? With a face like yours, you can get any woman. You don't need one who can't say no."

71

"I've decided I like her. And you know how I am. I won't allow you or anyone else to touch anything I consider my own."

"She isn't your bloody *coat*, Max!"

"True, but there is no way I would want Miss Hale back in my bed after she has been in yours. Why would I risk giving myself the Pox?"

"I don't have the Pox!"

"So you say."

"But you can't just *keep* her," he complained. "We gotta return her to her father. Might as well let me have a toss before that. She'll be no worse for the wear. I'll scrub her up clean as a whistle when I'm done, I swear it."

Abigail covered her mouth so she wouldn't whimper or do anything else to reveal her terror. Tom acted as if he were talking about a horse or . . . or a dog. In light of that, she was beginning to think she had made quite a bargain, arranging for Wilder's protection. There was little doubt that she was completely at his mercy, anyway. She would have traded just about *anything* before allowing him to hand her over to the likes of Tom.

"Go back to bed," Max said again.

There was a long pause. Then Tom cursed, smacked the door that much harder, and stomped away.

"Will he give us trouble later?" Abigail asked.

Despite everything that was going through her mind—all the panic and uncertainty—when Max looked at her, she couldn't help appreciating the unusual color of his blue-green eyes. He was far more attractive than the others. There wasn't a woman on earth who could argue that he wasn't.

"We will have to watch our backs," he said. "But so long as you don't get caught alone with him, you should be fine. I'm not particularly worried about Tom, Bill or Emmett."

A knot formed in the pit of her stomach. "Just Jack."

"Yes. He will be a challenge."

It made her even more nervous that Max seemed to be concerned. "What are we going to do?"

"Get up and go before we have to deal with him," he said and rolled out of bed.

"We're leaving? For good?" she asked hopefully.

"No." He pulled fresh garments from the trunk in the corner.

Rather than watch him dress, she got up too and walked over to the window, where she stared down at the weeds in the narrow separation between this house and the next. "Think of that poor woman on the settee downstairs," she said.

"Trust me, I have thought of her."

"And?"

He didn't answer.

"I know resurrectionists make far more than the average . . . silk weaver or what have you," she said, "but you could be much more than what you are now."

"You feel confident of that because . . ."

She took heart when he sounded more amused than offended. "I may not know your background or what brought you to these unfortunate ends, but you are obviously educated. You are handsome and charming as well, when you want to be and—" She turned, so intent on convincing him that she forgot he might not be fully dressed, and felt her jaw drop when she saw his bare backside. "And handsome," she repeated, suddenly too flustered to remember, until the words were out, where she had left off on his list of attributes.

He was so busy dressing he didn't notice that she was gaping at him. "Handsome serves me so well that I don't need to make a living?" he asked wryly.

When she couldn't seem to draw more words to her mouth, he glanced over his shoulder.

Feeling her face flush when he caught her ogling him, she whipped back around. Why was she trying to convince him of anything? What he did with his life was none of her business, and talking about his many physical assets made her a little short of breath. Seeing them had an even stronger effect. "Take me to Aldersgate," she said.

"We won't be going to the college, Abby. Not today."

She hadn't given him permission to use her first name, let alone the shortened version of it. Only those closest to her called her Abby. But nothing about this situation was usual. He had his trousers on now, but dear God, he was pulling the chamber pot out from under the bed. She could hear him. Considering that she had never been in the same room when a man urinated before, it hardly seemed she should comment on the fact that he was growing far too familiar with how he addressed her.

Fortunately, he had spoken with a touch of exasperation—like a brother might address his younger sister—and had the fortunate effect of offsetting her discomfort.

"And I won't have you constantly pleading with me," he added, scolding her.

"I'm not supposed to ask you to take me home? How am I to avoid it?"

He talked as casually as if he wasn't standing there, emptying his bladder. "We decided that *I* am in charge here, remember? You said you would listen to me, that you would trust me. Have I not kept you safe so far?"

The memory of Tom pounding on the door raised gooseflesh on her arms. But that only brought her thoughts back to the same old circle: How much gratitude did she owe Max when she wouldn't be here if he hadn't dragged her back into the house?

"It has been *one* night," she pointed out.

"I will keep my word. You can rely on it."

"Forgive my skepticism, but I barely know you." She had quite a bit more to say about how outrageous it was for him to expect so much of her, but she couldn't think straight with what was going on in the background. "Must I be subjected to hearing you . . . relieve yourself?" she snapped.

"Since I must keep you with me at all times, I have little choice." He didn't sound the least penitent—or even shamed.

"You could have used the privy. Surely you have a key."

"Everyone on this court uses that privy. I find it disgusting and only force myself to go there when . . . absolutely necessary."

"But I'm standing right here!"

"As close as we will be for the next couple of days, you may see and do a great many things you would prefer not to. You slept with me last night, didn't you?"

She relaxed, marginally, when he finished and started dressing again. "Should I have continued to suffer on the floor?"

"No. You made the better choice, and it didn't hurt you. I am merely saying that we will both have to be flexible. When this is over, you will go home in one piece—but that is all I can promise."

"How generous of you." She was pretty sure he was shrugging into his shirt.

"Perhaps I will be generous in other ways."

"Meaning . . ."

"I saw you watching me a moment ago."

"That was an . . . an accident. I turned too early."

"Most people don't accidentally *stare*, Abby. But, be that as it may, next time I disrobe, if you ask me nicely, maybe I will turn and let you satisfy that avid curiosity of yours."

Her cheeks grew even hotter. He had so easily recognized the degree of her interest! "That won't be necessary," she said, trying to save face by convincing him he was wrong. "Because it is easier to study the musculature of the human body on a male specimen, the college pays a premium for them. I have seen more men than women."

"Dead men," he pointed out.

They had been dead—and partly deteriorated. There was information to be gleaned there, of course, but a corpse didn't make a pretty sight. She had a feeling Max would look far more appealing, although she wasn't about to admit that. She had never discussed the male form with anyone else. It was indecent of her to discuss it now, especially with him.

And yet . . . she was intrigued. How many nights had she gazed at the ceiling of her bedroom, wondering what it would be like to have a man's hands on her body? To take a lover? She had no interest in a man's control. But his love? She couldn't say she didn't crave that.

"Dead men, yes," she conceded, "but by cross-referencing what I have seen with the diagrams in my father's books, I believe I have formed an accurate picture of the male penis and how it works. What I don't understand is why everyone makes so much of it."

"Everyone?"

"Men, mostly. The students . . . that's all they joke about."

"But you are not impressed."

"Should I be?"

He chuckled. "Maybe your opinion would be different if you knew the pleasure it brings a woman to ride a hard cock."

No one had ever used such language with her before. She wasn't offended that he had been so candid—he had said it matter-of-factly—but she was titillated all the same, and that somehow enhanced the taboo nature of the topic. Although she should have ended the conversation right there, he seemed so marvelously open and nonjudgmental that she couldn't help continuing. "I admit I can't imagine what . . . what sexual union would feel like, but one book had a—"

"To hell with your father's medical journals," he broke in. "If you have never been with a man who wants you, if you have never experienced real intimacy, you have no idea what *any* of it is about."

Why did he suddenly sound so impatient? Did her naïvité annoy him? "I can only learn from what is available to me, sir."

"Your education will be complete when you marry. Then you will understand." He spoke as if he would leave it at that, but she could hardly accept such an answer.

"I told you. I don't plan to marry."

"You also told me what you do plan to do."

"And?"

She expected him to point out how unlikely it was that her dream would ever come true. She knew he was thinking it. But he merely sighed and sat on the bed to pull on his boots.

"There is no reason a woman wouldn't make a fine surgeon," she said.

"Especially someone as relentless as you. So, if you behave yourself while you are here, maybe I will teach you a thing or two. At least you will go home wiser than when you arrived."

"Teach me a thing or two? You mean by exposing yourself? I'm not sure I can allow myself to participate in something so . . . improper!"

"Are you really going to let propriety stand in the way, when we are so far beyond the bounds of that? Once word gets out that you were held captive by a gang of resurrection men, most people will assume the worst. You might as well get *something* out of it."

"You are quite practical, sir."

"I think you are as practical as I am. Too practical to forgo such an opportunity."

She felt torn about what her response should be. Her father would be mortified, her aunt positively apoplectic if she took advantage of her capture in such a way. But how could looking at a live specimen be that much worse than looking at a dead one? "I'll consider it," she said.

"I thought you were scandalized." He laughed out loud. "You are an interesting woman, Abigail Hale."

She pressed her forehead to the glass of the window. "Don't say that."

From what she could tell, he was now brushing his teeth, but because she had seen too much before, she wasn't going to risk turning around.

"Say what?" he asked when he could speak.

Folding her arms to ward off the morning chill, she watched Borax, Jack's dog, dig in the dirt. "That I am *interesting*."

"What's wrong with *interesting*?"

"It means different." And experience had taught her that wasn't a compliment.

"Different isn't always bad."

"Of course it is. I've heard it enough to know."

"You called me a lout," he pointed out. "And a deceitful pig."

It sounded like he was combing his hair. "That was before we became . . . friends, of a fashion. I have since told you that you are an educated man and a handsome one. That is far kinder than alluding to my . . . uniqueness, especially in such a patronizing tone."

"There wasn't anything patronizing about it. I like a woman to be unique."

"No one likes a woman who is *too* unique." Because she refused to adopt the role society tried to press upon her, she had always fought to fit in, even at the college. Lecturers and students alike couldn't understand why she couldn't be content to sit in the corner and darn socks.

He set down whatever he had been using. "And why is that, pray tell?"

"She might have ideas and opinions of her own."

"I don't see a woman's ideas and opinions being a problem."

"They can make a man feel threatened."

"*Certain* men, perhaps. I am not so easily intimidated."

She was hardly convinced but wasn't angling for an argument. "If you say so."

"Are you ever going to turn around?" he asked.

"Are you covered?"

"I thought you *wanted* to see my cock."

Any other woman would have gasped at this comment, but she smiled at the humor in his voice. "I can't say I am entirely opposed to it."

When she turned, she knew she had succeeded in shocking *him*. He looked a little stunned, but he quickly rallied.

"You might want to think a little longer before you make a statement like that to an unscrupulous body snatcher."

At the moment, he didn't look unscrupulous. His clothes were basic and serviceable but better than what most men wore in these parts—and that only reminded her of how *she* must look, especially by contrast.

She confronted the mirror and gasped when she saw the red marks he had made on her skin. A deep purple bruise stood out on her neck like a brand. "Look at me!" she said. "Look at what you have done!"

"I noticed."

He didn't seem to be taking any pleasure in the harm he had caused, but she could detect no contrition, either. "I can't go out like this. Everyone will assume I am your . . . your whore!"

"Your clothes won't help. Where on earth did you find them?"

"The rag-and-bone bag. I thought they were the perfect costume."

"Indeed they are. You will fit right in. Just don't get separated from me or, pretty as you are, you might find yourself approached by any number of men." He came up behind her and lifted her chin to study, in the mirror, the marks he had made.

"Are you satisfied?" she asked.

The thumb of the hand that held her face moved over her bottom lip. "Hardly," he muttered, but he obviously didn't expect a response. Growing purposeful again, he let go of her and went to the door to peer out.

"Do you see anyone? Is Jack out there?"

"He doesn't seem to be up quite yet." He closed the door and waved her over to his toothbrush and comb. "It would be best if we get out of here as soon as possible. You have fifteen minutes, at the most. I suggest you do what you can to accomplish your toilette."

She recalled Tom saying Max wouldn't let anyone touch his things. "You don't mind if I use these . . . these personal implements?"

"Anyone who smells as good as you do can't be too dirty," he said.

"I am very conscientious about my cleanliness," she assured him.

"I believe that. But even if I didn't, some sacrifices have to be made." His gaze returned to the mark on her neck. "You won't be the only one making them, I assure you."

When she hesitated—it seemed so invasive to put his toothbrush in her mouth—he said, "Would you rather go without?"

"No," she replied and quickly availed herself of all he offered before he changed his mind.

He watched her while he waited, but she made him step out of the room and into the hall when she used the chamber pot.

Max strode down the street, his hand at Abigail's elbow as he propelled her along with him. He didn't like being out with the surgeon's daughter. He couldn't help worrying that someone might recognize him. On this side of town that wasn't likely, especially garbed as simply as he was and walking with a woman who could easily pass for a low-class prostitute—thanks to what she was wearing and what he had done to her face and neck. But he confronted that possibility whenever he went out, which was partly what made his situation so dangerous.

As if that wasn't enough to worry about, he wasn't sure he could trust Miss Hale not to grab some passerby and scream that she was being held against her will. He doubted she would be taken seriously, but her voice was quite cultured. Her education and intellect, should anyone listen for too long, would also be apparent. Both would work against him. If leaving the house to escape an early confrontation with Jack—Jack was never congenial the morning after a drinking binge like the one he'd had the night before—had been his only objective, Max might not have risked it. But he was eager to get a message to his clerk.

"Must you drag me along at such a brisk pace?" Abigail complained.

He wanted to reach the teeming docks of St. Catherine's and slip inside the cool, dark safety of the warehouse, just in case Jack had sent someone after him. He couldn't allow himself to be followed.

"You seem to be keeping up just fine."

"I'm nearly running! Perhaps you are *trying* to draw attention?"

That was exactly what he *didn't* want. Slowing, he shot her a disgruntled glance, and she smiled sweetly as if she enjoyed having achieved a victory, no matter how small.

"Quit being so smug."

She batted her eyelashes at him. "Why, whatever do you mean?"

"You know what I mean." He turned to glance behind them. All seemed as it should be, but . . . that could be deceiving. A disgruntled Tom could be trailing them even if Jack hadn't asked him to.

"Is something wrong?" Abigail craned her neck to follow his gaze.

He tightened his grip on her arm. "No, face front."

"*You* keep looking behind. Why?"

"Jack doesn't trust me much more than he trusts you, that's why."

"Must you always be so cryptic? *Why* doesn't Jack trust you?"

"I will answer your questions fully only if and when I want you to know something."

She rolled her eyes. "You can be terribly overbearing and autocratic, in case no one has ever mentioned it."

Had he not been sincerely concerned for their safety, he might have spared a smile for her pluck. There weren't many people in his life who dared to stand up to him the way she did. And what other woman could have weathered the past ten hours so well? "If you cooperate nicely, and stop questioning everything I do, I will buy you something to eat and maybe a sweetmeat on our way back."

"Are you bribing me with sugary treats, sir?"

Leave it to her to question him, even on that. "Consider it more of a . . . reward." He adopted a stern expression. "But we can forgo stopping if you don't care for being rewarded."

"I like being rewarded just fine!"

She assured him so quickly and unabashedly that he chuckled in spite of his anxiety. "As I thought."

"Just one more question."

He arched an eyebrow to let her know she was pressing her luck. "Where are we going?"

"To the docks."

"What business do you have there?"

When he didn't answer, she shivered even though it wasn't cold. "Whatever it is, I pray it has nothing to do with *death*."

"Those are my sentiments exactly," he responded.

She looked up at him. "You don't know?"

He *didn't*. He hoped to find Madeline alive and well, if not today, some day in the near future. But, considering it had been months since she disappeared and there had been no sign of her, learning of her death was far more likely.

"I can't say that I do," he said and quickened the pace again, desperate to escape the guilt that dogged his every move.

Chapter 9

Should she run? Scream? Plead with the man meeting Max Wilder to come to her aid?

Abigail shifted from one foot to the other as she stood in a dark corner of a large warehouse that smelled like tobacco, watching for her opportunity to escape. She had to do *something* now that she was out of Jack Hurtsill's house. When would she get a better chance? If she allowed Max to take her back to No. 8 Farmer's Landing, he would have the control he had before. She would also have to face Jack and the others and, while she hoped Max could protect her, she had no idea how long that would last or how far he would go.

Was he committed enough to risk his own hide?

Even if he was, the thought that he might be harmed while trying to defend her didn't sit well. They would both be better off if she could just slip away.

But how? He was keeping such a close eye on her. Although he had demanded she stay right where she was and moved some distance beyond her, he wasn't so far that he couldn't chase her down if she bolted.

If only the small, bespectacled man he had come to meet would acknowledge her in some way. Maybe she could send him a signal—with a fearful glance or a mouthed plea for help. But, from the beginning, Max's associate had acted as if she weren't even there. As soon as he had looked up to find her and Max approaching, he had hurried out of his small corner office, his focus on Max alone.

The low murmur of their voices reached her ears. She easily recognized Max's as the deeper of the two. But she could not make out the individual words. Both men seemed singularly intent on their subject.

What could they be going on about?

Max glanced over to be sure that she was where she was supposed to be and narrowed his eyes. "Don't you dare!"

She spread her hands as if she had no idea what he was referring to. Although his intermittent checks didn't make the task of escape any easier, she was secretly relieved that he had finally drawn his companion's attention her way. She implored the man with her eyes, but he bent his head back toward Max and the conversation resumed as though it had never been interrupted.

With a bolstering breath, she studied the large square of sunlight pouring in via the double doors through which they had entered. Freedom seemed *so* close. There were people outside—great masses, making barrels, crawling into and out of lighters, hoisting and searching cargo, collecting tariffs and doing other work for the customhouses. Could she make it to the wharf before Max set upon her? And, if she did, would anyone take pity on her?

With the way she was dressed and the marks on her neck, she feared not. Max would be right there to defend himself against her accusations, to tell any old lie he chose. He could claim she was his sister or some other close relation and he had merely come to get her off the streets and haul her home. Who would question it? And if she broke faith with him, she could lose his protection.

She couldn't even imagine how bad it would be if he abandoned her to the mercy of Jack, Tom or even one of the other two men who had delivered that cadaver to Aldersgate.

When Max handed his companion some money, Abigail decided their meeting was drawing to a close. She expected to leave soon after, but it was the little clerk who hurried out.

"Come sit down in the office," Max said, motioning for her to join him.

"What's happening?" she asked as she complied.

"Nothing. I am merely fulfilling my promise."

"To protect me?"

"To buy you a reward."

"But I thought"—she turned to look after the man who had darted out into the morning sun—"I mean, I assumed we would do the shopping ourselves." They had come down Ratcliffe Highway, which was lined with shops and taverns and doss-houses.

"That won't be necessary. We would be wise to stay out of the public eye as much as possible."

"Why? No one is likely to recognize me. Not in this end of town. I don't know a soul who lives near the docks."

"You have dealt with other resurrection men, have you not? One or more could easily live here."

"On occasion," she allowed. "But our contact has been so limited it would be highly unlikely for anyone to recognize me in such a setting and situation."

"Believe me, you are not so easily forgotten. Why take the chance?" He pulled out a chair for her. "My friend won't be but a moment."

Her hopes of escape wilted further as she sank into the seat he proffered. She had imagined them stopping at least twice on their walk back, which should have created two more opportunities for Max to become distracted enough so that she could break away and disappear. Now whomever he had sent would return with what he ordered, and Max would hurry her to Farmer's Landing, intent on nothing but her safe and secure return.

"I should have made a run for it," she said.

He surprised her with a cocky grin. "I knew what you were thinking. But there's no need to suffer too much regret. I would have caught you."

"Must you act so pleased with yourself?" she grumbled.

His grin only widened.

The items he had his clerk purchase did far more to mollify Abigail Hale than Max had expected. When Clive Hawley returned, and spread a small covering over his desk to make a place for them to eat, she accepted what he provided with the purest enthusiasm. She had two glasses of wine with lunch. Then she downed every pastry or sweetmeat he didn't eat himself, and seemed genuinely delighted when he presented her with a new sterling silver brush and mirror—so delighted that she gave the impression she had completely forgotten about trying to escape. She kept thanking him and marveling at the beauty of the set.

"Haven't you ever received a gift?" he asked, finally interrupting her happy chatter as they walked back. Hard-pressed to think of anything that might please a woman who had every reason to hate him, he had sent his clerk after the same set he had given his mother last Christmas.

"Now and then," she said. "My father would have given me more, but special occasions sort of pass like ordinary days for him. He is a very busy man."

Max had heard the *busy* part before. She offered that excuse for every shortcoming Edwin Hale possessed. "So you have said."

"But this . . . this is quite extravagant." She examined the mirror again. "Wherever did you get the money?"

He was considering how to answer when she stopped—so fast she jerked right out of his grasp.

"What is it?" he asked, turning to find her glaring at him.

"Tell me you didn't use what you took from the college for this!"

"I *didn't* use the college's money."

He could tell she wanted to believe him but remained skeptical. "How can I be assured of that?"

"You could believe me."

"And if I dare not?"

"I will gladly give you all forty guineas when I return you to your father," he said, taking her arm again. "Fair enough?"

She fell in step with him but wouldn't move quite as fast as before. "How is it that a man like you can spend a small fortune on me, someone who means nothing to you, without even blinking?"

He didn't want to go into that. What he had spent was a mere pittance to him, but practical considerations—like the fact that he hadn't wanted his clerk out shopping all day—had caused him to overlook how it might appear to a woman who had lived with far less. "As you have mentioned, my profession pays quite well."

"Not well enough to buy me baubles that are needlessly expensive."

"A card game on the side can make a tidy sum. Anyway, who says the expense was needless? Gifts aren't meant to be practical. They are simply meant to please the recipient." He hoped his attempt to charm her would be effective and was relieved when that seemed to be the case.

"I admit I have never owned anything quite so lovely."

He shot her a glance. Her obvious pleasure made him want to shower her with gifts. But he felt it only fair to warn her that his indulgence and affection could go only so far. "Don't feel too grateful, Abby. I owe it to you for what you are being forced to endure, since I can't return you to your rightful place quite yet."

"Have you decided *when* I'll be able to go home?"

"No."

If only he could find the answers he sought, he could take her to Aldersgate sooner rather than later. For the past several weeks, Hawley had been canvassing the medical schools as his emissary, asking about Madeline—even offering to pay handsomely for any information. But no one would admit to receiving or dissecting a specimen that looked remotely like his sister. And he could understand why. The scandal would put them all out of business. When they were dealing with a female corpse there was an even greater stigma, because of the sexual connotations. No family wanted their mother, sister or daughter's corpse exposed to the gaze of a roomful of lads, even in death.

So maybe his clerk would be able to glean some pertinent details on the middle-aged woman Jack had asked him to help carry in last night, since she wasn't yet at a college. Max had provided Hawley with her description, as well as the date of her demise. If his clerk visited enough workhouses and brothels, it was at least remotely possible that he could identify her and ferret out the circumstances of her disappearance or death. After all, chances were far greater, if she came from Wapping or any place nearby, that she was a member of the poorer class than not. Someone had to remember that artificial eye. Not every woman had one of those.

Then again, not every woman could afford one. He knew a sailor who had survived Trafalgar Square but lost an eye to shrapnel. A doctor replaced it with an enamel one, but that had been quite expensive. So if she had been poor at the end of her life, she hadn't always been destitute . . .

"What are you thinking about?" Abigail asked.

Max pulled himself out of his thoughts. "Nothing."

"Do you always frown like that when you think of nothing?"

Lately, there hadn't been a great deal to smile about. Not after everything he had decided about his own mother—and inadvertently let happen to Madeline. "Apparently."

"You are an unusual man," she said.

"Unusual as in 'interesting'?" He tugged her to the left to avoid a collision with two small street urchins.

She didn't reply with the same sarcasm. She seemed rather contemplative when she said, "Not quite."

He didn't ask her to clarify. Her excitement over such a small gift—small by his estimation, anyway—was affecting him strangely. He wanted to take down her hair and run his fingers through it . . . to make her laugh.

But such inclinations involved more personal interest than he could afford. His life was mapped out for him; it did not include a beautiful misfit like Abigail Hale.

At the curb, they paused to allow a hackney to go by before crossing the street. For the moment, Abigail seemed content to accompany him, which gave him some hope that he was winning a bit of the trust he had demanded from her. But as they drew closer to Jack's house, her step slowed and, once again, he had to pull her along.

"You had better hide your gifts," he told her as they came upon Wapping High Street. "Such items will assuredly draw the interest and attention of Jack and the others." Then they, too, would wonder why he would spend what he did, given that he had told them he had gambling debts to satisfy.

She put her mirror and brush in the brown wrapping they had come in and tied the strings.

"We will slide it under the house until I can bring it up to you later," he said.

Although she didn't seem to like the idea of parting with the package, even for a short time, he knew it was the idea of encountering Jack and the others that gave her pause. He couldn't blame her for that.

"I need you to continue to be brave," he said.

With a nod, she threw back her shoulders, let him take the brush and mirror and marched on.

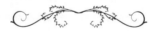

Jack and Tom sat at the table, eating what looked like potato pie with boiled bacon and drinking beer. Both men were wearing the clothes they'd had on the night before, which wouldn't have been so remarkable to Abby—most people in this part of town had only one set of clothing for every day—but it didn't look like they ever washed them. Only Tom had bothered to comb his hair.

As Max dragged her into the house, Jack glared at them with red-rimmed eyes—and Abigail nearly jerked out of his grasp and attempted to flee. So what if Max would chase her down? Maybe, by some miracle, she could elude him.

Once again, however, he proved cautious and tightened his grip, anchoring her to his side.

"Trust her enough to take her out, do you?" Jack said to Max.

Suddenly reverting to the boorish man he had been at the college, Max shoved Abby onto the bench across from Jack and went to the rack to hang his coat. "Didn't trust her enough to leave her behind."

Tom shot Jack a sullen glance. "Or he didn't trust *us*. He's gone sweet on her, like I told ye."

"Shut up," Jack snapped. "I don't need you to tell me anything when he's standing right here."

"He wouldn't let me get anywhere near her," Tom argued despite the rebuke.

"I can't say as I blame him for that," Jack responded. "But he made *me* a promise, too, and I expected him to fulfill it."

"I knocked on your door," Max said with a shrug.

Jack slammed his tankard on the table. "That so?"

"There was no response, but then you were pretty deep in your cups."

"I'm wide awake now."

Abigail's nails curved into her palms. She could tell the animosity between the two men wasn't entirely about her. Not this morning. Jack was challenging Max, testing his loyalties—she was about to learn if the assurances Max had given her were more than mere words.

Bowing her head, she studied the knots in the wood-plank table while awaiting his response.

"If you are craving a woman, I would be happy to help," he said and sat down with them.

Abigail jerked her head up. He hadn't even hesitated before giving in! But then he continued, "I saw Victoria and a handful of doxies, all painted and preening while I was out this morning. No doubt she, or one of her friends, would be happy to pay you a visit."

Jack fixed his eyes on Abby. "You'd hire me a pinchcock, when—"

"A pinchcock? You told me yourself that Victoria's better than the average prostitute. You said she was a 'toffer.'"

"But the surgeon's daughter is right here. Why spend the coin?"

Max crooked an arm around her neck, pulled her to him and slammed his mouth against hers. She had wondered what his kiss would be like, but there was nothing pleasurable about the brutality of *this*. "Because I'm not done with her," he said when he broke off the kiss.

Questioning her sanity for ever trusting Max Wilder in the first place, Abigail twisted to get away but froze when Jack came to his feet. "I didn't ask if you were done with her," he said. "I don't much care one way or the other. I expect you to pay me my due and see to it nicely."

"Then you don't know me very well." Max stood, too, and towered so far over the gang's leader that Abigail guessed Jack couldn't be planning to enforce his words with brute strength. A weapon would *have* to be involved—and there just happened to be one handy. A knife lay on the table, easily within his reach.

"That's the point," Jack said. "I *don't* know you very well. And I'm not convinced I can rely on what you tell me."

"Then kick me out—of this place, of the gang." Several pins fell as Max fisted his hand in Abby's hair and bent to inhale the scent of it. "Because this woman belongs to me," he said, "and no one touches what is mine. Not even you."

When Jack tensed, Abigail caught her breath. As the gang's leader, he had a reputation to maintain—and Tom was sitting right there.

But something—the fear of failure?—caused him to hold back. "And what would you do then?" he asked.

"There's no telling," Max replied. "I could join a rival gang—"

"I'd kill you first."

Max came off as unconcerned, but Abby sensed a level of awareness that belied that. "You could *try*. But I doubt you would succeed. Or maybe I wouldn't join another gang; maybe I would start my own."

"You think I'd let you compete with me? When I'm the one who taught you everything you know?"

"It isn't difficult to figure out how to steal a corpse, Jack."

"It takes more money to go it alone than you've got or you wouldn't have come to me in the first place."

"You think I can't find someone else to put up the bribe money and split my take? You pay off the sheriff for the remains of any criminal who's executed. You pay off any sexton who's willing to alert you to news of a recent burial. You pay off the directors of certain almshouses to look the other way when some poor bugger dies. Did I miss anything?"

"You'd start an all-out war between us," Jack warned. "I won't have you linin' yer pockets at my expense."

"I could always pay a visit to the police instead. They might be interested in hearing about the woman you brought home last night."

Abigail screamed when Jack grabbed the knife, but Max was prepared. He caught Jack's wrist before he could make any kind of slashing motion, and forced the blade out of his grip. It clattered on the table and remained there until he wrestled Jack around and put the knife to his throat.

"Surely, I make a better friend than foe," he gritted out. "Wouldn't you say?"

Jack's eyes flared wide. No doubt he could feel the power of the man behind him and knew he was no match for it. "I-I lost my temper is all, Max. You know how I can be. I can be rash when provoked."

Max made a clicking sound with his tongue. "I don't like it when you're rash, Jack. I don't consider it polite." He glanced up. "What about you, Abby? Wouldn't you say Big Jack here could improve upon his manners?"

Abby didn't know how to respond. She had no idea if Max would really hurt him or not, but she got the impression he wanted to—and that was frightening in its own right.

She backed away, hoping to get out of the house. But Tom came up from behind, slipped both arms around her and licked her cheek. "Relax, I got you," he murmured. "No matter what happens, you're not goin' anywhere."

"Can you blame me?" Jack asked Max. "First you want nothin' to do with the chit. Then you want her all to yourself."

"A man has the right to change his mind," Max responded.

Jack lifted his hands. "I see that. It was just . . . I had no idea she meant so much to you."

"I haven't had a woman warm my bed in quite some time and am loath to give her up too soon. You understand."

"I do," he said. "Of course I do. Just . . . put the knife away!"

Max let him go but held the blade at the ready in case he was threatened again. "Are you going to let a mere woman come between us?" he asked. "Or can I get you a doxy and we call it even?"

Jack swiped at a small trickle of blood on his neck. "*Never* do that again."

When he answered, Max was far from contrite. "It wasn't my idea to do it this time. As I have told you before, I need only fall in with you long enough to repay my debts. Then I will be on my way. But if you would rather I make other arrangements, say the word and Abby and I will vacate the premises."

"You held a knife to my throat!"

"The knife you first tried to use on me."

"Max isn't like us," Tom said, jumping in. "He doesn't belong here."

"Is that what you have to say?" Jack cried. "Because he's worth two of you."

Tom's voice took on a sullen note. "At least I'm loyal."

"You're only as loyal as you have to be." Jack jerked his head toward Max. "That makes you no different than him."

There were plenty of other differences, though. Even Abigail could name the most important one. While Tom was no challenge, Jack feared alienating Max.

"You can say that?" Tom cried. "After all we've done together?"

"I can say that." Jack slumped into his seat and took a long pull of his beer. "So put your tongue back in your mouth, let go of that bitch and finish your damn pie. Or I'll get rid of *you* instead of him."

Tom released Abby, but he didn't sit down. He stalked out of the house and slammed the door behind him.

"He'll be back," Jack said with an unconcerned wave. "Who else'll take him in and make it possible for him to fill his belly? He doesn't have a friend in the world, besides his brother, and his brother can't function any better than he does. They're both sons of a prostitute that left 'em on the street."

Abigail might have pitied Tom if she didn't dislike him so much. Unsure of what to do with herself—she was still reeling from the near stabbing she had just witnessed—she sank onto the bench.

Jack shoved the rest of Tom's meal at her. "Have some pie."

Chapter 10

To keep Abby safe and stop her from making another attempt to gain her freedom, Max locked her in his room and pocketed the key. He hated to do that, but he had to do *something*. At least he could go about the rest of his business feeling assured that she wasn't going anywhere—and that Jack or Tom wouldn't be able to reach her. But he knew better than to expect her to sit there alone, and idle, for hours. She would be that much more likely to plot some way to incapacitate him when he joined her later. So he carried up a tub of hot water and put her to work washing and mending his clothes. He was picky enough to want everything done right, and Abby admitted she had little experience with such things. She said her father hired a laundress for a few shillings a month, since they both worked. But any good Englishwoman could sew, and she was smart enough to figure out the rest.

If he could only get her to be patient long enough, he felt confident he could learn what he needed to know about Madeline. Not three nights past, while they were digging up a corpse at St. James's Burial Ground, he overheard the sexton ask Jack about the pretty redhead who had been with him the last time.

Jack hadn't given a clear answer. He had pretended not to know what the man was talking about. Even when Max asked Jack about it afterward, he claimed that the woman ran away.

Max wondered if that "redhead" might have been Madeline. His sister had dark auburn hair. She had also mentioned Jack's name the last time she came to visit, when she tried to convince him that one final purse, a small one, would be all she would ever require of him.

"I have found someone who wants to marry me," she had said. *"He may not be the most respectable man in London. He is not even a man I could ever respect, let alone love. But he makes a decent living, enough to keep a roof over Byron's head, and has promised to make us a family."*

"Are you sure you want to spend the rest of your life with a man you cannot admire?" he had asked her.

"Those finer feelings are luxuries I cannot afford," she had responded. *"At least I will get to be a mother to my son—at last."*

"And who is this man?" he had pressed.

"They call him Big Jack."

Because she had responded grudgingly, sparing all but that essential detail, Max had held the money he was about to give her just inches away from her fingertips when he asked, *"How does he earn this 'decent living'?"*

She had hesitated, bit her lip and mumbled something about body snatching being a necessary evil. Then she had grabbed the pouch and hurried out.

If not for that brief exchange, he would not have been able to trace her to the London Supply Company . . .

At least little Byron was now being looked after at Max's own estate in Essex, to keep him well separated from Max's mother, who lived at the London town house and was so displeased that Max would take him in. If the people Madeline had hired to care for him hadn't sent word that she hadn't paid them, that they hadn't heard from her in the week since they said they would turn her son out, Byron could have ended up in the street.

Max remembered how grateful he had been when Madeline left, how he had hoped she was right and he would never have to see her again—and chafed beneath the guilt that welled up. If only he had taken some pity on her over the last several years.

He would have, had he not been bound by the loyalty he felt to his mother—until he learned that loyalty was undeserved.

"Mr. Wilder. What a pleasure to see you."

Max blinked and focused on the man who had entered the parlor where he had been waiting, top hat at his side, after having taken an omnibus to Whitechapel. Ebenezer Holmes was an undertaker who sold coffins he advertised as "burglar-proof metallic grave vaults." They sported ten massive concealed locks designed to keep even the most determined body snatcher out—but, for a price, Mr. Holmes provided Jack with the key.

"The pleasure is all mine," Max said.

"Where is Jack?" he asked.

Max couldn't avoid thinking about Abby, and hoping Jack was far away from her. "I'm afraid he had other business."

Ebenezer's thick black eyebrows knitted together. "I am not important enough that he feels the need to come himself?"

"He knows that you are a wise man and will see reason, once I lay out our side of the argument," Max said, managing a placating smile.

Ebenezer yelled into the hall for someone to bring them tea and closed the door behind him before striding to the chair opposite the settee Max had been using. "What can you possibly say to change my mind?"

Max slid his hat farther to the right as he sank into his original seat. "You are unhappy."

"As I indicated in my letter."

"Because . . ."

"Since Burke and Hare ran amok in Scotland and killed those poor souls, the public has become so agitated, I could face a lynch mob should news of my . . . um . . . *arrangement* with your company ever come to light."

"Burke and Hare did their killing two years ago, and you have done plenty of business with Jack since."

"Public sentiment only gets worse. You've heard of the riots."

Adopting a somberness designed to mirror the concern the other man conveyed, Max leaned forward. "And more money for you will somehow soothe the public?"

"It will at least compensate me for the threat."

"Depending on gender and size, we already pay you a guinea or more," Max pointed out. "A guinea for little or nothing."

"While you make ten times that."

As Max had suspected, it wasn't the threat of exposure that bothered Mr. Holmes. That threat hadn't changed enough in the past several weeks to precipitate this meeting. His complaint revealed nothing but greed, which provoked little sympathy on Max's part. "We are the ones risking a public beating by slipping into the graveyards late at night, trying to break into the vaults you have created," he said.

"For which I provide the key!"

Max folded his hands in his lap to keep from ringing the man's scrawny neck. He didn't want to leave Abby vulnerable—couldn't quit worrying that he had. But he needed to see to Jack's business, as Jack had requested, or he'd only create more problems. "Ah, but if not for us, no one would need a burglar-proof vault, the sale of which provides the bulk of your income. To be so sought after also lends you a certain . . . respectability, which I know you enjoy. Have you considered the less tangible benefits to your association with the London Supply Company?"

Ebenezer lifted his pointy chin as if he had been expecting this line of reasoning. "I have. I have also considered that you are not the only resurrectionists in town. If you won't pay me more, maybe others will."

"We may not be the only resurrectionists, but we are probably the most successful." Jack did all he could to insure it. If competition arose, he took drastic measures to quash it, sometimes even denouncing whomever it was to the police. According to him, in order to put a rival out of business, he once left several empty coffins standing around the cemetery at Abbey Park, the graves from which they had been taken, unfilled. Jack had laughed when he said the borough where he did this was so outraged they wouldn't go near the cemetery for weeks, let alone bury anyone there.

"As long as I get what I deserve, I don't care," Ebenezer said. "Specimens are harder than ever to come by, and I am one of the few men left who can fill the pockets of *any* resurrectionist."

He was growing arrogant, which only made him that much more insufferable. "Unless that resurrectionist gets himself caught," Max said.

"At which point I will transfer my business to someone else."

"Providing he can be relied upon to keep his mouth shut about you."

Ebenezer shrugged. "Why would he talk? He wouldn't be held long. And, if he's smart, he has made arrangements with the various colleges to support his family while he is imprisoned."

Max idly turned his hat. "The desperation your fellow Englishmen feel to protect their dead is already providing you with a comfortable living." He indicated the new furnishings in the room.

"Indeed."

"So why press your luck by trying to renegotiate? Jack told me when he met you, you barely had two halfpennies to rub together."

He lifted a hand. "That was then. Unless you are prepared to offer me far more than you have paid in the past, I choose to discontinue our association."

Max was determined to make sure this man got everything he deserved—but not by paying more. He would expose him. He just couldn't do it too soon. Neither could he lose the business this man brought Jack, not after what had happened between them this morning. He had to prove his value.

Sitting back, he removed a speck of lint from his trousers. "How much are you asking?"

"Five guineas."

Max chuckled under his breath. "Jack will never agree to such a sum."

"Then he can find his corpses another way." The tea arrived, but Ebenezer told the bony servant who carried the tray to take it up to his study. He obviously believed their meeting was over—but Max wasn't finished quite yet.

"Are you sure you want to cross Jack?"

Ebenezer had gotten up and started for the door, but at this he froze. "*Cross* Jack? This is a business decision."

Max came to his feet. "You and I both know he won't see it that way. He feels you owe him a great deal. Without him, you would never have been able to start your coffin company. But I will pass the word along that you don't appreciate what he has done, if that is truly what you would like me to tell him."

The undertaker's Adam's apple bobbed as he swallowed. "This has nothing to do with appreciation."

"I can tell."

His expression hardened. "And so what if you tell him? He may not like it, but what can he do?"

"You can't answer that question yourself?"

They stared at each other for several seconds before Ebenezer wet his lips and ventured, "He wouldn't—"

"You know he would," Max broke in. "And should it become known that your burglar-proof vaults aren't burglar proof at all, that almost every one you have sold is actually empty—something that would be easy to prove should anyone have half a mind to dig them up and put them on display—you would be ruined."

He seemed to be having trouble breathing. "That-that's blackmail," he sputtered.

Max bowed. "Blackmail. Extortion. Call it what you will."

Such a cavalier response made him even angrier. "How dare you threaten me! That's against the law!"

"Believe me, Jack has committed far more heinous crimes."

"Then perhaps I shall turn *him* in!"

"If you do, he will only take you down with him."

He stood there, his chest rising and falling in conjunction with the flaring of his nostrils. "It was a mistake to get involved with him, to . . . to ever trust him."

"Yes. Just as it is a mistake for your clients to trust you," Max said. "I will convey to Jack the good news that we can expect twice as many corpses from you in the future. I predict he will be grateful."

"*What?* I said nothing about supplying you with more!"

"You agreed that business was better than ever. I said something about your fellow Englishmen providing you with a comfortable living in their efforts to protect their dead, and you said, *Indeed*. Why would we allow you to sell access to your 'burglar-proof coffins' to someone else?"

The undertaker pursed his lips so tightly that it expunged all the color from them. "How dare you . . ."

Ignoring this retort, Max moved on. "Several days ago, you mentioned you would have something for us this week, likely tonight. If that's the case, I should get the key while I'm here. Maybe it will ease Jack's concern over your near defection."

Ebenezer couldn't seem to bring himself to respond right away. But eventually he straightened his waistcoat, gave Max a curt nod and left the room.

He returned a few moments later. "It'll be at St. Andrew's tonight," he said as he handed over the key.

"That's near the cemetery we went to last time, at St. George's?"

"Yes. Off Gray's Inn Road."

"Fine. You will receive your guinea as soon as we have successfully squired off the brother, sister or other loved one of your latest client." Settling his hat on his head, Max started out as though his business was done. But now that he had Mr. Holmes alone, for the first time, he had more to say. He just had to be careful how he said it.

"By the way." He turned back as if a new thought had occurred to him. "There is one more thing."

"And that is . . . ?" His mouth barely moved for the stiffness of his jaw.

"This squabble over money. It didn't come up because you have been approached by someone else with a better offer . . ."

"No," he said quickly. "No, of course not. I was hoping to work things out with Jack all along."

At least the man was wise enough to be somewhat diplomatic in his defeat. "Then you haven't heard from the redheaded woman who was to marry him?"

"Marry *Jack*? I never heard that she and Jack were planning to marry."
Hope caused Max's heart to pound in his chest. "But you have met her."

"Once. Maybe . . . two months ago? She came by with Jack but
hasn't been back since. I swear it."

Here was someone else who had seen a redheaded woman with Jack.
"Maybe we're not talking about the same person. Did you catch her
name?"

"No."

"Are you certain? Could it have been Madeline?"

"Perhaps. I don't remember, but"—he paused and frowned—"now
that you mention it, I do believe I heard him call her *Maddy*." He lowered his voice in disbelief. "Don't tell me she has gone out on her own.
A woman in the resurrection business? Without a man? Where would
she get the physical strength for such work? And the nerve?"

"It's possible she has help."

"Still! A female body snatcher! What's this world coming to?"

Max knew he should let it go at that. He didn't want Holmes mentioning his query to Jack when they next spoke, but the pressure he felt
to return Abigail to the college, and to find Madeline before it was too
late—if it wasn't too late already—forced him to press a little harder.
"Is there any chance you might know where I can find her?"

"No. But if she contacts me, I will be sure to send word straightaway."

"It's a bit of a sore subject with Jack, the way she jilted him."

"He must have been furious!"

"Indeed, so if you happen to see or hear anything about Madeline,
I would appreciate you alerting me and me only. I would even pay you
a few guineas for your discretion." He would have said he'd pay handsomely. He was willing to part with just about any sum. But it would
not serve him well to let Mr. Holmes know how desperate he was.

When Ebenezer narrowed his gaze, Max feared he had already
revealed too much.

"You aren't planning to oust Jack, to take over the London Supply
Company by joining forces with this woman?"

"No." Max breathed a sigh of relief that the undertaker hadn't guessed the real reason for his interest. "I am too loyal for that."

"Loyal? In this business? That won't get you very far. You should take control. *You* are the stronger leader. Think of how much more you could make."

"Greed often leads to trouble," he warned and left.

Abby listened for any creak, rattle or footfall, any indication at all that Jack or Tom might be hovering outside the door, hoping to find some way into the room. She knew, without being told, that they would love nothing more than to prove Max wrong in his belief that he could keep her to himself. The challenge he had created, not to mention the insult, strengthened their desire and determination. But, other than a few settling noises, she heard nothing.

Before long, she became convinced that she was in the house alone, which made her almost as frustrated as she was relieved. This would have been the perfect time to escape! If only Max or Jack hadn't tied Borax to the tree outside her window. Even if she was willing to risk breaking her neck by climbing out, the second she dropped to the ground, she would be eaten alive. Whenever she appeared at the window, Borax stared up at her as though salivating at the thought.

She was stuck stewing and washing Max Wilder's clothes—or what was left of them.

Preening in the mirror, she admired the simple dress she had created by disassembling one of his coats, incorporating one of his shirts and using the fabric of a cravat and a pair of his trousers for trim. If she had to continue to share a room with him, at least now she had something better to wear than her gypsy rags.

She was proud of her resourcefulness. But, in her more reflective moments, she was also frightened as to how he would react when he saw the results of her day with a needle and thread. His clothing had been better quality than the average person's; no doubt those garments had cost him a goodly sum. But he had every other advantage the situation could offer. He could hardly begrudge her a decent change of clothes.

A noise from downstairs brought her to the door. Someone was home.

Was it Max?

She pressed her ear to the wooden panel but, unable to hear anything else, crossed over to the window to look out. She couldn't see the courtyard from her vantage point—only the dog. By the way Borax strained against his leash, however, something was going on.

Sure enough, a second later she heard Max, Jack or Tom rummaging around.

Or was it her father? Had he finally come?

Feeling a burst of claustrophobia and desperation, she was tempted to call out, but Max's warning about her father's safety kept her quiet. Her father didn't need to become embroiled in the mess she had created. It would threaten everything he loved—cost him the school and maybe even his knighthood. Max had said he would return her to the college eventually, and since he had protected her on two occasions, she was beginning to believe he would keep that promise.

The question was . . . when?

The stairs creaked as someone climbed them. Then the knob on the door to her room turned and rattled when whoever it was realized it was locked.

She pressed a hand to her chest in a futile attempt to push down the fear that sprang up. "Who is it?"

"Where's Max?" a terse voice replied.

Jack. Fear made her skin prickle. "I haven't seen him since he locked me in this room."

"If you'd rather be locked in *my* room, all you have to do is say so. We'll figure it out, you and I. And I'll make damn sure you get that elephant back—that and a lot more."

As much as she longed for her beloved keepsake, he couldn't bribe her, not even if he offered her the moon. She would rather die than let him lay a hand on her.

Laughing softly when she didn't answer, he said, "What if I gave you a few shillings of the money we took *and* that fancy bauble?"

No doubt, to a common prostitute, that would sound like a generous offer. But she prayed he would just move on down the hall. "I want to go home."

"I could arrange for that, too, in due time. How much is it worth to you? Would you spread your legs for me first?"

Afraid he might try to bust in, she cowered against the far wall, amid all the wet laundry she had draped on the furniture. Was he serious, or just trying to harass her? "Leave me alone."

"You haughty bitch!" he snapped. "You seem content enough to let Wilder have a go!"

If she had her guess, the fact that he believed his rival had taken liberties bothered him more than anything. He wanted to be able to compete with Max, wanted to compare favorably. But he stood no chance. As far as Abby was concerned, it didn't matter that they were both criminals of a sort. Jack wasn't a fraction of the man Max was. Whenever she let her mind wander, her thoughts invariably turned to Max and the comfort he had provided when she finally crawled into bed with him the night before. The more she considered him, the more she began to look forward to seeing him again—ironic, given he was partly to blame for her predicament.

"You're taken with that pretty face of his, eh?" Jack said.

Max's physical attributes were certainly appealing, and seemed to be growing more so the longer she was around him. "I don't know where he is. But he should be home soon," she said. *Please let that be the case.*

"He better be," Jack responded. "Because if he doesn't come back, there will be no more asking you nicely. I'll lift your skirts whenever and wherever I decide."

Feeling sick, Abigail slid down the wall. As far as she knew, her father hadn't come looking for her as expected. She had never felt more alone, and she had felt alone for most of her life.

Where was Max? Why would Jack suggest that he might not come back? Did he know something she didn't?

"You . . . you wouldn't seriously hurt a member of your own gang, would you?" She hated the tremor in her voice, but she knew he would. He had already pulled a knife on Max once.

"A man like that is going to get what's comin' to him eventually. That's all I'm sayin'. And maybe it'll be sooner rather than later." He rattled the doorknob again. "Maybe it'll even be tonight," he said and whistled while he walked away.

Chapter 11

Someone was following him. This time, Max felt sure. He didn't recognize any of the faces he saw when he turned to look, but the hair stood up on the back of his neck. It was almost as if he could hear footsteps that fell in stride with his own. Every time he walked, someone else did, too.

He stopped in an alcove and waited, hoping to take whomever it was by surprise.

No one suspicious passed by.

Leaning out, he gazed down the narrow street. But it was raining and far too dark in the warrens off Whitechapel Road to distinguish one individual from the next. It could be Jack who was trailing him, or another member of the London Supply Company. Or it could be nothing more than a desperate or greedy pickpocket hoping to lift his purse.

Pulling his coat tightly closed to avoid the wet, he shoved off the grimy brick building, hurried around a small bend and ducked into a dimly lit brothel on Berners Street.

A stout woman, dressed in a red velvet, low-cut gown—the procuress, no doubt—introduced herself as Jane Davenport and offered him an eager smile. He had seen similar smiles—far more shrewd than they were meant to appear—on a hundred women or more as he combed through the seediest parts of Wapping, Covent Garden and Whitechapel.

"What can I do for you tonight?" She got up from her desk and came around to meet him. There was a sitting room to one side, where a cat lounged on a chaise next to a table bearing tea and cakes. "Would you like to start with something hot to drink?"

"No, thank you." He preferred to get right to the point, to ask if she had seen Madeline and describe his half sister while studying her face for any hint of recognition. But if he had been followed, he dared not make his purpose so obvious lest someone from the London Supply Company question her after he left. As anxious as he was, as cognizant of the passing days and the fruitlessness of what he had accomplished so far, he could not grow careless. He had to be prudent—and not just for his own sake. Abby was at Farmer's Landing. She was depending on him, too.

"I'm looking for a young woman."

"Most of the men who come in here are," she responded, batting her eyelashes. "Have we met before?"

He feared maybe they had, in his wilder days. To his parents' dismay, he and his best friend, Ethan, hadn't always kept the best company while they were getting an education at Cambridge, and she looked vaguely familiar. But it was important she not recognize him.

"No, I'm sure we haven't. I'm new to Whitechapel," he said and scowled in concentration, pretending to study the handbill posted on a sign next to her desk. This handbill gave a physical description of the prostitutes within her establishment, including each woman's sexual specialties. It reminded him of the notorious gentleman's guide to the current brothels and prostitutes in London—*Harris's List of Covent Garden Ladies*—even though it hadn't been published in some years, since The Proclamation Society brought the publisher up on charges in an effort to stop the dispersing of "poison" to the young and unwary. He'd barely been born when that happened, but he'd seen a copy while he was at Cambridge.

"Then let me be one of the first to welcome you and to assure you that you will receive nothing but pleasure here—all my girls are clean."

Judging by the smell of the brothel, that was nothing Max could ever take for granted. He pitied the fools who did. But this establishment was definitely a cut above the competition, especially for these parts. He could see why so many recommended Madame Davenport's.

She slipped her arm through his as she guided him across the room to a high-backed chair. "Here, sit. Let me get you a handbill you can study more closely." She stepped back, making him uncomfortable again by eyeing him carefully. "Although . . . maybe I can make the decision an easy one. I have recently acquired a new girl, a virgin of only fifteen. I'm guessing a man as virile as you might enjoy the taking of such innocence, yes?"

Virgins were so sought after that some women physically altered their bodies in an attempt to pass themselves off as never having been with a man. Procuresses liked virgins, too, because they sold for a premium. But Madeline had had a child. Max doubted she would ever try to pass herself off as untouched, even if she had sunk as low as prostitution.

"I prefer a woman with some experience," he said. Those words weren't simply his way of furthering his search. They were true—or used to be. Almost as soon as he said them, he thought of Abby. She had no experience whatsoever, and yet she appealed to him just as she was.

God, Abby again? He couldn't seem to get her off his mind. At random moments, her pleasure over the mirror and brush set he'd bought her would pop into his head—and he'd smile. Or he'd remember the no-nonsense way she had described sexual intercourse, as if she knew so much when she knew next to nothing, and he would chuckle to himself.

"Rather than have me choose from a piece of paper, why don't you bring them all out?" he asked Madame Davenport. "I'll know what I want when I see it."

She blinked in surprise. "I'm afraid that's impossible. Some are already working."

"Then show me what you've got." Since he couldn't *ask* if she had seen someone of Madeline's description, he would have to check for himself.

"As you wish." Stepping back so he could sit down, she gave him a nod and bustled off.

When she returned some fifteen minutes later, she had ten women in tow.

Max nearly jumped to his feet when he spotted one, entering the room behind two others. She had hair the same color as Maddy's! That shade was so unusual, he felt sure he had finally found his sister, so sure that his breath caught as he anticipated whisking her away.

But . . . no. As he shifted in his seat to see her face, he realized the girl was far too young. She wasn't nearly as pretty, either.

The bitter taste of disappointment rose in his mouth as he pretended to consider the selection. "How many more possibilities do you have?" he asked.

"Six," Madame Davenport informed him. "And we get more every week if we don't have something here you like."

He would have to come back to see the other six—just like he had to revisit all the other places he'd been, in case something had changed since he had been there before. He wanted to dismiss them all so he could move on, but he couldn't leave the premises quite yet. He had to stay long enough to convince whomever had been following him that he had come for the usual reason.

After selecting a woman who reminded him, although remotely, of Abigail, which was somehow a positive association, he let her lead him into the back.

The girl told him her name was Kitty and wound her arms around his neck as soon as the door closed behind them, but he set her aside. Whatever he had imagined in this woman to be like Abigail—he could already tell she was nothing like her in reality. "I'm too tired for anything more than a good rub," he said.

"A *rub*?" she echoed as if it were a disappointment.

"Yes."

"That's a lot of work," she complained. "Takes longer, too, so it'll cost you extra."

"I'll pay it."

"Why? Why not use what you got 'tween your legs instead? Let me enjoy my work, for a change?"

"For a change?" he repeated.

Her lips curved into an appreciative smile as she cupped him. "It's not often we get a man handsome as yourself. It'll give me something to dream about later, when the next guy's fat as butter."

He stopped her from fondling him. "I just want the backrub."

Offended that he would refuse, she stuck her bottom lip out. "Suit yourself, then." She indicated the bed. "Lay down."

Unwilling to touch the linens, he pulled a chair into the center of the room.

"What's that for?" she asked.

"That's where I'm going to sit."

She looked confused. "You don't want to stretch out? If you lay down, maybe I can prove that you're more interested than you thought."

"I'm afraid not."

"No one'll believe you were such a disappointment," she grumbled, but once she started to knead his shoulders, he thought he was the one who had the right to complain. He'd never had a worse backrub.

But her lack of skill didn't matter. He was just biding his time. In another quarter of an hour, he could walk out without worrying that whoever had been nipping at his heels might find it strange that he had stayed for only a few minutes.

"Do you like this?" the girl asked.

He made a noise indicating assent.

"It would be nice if you remembered I'm in the room once in a while, you know."

His mind had been drifting—he'd been thinking of Abby again, wondering what she was doing. He needed to hurry home so that he could make sure she had what she needed before going to work with Jack and the others.

"I'm paying you; you're not paying me," he reminded her. "I owe you no favors."

She shut up after that, and they managed to whittle away twenty minutes. But after making himself dally that long, he walked out and headed down the street—and it was only a few minutes later when he felt that same creeping sensation that he was being followed.

Determined to figure out who it was—and to put a stop to it—he ducked into the alcove of a tavern but didn't go inside. He slipped around a knot of men who were just exiting instead—and waited.

Sure enough, Emmett came skulking up, hesitant lest he be overeager and get himself caught, but so intent on seeing inside the entrance when the door opened again that he didn't notice Max standing to the side.

"Why are you following me?" Max asked as he grabbed his arm.

Emmett didn't seem overly concerned. He merely flipped his wet hair out of his face. "Why do you think? Jack asked me to. He's asked me to do it a number of times."

Max had expected him to lie. He liked Emmett much better when he didn't. "I left Farmer's Landing well before you."

"No. I started out immediately after, just as soon as we divided the money from Aldersgate."

Max studied him. Did he know anything? Did he seem concerned or overly suspicious? "And?" he asked. "Have I done anything particularly interesting this evening? Or before, for that matter?"

"Not that I can tell. You do a lot of walking, I can say that."

He hadn't been *walking*; he'd been searching. Besides Madame Davenport's brothel, he had visited several taverns. He'd asked about Madeline at each. Had Emmett gone in afterward to inquire as to his business there? Or had he simply continued to follow? "Why would Jack be interested in what I do on my own time?" he asked.

"He thinks you're up to something." Emmett spat at the ground. "You know Jack. He always thinks the worst."

"That's true enough, but I'm a little surprised you'd tell me. You know he wouldn't like it."

Emmett kicked a stone as they started down the street together. "You gonna give me away?"

"I haven't decided yet. Answer my question, and we'll see."

"You're a decent chap, not angry like Jack and not weak like Bill. I like having you around; I don't want him to run you off."

Max couldn't help feeling sorry for Emmett. He'd been born into the squalor of Whitechapel. After being abandoned by a destitute mother, he'd had to shift for himself on these streets—by begging, trading sex for money or pickpocketing. Emmett knew Aldgate, Bethnal Green, Mile End, Limehouse, Bow and the other villages east of London better than the rats that infested the area.

"He won't run me off for visiting a brothel, will he?"

"Not normally."

"Is this somehow different?"

"Can't say as he'll understand it now that you got that pretty surgeon's daughter he wants so badly for himself. I mean, what would you want with a common whore when you can dip your wick in something like her—especially you, clean as you are?"

Max had pulled on his gloves before leaving Madame Davenport's. He smoothed them on tighter as they reached Whitechapel Road. "Maybe I have a predilection for things Abby doesn't know how to do."

"A pre . . . what?"

Emmett might not know what the word meant, but he certainly understood more about human fetishes and perversion than most people. After he had worked as a mudlarker—a child who scavenged the coal that spilled from coal barges down at the docks—he had become a male prostitute until he grew too old to be attractive to the type of man who typically hired him. "A common whore will perform certain . . . favors a man can't ask of a regular woman."

"Oh. Aye. But you don't seem the type to need . . ." He stretched his neck. "Never mind. I'm just glad you came out of Madame Davenport's when you did. Jack remembered something right after you left and changed our meeting spot for tonight. He wouldn't have been happy if you didn't show up for work tonight."

Max thought of Abby. He'd assumed he would have the chance to take her more food before going to work with the others. What he had left couldn't be enough to keep her from going to bed hungry. "I just need to head home and make sure Abby has everything she needs. Then I'll join you."

"I'd let Abby wait, if I were you."

"Excuse me?"

He shoved past two men who were haggling over something and standing in their way. "If you go all the way to Wapping, you won't get back in time. And it'll seem strange that you've got so much to do you can't make a midnight rendezvous, especially when you need money as bad as you do."

Something about the way Emmett said that last part made Max uneasy. Was he simply trying to be helpful, to look out for him? Or did he know more than he'd let on? "Why wouldn't I make it back? Where are we meeting?"

"Just down the street here, at St. Mary's. We're almost there now."

But Abby had to be getting hungry . . . "I'll have to be late. We have a corpse on the sofa. We have to deliver that, anyway—before it starts to putrefy."

"Jack and Bill said they'd take care of that. I'm guessing they already have."

Max got the impression that this was some sort of test—and figured he and Abby would probably both be safer if he complied. "Fine. She won't starve in one night. We'll go now and get it over with."

They traveled the remaining blocks in silence. But once they could see St. Mary's, Emmett pulled Max to a stop. "So . . . what is it you wanted that whore to do?"

Max hid a smile. He had the boy's imagination going. "I guess you should have followed me inside."

He offered Max a sheepish look and wiped the rain out of his face. "I was afraid you might break my jaw if I did."

"You're smart to trust your instincts there," he said and clapped him on the back. "Because if I ever find you following me again, I *will* break your jaw."

Emmett's eyes widened when he realized that Max was serious. "I was just doing what I was told."

"Then you might want to apprise Jack of the danger."

"That means tell him, right?"

Max dipped his head to confirm it. "That's exactly what it means."

The house had been silent for some time, making Abby believe Jack had left. She didn't hear from him or Tom, but as the hours inched along on leaden feet, she grew more and more worried about Max. Darkness fell and he didn't return. He had left her a platter of bread and cheese and a pot of tea, but the food was gone. Surely, he would remember that she needed more to eat and would arrive soon to tend to her needs, since she had no way of tending to herself . . .

Where are you? Why aren't you back?

While she'd spent her day worrying about how Max might react to the dress she had made at his expense, or remembering how warm and oddly content she had been at various moments when she was pressed up against him the night before, she'd spent the evening consumed with imagining Jack, or someone Jack had put to the task, trying to prevent Max from returning to Farmer's Landing, possibly for good.

Had he been murdered like that woman downstairs probably was? Were Jack and Tom out right now, selling *Max's* corpse to one of the colleges for ten guineas?

If so, he would soon be dissected and, more likely than not, no one would ever be the wiser . . .

Pivoting at the window, she recalled Max checking behind them repeatedly when they were walking to St. Catherine's that morning.

She could only hope he was still watching his back as carefully—because if he didn't return, she may never see her father again.

Chapter 12

Abigail must have fallen asleep. The next thing she knew, it was pitch-black, with just a thin sliver of moon grinning through the window and Max was climbing into bed with her. Knowing he was safe doused her worry. Thank God! But where had he been? And why would he leave her for so long?

"What time is it?" she mumbled.

"Late," he replied. "I've brought food. Are you hungry?"

She could smell it, but she was too upset to eat. "I don't want anything."

"Are you sure? Do you need to go to the privy?"

"*Now* you ask?" She was secretly so relieved to see him she could cry, but she wasn't about to throw her arms around him like she wanted to—not after what he had put her through.

He tried to pull her into the cradle of his body, to settle her for sleep as they had slept the night before, but she wouldn't let him. She had taken off the dress she made—she still didn't know how he was going to react to *that*—and was in her drawers and shift. She had decided to help him keep the linens clean since he was so meticulous about it, but that didn't leave her with a lot of modest options. She didn't want to sleep in her new dress and her gypsy rags were too filthy. She would have washed them but she didn't want them to be wet when Max returned. Then she wouldn't be able to wear them, and she wasn't quite ready to show him that she'd cut up his clothes to make a dress.

"You scared me." She kept her back, which was turned to him, ram-rod straight.

"I know. You must have been terrified when I was gone for so long. I'm sorry. I came as soon as I could." He caressed her arm, obviously trying to get her to forgive him, but she told herself she shouldn't do that too easily. He deserved to be rebuffed after leaving her for hours and hours.

"Jack won't let you get away with humiliating him in front of Tom," she voiced, now that she had the chance, what had been going through her mind all evening. "He . . . he wants to best you in some way. Show you that you can't outdo him. Maybe he even wants to . . . to seriously harm you."

"Nothing's going to happen to me, Abby," he assured her. "Or you."

She turned to look at him but could make out only the gleam of his eyes and a few of the planes and angles of his face. "How can you be so certain?"

"I will see to it."

He had promised her safety, but he couldn't control *everything*. With the animosity she sensed coming from Jack, it was difficult to believe Max would be able to keep *himself* safe, let alone her. "You don't have eyes in the back of your head. Anything could happen."

"Shh . . ." He stroked her hair, smoothing it away from her face. "If I don't check in regularly with that man you saw me meet today, he will go straight to the police *and* your father. I have instructed him to do so."

"*Instructed* him? Why would he listen to you?" Her voice cracked, offering proof that she was suddenly and inexplicably battling tears.

He must have noticed because he pulled her closer in spite of her resistance. "He has good reason. Don't cry. That makes me feel even worse."

"My father didn't come today," she blurted. "Do you think he doesn't care that I'm gone?" It was Thursday. Maybe he had been too busy to notice. He and Mr. Holthouse had their general and morbid anatomy lecture at half past two, but surely Mr. Holthouse could have covered the class. They didn't even have a cadaver for their lectures this year, which was why she had been trying so hard to procure one. They had been limping along using various well-preserved samples her father had collected through the years, as well as some exhibits loaned to him by Sir Astley Cooper.

Max leaned up on one elbow. "I'm sure nothing could be further from the truth."

"It could be that he's glad to no longer be saddled with the burden of a daughter who should be married but isn't."

"He's pushing you to marry?"

"Of course. What else is there for a woman?"

"That's true. Perhaps you will be more amenable to it after this little adventure," he said as he lay back down.

"Are you suggesting that being abducted should endear me to men?"

"I haven't abducted you! You came to me."

"You are holding me against my will. And I don't even know why."

"I am keeping you here for your own safety—and to guard against a surge of conscience. The more variables I control, the better off I will be."

"And me? Will I be better off, too?"

"You won't be here for very long."

"I could be, if my father doesn't care enough to even look for me."

"Your father is probably searching right this very minute. No doubt he will be here by morning."

She swallowed against the lump that clogged her throat. "If I were a son, I would be a surgeon already." She wasn't sure why she volunteered that—except she feared her father lamented her gender as much as she did.

"You are every bit as good as a son," Max said. "And I bet your father would be the first to admit it."

How could she be as good as a son? Her father couldn't share his love of medicine with her as he would have with a male child. How many times had he admitted that he didn't know what to do with her—or for her? She had done her best to meld into his world, but even there—*especially* there—her femininity stood between her and true integration.

But she had revealed more of the insecurity that plagued her than she had ever revealed before and didn't want to say more. It was this situation, her vulnerability, that caused her to be so fearful and doubting. Otherwise, she would never question her own father's love.

She changed the subject so she could salvage *some* of her pride. "Did you get that . . . that corpse off the sofa downstairs?"

"We did. It's gone; you can forget about it."

Forgetting would be impossible. Abby had seen a number of dead people over the years, but never had she been forced to contemplate the possibility of someone being murdered for the sake of anatomy—at least not so close to home. Burke and Hare had operated in Edinburgh, which was half a country away. It turned her stomach to think her willingness to pay for a corpse from this very gang might have caused such a heinous crime. "You didn't take her to Aldersgate."

"Of course not. Sir William Blizzard has a surgery coming up, on a gentleman of consequence, and wanted a cadaver to practice on."

"He settled for a woman?"

Max hesitated but eventually responded. "He didn't pay us as much, but . . . yes."

"So you're pleased with your night."

"I'm tired, if you want the truth. And relieved to be back and find you safe."

He sounded sincere, but how much could he really care? He was the one who had kidnapped her! Her own father hadn't even bothered to track her down. If her father was concerned at all, surely he would have arrived at Farmer's Landing by now.

"I have to go to the necessary-house," she announced, rustling the bedding to cover a sniff.

"Come on. I'll take you." He got up and waited while she pulled on her gypsy rags. Then he lit a lamp and draped his coat around her shoulders. Why he hadn't hung it on the hall-tree downstairs, as usual, she didn't know. It made her wonder if he had been telling the truth when he said he had been worried about her. Maybe he had gotten home and immediately hurried up to see her . . .

That was probably nonsense, she told herself, something she made up to feel important to *somebody*.

"You should let me go," she said as they stepped outside, but she didn't sound all that convincing, even to herself. She was beginning to wonder if she didn't belong at Aldersgate, either. After all these years of giving the college such dedicated service, hadn't anyone missed her?

Maybe her father didn't even realize she was gone.

Or had she been kidding herself all along, trying to fit in where she would never be accepted?

It was chilly and starting to rain when they trudged to the privy. Borax was taking cover under the eaves. He snarled to let her know he noticed that she had finally abandoned the safety of her room, but after a quick rebuke from Max, he whined and curled up to sleep. Even a dog could sense Max's authority.

The weather and Borax's reaction seemed fitting, given Abigail's mood. Never had she thought she would be at such loose ends—grateful that her kidnapper had returned to curl up beside her (wasn't a kidnapper someone she should hate?), disappointed that no one had come to find her (how could her father and her other associates at the college not have noticed she was gone?), afraid to remain where she was but too sad to fight for her freedom (where else would she go if those at the college didn't want her?).

"Are you coming out anytime soon?" Max asked.

Once she had gone inside and taken care of her business, she had remained there despite the stench. It made her feel slightly better to make Wilder wait in the rain after what he had done to her. "Coming."

Dashing a hand over her cheeks, she took a few more minutes to compose herself. Then she straightened her clothing and emerged.

"I'm soaked," Max grumbled.

"If you want to have something to complain about, try being locked in a room all day without sufficient food," she responded tartly.

"Was that eternity in the privy your attempt to punish me?"

"It was subtle, but I'm hoping it was effective."

He chuckled as they approached the house. "I have a feeling I am going to miss you when you're gone."

"Are you trying to get my hopes up that I will be leaving soon?"

"Merely encouraging you. Your father will be here tomorrow, Abby. I can't let you go with him, but at least you will be reassured that he is looking."

When she said nothing, he sighed. "Wait here. I'll get your mirror and brush set. Maybe that will cheer you up."

When he crawled under the house to retrieve it, she didn't even try to run. Borax would have sprung into action and taken a chunk out of her leg if she had. But that wasn't the only thing holding her. Trying to escape suddenly seemed like it would require too much effort.

"Here," he said when he returned with her package. "It made you happy this morning."

"Because no one had ever given me anything like it," she grumbled. "But now maybe I understand why."

He took hold of her shoulders. "You are jumping to conclusions— the *wrong* conclusions," he said with an emphatic shake.

He had a point. She needed to quit thinking and doubting and sleep, so she could gain some control over her emotions. Maybe her father had tried to find her but Bransby, thinking she wouldn't want him to, hadn't come forward to help.

Although such a scenario was almost inconceivable, she supposed that *could* be the case. Regardless, no amount of self-pity would change the situation.

Her prospects would look better in the morning, she told herself. She felt somewhat better after she had eaten. But once Max changed into some dry trousers—apparently he didn't have a nightshirt—and she removed her outer garments and climbed into bed, it wasn't long before she noticed something hard pressing against her backside. And the more she shifted around, the bigger it grew.

"Lie still," he finally snapped.

But with her blood suddenly rushing through her veins and roaring in her ears, it felt as if she had slept long enough.

From the moment he had fallen into bed with Abby, Max had been fighting the desire to run his hands up under her shift, to seek out the soft mounds of flesh that strained against the thin fabric. The fact that her behind kept brushing his lap made the impulse that much stronger.

"Are you not tired?" She shifted again.

"I said I was, didn't I?" He didn't mean to be terse, but it was difficult to be polite when he was waging such a battle against his body.

"I guess you did."

She sounded chastened, as if he had struck her, so he softened his voice. "I thought you were tired, too. You were asleep when I arrived."

"That was before we went out in the dark and cold."

"Might I remind you that you are the reason we were out for so long?" In spite of that small rebellion, he would have hugged her tighter. He felt terrible that he had to keep her from her home and wanted to offer as much reassurance as possible until he could return her to safety. But if she wasn't aware of his arousal, he preferred she not encounter evidence of it.

"Do you really think my father might come tomorrow?" she asked.

Did they have to talk about this again? Max wasn't sure how he was going to handle the surgeon when he arrived, but he knew it would involve a great deal of lying, and he wasn't looking forward to the encounter. "It's a possibility."

"So tonight could be our last night together."

"I doubt it, but no one can predict what might happen." As depressed as she had been a few moments ago, he didn't want to extinguish *all* hope.

"Then maybe—"

"Abby!" He spoke her name through gritted teeth when she brushed against him yet again.

"What?"

"You need to hold still."

"*Why?*"

"Because I can't relax unless you do."

"But as long as you're awake, maybe I will take you up on the offer you made this morning."

His entire body went stiff as he blinked against the darkness. "What offer?"

"You don't remember?" She didn't seem embarrassed, only taken aback that he wasn't as eager as he had come off earlier. "Or is it that you weren't serious?"

Mostly, he had been amusing himself by teasing her. He liked that her reactions were so atypical of her sex. He had thought that *maybe* there would come a time when he satisfied her curiosity regarding the male anatomy—but he had never dreamed she would press him to act on those glib words when he couldn't be as objective as she was. "I was serious, more or less," he added to allow himself some wiggle room. "But . . . maybe another time."

"Why not now?" she asked. "Your cock feels as if it's erect, which would be much more interesting to see, since I have viewed many in a flaccid state already."

Her approach was purely clinical. But as he snuggled against the warm softness of her body, he was having a difficult time keeping the same perspective. "I need my sleep."

"It would only take a second."

He was throbbing with the desire to enjoy her intimately, and she merely wanted to examine him like she might an unusual bug.

"If I don't take this opportunity, I may never get another one," she added.

He almost refused in no uncertain terms and rolled over. But he was too tempted to put her at the same disadvantage he was, to demonstrate what it felt like to be so aroused. Just the thought of obliterating her emotional detachment, of making her gasp and moan and strain to join her body with his, made him short of breath.

But she was a novice. It wouldn't be fair to capitalize on her innocence. So he tried to distract her instead. "Tomorrow."

"Why wait? Is there something *wrong* with you, something you are embarrassed to show me?" she asked.

His surprise distracted him. "Like . . . ?"

"According to what I have overheard from the students at the college, some men are very sensitive about the size of their . . . their manhood and whether or not it is sufficiently . . . impressive."

He drew in a lungful of air as he attempted to calm down. "I assure you I have never had any complaints about my manhood."

"Even if you are less than what you might wish when it comes to . . . to size or what have you, I want you to know you are completely safe with me. I won't say one demeaning word, especially to Jack and Tom. Not one. I swear it."

"That's it," Max said.

She widened her eyes in feigned innocence. "That's what?"

He could tell she wasn't so naïve that she didn't know how she had challenged him—and a woman wily enough to try to manipulate a man in that way deserved to get what she was asking for, and then some.

Only he would deliver the education she wanted on *his* terms. "I'll remove my trousers," he announced. "On one condition."

Her lips curved into a victorious smile. "And that is . . . ?"

"You have to give *me* something first."

Her smiled faded. "Surely you have seen a naked woman."

That would be a logical trade, but . . . his conscience wouldn't allow it. "I commend your sense of fair play. However, there will be no need for you to disrobe. I am merely asking for a kiss."

When she didn't respond, he said, "So? What do you say? Do you agree?"

"I . . . don't . . . know." The slowness of her speech revealed her uncertainty. "You have kissed me once, have you not? And it wasn't very pleasant. Is the sight of your cock worth tolerating more?"

There she went again, challenging him. He would shut her up on that score in a moment. But first, *when* had he kissed her? He couldn't recall any such contact. Surely he would have remembered, since he had hungered for a taste of her ever since he had chafed her skin the night before.

He was about to ask her to clarify when his brain seized on the moment he had crushed his mouth to hers, and then he understood. "That wasn't a kiss, Abby."

"What was it?"

"An act of desperation. A show I was putting on for Jack to establish my dominance and control."

"I see. I didn't like it."

"You weren't meant to."

"You can do better?"

"Why don't we let you be the judge of that? Unless you're too self-conscious in your own right," he added quickly.

"About . . . ?"

"Your inexperience, of course. Some virgins are very sensitive about the way they fumble around."

"You don't think I can please you?"

"I wasn't suggesting that. Merely allowing you to back out if you are too afraid I will find you lacking as a partner."

"You won't find me lacking," she said. "I have always been a quick learner."

"I bet." Hiding a smile, he cupped her face with both hands and tilted it to where he could see her profile in the moonlight streaming through the window. "Does that mean we have a deal?"

She seemed slightly unsure, as if she could sense that he had just baited a trap for her. But she was too curious—or confident in her ambivalence—to avoid it. "Yes," she said. "Yes, we do."

He wanted to take her mouth as he wanted to take her body—with decisive authority. To show her what it felt like to get swallowed up in the pleasures of the flesh. But he forced himself to hold back and be as gentle as possible.

"Not bad." She pulled away as soon as he touched his lips to hers, but he wasn't about to let her off so easily.

"I'm not finished yet," he said. "Close your eyes and, whatever you do, *don't talk.*"

When she did as he asked, he moved his lips over hers with just a little bit of moisture, wordlessly coaxing her to feel the warm, languid heat that was pouring through him and was rewarded for his efforts when she began to relax and mold to his body.

"That's it, Abby. Now maybe you'll try a real kiss," he whispered and parted her lips, touching her tongue with his to see if she might want to taste him, too. He knew such sensations were foreign to her, that she might need time to acclimate and tried not to go too fast. If she liked what he was doing, she would give him some kind of signal. . .

That signal came when she moaned and slid her arms around his neck, effectively holding him in place.

"You are indeed an apt pupil," he told her.

"And you, a gifted tutor," she breathed.

That was when he rolled her beneath him. He thought she might resist. This was beyond a mere kiss. But, no. She was clearly enjoying his ministrations with the same unbridled joy she had exhibited when he presented her with the sweetmeats and the brush and mirror.

The moment she spread her legs and arched into him, the fire inside him threatened to burn out of control. Soon they were kissing so feverishly that they were both panting for breath when he lifted his head.

"I like kissing," she told him, as if he had merely stopped to check, and guided his face right back to hers.

That was when Max began to feel his restraint slipping. Already settled between her legs, he began to thrust against her, and she lifted her hips to meet his, instinctively mimicking the joining of their bodies as much as he was.

It was her eager response that goaded him on. Only when he started to suckle her through her shift, and she cried out as if it was the most exquisite thing she had ever experienced, did he realize how quickly he was approaching the point of no return. And that brought him back to his senses. With a groan of frustration and regret, he rolled off her and faced the other direction for fear he would only reach for her again if he didn't.

What had he been thinking? He was keeping this woman against her will. He couldn't ravish her, too. That would make him no better than Jack and the others.

"Max?" she whispered. "Did I do something you didn't like?"

No, she had managed to get him good and love drunk, despite her inexperience. That was the problem. She had him so desperate to steal her innocence he feared the slightest touch might cause him to forget who he was and why he needed to salvage at least a thimbleful of his integrity.

Squeezing his eyes closed, he tried thinking of Madeline, his deceased father, his mother, his obligations—anything to escape the clutches of the desire that drove him to scoop her back into his arms and finish what he had started.

"Max?" she said again when he didn't reply.

"No. Nothing," he managed to say.

"Then why did you stop? That isn't where it ends. Even if I hadn't read about sexual congress, I would know. My whole body aches for more . . . for *you*, in some way."

He gritted his teeth against an avalanche of fresh temptation. It didn't seem giving in could be too bad if she wanted the same thing. But, on some level, he knew better. "Don't say things like that, Abby."

"Why not?"

"Because I won't be able to return you as I found you if you do. Don't you understand? Unless you want to lose your virginity right here, at my hand, we need to put some distance between us."

He thought she might press him to fulfill his side of the bargain, at least. She was as indomitable as she was insatiably curious, and he had made a deal with her. But she seemed to understand that such a request could be the spark that burned them both to ashes, because she didn't demand that he follow through.

"I don't think I would be opposed to that," she whispered.

"Abby, you can't make such a monumental decision right now. Neither of us is in a position to think clearly at the moment."

"Can we talk about it in the morning, then?"

"That would be advisable."

After several seconds of silence, she said good night and slid toward the far edge of the bed, but it wasn't two hours later that they found each other again. All it took was for Abigail to slide her hand down his arm and entwine her fingers with his, and it was as if those two hours had never elapsed. In the matter of a few short minutes, he had her clothes off, his mouth at her breast and his hand between her thighs.

Chapter 13

Abigail had never felt anything like the pleasure pouring through her—and not just because of the sexual nature of Max's touch. Since her mother died, she'd had so little physical affection. Her father had occasionally patted her on the head when she was a girl and, in those first years, there had been a nanny to bathe and look after her. But, like her governesses, her nannies had come and gone so often that she hadn't grown attached to any of them. One left to marry after only two months. Another moved to the United States before the year was out. Yet another, caught stealing from the larder, was sacked. After that, it was the servants at the college who kept an eye on her for her father, but they remained so distant and formal that she never felt they truly cared. Until now she hadn't even realized how desperately she craved human contact and could hardly believe that Max, of all people, was making her feel important, even vital in some way.

Although she hadn't meant to tempt him beyond his resistance when she reached out a few minutes earlier, she certainly hadn't done anything to discourage him when he drew her back into his arms. *He* kept trying to break contact, however—at least at first. Every few seconds, he would pull away, try to catch his breath and overcome the temptation she posed. She probably should have done more to help him, since his self-respect seemed to hinge on his resistance. But they were locked in the same small room, where there was no way to escape such poignant desire. It simply would not recede no matter how long they stared into the darkness, willing their heartbeats to slow. As soon as she touched him, he had turned into her as if he had been lying there, battling the same impulse.

"What's one night?" she asked. If she was never going to marry, she didn't see why she shouldn't take this opportunity to learn what it would be like to lie with a man. Max was a resurrectionist, which wasn't an occupation anyone could admire—even her, despite the college's dependence on the specimens they provided—but she liked him in spite of that. Truth be told, he was unlike any man she had ever met. He seemed so knowledgeable, so worldly and capable.

The rasp of his breathing sounded in her ear as his fingers sought out various places on her body she hadn't even known could be so receptive to a man's caress—and before long, the only thing that mattered was obtaining the satisfaction her body sought. Max could provide that. But when she started to undo the buttons on his trousers, he stopped her.

"Abby, no. We can't."

She froze, startled by his refusal. "*Why?*"

"Because what I have done is bad enough."

"You don't want me?" she asked.

He framed her face with his large hands as if he was trying to convey more than the words he was saying. "I want what is best for you. That means I have to think beyond this night."

"You're afraid I might conceive."

"That's part of it, yes. I won't risk a bastard. And there can be no future for us. You understand, don't you?"

She wasn't asking for a future with him. Her father would never allow her to marry a member of the London Supply Company or any other sack 'em up man. When she returned to the college, whatever happened at No. 8 Farmer's Landing would have to be forgotten.

"There isn't any preventative we can use?" She had heard about sponges and something called a *womb shield* from Dr. Bartello, who taught midwifery every day at the college—at half past ten. But she had no idea where to get such items, especially late at night. She would have listened more carefully to that part of his lectures if she had ever dreamed she would have a need. But she had been more interested in *birthing* babies than preventing them.

He rested his forehead against hers. "Nothing at hand. And even if there were, abstinence will protect you far better. Besides, I have no experience with virgins, Abby. If I pressed inside you as I am dying to do, it would only hurt you."

"You said it was pleasurable for a woman to ride a hard cock. And yours is certainly hard."

"Indeed it is," he said with a ragged chuckle. "But it's something you have to grow accustomed to. Your body isn't used to accepting a man."

"I will adjust," she insisted. "That is what women have done since the beginning of creation, isn't it?"

"That's your damn curiosity talking again," he said gruffly. "But I can't listen to that. I know you will live to regret giving me something so precious just for the sake of experience."

She stared up at him. "That's it, then?" She started to push him away, but he held her fast.

"Wait, it doesn't have to end quite as badly as this."

"Just go to sleep," she said.

He had thought he would enjoy turning the tables on her, but that wasn't the case—not if he couldn't fulfill the desire he had created. "Abby, stop."

"I don't understand your refusal. You're shaking with need."

"I don't deny it. But I would rather not hate myself when this is over."

"Fine. Sleep, like I said."

"In a few minutes. First, I'm going to give you a little something to remember me by, something to show you that making love can be every bit as pleasurable for a woman. That way, if you do marry, you will know to demand more of your husband. He should meet your needs as you should meet his."

"What are you talking about?" she asked. "You just refused to go any further."

132

He didn't answer. He was too busy creating a trail of kisses down her abdomen.

Although she expected him to stop before he moved much lower than her belly button, he didn't. He continued on that downward path.

Shocked, she tried to cross her legs. She felt so exposed and . . . and embarrassed. But he wouldn't have it.

"Don't fight me." He held her thighs apart. "I promise you will like this," he said—and she did. From the first wet glide of his tongue, she could hardly lie still and her enjoyment grew from there.

When she couldn't take any more, Abby fisted her hands in the bedding and began to plead with him. "Max! Max, please. You are driving me mad, making me want . . . making me want . . ."

"I know what you want, and I am going to give it to you," he promised. "All you have to do is trust me—trust me and forsake all inhibition and reservation."

She was no longer resisting. She just didn't know how to do as he said, couldn't make it happen—and then . . .

A flood of sensation welled up and swept through her body, and she knew nothing could ever feel better.

When the first delicious spasm hit, she cried out in surprise—and heard Max make a similar sound, only his contained more frustration than exultation. He undid his trousers and lifted himself over her as if he would bury himself inside her. But, with a muttered curse, he dropped down beside her and guided her hand to what he had exposed instead.

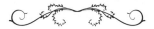

When Abigail woke, she and Max were naked and tangled up in each other. She knew, as the daughter of the head surgeon at Aldersgate College, she should get up right away and put on her clothes. Only a strumpet could be so indifferent to the fact that she was lying with a man she had barely met without so much as her shift. But she was so satisfied and comfortable that it was hard to care enough to drag herself away from him. They had their privacy. And Max felt better against her bare skin than a yard of silk. Although he had refrained from taking her maidenhead, what they had done felt just as intimate. He had told her that those in the bawd-houses called it "tipping the velvet." She wondered if those higher born knew about such a thing—but couldn't imagine any of the wives of the surgeons she had met allowing their husbands to kiss them where Max had kissed her.

When she lifted a hand to smooth the hair out of her face, she realized Max was awake and watching her beneath the fringe of his dark lashes.

"You were right." She offered him a smile.

He arched an eyebrow in question.

"A live cock is infinitely more interesting than a dead one."

"For the love of God, Abby." He rubbed a hand over his face, then pinched the bridge of his nose.

"That was a compliment," she said, slightly put out by his reaction. "You have every right to be proud. Although I don't have a great deal to compare you to, you are certainly not lacking in size—"

"Abby!"

He had choked out her name as if she had said something terribly wrong, which was puzzling. He had been willing to discuss his cock the morning before. So why was it wrong to mention it now that she could actually offer an opinion?

"You seem to have awakened in a sour mood," she said.

"I've got to get you back to the college before I ruin your life. But if I return you . . ." He sighed. "Never mind."

She might have promised him that she wouldn't tell anyone about him or the gang so long as he freed her. But she wasn't entirely sure she could keep that promise. Someone had to investigate the circumstances surrounding the death of the woman who had been on the sofa. If she maintained her silence that might never happen.

She studied Max's handsome face, telling herself it wasn't because she was suddenly reluctant to leave *him* that she had less interest in returning home.

"That sounds like the same problem you had yesterday," she said, "so I don't know why you have to be so gruff."

"Today the problem is worse than it was yesterday."

"Because . . ."

A muscle moved in his cheek as his gaze lowered to the place where the sheet barely covered her breasts. "I hadn't bedded you yesterday."

"You didn't bed me last night, either." She slid on top of him and felt gratified when his member stiffened in response. She loved that she had the power to arouse him so quickly.

"You're flirting with danger, Abby," he warned as he watched her with heavy-lidded eyes.

She gave him a sultry look. "So push me away."

When he lifted his hand, she thought he was going to do just that. Max was not a man to be trifled with. But he didn't. He cupped her breast while grabbing a fistful of her hair and dragging her mouth to his.

"Do you really want to provoke me?" he asked against her lips.

His kiss wasn't nearly as gentle as those he had given her in the night but, after spending much of the past thirty-six hours with him, she knew he wouldn't hurt her. He was merely frustrated. He wanted her as much as ever but wouldn't let himself take her.

"If you are trying to frighten me, it won't work," she said and ran her tongue against his as he had taught her hours before.

With a curse, he let go of her hair and devoured her kiss. Then his hands circled her waist, positioning her such that she could slide onto his hard shaft if she wanted to take the initiative.

Her heart pounded with the daring of it. She lifted her head to stare into his eyes, but he seemed to realize that she would indeed give him her virginity and lifted her to one side before rolling out of bed.

"Why am I letting you torture me?" he grumbled.

She made a face at his back. "You're the one holding me here against my will."

"No wonder it's strange to me that you should be so happy!"

"You have introduced me to a new, sensual world. Is it so terrible that I am eager to explore it while I have the chance? Can you honestly tell me that any woman wouldn't like . . . what did you call it? *Tipping the velvet?*"

"That is not a term for you to repeat," he said.

He sounded a great deal like her father. "Fine. I won't. Apparently, it would please you better if we pretended to still be strangers this morning, which makes no sense—not now that we have been so intimate."

"Don't talk like that, either."

"*Why?*"

He grimaced. "Because it reminds me that I have not acted honorably!"

"I thought you didn't care about honor."

"My honor was lost when I held you against your will. But I have to draw a line somewhere."

"Then be miserable, if that's what you want. But must I be miserable with you? Would you rather I was *un*happy?"

He sighed. "I fear I am setting you up for just that."

She combed her fingers through her hair as she watched him dress, which was enjoyable in itself. "Because you were right?"

He wouldn't look back at her. "About . . ."

"The fact that I would like your cock?"

"Abby, you have no idea what that kind of talk does to me," he growled. "You *must* stop!"

She laughed that he could be so easily flustered. "*You* can be vulgar in an attempt to shock me, but I can't do the same to you? Who would have thought that a body snatcher could be such a prig?"

He shook his head. "I never should have touched you."

Suddenly, Abby felt a little sick. "Do you regret it?"

"Yes! No! I mean . . . I *should.*"

"But . . ."

Finally dressed, he whirled to face her. "I can't feel good about it because you don't know, damn it!"

"Don't know *what?*"

"Anything!"

"Are you disappointed in my lack of experience?"

"Of course not."

"It seemed to me you liked it when I touched you, when I kissed you—"

"Abby, that goes without question. You saw and felt what you did to me. But you cannot leave yourself so vulnerable, so—"

He never got the chance to finish. Borax began to bark. Then there was a rap at the door downstairs and a male voice rang out, "Open up! This is the Metropolitan Police."

When Max hurried out of the room, he happened to meet up in the hallway with Jack who, surprisingly enough, seemed more excited by their unwanted visitor than concerned.

"I guess now you're gonna have to answer for treatin' the surgeon's daughter like a dirty puzzle, huh?" he said and chortled, rubbing his hands in anticipation.

Max wasn't always familiar with Jack's slang. They hadn't grown up in the same class. But he knew a *dirty puzzle* probably wasn't much different than a *bob tail*, or disgusting whore, which is what Jack called most women. "Don't talk about Abby like that," he said, "or we're going to have a problem long before we make it downstairs."

A blast of sour whiskey breath hit Max as Jack laughed. "You got that girl's quim on the brain, I tell you. Let's see what this constable thinks of you wapping the surgeon's little beauty."

Max cut Jack off before he could get past him. "You realize we're in this together."

"*I* haven't touched her!" Jack said.

"Only because I wouldn't let you. Anyway, if Edwin Hale isn't at the door, too, it's possible this isn't about Abby."

Jack looked perplexed. "Of course it's about Abby. What else could it be?"

"Remember that maid we ran into approaching Sir William's last night? It could be an inquiry into what we were carrying in the bag. Given the size and shape, and Sir William's occupation, it wouldn't be hard to guess our purpose there. It could even be that the police have already visited Sir William, ascertained the identity of that corpse and want to find out where and how we got hold of it."

The levity fled Jack's face.

"I suggest you spend a few minutes thinking about what you might say if that woman didn't expire of natural causes," Max said.

"Did you lock the surgeon's daughter in?" Jack whispered, now somber as a priest.

"I did," Max replied and took the stairs two at a time.

Another knock resounded, this one more impatient than the last. "Open up!"

When Max did just that, the constable standing on the stoop shifted on his feet as if he wasn't quite comfortable in his stiff blue uniform. Edwin Hale wasn't with him; he was alone.

"Is there a problem, sir?" Max asked.

The constable angled his head to peer past him and seemed to take note of Jack, who was making a show of putting water on to boil. "I'm looking for two men—Maximillian Wilder and Jack Hurtsill."

"I'm Wilder." Max pressed a hand to his chest before indicating Jack. "That's Hurtsill."

The constable's lips curved into a smug smile. "I'm afraid we have received a complaint against the both of you."

Max cleared his throat. "Regarding . . ."

"A certain young woman you are holding against her will."

This *was* about Abby. "I don't know what you're talking about." Max spread his hands to signify that he had nothing to hide.

"Is that so?" The constable's eyes narrowed; he had pegged that response for the lie that it was. "Because a bloke by the name of Tom Westbrook claims he has been living here with you and has seen the woman with his own eyes."

Max had expected the mention of Edwin Hale's name. But *Tom* was behind this?

He cast a glance over his shoulder to make sure Jack had heard—and saw Jack's mouth tighten. With Tom implicating them both, Jack would be even more hard-pressed to establish his innocence, should he try to blame the whole thing on Max. Abigail's elephant was in his room this very instant.

"Tom is merely trying to cause trouble," Max said, doing his best to appear nonplussed. "We had an argument yesterday, and he walked out. This must be his revenge."

"Then you won't mind if I come in and have a look around? Mr. Westbrook has indicated that the woman is Abigail Hale, the daughter of the surgeon at Aldersgate School of Medicine."

Max didn't move out of the way but he didn't refuse the constable entrance, either. "I have never met a Miss Hale."

"Then how would Mr. Westbrook know she's gone missing? I just came from the college. They have been searching for her ever since they noticed she was not about her usual duties sometime yesterday afternoon."

It had taken those at Aldersgate most of the day to realize Abby wasn't there? That bothered Max almost as much as the fact that Tom was the one who had brought the authorities down on them.

"I don't know what to tell you," he said. "Maybe she ran away."

"A porter at the college has indicated that she attempted to purchase a cadaver from you and your associates the night before she went missing. Is that true?"

Max was growing more worried by the moment. He had never had a great deal of confidence in Sir Robert Peel's new police force, but he was beginning to believe he had underestimated them. "If she was trying to buy a corpse, she must have been dealing with someone else."

The constable stood back to survey the dilapidated house. "You are not a bunch of resurrectionists?"

"We're a bunch of rat catchers," Max said.

"Rat catchers," he repeated, clearly skeptical.

"It's a noble enough profession. We supply many of the taverns."

"With *that* dog?" He gestured at Borax, who was still making a racket.

"No. We have several well-bred terriers, and even a few ferrets, at Jack's brother's place. Bill's the trainer."

"Then maybe he's the rat catcher, too, because Mr. Westbrook claims you sell corpses for a living. He says that when some disagreement arose over the price of a dead body at Aldersgate, the exchange did not take place. So Miss Hale came here to continue negotiations, hoping to procure a specimen for the college at long last and was taken captive and locked in your bedroom."

Tom had conveniently left out the theft for which he would have been partially responsible, Max noted. "Mr. Westbrook doesn't know what he is talking about," he said.

That Max would continue to deny the accusations in the face of such a strong argument caused the constable to study him with a condescending sneer. "I would be much obliged to have you prove that, if you wouldn't mind showing me the room in question?"

Afraid of what Jack might do if the constable entered the house, Max shook his head. "I'm sorry. You will have to come back after visiting a magistrate. I believe you need a warrant in order to enter this house without our express permission." Thankfully, the public's fear of an organized police force had caused parliament to limit their power.

But that didn't make the difference Max was expecting it to. The constable's smile turned almost gleeful as he held up a piece of paper. "I went directly to the magistrate from the college."

Damn it! Max had expected a few rudimentary inquiries before the investigative process reached this point. Just because Abby had done business with them the night before—even business that had not gone well—didn't mean they were responsible for her disappearance. Her own father had seen her after they left; Max, Jack and the rest of the gang had watched through the window as the two conversed in the office before they stole the cadaver from the dissection theatre. There was no proof of the London Supply Company's involvement. He'd hoped trying to establish a link between their visit and her disappearance, and searching for her elsewhere, would give him the time he needed to find out all he could about Madeline—or at least provide sufficient warning that he should sneak Abby out of the house. Never had he dreamed that Tom would betray them.

"And where is Tom?" Max asked. "If he has not sent you on a fool's errand, why is he not here, ready to point a finger?"

For the first time, the constable appeared to lose a bit of confidence. "He refused to come. He is terrified of you both."

Max knew he should be doubly terrified now.

"There's no woman here," Jack piped up. "No woman that doesn't want to be."

The constable remained far from convinced and, considering what Tom had told him, Max could see why. "I will gladly determine that for myself," he said.

Memories of the day before, when Jack had pulled that knife, made Max nervous. He didn't want anyone to get hurt. Regardless of whatever else happened, he had to make sure this bobbie left unharmed. So he blocked Jack with his body in order to let the man in.

"You bloody idiot! Do you want to hang?" Jack whispered below the pounding of the constable's feet as he headed straight up the stairs.

"I'll take the blame." Max figured he would muddle through an arrest somehow. He had friends in high places. He could go to them, tell them why he had been in Wapping and get himself released. But he had enough notoriety in certain circles that if he did that, word of his exploits would spread—and Madeline would very likely be lost to him forever. He didn't want to die in his old age having never solved the mystery of her disappearance, still feeling responsible for it.

If he maintained his cover and allowed himself to be tried as Max Wilder, on the other hand, he *might* be able to return to the London Supply Company when the ordeal was over. If he received a gaol sentence instead of a public beating, he doubted he would spend too much time behind bars. Lining the right pockets would help. Having spent some time in the clink might even lend him added credibility— if no one recognized him during the process.

But by then Madeline's trail would be so cold . . .

"This door's locked," the constable called to them. "You will produce the key immediately, or I will break it down!"

The look on Jack's face made Max shake his head and murmur, "Trust me."

"You better know what you're doing," Jack said and followed Max up the stairs.

Although Jack was angry and just defensive enough to be dangerous, Max felt slightly relieved that Abigail would be rescued and returned to her father. What had happened to her, how she had gotten involved, wasn't fair. He even felt some relief that he would no longer be faced with the moral dilemma that his desire for her posed.

But he couldn't help the lingering disappointment that he was *again* letting Madeline down.

Abigail had been a costly miscalculation . . .

Swallowing a sigh, he shot Jack a final, quelling glance as he nudged the constable to one side and opened the door.

Chapter 14

Abigail held her breath as the hinges on the door whined. Thanks to the constable's loud voice, she had heard most of what had gone on below—enough to know that this was her chance. Help had arrived and she could escape the London Supply Company.

But what would happen to Max if she admitted that she was, indeed, the missing surgeon's daughter?

He would be beaten, or go to gaol. She wanted that for Jack. *He* was twisted. She could feel it in her bones. But Max was not.

As the constable rushed in, Max and Jack fell in step behind him. "Miss Hale? Are you all right?"

She should have been more than eager to fall into her rescuer's arms and be whisked away from such a dangerous place. Any normal woman might even have cried in relief. But she felt only the panic that had sliced through her the moment she realized the police had arrived.

With her heart beating loudly enough to echo in her ears, she turned in her seat at the vanity and conjured a blank but slightly surprised expression. "What did ye call me, gov'na?"

The constable came to an abrupt halt. His gaze lowered as he took note of her gypsy rags, which she had gotten up and donned instead of the dress she had sewn from Max's clothes. Then he focused on the mark on her neck. Anything could have happened to a kidnapped woman in three days—her own clothes could have been taken from her and she might have been used by any number of men—but the accent and language she had employed didn't fit that of an educated, middle-class surgeon's daughter.

"I'm looking for a woman by the name of Abigail Hale," the constable explained, clearly confused by her lack of recognition.

She continued running Max's brush through her hair as she regarded them in the mirror. "Beggin' yer pardon, sir, but I ain't never 'eard of a whore by that name. She from around 'ere, then?"

"She is *not* a whore," he replied, his voice clipped. "She is the daughter of a surgeon in Smithfield."

"Ah, that explains it." She gave an unladylike snort. "I 'ave no reason to 'obnob with that sort."

The constable glanced behind him, at Max and Jack. "You don't understand," he said when he returned his gaze to her. "I suspect she's here, in Wapping. I thought maybe . . . maybe *you* were her."

She put down the hairbrush, stood and sidled up to Max, who tensed but didn't rebuff her. "Maybe she is . . . somewhere. But I'd rightly know me own name, eh?"

The policeman scratched his head. "Then . . . who are you?"

"For the right price ye can call me whatever ye like," she said with a throaty chuckle.

Grabbing her by the arm, he jerked her away from Max and gave her a hard shake. "But you were locked in this room! Getting in required a key. Surely, you can't be happy about that!"

"There's no need to be so rough." The growl in Max's voice was as much of a warning as his words.

The constable let her go and turned to glare at him. "Why, in God's name, have you imprisoned this woman?"

Abigail hurried to speak before Max could say anything that might contradict her. "I'll let a man do most anythin' 'e wants, long as 'e pays me enough. If 'e chooses to lock me up and pretend I'm 'is captive, all I say is, 'I charge by the 'our.'"

She winked, even though she was secretly afraid he might arrest her. It was one thing to pretend to sell her body, another to be so brazen about it. But prostitution was rampant in London. Unless something else was also involved—theft or violence or repeated complaints—the police usually turned a blind eye to such commerce. If they ever decided to lock up all the "working girls" in the villages east of London, they would be busy for days and the gaols would be full to overflowing.

Jack, seemingly recovered from the shock of how she had handled the situation, spoke up. "Told you there wasn't anyone here who didn't want to be."

Max was wearing a dark scowl but remained silent. If he was grateful that she was trying to save him from arrest, she couldn't tell. She got the impression that maybe he *wasn't* so pleased, that her protection was somehow more than he wanted to accept from her.

"You're aware of the many dangers that can befall an . . . an unfortunate female such as yourself," the constable said. "That certain charities exist to offer you assistance?"

"Assistance with what?" She batted her eyelids at him. "I'm fine just as I am."

"They can help get you off the streets, for one." He stood taller to convey his condemnation. "Many women, such as yourself, have been able to find honest work."

At that, she laughed outright. "As a needlewoman, ye mean? Where I'd stitch for eighteen hours a day, still not make enough to feed meself—an' go blind to boot? Ye can 'ave yer bloomin' charity, that's what I say."

"Then maybe there is a poorhouse that has room—"

"'*Ell* would be more comfortable," she scoffed. The almshouses provided such a cruel and meager existence that no one wanted to end up there, so he could hardly act surprised.

Having received the sharp edge of her tongue instead of the gratitude he seemed to expect, he gave up trying to rescue her. "I will leave you to your own devices then," he ground out and started to leave, only to turn back at the last second. "Are you *sure* you have never heard of Abigail Hale, or the Aldersgate School of Medicine? I cannot fathom Tom

Westbrook telling such a story if it wasn't true. And it matches what the porter said at Aldersgate perfectly."

"I've met Tom. 'E's not quite right in the 'ead. I mean"—she dipped into a facetious curtsy—"do I look like I'm being held against my will to you?"

When Jack guffawed, the constable hung his head and walked out.

Jack followed, but Max stayed with her—and shut the door as soon as the others passed through it.

"What were you thinking?" he asked, his voice barely audible so he couldn't be overheard. "He would have taken you home. You could have been reunited with your father inside the hour!"

She raised her eyebrows. "You sound disappointed."

"Aren't *you*?"

"I miss my father, and . . . and my duties, but . . ." Clasping her hands together, she stopped.

"But what?"

She couldn't bring herself to admit that the college had lost some of its appeal since she had come here, particularly in the last twenty-four hours. The ramshackle house where they were sleeping was nowhere anyone would aspire to live. But the longer she stayed, the more she came to view the *college* as restrictive. For the first time, she was experiencing life beyond it, and while that life was more frightening and dangerous, not to mention dirty, it was also more exciting, liberating and full of potential.

"You would have gone to gaol if I had done anything other than what I did," she said.

"I am not your concern," he responded.

Apparently, the constable hadn't left yet. She could hear Jack arguing with him below, talking about Tom.

"You *want* to be locked up?" she asked Max. "To live on little more than bread and water?"

"Look, Abby, I admire you for what you just did. I don't know another woman who would have tried to pull that off. But last night . . . you can't take it to mean too much. You have to look out for yourself. Do you understand?"

"You think I protected you because of the pleasure you provided?" Even now, her skin burned with the desire to be touched by him, but she didn't want to let him know she viewed him as anything more than a learning experience—not when he repeatedly warned her not to get attached. "If I had answered to my own name, that constable would have dragged you away."

"I realize that, but"—his scowl deepened—"what now?"

She hadn't thought that far into the future. There hadn't been time. She had merely done what she felt she had to do. "Now I . . . leave. I return to Aldersgate, where I belong."

"And what will you tell your father?"

"That I was abducted on my way to the college after making arrangements with you and Big Jack to deliver another corpse. That keeps you from being blamed and makes it possible for me to return with the college's money."

"But your father will want to know how you escaped from your captors, who they were—and how you managed to walk off with so much worth robbing."

"I'll make up something. I have a vivid imagination."

"You have no idea the pressure he will bring to bear. If he is anything like me, he won't rest until he finds the culprits."

But that was just it—Max wasn't anything like Edwin Hale. She had no doubt her father would make an honest attempt to seek out her captors and see them punished, but she also had little doubt that he would give up if those first efforts proved unsuccessful, especially if he felt comfortable that she was safe with his sister in Herefordshire. Then he could return to his schedule and his interests. He wouldn't want to dwell on something so negative, wouldn't appreciate the distraction nor the reminder that the daughter he was responsible for had ended up in the wrong hands because he had let her talk him into staying on at the college instead of making her go where she was "better off."

"I can manage my father," she insisted.

"You won't break down and reveal the truth?"

"Didn't I just prove my discretion?"

"You were acting in the name of expediency, but have you considered living with your conscience once you get back? How will you go on as if you never saw what you saw, never heard what you heard? What about the corpse that was on the sofa? Will the memory of that poor dead woman never get the best of you?"

He was right. When she had lied to the constable, she hadn't even thought about the woman who might have been murdered for the money her body could bring. But even when she *did* think of that possibility, she knew from the way Max had reacted the night Jack brought the body home that Max wasn't involved. He had been shocked, suspicious and upset, which made her feel she was right to do what she had done. He was *not* the one who deserved to be punished.

"That was Jack, not you," she said.

"It doesn't matter. I can't have you telling anyone about it."

"*Why?*" she cried. "Why would you protect *him?*"

"I have my reasons."

"You need the profit this nasty business brings that badly? Badly enough to remain silent about a possible murder? How high are your gambling debts? Enough to sell your soul along with the corpses you deliver?"

He looked pensive as he paced across the floor. Then, after locking the door, he leaned against the panel as if he would bar the way even if the lock didn't hold. "Abby, I am not what I appear to be."

She could still hear the hum of Jack's voice as he spoke to the constable, but she couldn't concentrate on what they were saying. Max had captured her undivided attention. "What does that mean?"

"I am not a resurrection man. I am merely posing as one. You see . . ." He let his words fall off, suggesting he was thinking twice about making any revelations.

"Go on," she prompted. "I won't tell a soul, I promise."

He hesitated but ultimately continued, "Not long ago, maybe a month or so is all, my sister was seen with Jack."

His *sister*? He hadn't mentioned having a sister, but she didn't know much about him. "And?"

"She has since disappeared."

Abby covered her mouth. "No . . ." she said through her fingers.

"It's true. That's why I'm here: to find her."

"But . . . where could she be? You're not thinking—"

"Anything is possible," he broke in.

That explained so much—why Max looked, acted and even dressed so different from Jack and the others, why he had done what he could to protect her and couldn't have let her go for fear she would bring down the authorities before he found his sister.

Abby dropped her hand. "And your gambling debts?"

He shoved away from the door and came toward her, stopping only a foot or so away. "I have no gambling debts. Jack is right to suspect me, which puts me in a very precarious position."

The memory of Jack returning with that corpse played through Abby's mind once again. "You are risking your life!"

"Perhaps. I don't fear Jack in an even fight. But . . . if he figured out who I am, I doubt it would be an even fight."

"You shouldn't be here!"

"I have no choice."

Those fatalistic words told her how much he had agonized over his sister. "The police can't help?"

"I refuse to leave a matter of such importance in their hands. You have seen what it's like here in Wapping. No one would talk to the police. They are too afraid of recrimination. And then Jack would know that there are people searching for Madeline. If she is alive . . . I don't want to make her situation any worse."

If was the key word. Knowing Jack, Abby couldn't help assuming the worst. "Are you making any progress?"

"Not as much as I would have liked. As a newcomer to this world, it has been hard for me to establish the trust I need to acquire useful information. I've been here the better part of two weeks and only now am I starting to make some headway."

"Then it's more important than ever that you do all you can to convince Jack you are here for the reason given."

"Yes." He reached out and touched her neck, where he had left that purplish mark. "But I'm afraid *you* have been a complication I never anticipated and I have not handled our association well."

Neither of them had planned for their lives to intersect, especially in such an explosive way. "You realize chances are far greater that . . . that your sister is already dead."

He blanched as he went to the window. "Of course. That's exactly why I jumped to the conclusions I did when I saw the corpse of the woman Jack brought home."

"I heard you say she was still warm."

"She was. She didn't come out of any grave. But I can't lodge an accusation without proof, or an eyewitness. I have to bide my time, be smart, learn more. Providing Jack is indeed involved in something as sinister as murder, I need to know if he has been acting alone and whether there have been other victims. If so, I'm sure the families of those victims would like to discover what happened to them as much as I would like to discover what has become of Madeline."

So he was taking on more than just the search for his sister.

Abigail sank onto the stool of the vanity. "How old is Madeline? And how in the world did she ever become acquainted with Big Jack?"

The lines that creased Max's forehead grew more distinct, suggesting it pained him to talk about this, to even think about his sister, but he answered the question. "She is younger than me by six years, so twenty-three." He closed his eyes as he shook his head, obviously remembering. "And she has had a rough life, was not nearly as well protected or cared for as I was."

"Why would there be such a difference?" Abby asked. "Was she . . . difficult?"

"Not especially. She was born to a different mother. Her mother died ten years ago and my father insisted we take her in, but . . . it was never a decision that rested easy with my mother. I fear she was cruel in myriad small ways."

Abby sifted through the puzzle pieces he had revealed to her thus far, trying to form a complete picture. "Your sister was illegitimate?"

He nodded. "When she first moved in, my father did what he could to stand by her, but then he grew ill. By the time he died, Madeline was pregnant with her own bastard child and my mother simply would not abide her any longer."

"What happened?"

"She was tossed out to scrape by on her own."

"With a child."

He winced. "Yes."

"And you . . ."

"I did nothing to stop my mother." His words sounded hollow. "I felt I owed her my loyalty, allowed her to poison my brain." He sighed as he ran a hand over his face. "Never mind. Excuses change nothing. Suffice it to say that I sincerely regret my inaction."

"I see." Max's place in *this* world was finally making sense to Abby—but who was he really? What was his other life like? He was obviously educated, and his clothes and the sterling silver brush and mirror set he had bought for her suggested he didn't come from an impoverished family, like Jack and the others. "So that man at the warehouse . . . he is helping you with this search? Is that what you two were talking about the day we went there?"

"Yes. Mr. Hawley is my clerk."

More clarity. "Then . . . that warehouse is yours?" She was guessing, given the treatment he had received from the clerk, which had seemed slightly deferential. "You're a merchant?"

He returned his attention to some point beyond the window. "You could say that, yes."

"Then you were telling the truth when you said you don't need the money you stole from the college."

"If Jack hadn't come back when he did, I would have given you all forty guineas and sent you home." He gripped the windowsill. "I would have figured out a way to return your elephant, too, if doing so would have kept you out of this." He let go. "I'm sorry."

But . . . she wasn't absolutely convinced that life as usual would have been the best thing for her. It wasn't until she came here, until she experienced what it was like to sleep in his bed, to taste his kiss and experience his touch, that she felt she had truly lived. She'd thought she wanted to be a surgeon. She was pretty sure she *still* wanted that. But mostly, she wanted to help others, to make a difference in the world, *to matter to someone.*

"You wish we never would have seen each other again?"

"I wish you were never involved," he said. "This has been no place for a woman. And surely what's happened will make your situation harder at home."

"You don't need to worry about me. I am an independent woman. I can take care of myself."

"Abby, Madeline probably thought the same thing. But *something* terrible has happened in spite of that confidence. She would not leave her son without so much as a good-bye. Not unless she had no choice."

A chill ran down Abby's spine. Jack had always frightened her. He frightened her even worse now. "Who is caring for the boy?"

"I am."

"How? Where?"

"He is at my home. I have hired a nanny as well as a tutor."

Abby had more questions than ever, but before she could ask them, she heard Jack's tread on the stairs. He was coming back after seeing the constable off.

Max motioned in case she hadn't noticed and fell silent. Together, they listened to his approach and, when he sounded close, Max unlocked the door.

Chapter 15

"That was bloody genius!" Jack clapped Max on the back as he walked in. "Whatever did you do to get her to lie like that?"

"Nothing," Max said.

"You didn't threaten her? Or her father?"

"No. I was relying on being able to dodge the authorities if they showed up. And I'm confident that would have been enough—without Tom. His betrayal changed the situation considerably."

"He's a fool," Jack grumbled. "Does he think I'll just let this go? I'll find him. I know where his no-good brother lives."

Abby believed Tom would indeed pay a high price should Jack ever have the opportunity for revenge. She wasn't pleased with Tom herself. If he were still in the house, still in Jack's good graces, he wouldn't have done anything to help her. But, in spite of that, part of her—the part that identified with his isolation and loneliness—was proud that he had found the nerve to stand up to Jack, who had been so assured he would return cowed and beaten.

"We need to let Abby go," Max said to Jack. "The sooner the better."

"Why now?" Jack demanded.

"Because her father will be here shortly. Get her elephant and the money we took from the college, and we'll send her on her way."

Jack's expression darkened considerably. "I can't give her the money. I've already passed everyone their fair share."

"We could all give it back or, barring that, replace as much of it as possible with what we earn tonight."

"There's no need to go so far," Jack argued. "She told the constable herself that she wasn't Abigail. That should be the end of it."

"It won't be," Max insisted. "Her father will come here, if not today then tomorrow."

"How do *you* know?"

"Imagine sitting at the college, awaiting word of *your* daughter," Max said. "You believe she has been found and will be returned to you shortly. Instead, you hear some strange story about a prostitute being locked in a bedroom at the location where your daughter was supposed to be—a prostitute with the same physical characteristics. Mr. Hale might take that as an odd coincidence, don't you think?"

"So what if he does? He'll have the constable's word it wasn't her. The constable heard it from her own lips."

"I'm telling you that's not enough," Max said.

"It'll have to be!" Jack retorted. "We gotta live somehow. Hale doesn't have the bollocks to come down here, regardless. Even if he does, I can make damn sure he doesn't make it back."

"No!" Abby cried but Max motioned her to silence.

"And risk a noose around your neck? For forty guineas? Why? We would be much smarter to give her some money and let her go."

But, as long as she could let her father know she was safe, Abby wasn't sure she *wanted* to go back to Aldersgate. Not so soon.

"What if she opens her trap, if not now then later on?" Jack asked. "What's to stop her from telling her father it was us all along? That constable could come back, you know. I say we keep her *and* the money. We're in the clear, Max!"

"No, we're not!"

"If Hale comes here, we'll tell him to bugger off. *He* won't be toting no warrant."

Abby knew what she was about to suggest was lunacy, but she couldn't imagine leaving Max here to figure out the mystery of his sister's disappearance alone. Remote though the possibility was, what if

Madeline was still alive? What if they could save her if they reached her in time? Certainly two pairs of eyes and ears would be better than one. Abby could always go to her aunt's bucolic village of Ewyas Harold in Herefordshire *after* they did all they could to save Madeline. "If you will give me the money you took so that I can return it to the college along with a note for my father, letting him know I'm safe, I will stay and . . . and help you make far more than forty guineas."

Both men gaped at her. Then Max shook his head. "That's impossible."

"It's not!" she said. "I didn't give the constable a name. All we have to do is find a prostitute of similar height, hair and eye color, pay her to say she was here when the constable arrived and direct my father to her if he comes. As long as I remain out of sight, he should be convinced."

"*What?*" Max obviously couldn't believe she would go so far as to join *Jack's* side of the argument when he had been fighting for her release. But what was waiting for her at home that wouldn't still be waiting in a few days or weeks? By now Bransby would have told everyone at the college that she had been dealing with body snatchers the night before she went missing. To salvage his knighthood and maybe even his career, her father would *have* to send her into exile the moment she returned. And there was nothing for her to do in the country, except submit to her aunt—a religious zealot bent on reforming her so that she would one day become as docile as a woman should be.

"I want to stay here, to take Tom's place," she said.

Again, Max spoke before Jack could. "Absolutely not!"

Abby held up a hand. "Listen to me before you decide. I can do things Tom could not."

"And he can do things a woman cannot," Max responded. "Like go out alone."

"I can go to certain places, during the day. A cemetery would be one of those places. Women, even in these parts, do it all the time. But where Tom stood out in a crowd and looked . . . disreputable, even alarming, I don't. In the right clothes, I would appear quite respectable, which means I should be able to fall in with almost any mourning party." She grabbed the dress she had sewn from where she had it stowed under the bed. "See this? I could wear this."

"Where the hell—wait a minute!" A murderous expression descended on Max's face. "That's the fabric from my coat! Don't tell me you—you did!" he breathed in sheer disbelief.

She shied away from his anger. She could tell he wasn't used to having anyone appropriate his belongings for their own use, which again made her wonder about his life outside of the role he was playing here in Wapping. "You wanted me to stay busy."

When Jack threw back his head and laughed, Max's jaw tightened. Jack's pleasure in what she had done wasn't helping her cause. "I'm beginning to like this wench," he said.

"I don't care if you like her or not, she can't stay," Max responded, getting back to the business at hand. "It's not safe. Would you see her arrested along with us if we are ever caught?"

"That should be *my* decision." Abigail tried to interject, but Jack spoke over her.

"No one's goin' to be caught."

Max sneered at his words. "You can't promise that."

"Maybe not," he allowed, "but I say it's worth the risk. Like she said, a woman can get much closer to a mourning party than we probably could. You don't want to get blown to bits, do you?"

Confusion momentarily trumped the other emotions Max was exhibiting. "Blown to bits?"

"I'm talking about the booby traps some of the families set to protect the deceased. Or maybe you didn't hear about the father who filled his child's coffin with gunpowder and fused it so that it would explode if anyone tried to pry it open." He made a clicking sound with his mouth. "Times are hard, Max. But we wouldn't have to worry so much about running into gunpowder and the like if an innocent like Abby does our scouting. Who wouldn't trust a face like hers?" He lowered his voice meaningfully. "And think of the comfort and pleasure she'll bring you at night."

At that, Max seemed more adamant than ever. "I said no."

Abigail propped her hands on her hips. "How much easier would it be to pay off your gambling debts if you were to sell two or three more corpses a week? That's the entire amount in the college's purse, but you would be making it again and again."

"Why would you want to help with such work?" Max asked.

For Jack's sake, she pressed a hand to her abdomen and pretended to be fighting tears. "Because I might be with child. You can't expect me to go back to my father this way. I'll be a disgrace!"

Max was so stunned he seemed at a loss for words, but Jack spoke up. "A woman with child would be even less suspicious."

"You are *not* carrying my baby," Max said, ignoring him.

Abby lifted her chin. "It's too early to tell but . . . it's a possibility, right?"

He couldn't argue, not without giving away the truth. Jack believed they had been intimate—Max had made sure he believed it. "Having you here would never work," he said instead.

"Why wouldn't it?" Jack wanted to know. "She's a clever one—far more clever and brave than Tom. It took nerve for her to come all the way from Smithfield, at night, on her own. And if she becomes one of us, we won't ever have to worry about her going to the police, because she'll be in it just as deep."

In it just as deep . . . Truer words had never been spoken, Abby realized. If she got caught helping this gang steal bodies from the various cemeteries, no one would ever believe she had been kidnapped.

She wasn't the least bit sure she was making the right decision, but she wanted to help Max find his sister. She also wanted to do something to avenge the poor woman who'd been on the couch and might have been murdered by Jack or someone associated with him. And since her father would be better off if she kept her distance from him and the college, at least for a period of time now that things had gone so far, why not aid the cause of justice instead of sitting in her aunt's parlor, tucked away in the middle of nowhere, doing needlepoint?

Remaining in her current situation involved a degree of risk. She would be a fool not to acknowledge that. But it was exciting at the same time—and lending a hand was the right thing to do. If she was no longer being held against her will, perhaps she would have the chance to leave if her situation became *too* tenuous.

"What will you tell your father?" Max asked, as if that alone was an insurmountable obstacle.

"In the letter? That I'm fine. That I will return soon. That I'm sorry about publicly humiliating him and causing him to worry. That's all he needs to know. Anything more will cause bigger problems. And we will have it delivered by a messenger that can't be traced back here. At least then he will have some word from me, and the money the college needs to get supplies this month."

Jack seemed to view her with fresh suspicion. "I didn't agree to return the money."

"You *have* to return it, or I won't stay," she said. "With my help you could easily double that amount. You heard me a moment ago—that's only three or four corpses."

"Three or four corpses ain't as easy to come by as you think."

"We could easily do that much additional business every week," she insisted.

Although he took a second to think about it, her reasoning seemed to penetrate his greed and resistance. "Would you listen to that?" he said. "The chit wants to join up with us. I say she'd be a good investment."

"You're making a mistake, Abby," Max warned.

Maybe so, but she felt better about staying than confronting her father's disappointment and displeasure—and then her aunt's. "If it doesn't work out—if I'm not as much help as I have promised, I'll leave," she told Max. "Fair enough?"

Hoping to avoid another refusal, she added, "Sometimes a woman can see or hear things a man may not."

She wasn't talking about locating corpses; she was talking about Madeline, and she hoped he realized it.

Either he was afraid she would say more and give them both away, or he caught her meaning, because he finally relented. "You will stick by my side at all times." He pointed a finger at Jack. "And if you so much as touch a hair on her head, I won't be responsible for what I do to you. I swear to God. Understood?"

Jack didn't take easily to being threatened. Abigail feared Max had once again stirred the other man's jealousy and ire, feared that they might erupt in violence just as they had at the kitchen table the day before. But Jack managed a slight shrug.

"I won't touch her," he snapped and stomped out.

Max regretted giving in almost the second he did it. "Abby, do you realize what you have done?" he asked after he closed the door and turned to confront her. "If I have to protect you, it could compromise everything I have established here so far, make all the risks I have taken pointless. It could also—"

"Be a great benefit," she broke in, lifting her chin. "For all you know, *I* could end up protecting *you*. At least you will have someone to watch your back, and to get help if you need it."

Although he appreciated her courage and confidence, he would hate to see her hurt, especially while trying to help *him*. And there was that other matter. He couldn't let her sleep anywhere besides his bed for fear of what might happen in the night, but he couldn't trust himself to lie with her, either.

"Jack might insist that we won't ever get arrested, but we could," he said. "If we happen to steal the corpse of someone attached to a powerful family or someone with powerful friends, the backlash could be severe."

"I understand that."

"And what of your reputation? What of your *father's* reputation?"

"My reputation has to be damaged beyond repair already. I'm sure Bransby told everything as soon as he learned I was missing."

"He did," Max confirmed. "The constable said as much."

"Then I'm probably the talk of the whole college by now—and St. Bartholomew's Hospital, too, since it's so close and so many of the doctors and surgeons that lecture at Aldersgate work there. It won't take long for the news to spread through the entire medical community and maybe beyond."

"That could ruin any hope your father had of achieving a knighthood."

"Which is exactly what I was trying to avoid from the beginning. But there will be less chance of my actions reflecting poorly on him if I stay."

"You would rather be perceived as a willful, rebellious daughter?"

"Yes! At least then what has happened here will be my error and not something he can be faulted for. Being accused of failing to control me is hardly the same as being accused of charging me with the task of acquiring a specimen for the college, which is what some would assume. Not many people would expect a daughter to involve herself as I did."

Although Abby was different from most women, not everyone would know that. Max had to agree that most would blame Edwin for what she had done, since he stood to benefit the most, had it gone well. "But will your father hold this against you when you do go back? Almost every move you have made has been designed to help him and the college, but will he see it that way?"

She would no longer meet his eyes, which told him the answer before she could even speak. "Would you want your daughter involved with resurrection men?" she asked.

Max didn't respond. It was a rhetorical question, and one he didn't care to think about. But he was looking at her stay a little differently. "Then you are determined."

"For now. I say we see what we can come up with on your sister over the next few days and then reevaluate. Can you agree to that?"

"You promised Jack much longer, said we could steal three more corpses per week with your help."

"I had to convince him, but we will stay only as long as we have to, of course."

Somehow such a short timespan made her continuing on at Farmer's Landing more palatable. It would be a struggle to keep his hands to himself, but at least he now had a noble reason for continuing down the path of temptation. Maybe they would be able to preserve her father's reputation, as she was hoping. And having her help *could* prove beneficial. She might get more out of Jack and the rest of the gang than he could. It was even possible that *he* would be more fully assimilated into the group, thanks to *her* credibility.

Anything he could do to get Jack to lower his guard would be wise.

"Then you had better put on your other dress. We have people to see."

When she grabbed what she had sewn from his clothes, he couldn't help frowning. "I can't believe you destroyed my coat."

"I told you I wasn't a worthy laundress."

"I see you are, however, a talented seamstress."

"Mrs. Fitzgerald saw to my education on that. She's quite accomplished with a needle. There was no way she was ever going to send me to my aunt without the skills befitting a good English girl."

"And Mrs. Fitzgerald is . . . ?"

"The housekeeper at the college," she reminded him.

He felt a fresh dose of curiosity about what her life had been like before. "Are you close to her?"

Abby shrugged. "Not particularly. She's rather . . . stern, definitely more in keeping with my aunt's approach to life than my father's, but she means well."

He fingered the fabric that had been his coat. "You could never tell she was stern by how easily you assumed ownership of my coat and whatever else you used to make that dress."

"It's a good thing I took the initiative," she said. "Otherwise, I would have nothing to wear."

"I could have bought you something."

"And how would you explain to Jack having the money for that?"

"I'm not a pauper, even as a resurrection man," he grumbled.

She gave him a sheepish look. "I'm sorry."

"It's fine. It will be easier to replace my coat."

When she smiled at how quickly he had softened, he rolled his eyes and walked out before she could disrobe. There was no way he wanted to be buried in another wave of the frustration he had suffered for most of the night.

A few days, he told himself. *I can last a few days.*

Chapter 16

The morning after she joined the London Supply Company, Abby wrote her father to let him know she was safe. She hated the thought of causing him pain, and she didn't want Bransby to worry, either. Chances were, the aging porter blamed himself for not telling Mrs. Fitzgerald about Abby's plan to buy another specimen, as he had threatened to do. Before everything went so horribly wrong.

Abby also returned the college's money—minus Tom's share. Tom had wisely not returned to the house. Although she felt better where her father was concerned, she was beginning to wonder if she had made an even worse decision than she had thought by choosing to remain in Wapping. She had told herself that staying with Max and Jack increased the chances that *she* would be criticized instead of her father. She had also told herself that it would give her a window of freedom before he could react to what she had done. Both were true. But, deep down, she knew that Max was the real reason she stayed.

If only he wasn't suddenly acting so . . . remote. The night before, as soon as they went to bed, he faced away from her and remained in that position even when she slid a little closer, hoping he would turn and curl into her as he had the two nights previous. She missed having him hold her. Those hours constituted one of the few times in her twenty-one years that she hadn't felt as if she were drifting through each day on a one-man raft, bumping up against others but never really connecting.

"Steady . . ." She was stirred from her thoughts and brought back to the present when Max whispered in her ear. Somehow she had just swayed toward the hole he and Emmett were digging. It was bad enough that she was standing in a cemetery in the middle of the night. Add the fog that had rolled in an hour or so earlier, and being there for the unsettling purpose of disturbing the dead, and it became a positively unnerving experience. She was so busy peering around she hadn't noticed that she had inched so close to them they scarcely had room to work.

Hauling in a lungful of the moist, chill air, she stepped back and nodded. Fortunately, Max and Emmett were the only ones at St. George's with her, so she didn't have to deal with Jack. Jack and his brother, Bill, had gone elsewhere. Jack had said they were meeting a gravedigger who had a lead on another corpse, but she had heard Emmett mumble to Max that they were going after Tom.

She wondered if they had found him—and what they might be doing to him if so. The images her imagination offered up further unsettled her.

"Why don't you go sit on the church steps while we finish?"

Max sounded concerned. Although he had ignored her the night before, he had been friendly enough once they left the house that morning. It was Max who had taken her around to the various cemeteries they monitored. Max who had pulled her aside to warn her to stay away from any other burial places for fear she would anger rival gangs. Max who had told her not to ever allow herself to be caught out alone after dark.

Following that bit of training, he had sent her into St. George's cemetery and stood at a distance while she joined her first mourning party. Knowing he was watching over her proved comforting—except that he showed no special interest. Not like she wanted him to.

Perhaps she should have gone home. Body snatching was even more disgusting and gruesome than she had imagined. The cemeteries were so overcrowded that a corpse barely had time to decompose before another corpse was placed on top of it. Most graves were stacked four or more deep, making some cemeteries higher than the street!

But without joining the London Supply Company, she would never have talked Jack into returning the college's money, and she could not have gone back empty-handed. She had far too much pride for that. Her father would take such a loss and have the proof he needed that a woman shouldn't meddle in a man's workplace.

"Abby?" Max prodded.

She must have pressed closer to them again. "I'm fine."

He had told her to stay at the house. She probably should have. But Jack had said that her father went to the house while they were out that afternoon. Although he let Edwin in to search the house and named a local prostitute as the woman the constable saw, she feared that wouldn't be enough to keep her father away. Maybe the letter she sent would help. If not, he could come back, and she didn't want to be home alone when he did. So she had insisted on changing into her gypsy rags and tagging along with Max and Emmett.

"You're about to keel over," Max said. "Set down that lamp and take a break. We don't need you for this."

"Max, quit worrying about her!" Emmett snapped. "Do you want to get caught?"

To Abby's infinite relief, the younger man paused in his work. They were using wooden shovels to mitigate the noise, but every scrape and plop seemed to echo against the stone church that cast an invisible shadow across the ground.

"Mind your own business," Max growled.

"You need to let that bit of fluff take care of herself," Emmett responded. "We don't have time to coddle a woman."

Abby didn't appreciate how dismissive he was being, and she definitely didn't want to be the weak link. So she summoned what strength she had left and held the lantern closer to the head of the grave. They had done this without her before, but the fog was so thick they wouldn't be able to see if she didn't angle the light exactly right.

"This isn't helping?" she asked.

Max hesitated but ultimately went back to work, and Abby shivered as she watched the loose dirt they were piling on top of a sheet grow into a large mound.

"How will you get the body out if you don't uncover the entire coffin?" she whispered, surprised by the small size of the hole, which was more of a tunnel.

Breathing hard from the exertion, Emmett stopped long enough to wipe the sweat from his brow. "We break the lid, tie some rope under the arms and haul the bugger up. What do you think?"

The bugger. This was *so* disrespectful.

Once again Abby's eyes strained as she did her best to see beyond the small circle of her lamp. She thought she heard voices. Were they real—or only imagined?

The funeral party had been subdued and had made no mention of an all-night vigil or other attempts to protect the body. She got the impression, poor as they were, they didn't have the time, the coin or the energy. But that was partly what made her so nervous. It shouldn't be this easy to do what they were doing—not since Burke and Hare had made entering a graveyard at night such a dangerous endeavor.

Feeling extremely out of place, Abby adjusted the light yet again. Body snatching felt so much worse when she was participating in the procurement instead of waiting at the college. She had been among this man's family and friends, had witnessed their grief and distress. No one had seemed to suspect she might double-cross them; they weren't even leery enough to question her presence. Although several had glanced up when they saw her walking or standing nearby, they had ultimately assumed she was there to pay her respects, just like they were. She looked respectable, as she had told Jack she would.

She was about to say that she couldn't go through with their plan any longer when Max's shovel struck something besides dirt.

"There it is." Emmett, too, had heard the solid thud. Tossing his shovel on the damp earth, he said, "Let's hurry. Somethin' doesn't feel right."

Apparently, she wasn't the only one ill at ease. But Abby got the impression it was *her* presence that was making young Emmett uncomfortable.

From the beginning, he hadn't been happy about having her accompany them. Despite the fact that she was the one who had scouted this particular grave, he seemed to consider her involvement a bad omen.

The wind whistled through the trees, stirring the thick fog like an invisible hand as they dragged the "adult male" to the surface. This part of the theft was nerve-racking, but at least they were finished with the telltale digging.

Emmett removed the shroud and stuffed it back into the grave. Then Max helped him load the body in the cart they had brought with them and they all three replaced the dirt.

"That's good enough, ain't it?" Emmett said before Max could even finish tamping it down.

Max didn't argue. He seemed equally anxious to be gone. But just as they grabbed hold of the cart, the voices Abby thought she had heard grew far more distinct.

"I told you I saw a lamp!"

"They're in the blasted cemetery!"

"Joseph's funeral was today."

"It's gotta be the damn resurrectionists, after his bloody corpse!"

"Go to his house and wake his son! Hurry!"

"Douse the light," Max barked.

Given the impatience in his voice, he might have said it before. Abby couldn't be sure. She'd had ears only for those who were coming. But she didn't get the chance to remedy her lapse. The next thing she knew, Emmett had blown out her lamp.

As the dark and fog closed around her like a fist, she had no idea how they would escape. Without a lamp to guide their way, they wouldn't get far without running into each other, a headstone or a tree. But they had to do something.

The meager light of someone else's lamp appeared, fuzzy and indistinct, at the entrance of the graveyard. As the fog shifted, she caught glimpses of the dull black mourning clothes of those who were coming—and various faces contorted with rage.

"Stay here," someone called out. "Whatever you do, don't let the bastards out!"

"If you catch 'em, hold 'em tight," someone else responded.

"They'll never steal another corpse as long as they live, not once Joseph's son gets through with 'em."

The panic that rushed through Abby nearly caused her knees to buckle. She couldn't run, couldn't move. She was frozen in fear, sure they were about to be caught.

But then Max grabbed her hand. "I've got Abby," he whispered to Emmett. "Get yourself out and we'll meet at the house later."

Emmett didn't bother to answer. At least, Abby didn't hear his response if he gave one. When he pushed them out of the way to take hold of the cart, Max whispered that he should leave it, but Emmett wouldn't listen. She heard the creak of the wheels as he took the corpse and headed into the fog.

"Where can we go?" she asked Max as he started dragging her along with him. Fortunately, he and the rest of the gang worked this cemetery often enough to be able to navigate it in the dark. She, on the other hand, had only visited it for the first time that morning. Even so, she knew they were encircled by a tall, wrought iron fence, and he was heading straight for it. They would never be able to scale those iron bars, which were tipped with sharp points.

"The entrance is the other way," she said, although he had to know that.

"Didn't you hear them? They've posted a sentry there," he bit out.

Judging from the commotion, several people were rushing through the arched entrance. Those men, together with whomever had been asked to stand guard, effectively blocked them in. But she couldn't see how getting trapped against the fence would serve them any better.

No matter what they did, this wasn't going to end well. The cemetery was only about two thousand feet square. That didn't leave them many options.

Was Max planning to fight? If it came down to an altercation, she was willing to bet he could manage one, possibly two men. But with all the voices calling out in the night, she guessed they would be up against four or more.

For a second, she imagined her father receiving word that she had been arrested. He would be shocked and humiliated—again. But that would be far better than the alternative. *They'll never steal another corpse as long as they live, not once Joseph's son gets through with 'em.* These people were more likely to mete out their own justice, just like William Hare's work associates did when they blinded him by throwing him into that pit of lime.

Abby pulled on Max to get him to stop. She had just smacked her knee on a headstone and could barely move for the pain. She didn't want to continue to stumble into obstacles she couldn't see through the fog. "Is there someplace we can slip *under* the fence?"

She could only hope . . .

He didn't answer, but his hand tightened on hers and he continued to drag her along.

"Over there!" That shout came from the other side of the church, so Abby guessed whomever it was had to be talking about Emmett.

"They'll catch him if he doesn't leave the body so he can run," she said, barely able to speak, she was so frightened and out of breath.

"He should have left it from the beginning," Max responded. "Whatever happens to him happens; I'm getting you out of here."

He spoke so low she couldn't hear each individual word, but she understood his meaning. "But he's so young."

"He knows this place far better than we do."

How could they help him, anyway? They were all going to be caught. Or did Max think it was possible to double-back toward the entrance and slip past whoever had been stationed there?

Evidently that wasn't his intent, because he didn't go that direction. He pulled her up against the side of the church, under the portico.

"What now?" she whispered, her heart thudding in her ears.

"We stay still and quiet, and we wait. Hopefully, they will assume we fled."

She could feel his warmth, his closeness, but she could also sense the tension gripping his body. "They'll find us here." How could they not? The church was the only structure that provided cover. Surely, their pursuers would search all around it. Already, she could hear them getting closer.

"Max!" she whispered in panic as a lantern cut through the fog only about ten feet away.

When she heard Max's quick intake of breath, she knew he saw the same thing. But he didn't drag her off again, didn't try to outrun them. He couldn't move fast enough, not with her stumbling behind him—and she couldn't improve on her speed. She wasn't familiar enough with the cemetery.

"Go." She tried to shove him away. "Leave me. You might be able to escape on your own. There's no reason for us *both* to be caught."

Although he released her, he didn't abandon her as she suggested. She could hear him rustling around, moving with a sense of urgency, but she wasn't sure what he was doing until she felt him lift her skirts and shove her up against the stone building.

"What are you doing?" she whispered.

His hands palmed her bottom through the thin fabric of her drawers as his mouth moved down her neck. "What I wanted to do last night."

She had expected this then, hoped for it—and he hadn't even touched her. *Now* he wanted to kiss?

Abigail could feel the muscular contours of his bare chest, knew he had opened his coat and unbuttoned his waistcoat and shirt. She thought his pants might be undone as well but couldn't tell through all the layers of her skirt.

"Max!" She tried to push him away, but he wouldn't allow it.

"Just play your part," he whispered as his mouth reached her ear.

There was no time to say more, but she finally understood. He wanted her to act like a strumpet he had brought into the cemetery for a quick thrill.

There were enough desperate prostitutes walking the streets of Wapping and nearby villages that it wouldn't be unusual to come upon such a scene in the middle of the night in some dark cove or alley—even up against a church in a cemetery. But the timing—that they would be so engaged while resurrectionists were snatching a body not far away—would be suspect.

Abby wasn't sure they would be able to convince anyone, but it was their only chance. Dropping her head back to give him better access to the skin he was baring by pulling her dress down over one shoulder, she moaned. "That's it, guv'na. Ye know 'ow to make a girl beg for more, that ye do."

It was a risk to speak in a normal volume, but they couldn't act as if they were hiding.

In spite of that logic, she felt her stomach muscles tense when the person carrying the lamp called out, "I found somethin'! I think it's a man and a woman!"

When the lamp carrier came to investigate, Max lifted his head and scowled as if he didn't appreciate the interruption. "Bugger off!" he snapped, but the interloper didn't go. He hesitated, obviously suspicious.

"What'd you find?" Someone else stepped out of the fog to join him, someone who was surprisingly familiar to Abby . . .

Angling her head to see the newcomer more clearly, she recognized him as one of the three individuals who had been talking in the street when she got out of the hackney the night she first came to Wapping. It was the man who had taken her for a beggar.

The lamp owner shrugged. "Not sure. Just some bloke tupping a threepenny upright, I think. But she's the prettiest whore I ever saw."

The man who had tossed her a coin that first night took the light, lifted it to peer at her and nodded. "Aye, I've seen that woman before. She's no resurrectionist—just another pinchcock."

His endorsement gave Abigail hope. Still, that might not have been the end of it. From his expression, the first man was not entirely persuaded—but at that precise moment, another voice rang out from across the cemetery.

"Over here! Hurry!"

Other cries arose too: "There he is!" . . . "Is he alone? . . . "Looks like it." . . . "Grab him!" . . . "He's got Joseph's body!" . . . "Cut him off."

That seemed to be the deciding factor. The two who had come upon them rushed off to see what all the excitement was about.

Sagging in relief, Abigail buried her face in Max's warm neck. "Thank God."

He dropped her skirts, which was a separate relief, given the cold. "Are you all right?"

"I've never been called a . . . a pinchcock or a threepenny upright."

"Granted those aren't flattering terms, but at least they could tell you were pretty."

His wry humor was somehow bolstering.

"Where have you met that man before?" he asked, leaning back to look at her face.

"We've never met—never been introduced, I mean. He saw me on the street when I was first trying to find Jack's house and took me for a beggar."

"I'm glad he remembered you. That helped." He let go of her far too soon. Even in this situation, she enjoyed his touch, felt strangely bereft without it. Was all that ardor truly an act? It had flared up so quickly and felt real despite the deception behind it . . .

"Let's go," he said as he fastened his clothes. "Maybe we can slip out while they're chasing Emmett."

Abigail let him lead her from the church. She couldn't wait to be safe and warm in their room at Farmer's Landing, couldn't wait to put this nasty business behind them. Maybe Max would kiss her again. Maybe he would do more. Her mind constantly returned to those few moments when he had used his mouth in such an expert fashion . . .

The commotion seemed to have drawn even the sentry from his post, if anyone had followed through and stood guard to begin with. But as they approached the arch that signified the entrance—and their escape—they discovered the cart bearing the corpse they had dug from its grave.

"They'll be back," Max promised when she hesitated. "Come on."

"But we could take it, and they would never be the wiser," she said.

"We don't want it. Emmett will vouch for what happened here. Jack will think we did all we could."

Abigail wanted Max to find Madeline. But maintaining his cover wasn't *all* that mattered. Max didn't understand how dire things were getting at Aldersgate. If the college went much longer without a specimen, they would have to close their doors. Abby saw no way of avoiding such an end. Her father's sterling reputation had attracted a number of students, but anyone planning to apply for a license had to complete two full courses of anatomy *including dissection*. That meant those students would *have* to go elsewhere if they were serious about the future.

Although it had been only minutes earlier when she felt she couldn't go through with the disinterment, the worst was over and she was back on the other side of the argument. She wished there was a better way to meet the needs of the college, but there simply wasn't, not as the system was currently set up.

"Hurry!" Max gave her arm an insistent tug—but she resisted. Those who had discovered them were at the back of the cemetery. From what Abby could tell, they had Emmett trapped on the fence or in a tree.

"I can't just . . . leave it here," she told Max. "I owe it to Aldersgate."

"I'll give you the amount you had to short them. I told you I would, as soon as I can meet with my clerk. I can't carry a lot of extra coin without giving myself away."

"They need a specimen more than they need that last eight guineas—and as I told you before, it's not your debt. You repaid what you took." She tried to get behind the cart and push it herself, but it was heavy and slow-going on the turf. Not only that but she still couldn't see anything except the arch, which appeared and disappeared in the patchy fog.

"You'll get us caught," Max hissed.

They had only a matter of minutes before the men who had flowed into the cemetery would be heading out of it again—likely dragging Emmett with them. She understood that. But she saw in this brief interlude a way to make amends for the loss she had caused the college.

"Please?" she said.

"Abby, there are *two* shovels in there. One man would not need two shovels. Once they have Emmett, they will remember the couple they saw up against the church and start looking for us."

"They may not have noticed that there were two shovels—and they won't see them if we take them as well as the body!"

"For the love of God," Max snapped and nudged her aside so that he could push the cart himself.

Chapter 17

It was nearly three o'clock in the morning by the time they returned to Jack's. Abby wondered if they would find Emmett there. She hoped so; she wanted him to be safe and knew Max did, too.

On the way back from Aldersgate, they had gone by the cemetery looking for him, in case he was lying hurt on the ground. But St. George's had been dark and quiet; they couldn't find any trace of him or anyone else.

Despite the late hour, no one was at Farmer's Landing, either.

"Maybe he'll show up by morning," Max said, letting her know that he had been thinking the same thing.

Worried for Emmett but relieved that she didn't have to face Jack, Abby went back to imagining Bransby or someone else discovering the cadaver she and Max had put in the cellar at the college. Bran would know she had brought it. After her letter, even her father would likely guess. Max had argued that it would only bring him back to get her. But, because she cared so much about the college's survival, she had managed to convince him to let her do it.

Max wasn't nearly as resistant to giving her what she wanted as he preferred her to believe, she decided. That was another reason she liked him. Maybe he didn't realize it, but he liked her, too. She was convinced of that—and she was determined to make him acknowledge it.

"Are you hungry?" he said.

They had already eaten the sandwiches they had wrapped in paraffin paper and taken with them in the deep pockets of Max's greatcoat, so she wasn't hungry. She was tired—but as soon as he removed his waistcoat and cravat, she announced that she simply *had* to have a bath.

"*Now?*" he said.

Farmer's Landing lacked many of the luxuries she had taken for granted at the college. She and Max sponge-bathed every day, but after participating in the disinterment of a corpse—what the washbowl offered wasn't enough. And maybe if she took off all her clothes, it would stop Max from falling into bed and turning away from her again. He had made a comment at the church that led her to believe he wasn't as indifferent as he pretended.

"I can't wait another day," she said.

"Fine. I'll manage it." He left and returned with a large barrel-shaped tin tub.

She frowned at the sight. "This is it?"

"It's all we've got. Jack and the others don't bother to bathe very often."

"Which is why they smell the way they do," she grumbled.

They made quick work of building a fire, but the water took time to heat.

"Tonight was pretty harrowing." Max watched her in the flickering firelight as they waited. "Do you regret staying here instead of going with that constable?"

What had happened at the cemetery was frightening. But she had never felt more alive than she had the past several days. "No."

"I hope you don't regret it later."

"Someone has to stop Jack," she said.

"That someone doesn't have to be you."

She met his gaze. "You would rather be here alone?"

"Would you go home if I said yes?"

She braced herself. "If you truly meant it."

He shoved a hand through his hair. "Abby, as much as I want you, you would be far better off with your father. It's unconscionable for me to be so selfish—"

"It's selfish if I want the same thing?"

An intense, hungry expression crossed his face as he stepped toward her. But then he closed his eyes, and his chest lifted as if he had just drawn a deep, bolstering breath. "The water must be ready," he said and pivoted instead of closing the distance between them. "I'll get it."

"That's it? You're walking away right *now*? Can I be so alone in this . . . this terrible craving I have to feel you inside me?"

His eyes lowered to her breasts, and she felt a corresponding tingle. "For the sake of decency, I can't."

He seemed to be trying to convince himself as much as her. But it definitely wasn't what she wanted to hear. "Make love to me while you can, Max."

"Be careful what you ask for, Abby."

Slowly, she unbuttoned her blouse. "Or . . ."

He stared as if mesmerized by the movement of her fingers. "You might just get it," he said. "When all is said and done, I am not made of stone."

"I don't understand what's stopping you."

"And I can't explain." He tore himself away after that, and carried up bucket after bucket of hot water. Then he insisted Abby take her bath first and left the room.

Abby made a face at the closed door. "Coward!" she called after him.

When she didn't receive a response, she assumed that would be the end of it and finished stripping off her clothes. But he startled her by throwing the door open so hard it banged against the inside wall.

"*What* did you call me?" he demanded.

She swallowed hard. "A c-coward."

He certainly didn't seem ready to run from anything now. Had she finally snapped his restraint? The naked lust in his eyes made her wonder. It was almost as frightening as it was exhilarating. She had never seen him like this.

"For trying to *protect* you?" He stalked closer, causing her to back up, against the wall. "For going to bed every night aching to touch you and yet resisting, all because I know you will be better off if I leave you alone?"

"For denying what you feel, what we *both* feel."

"If you truly understood what I'm feeling, how desperate I am to feel you beneath me, you would be terrified."

"Because . . ."

"My thoughts do not revolve around touching you gently or taking it slow, my little virgin."

"Then take me as you want me. I would rather that, rather you approach me with honest emotion than constant denial."

He scooped her into his arms and carried her to the bed, where he kissed her with such wild abandon, with such single-minded determination, she thought he would finally take her maidenhead. But he didn't. He used his hands in the same way he had used his tongue—touched her until she was wracked, again and again, with the most exquisite pleasure. And she touched him, freely and openly, reveling in the beauty of his form and the smoothness of his skin as it slid against hers. Then they bathed each other and curled up in bed. Abby was satiated but as she fell asleep in his arms, she was also curious.

Why did he continue to deny them both?

Max woke with Abby's soft bosom pressed up against his arm and the smell of her sex on his fingers. He breathed deep, taking in that heady scent and remembering. She satisfied something inside him no other woman ever had. And yet, no matter how many times he brought her to orgasm, or achieved orgasm himself, it wasn't enough. Apparently, there was no substitute for fully possessing her. Even now, he longed to roll her onto her back and press himself inside her, to feel her close around him, warm and tight, while she stared up at him with those beautiful eyes.

But he could not justify taking her virginity—not when she didn't even know who he was. He had already gone much further than his conscience dictated. It would be different if he had any hope of continuing the relationship. But that was out of the question.

"Am I still a virgin?" she mumbled.

She was certainly unafraid to say whatever was on her mind. Not many women were so bold. But he liked her honesty. She bravely wore her heart on her sleeve. That was another reason he had to do all he could to protect her. He didn't want to destroy her emotional courage. It was one of the things he loved about her.

"Through no small feat of my own, yes."

"And that is supposed to be some sort of favor on your part?"

He smiled that she would sound so disappointed. "Someday you might thank me."

"That day isn't today."

"You are not satisfied *yet*?"

"Are you offering me another substitute? Maybe I will be lucky enough to meet a man who will not be so stingy with me."

Max could tell she was teasing, but he didn't like the sound of another man taking what he so desperately craved. "Are you such a lusty wench?"

Her lips curved into a lazy smile. "Only when it comes to you."

"I wish things could be different, Abby," he admitted but a noise from downstairs broke into the conversation.

"Jack's home," he said.

Hearing the same noises, Abby propped herself up on her elbows. "Do you think Emmett is with him?"

"I hope so."

"Max! Max, get down here," Jack called. "And bring that bitch of yours. Emmett didn't make it home last night."

With a curse, Max rolled onto his back and stared up at the ceiling. "I guess that answers our question."

"He won't be happy to hear what happened," Abby said.

"He's never happy regardless," Max grumbled as he got out of bed.

Abby admired his body as he dressed, and grinned when he caught her looking.

"If you are trying to make me want to come back to bed, it's working."

She arched her eyebrows. "You are all talk."

"If only I could do as I wished."

"Someday I will have you so desperate for the feel of me that you will give in."

"That's what I'm afraid of," he said and headed down.

Abby couldn't go quite yet. She hadn't braided her hair before falling asleep with Max and needed to do so. After the night they had spent, it was tangled about her face.

When she did go below, she found Max leaning against one wall, Jack slouched at the table with a beer and Bill drinking with him.

"So you have no idea where he is," Jack said.

Obviously, Max had already indicated that they had encountered some difficulties at St. George's. "No."

The glower on Jack's face made Abigail uneasy. She purposely kept her mouth shut as he turned his tankard in a circle.

"*What* happened again?"

"I told you. We were spotted in the cemetery."

"And?"

"Set upon," Max replied.

Bill's eyebrows shot up. "Hasn't this been a week!"

Jack ignored his brother. "The police came after you?"

Max shook his head. "Not the police—friends and family of the deceased."

"I'm not sure I understand how that happened." Jack thrummed his fingers on the table. "Wasn't Abby supposed to make sure the coast was clear?"

A fissure of alarm snaked through Abby. Jack hadn't yet made it to bed. He was drunk, and looking for someone to blame. And she had a feeling *she* would be the scapegoat. She was certainly easier to blame than Max. Jack always picked on the weakest member of the group, and he perceived her as the weakest now that Tom was gone.

"Abby did her part," Max said. "She was supposed to find out if there were any booby traps. She told us there weren't, and she was right. Last night's should have been an easy take. It was just bad luck that things went as they did."

"We seem to be having a lot of bad luck since Abby came here," Jack said.

"You're the one who didn't want to let her go," Max pointed out and shoved off the wall to pour two beers.

Abby didn't like the sound of that. But she could see why he would say it. She hoped it was only for Jack's benefit. Max was such a contradiction. He wanted her—but something stood in the way.

Accepting the mug he handed to her, she sat next to Bill. Max acted as if he expected her to behave as any other member of the gang—and she instinctively understood she had to let Jack know she wasn't that easily intimidated, or his abuse would continue.

"You seem happy enough about that decision, Max," Jack said. "And it's no wonder, since you're the one who gets to sleep with her."

Abby didn't dare look at Max for fear he would act as if that held no value to him.

"This isn't about who I sleep with," he responded. "You're upset about how it went at St. George's, and you have every right to be. We're all upset. Someone must have been looking out—"

Jack came to his feet. "So there *was* someone guarding the body."

At the accusation in his tone, Max grew impatient. "Calm down."

Hoping to distract Jack, to keep him from getting angry at Max's tone, Abby came to her own defense. "Not specifically. Not that anyone talked about at the burial."

She cringed when Jack turned his bloodshot eyes on her, but Max stepped in again, drawing Jack's attention back to him. "Someone spotted our lamp and called out an alarm that brought down what felt like an army. It could happen any night. We could have been arrested, or beaten, or . . . only God knows. You're well aware of the risks."

"An army, eh?" Jack focused on that part and ignored the rest. "One would think you'd be done for."

"That's what we thought," Max said.

"Then how is it the two of you got away?"

There was that doubt again, that underlying suspicion that kept them in constant jeopardy. Abby held her breath while she waited to hear what Max would say.

"We broke up, spread out, and did the best we could."

"And Emmett? You don't know what became of him?"

"I've already told you I don't," Max said. "We were too busy doing everything in our power to escape."

"I'm sure he'll thank you for running out on him."

Max grabbed his mug and stood. "I wouldn't call that running out. I had Abby to consider. Would you have wanted her to be arrested? For it to come out that she has been here with us the whole time?"

"With *you*, Max. You're the only one who's had any benefit from her being here. So far, she's only cost me money."

"Makes no difference," Max argued. "I couldn't let her fall into their hands. There's no telling what they would have done."

"I wonder if Emmett knew you'd put her first, that's all," Jack said.

Bill chuckled uncomfortably. "Come on, Jack. Emmett might be young but he can fend for himself. She's a woman."

"So?" Jack challenged. "Emmett's more valuable to me than she is."

"We went back later," Max told them. "We couldn't find Emmett."

"Listen to that," Bill said. "They did all they could. Emmett will show up eventually. There's no need to cause a row with Max, or before you know it, we'll be a gang of only two. And what we do is too hard for that."

"We could manage. At least I can trust *you*," Jack grumbled.

"You think Abby and I *wanted* this to happen?" Max asked.

Jack took a long pull on his beer. "I can't figure out what you want."

"I've told you. I want the money to pay off my debts."

"Then you'll have to be more successful than you were last night, won't you!" Jack glared at him over the rim of his cup. "Where's the corpse you went after? If it's still in the ground, we should go back there tonight, before it can decompose any further."

Max shook his head. "It's not in the ground. Emmett hauled it away."

Abby wondered what Jack would do if he learned that they had taken the body to Aldersgate. She had been grateful for Max's help last night, but only now did she realize just how much he had done for her, and why he had insisted they not dispose of the cart until they were well away from Smithfield. Jack had regretted letting her return the college's money almost from the moment he agreed to it. He would not be pleased that she had cost him even more.

"You gotta love that kid," Jack said. "You're protecting your willy's interests while he's seeing to business."

"In all likelihood, trying to take the body is what got him caught," Max pointed out. "That cost us a good cart."

"*Now* you're seeing the wisdom of it. Maybe we can find it."

"I told you. We went back to the cemetery. There was no Emmett and no cart. So why return again? They'll only be waiting for us next time."

Jack sneered at him. "They were waiting for you last time. Maybe tonight we fight back—teach 'em a lesson for Emmett."

Although it wasn't unheard of for mourners to get into a skirmish with resurrection men, Max rolled his eyes. "You're drunk."

The contempt in those two words made Abigail fear how Jack might respond. Bill must have had the same reaction because he stepped in to smooth things over. "We made up for the loss, Jack. Got fifteen guineas ourselves last night, didn't we?"

Instead of ratifying what he had just heard, Jack sent Bill a quelling glance. "Shut the hole in your face before I shut it for you."

Bill's placating smile withered and he went back to drinking.

"You sold another corpse? Where'd you get it?" Max's questions were directed at both of them, but Bill kept his eyes on his cup and didn't answer.

"There was no other corpse," Jack said.

"You got fifteen guineas for something," Max responded.

"Bill doesn't know what the hell he's talkin' about," Jack said. "He never does."

Max sat back down and stretched out his legs. "Emmett told us you went looking for Tom. Did you manage to find him?"

Jack glowered at him. "Emmett doesn't know what he's talkin' about, either. We met a gravedigger who led us to his last few graves. Right, Bill?"

When Bill grunted in agreement, Max pursed his lips, considering. "You just said you didn't sell another corpse."

"Doesn't matter. What we did tonight is none of your damn business," Jack snapped.

Max leaned forward. "And Tom?"

"Forget Tom! He left of his own accord, and he won't be coming back."

"Because . . ."

"He knows better than to show his face around here after what he did."

He sounded so certain . . .

Abigail noticed how Max's knuckles whitened on his cup and guessed he was thinking the same thing she was: Tom knew better than to come back—or, now that Jack had finished with him, he *couldn't.*

Chapter 18

When Abby entered their room, she expected Max to follow her. But he didn't. He continued down the hall, only to return a moment later—with her elephant.

Suddenly homesick, Abby took it and hugged it to her chest. "Thank you."

He didn't respond. He just stood there, watching her.

"What?" she said, growing self-conscious beneath his unwavering regard.

"I was wrong to let you talk me into bringing you back here, Abby. It's not safe."

"I told you I won't go out again, not at night. I'll leave the body snatching to you and the others."

"But you're not safe even in this house! I was deluded to think you might be. Maybe Jack has accepted your presence, but he can't be trusted. You saw how he acted a minute ago. And there's no telling what he and Bill did to Tom."

"Tom betrayed him."

"And what are we doing? What if he were to find out? Tom's probably dead!"

"That's one of the many reasons Jack must be stopped. I'm trying to help you accomplish that." After last night, he had to know that *he* was the real reason she had stayed. But he was suddenly acting as if her presence was all about the practicalities of their situation.

"I've told you, this is not *your* fight. The college has its money and its cadaver, and you have your mother's last gift. Let me take you back to Aldersgate right this minute, while it's still possible to get you home unharmed."

She could hear Jack and Bill downstairs, and lowered her voice so they wouldn't be able to hear her. "If I wanted to be at Aldersgate, I would have stayed when we were there delivering that corpse."

He had tried to convince her to do just that, and she had briefly considered it. What they had encountered at the cemetery had scared her enough to make her realize that she was in real danger, and not just from Jack. Anything could happen.

But after they put the corpse in the cellar and she pressed her hands up against the brick building that had been her home for so many years, deliberating, she no longer felt as if she belonged there. Something had changed in the brief time she'd been gone—*she'd* changed. She felt like a butterfly that had been let out of a jar. She was no longer provided for—but she was no longer caged, either.

There was also the fact that she couldn't bring herself to let Max walk away, of course. She feared if she did, she would never see him again.

"Surely, after all that's occurred, you must see that this is no place for a woman," he said. "No business for a woman to be in."

She put her elephant on the vanity with the brush and mirror set he had given her. "Without me, you would have been caught at St. George's."

"You don't know that."

"They caught Emmett. They only let us go because they thought we were . . . you know." After the pleasure they had given each other, she could no longer address those issues from a clinical standpoint. He had been right that first night when he told her intimacy was nothing like what she had read in her father's medical journals—at least it wasn't when the heart was as engaged as the body. And, for her, that had definitely been the case.

His beard growth rasped as he rubbed a hand across his chin. "Emmett tried to escape while encumbered with a corpse. He's young enough to feel invincible. I would not have been so stupid."

"That doesn't mean you would have escaped without me. Anything could have happened."

"That's what frightens me!" he said, exasperated. "I'm afraid if we ever get into another situation like that, I won't be able to protect you!"

"So you'd like me to leave."

"Yes! Jack resents the fact that I have you in my bed. He won't let it go."

"What about us?"

A pained expression crossed Max's face. "Abby—"

"I know you care about me," she insisted.

"Let's not go into that."

"Why not? What are you so afraid of?"

"I'm afraid of hurting you! We have no future together!"

It was difficult not to wince. He had told her that before but . . . she had been certain she could get him to change his mind. The way he looked at her had to count for something, didn't it?

Or had she misjudged his many kindnesses? The way he protected her from Jack? The desire he seemed to feel when they touched?

"That could change, couldn't it?" she said. "I mean—"

"No!"

He was so absolute she could scarcely breathe. "*Why?*"

"Because my plans don't include you! I thought I made that clear."

He had—but he had also made her feel as if she were the only woman in the world. Last night had encompassed so much more than the physical. She *knew* it did. "You have to feel more than you're admitting."

With a muttered curse, he put his back to her.

"Max?"

He didn't respond immediately. When he did, his voice was so low she could barely hear him. "Abby, this isn't about what I feel."

"Then what is it about? Tell me! Tell me at last!"

With a sigh, he faced her. "I'm afraid there's someone else."

She could only hope she had heard him wrong. "*What did you say?*"

"It's true," he replied, but she could tell that from his face. "I'm engaged to be married."

She pressed a hand to her chest as she tried to absorb this revelation. She had thought he would blame the situation he was in, the fact that his own future was uncertain, that his stint in Wapping could drag on. She had not expected another woman! Why hadn't he mentioned being in love? And that woman was going to be his wife!

"Who . . . who is she?" Dear God, she could scarcely form the words.

He pinched the bridge of his nose. "Does it matter? The less you know about me and my life, the better."

She blinked at him as she struggled to rally. Was this her fault? He *had* warned her not to get her hopes up, just as he said. She was the one who had blown sexual interest and compatibility into something more—because of her naiveté.

No wonder he had been trying so hard to keep his hands to himself.

Embarrassed by how forward she had been, how wanton, she managed the best smile she could under the circumstances, and politely dipped her head. "I see and I . . . I nearly forced myself on you on two separate occasions. I sincerely apologize. I didn't realize your heart was taken." She turned to get her elephant.

"What are you doing?" he asked.

"I'm leaving, of course. As you wish." She abandoned the mirror and brush he gave her—obviously she had been deluded to think that was any kind of real gift—as well as the dress she had made from his clothes (*how angry he must be about that*), and tried to skirt past him.

He caught her by the arm. "Wait, please. I'll take you after Jack goes to sleep."

He had asked her to vacate the premises and she had agreed, but he didn't appear to be pleased by the victory. If she had to guess, he was angry, and it was no wonder. Thanks to her silly infatuation, and the vain imaginings of her virgin heart, she had made fools of them both. If only he could have explained earlier . . .

"There's no need to trouble yourself," she said. "I will be fine."

"You *can't* go alone." His fingers bit into her arm when she tried to pull away, but she could scarcely feel the pressure. There were too many things going on elsewhere in her body. Her chest was tight, her eyes burning.

She cleared her throat, trying to remove the lump that made it difficult to speak. "It's broad daylight. Besides, I came down here on my own, didn't I? Unhand me, sir."

He looked strangely crestfallen when he gazed down at her. "Sir? I am *sir* to you now?"

"I don't know what else to call you! I have already apologized for my . . . inexpert attempt to . . . to turn our relationship into more than you wish it to be. I can only beg your forbearance and understanding, given my lack of experience, and ask you to let me go so that I no longer have to suffer the humiliation of sitting here with you, knowing I encouraged you to . . . to act on certain base desires I misconstrued."

"You didn't misconstrue anything. I—never mind," he said with some impatience. "There is nothing to be gained by trying to explain my actions. Just know that I assume full responsibility and lay no fault at your feet."

"Thank you." Again, she started to go, but he stopped her.

"That doesn't change the fact that you won't be leaving this house until I can escort you." He glared down at her, his expression unyielding. So she backed up in order to get him to release her—it was too difficult being in such close proximity, too embarrassing to think she had flirted so terribly with a man committed to marrying another—and sat down to wait.

Silence settled over them. She tried to draw some sort of calm from it, but the tears she had been fighting began to slip down her cheeks. Mortified that she would embarrass herself further, she bent her head to stare at the floor. She hoped he wouldn't notice, but when he cursed, she guessed he had.

"You love the college," he said.

It was almost an accusation. She didn't respond. What could she say? This had nothing to do with loving the college and everything to do with loving a man—loving *him*. In spite of all her previous opinions about marriage, she had begun to believe that she had found her place in the world, at last, and it was by his side.

"Someday they might admit you," he added. "I mean . . . it's a possibility, however remote."

She wanted to wipe her cheeks, but she feared that would only draw attention to her distress.

He cleared his throat. "And think of how happy your father will be to see you."

Her father would indeed be relieved. She missed him, and she missed others at Aldersgate. But what had happened over the past several days had radically changed how she viewed her future. There would be no going back to the way things were—even if her father allowed it. She was too aware of her own loneliness. This stint as a body snatcher—as loathsome as the job was, as loathsome as Jack and the rest were—had somehow brought her more fulfillment than she had ever known before. And what did she have at the college? She couldn't even count on having a career, like her father.

There was no point in explaining any of that to Max, however. Why would what might become of her be any of his concern?

"Abby, are you listening? Everything will be fine."

She didn't look up.

"Because even if they don't admit you, someday you will meet the right man—someone who will marry you and make you happy to be a wife and mother."

As if taking too much for granted wasn't humiliating enough, she had to sit there, crying as he told her how happy she would be with another man? Was he picturing how happy he would be with his betrothed?

Her gaze cut to the door, but he stepped in front of it, cutting her off before she could even make the attempt.

When she realized how carefully he was watching her, she dashed a hand across her face. What was the use of trying to hide her emotions?

He could tell she was in tears, or he wouldn't be trying so hard to console her.

"Don't cry," he said then, softly. "I never meant to hurt you. I never meant for any of this to happen."

She sniffed. "I'm not blaming you. *I'm* the bumbling halfwit. I understand that. I'm not sure how you avoided laughing at my clumsy attempts to . . . to make love to you."

He seemed stricken by her last comment. "Don't say that. I wasn't tempted to laugh because there was nothing clumsy about it. Your touch, it . . . it tested me almost beyond my ability to resist."

She laughed humorlessly. "Of course it did. A man here, alone in this room with his . . . his betrothed elsewhere. I'm sure any woman would have been a temptation. So put us both out of our misery and let me go. Once I walk out that door, you will never have to see me again."

His face fell as if the thought of that made him feel as bad as it did her. "I'm not in such a rush that I would risk your safety."

"Oh bother! You have no say in the matter!" She got up in spite of his refusal—but before she could take a single step, someone banged on the front door downstairs.

"Jack! Damn you! What have you done to my brother?"

Her own troubles momentarily forgotten, Abby looked to Max.

"It's Peter, Tom's brother," Max said. "I've met him before. And from the way he's slurring his words, the poor bastard's drunk."

A keening wail rose to their ears. "You've killed him. I know you have. Open up for what you've got comin', or I'll break down the blasted door!"

Jack or Bill—Abigail couldn't tell which from up in the bedroom—must have let Tom's brother in, which was a mistake. Max knew it was, too, because the second that happened, he barked at her to stay put and hurried down the stairs.

"He told me you'd be after him!" Tom's brother went on, his voice ricocheting through the house. "He said you were the devil hisself!

What have you done with him, huh? Did you sell him to the bloody anatomists?"

"I haven't seen him." Jack sounded rather complacent for being falsely accused of murder, and he maintained that smug complacency throughout the argument that ensued.

Worried about Max in spite of her previous pique, Abigail moved out of the room. She stood at the top of the stairs, listening, as Tom's brother insisted that a friend of his *saw* Jack and Bill dragging Tom through an alley.

Both Hurtsill brothers denied it. Max tried to act as mediator, tried to get Tom's brother to put down a pistol. But then a blast rang through the air and there was a scuffle—what sounded like a few overturned chairs and two or more men wrestling.

Max managed to get the gun away from Peter, but it hadn't been easy with Jack trying to retaliate by coming after the man with that knife of his.

"Stupid bastard." Jack glowered at Peter while Max pinned him to the wall.

Max thought Bill had been seriously injured. Jack's brother sat slumped on the floor, where he'd fallen when the gun went off. But a closer look revealed that the bullet had only grazed his arm.

"That bloke shot me," he said, eyes glazed.

"Don't you worry, brother, he ever comes at us again, he'll get what's comin' to him." Jack turned the knife in his hand. "Then we'll have us *another* corpse to sell."

"Sometimes I think you'd sell mine, Jack," his brother mumbled.

"Just don't die on me," Jack said with a laugh.

Feeling as if Jack could finally be trusted to restrain himself for the moment, Max turned his attention to Tom's brother. "Are you finished here? I dare say it's time for you to go home while you can still do so with all your body parts intact."

"You should have let me kill him," Jack said. "It would have been self-defense, clear and simple."

"No one's going to hurt him," Max said.

"What have you done with my brother?" Peter asked, but he looked deflated, more distraught than dangerous.

Max addressed Bill and Jack. "Where does he belong? I'll take him to his wife."

"He has no wife—or other family," Bill said.

"Except Tom," Max reminded him.

The Hurtsills exchanged a look that made the blood run cold in Max's veins. There was no more brother—no more Tom. Max felt certain of it. But just as he was about to call Bill on the slip, he saw Abby standing on the steps, gaping at the scene below her.

"Go back upstairs," he said.

She didn't do as he directed. She shook her head. "No. I'm leaving. I'm finished here."

She hurried down the final three steps and attempted to circumvent them, but Jack intercepted her.

"You're not goin' anywhere," he said. "You had us give that money back to the college, said you'd help us replace it and you're gonna do just that. I won't have you betray me like this bastard's brother did. We're goin' to be a mite more careful around here. So get your pretty little arse up those stairs before you wind up in my bed instead of Max's."

Her gaze riveted on the blood seeping down Bill's arm. "I want no part of this."

"What, you can't take a little blood?" Jack scoffed.

"It's not the blood I'm worried about." When she met his gaze, her eyes narrowed with scathing accusation. "I'm afraid you killed Tom."

"It's that kind of talk that'll get you in trouble," he warned. "I don't know where Tom is. I haven't seen him, and I won't have you saying otherwise—to anyone. You understand? You decided to become one of us. It's too late to back out now."

She licked her lips, obviously nervous. "You're not . . . you're not going to have Max lock me in the room again."

"That won't be necessary," Jack said. "If you go missing, I'll hold Max accountable—and I'll do everything I can to destroy your father."

Max dragged Tom's brother to the door and pushed him outside without the pistol he had brought. That lay on the floor, where Max had forced him to drop it once he got off that first shot. "There's no need to threaten either of us," he told Jack while keeping one eye on Tom's brother to be sure he scrambled away and wouldn't cause any more trouble.

All the excitement set Borax off. He strained against his leash, barking and jumping in an effort to reach Tom's brother, but, even drunk, Peter managed to avoid the dog.

"I won't be having you tell me my business ever again, Max," Jack said above the din. "You've crossed that line one too many times—do you understand? You mind that bitch of yours and do your job, and we'll get along just fine. 'Cause if you don't"—he used his knife to punctuate his words—"one way or another, I'll make sure you regret it."

Max closed and locked the door. "Like you did with Tom?"

Jack's eyes narrowed. "Don't tempt me to take this any further. Tom got only what he deserved."

Max measured his chances of wresting that knife away. He felt as if he could overcome Jack; physically, Jack was no match for him. But he feared Bill would grab Abby. Jack's brother was already standing up and moving closer. And if it came down to a standoff, it would cost him any chance he had of finding Madeline. He wouldn't be able to achieve justice for that woman Jack brought home—or for Tom, either.

Max wanted to see Jack properly punished for whatever he had done, so he clenched his jaw and overcame the impulse to act. First, he would get everything he wanted out of Jack and Bill—so that he could save Madeline, if she was still alive.

"Abby, go back upstairs," he said, and this time she did as she was told.

Chapter 19

Jack refused to go to bed even though he clearly needed some sleep. Max wasn't sure how the man remained on his feet. He was running on gin, and gin alone. But Jack was odd like that. Sometimes he would stay up for several days in a row. He said he *couldn't* sleep, especially during the day, didn't like feeling as if the world was going on without him.

Max wished exhaustion would take over—or that the man would simply pass out. But that didn't happen. He insisted they all go out together and search for Emmett. Although Max argued that Abby should be allowed to stay at the house, and then that they could cover more ground if they split up, Jack rejected both propositions. He said no one was going to be anywhere he couldn't see them.

Jack was growing paranoid, Max thought. And that concerned him. It made the gang leader even more volatile and dangerous than he already was.

Besides checking the garret where Emmett lived, not far from Execution Dock, they visited several brothels and taverns and talked to people in the streets. No one had seen Emmett.

"Maybe Tom knows where he is," Max suggested, trying to get Jack to reveal more about what might have happened to Tom. But that achieved little. Jack didn't even answer. And his mood seemed to worsen as the hours passed. No doubt he didn't feel well after being up for so long. But the way he watched Abby made Max nervous. Max should have gotten her away from the London Supply Company while he could have. Instead he had let her lie to that constable and join the gang—and now he feared it was too late. Even if he took her home after Jack went to sleep, Jack knew where she lived. Max feared he would only become determined to punish her as he had punished Tom. That meant her father or someone else at the college could get hurt, too.

He would have to keep her by his side a little longer, Max decided. But he already knew it wasn't going to be easy to lie beside her each night and not touch what he had grown so familiar with. She would scarcely look at him now, but the memory of her body, rising to meet the thrust of his hand, played in his mind over and over again, making his heart pound in his chest.

When they finally abandoned the search and returned to Farmer's Landing, Abby ate a small dinner and went up to their room. They had gotten in late the night before. Then they had been so caught up in each other that they had slept for only a few hours. She had to be almost as exhausted as Jack was. Max knew he was.

Sure enough, when Max joined Abby, he found her in bed, facing away from him. She gave no indication that she even heard him come in.

He closed the door and locked it for good measure. Bill was gone but Jack was home. Max didn't want him to wake before they did, didn't want him coming in while he and Abby were sleeping. They had to be extra careful going forward. Jack had drawn battle lines—and was waiting to see if Max would cross them.

Max hoped he would be able to avoid doing so for as long as it would take to learn Madeline's fate—for as long as it would take to get them all out of there alive. But there were no guarantees. He would have to cross those lines eventually, and once he did, anything could happen.

"I should have left you at Aldersgate when we delivered that corpse," he said. There was an edge to his voice; no doubt she heard it. But he wasn't angry with *her*. He was angry with himself for ignoring his better judgment. As much as he wanted to blame Abby for insisting on returning, he knew that wasn't entirely fair. If, deep down, he hadn't wanted to keep her with him, he would have made her stay at the school.

She said nothing, and yet he could tell she wasn't asleep.

"Are you not speaking to me?" That was all he could guess. She had barely said a word to him since they left earlier.

"What do you want me to say?" she asked. "You've already made it clear you don't want me here. I would go if I could."

He wished he could see her face. How upset was she?

He couldn't tell, because she didn't roll over. "I just want you to be safe."

"Then it's a good thing I *didn't* stay at Aldersgate last night."

"Excuse me?"

"Who knows how Jack might have reacted if I didn't come back? We're in the middle of this now. We have to see it through."

He removed his coat. "If Madeline's dead, I'm risking your safety for nothing. That's what bothers me."

"We don't know she's dead. We have to assume the best. It might be the only chance she has. You said she would never willingly abandon her child."

But, even if she was alive, would he ever be able to find her? Or was he grasping at thin air?

Probably the latter, but he couldn't extinguish the hope that burned so brightly inside him—the desire to achieve her forgiveness and, more than anything, restore his nephew's mother.

"I'll give it another week," he said. "If we don't find her, or something that gives some indication that we can expect the best possible outcome, I'll go to the police with what I know."

Finally, she rolled over. "And what do you know?"

"Not enough," he admitted. That was the problem. The police would come. Thanks to who he was, they might even perform an investigation. But Max had no confidence their efforts would amount to anything, or he would have handled the situation that way from the beginning. He had been living with Jack for three weeks and hadn't yet found the answers he sought. What more could *they* do? And if he went that route, Abby could still be in danger. Thanks to his deception, she might be in even *more* danger, because if Jack learned the truth, it would only provoke him. It wouldn't be unlike Jack to use Abby to hurt Max.

Stifling a sigh, he piled his waistcoat and shirt on the chair where he had just draped his coat, and climbed into bed. It had been a long day and what had happened with Tom's brother left him uncertain that he had chosen the most prudent course, especially when it came to Abby.

"I never liked Tom," he said, voicing what had been going through his mind since Peter showed up with that pistol. "But I can't help feeling sorry for him. His background played a big role in the type of unfortunate adult he turned out to be."

"He was weaker than Jack and Jack preyed on him. That's why you pity him. Tom deserves justice the same as Madeline."

"I hope we can get that justice."

He could see the fat rope her braid made in the moonlight and couldn't help remembering what her hair had felt like, falling freely across his chest.

"Are you cold?" He hoped she would say yes so he would have an excuse to provide her with his body heat.

"I'm fine," she said stiffly.

He could tell that, no matter what he did, she wouldn't allow him to touch her, not after what he had told her earlier. She wanted his heart as well as his body—and that was what he couldn't provide.

"Do you think Emmett's in gaol?" she asked.

"I can't imagine he wouldn't come here to let us know, had he escaped the cemetery."

When their eyes met, she pulled the blankets up that much higher. "I'm worried about him."

"I am, too—and yet I can't help being relieved that he inadvertently distracted those men at St. George's. I doubt we would have gotten away otherwise, and I shudder to think what they might have done to you."

They certainly wouldn't have been able to squire off the corpse they had disinterred.

"Why doesn't Emmett board here like Tom did?" she asked. "He seems so young. How does he get by on his own?"

"Emmett's willing to work with Jack; he's not willing to live with him."

"Tom would've been smart to stay elsewhere, too—with his brother or, failing that, at a common lodging house. Why would he subject himself to Jack's abuse?"

"Who knows? Emmett's life, hard though it has been, has probably been easier. At least he's been able to make friends. I don't get the impression Tom ever managed that. And Tom's brother isn't any more stable than Tom is . . . or was, if he's no longer alive."

When she didn't say anything, he almost reached for her. He longed to forget everything that had transpired between them that day, wished they could go back to the night before. After the liberties he had taken, it felt so natural to draw her to him. He wanted to slip off whatever she had on and kiss her until he could no longer think about Madeline or Jack or anything else.

But every time he shifted, she inched away from him, as if she was opposed to encountering him even by accident. He feared if she moved any farther she would fall out of bed.

"It surprised me that his room was so neat and clean," she said.

"That's probably another reason he's not willing to live here." Max hated living in such squalor.

"Does he have a sweetheart?"

"From what I can gather, he prefers a good whore to anyone he might become responsible for."

"How admirable."

At the sarcasm in her voice, Max wished he hadn't been quite so candid. After all, she hadn't had the best experience with him—and he was her *only* experience. He didn't want to poison her against men. "You have to remember who he is. He doesn't know any better. He spends most of his time just figuring out how to fill his belly each day."

"I'm ready to return to the college."

He had finally convinced her that she would be better off there. So why, despite all his talk to the contrary, was he so reluctant to see her go?

Stifling a sigh, he moved onto his back and tried to fall sleep. But it didn't happen right away. He stared at the ceiling for a while, then he turned to watch Abby sleep.

"Why didn't you tell me you were in love with someone else?" she asked at length.

Apparently, she wasn't sleeping after all. He was glad—until he reached over to smooth her hair back, and she recoiled.

"Because love has nothing to do with it," he said and dropped his hand.

"Are you awake? We need to get up."

Abby felt as if she had barely closed her eyes. "Why so early?" she grumbled.

"It's not early. It's midmorning."

It didn't look like midmorning. When she rolled over to face the window, she saw that it was a dark and dreary day. "It wasn't all that long ago that we went to bed."

"I have to check in with my clerk. I prefer to do that while Jack's sleeping. With Tom . . . gone"—she noticed that he didn't say *dead*, even though that was what they both believed—"Emmett likely in gaol and Bill home with his domineering wife, there will be no one to follow us."

"Fine. I'm coming." She didn't want to be left behind with Jack—or locked in the room. Besides, maybe she could learn something from Max's clerk. She couldn't get a word out of Max about the woman he planned to marry. Who was she? Where did she think he was? Did she know he was sharing a bed with someone else? What was their relationship like?

Abby certainly wondered—especially when she pushed the blankets away and Max's gaze riveted on what the thin fabric of her chemise revealed.

Covering her breasts with her hands, she gave him a starched look. "Is there some reason you feel free to ogle me, Mr. Wilder?"

He frowned, obviously disappointed by her reaction. "If I can't touch you, at least let me look."

"You can look at your fiancée." She smiled with feigned sweetness. "Have you told her about me, by the way? Or are you excusing your behavior because you have pleasured me with your mouth and your hands but have saved your cock for her?"

"Don't provoke me, Abby," he growled. "I preserved your maidenhead for *your* sake, not hers."

"Still, I'm sure she will appreciate your restraint."

"My fiancée and I aren't exclusive. I can take my pleasure wherever I like. What she and I have is more of a . . . a business arrangement."

"And that's supposed to make what we have done less of a betrayal? Or is it designed to make me want to spread my legs and stupidly beg you to take me as I have done before?"

A muscle moved in his cheek. "Only if you feel, as I do, that taking advantage of this time, this chance to be together, is better than walking away with nothing."

"From what you have said, I *will* walk away with nothing. Isn't that what you have been trying to convey?"

He lowered his voice in entreaty. "I have been trying to convey my honest limitations. Anything short of that would be unfair to you."

She slipped off her chemise and let him look, secretly gratified by the hunger in his eyes. "So now that I know I will be cast aside, your conscience is clear and I can throw myself onto the rocks if I want to?"

"It wouldn't be like that." He stepped forward, no doubt eager to convince her, but she held up a hand to stop him.

"I appreciate your generous offer. But, surely, someday I will meet a man not promised to someone else who might want to touch me here"—she ran her own fingers over the tips of her breasts and moved lower—"and here."

"You want what I want," he insisted.

She turned away to wash with the pitcher and bowl. "I want what I can't have. And now, so do you."

Chapter 20

This time Max let Abby join him in Mr. Hawley's office. She was wearing the dress she had fashioned out of Max's coat in place of her gypsy rags, and the mark he had left on her neck was almost gone. In her own estimation, she had to look a lot more respectable. But, like before, Mr. Hawley didn't take much notice of her. She could only hope he remained as oblivious of the tension between her and Max—although she couldn't imagine how that was possible. There was so much emotion flowing under the surface they could scarcely look at each other.

"I've found a few things," the clerk announced, getting right to the point.

"It's about time we have a change in fortune," Max responded. He was in no mood for further disappointment, and Abby could easily tell. "What have you learned?"

"That woman who died? The one you were worried about being murdered?"

"With the glass eye?" Max slid forward in his seat and Abby caught her breath.

"Her name was Anna Harper. She was a widow who boarded with a Mr. Bolstrum and his wife."

"How do you know?"

He rubbed his hands in apparent eagerness. "I found a shopkeeper who recognized her description."

"You've spoken to this Bolstrum and his wife, then?"

"I have. They claim she fell ill and passed unexpectedly."

"In their house?"

"Yes. In her own bed."

Max's gaze strayed to Abby. He was obviously eager to celebrate this small victory with her. At least they had discovered *something* about the woman, something that might lead them further. But then he must have remembered that they were at odds, because he jerked his attention away. "Then how did Jack gain possession of her body?"

The door slid open with a bang, and a stocky, tattooed sailor came into the warehouse. Mr. Hawley got up to see what he wanted, gave him directions since he seemed to be in the wrong place, and returned. "Mr. Bolstrum said her family lives in India," he told Max. "She has stacks of letters from them, which he showed me. He said that of course they couldn't wait for someone that far away to make arrangements for her burial. It would take weeks just to notify them."

"So they did . . . what?" Max asked.

"She was a member of a friendly society. After paying twopence a week for the past several years, she should have been afforded a decent funeral—an elm wood coffin with a coffin plate and handles, a velvet pall, even hatbands, hoods and scarves for the attendants."

"How do you know?"

"I spoke with Mrs. Shrewsbury, who runs the society she was in."

Max took a moment to digest Hawley's response. Then he asked, "Why didn't Anna Harper get what was due her?"

"Mr. Bolstrum claims he contacted the society and they came for the body. As far as he is concerned, she did get it."

Abigail couldn't stop herself from jumping in. "How long did she live with the Bolstrums?"

"Ah, your mind is going where mine did." Mr. Hawley didn't seem the least put off that she would be the one to ask this question. He was too pleased that he had an answer. "I wondered the same thing, so I asked him for his rental records."

"And he complied?" Max asked wryly.

"He was eager to convince me that he had nothing to hide."

"What did the ledger show?"

"She had been staying there since October of 1827."

"After three years, he and his wife should have known her quite well," Abigail mused. "Wouldn't they be aware of her funeral? Wouldn't they have wanted to attend?"

"Mr. Bolstrum mentioned that it was difficult to endure her company," Mr. Hawley replied. "They weren't on speaking terms at the time of her death."

Abby looked to Max but only briefly, as he had looked at her before. "So it's Mrs. Shrewsbury who sold her body to Jack?"

"It sounds like she would certainly have been in a position to do so." It was Max who answered her question and yet his attention remained on Mr. Hawley.

The clerk seemed oblivious to the fact that they were so hesitant to engage each other directly. "I don't think it was her," he said. "Mrs. Shrewsbury insists she was never notified of Mrs. Harper's death."

"That merely makes it Bolstrum's word against Mrs. Shrewsbury's," Max pointed out.

Mr. Hawley dipped his head in agreement. "Still, I believe Mrs. Shrewsbury—"

"Why?" Max broke in, sounding slightly irritated. "We can't assume she's honest just because she's a woman."

"Although a woman is probably more reliable than a man," Abigail added.

She had spoken under her breath, but Max heard—and scowled at her. "You can't intimate that I haven't been honest with you."

"That depends on your interpretation of *honest*. What you have told me came a bit late."

The clerk's eyes widened at this exchange.

Max arched his eyebrows. "And she's the daughter of a surgeon," he said as an aside. "Presumptuous, isn't she?"

Provoked by his condescending manner—as if it was beyond shocking that she would dare speak to a successful man of business when she was *merely* the daughter of a surgeon—Abby regarded Mr. Hawley with a level stare. "Mr. Wilder has his own flaws."

"The most grievous of which is the fact that I have a fiancée," Max added dryly.

Abby gaped at him. "I wouldn't want you, anyway!"

When Mr. Hawley coughed, Abby realized that she had gone too far. Finally feeling some of the embarrassment she would have felt much sooner, if not for the jealousy that poked her like a sharp stick, her cheeks flushed hot. "But . . . continue," she said, trying to back away from the scene she had just caused in front of Max's employee. "I will . . . I will say nothing more."

There were several moments of silence. To Abby they felt as if they stretched on for an eternity, so she attempted to guide the conversation back to where it should be. "You were saying you believe Mrs. Shrewsbury and not Mr. Bolstrum," she murmured to Max's clerk.

"Right. Yes. So I was." He seemed to be having difficulty getting over what he had just witnessed but, to Abby's relief, he managed to resume. "It seems logical to me, given that it is Mr. Bolstrum who lives down the street from Bill Hurtsill."

Thankfully, this piece of news was sufficient to propel the conversation forward, beyond her gaffe. Not that anyone was likely to forget her behavior, especially Abby.

"So after they left the Lion's Paw, Bill, Emmett, Tom and Jack probably walked past Bill's house on their way home," Max said. "No doubt they expected to drop him off and continue. Instead, they received the 'happy' news of Mrs. Harper's death, paid Mr. Bolstrum a few shillings and took her off his hands."

"That's a plausible scenario," Mr. Hawley said. "Perhaps Mr. Bolstrum assumed, with her family in India, he could do as he pleased—and might as well make up for the rent he would lose while he advertised for a new boarder."

Max studied his clerk. "He didn't like her anyway."

"He admitted as much."

"So you don't think she was murdered . . ."

Mr. Hawley kept his attention on Max. Abby couldn't blame him. She had embarrassed them all with her outburst. Max had, to a point, provoked her. But she had overreacted.

"So far, we have no proof either way," he said. "Given what you have told me about the London Supply Company, and Mr. Bolstrum's apparent lack of feeling where Mrs. Harper was concerned, it is just as likely that they killed her and agreed to split the money her corpse could bring."

A frown tugged on Max's lips. "Jack told me that someone supplies him with a body here and there. That makes Mrs. Harper's appearance at Farmer's Landing sound like more than sheer luck. He even mentioned paying this person. That's a business transaction. So what we need to learn now is whether or not he was speaking of Mr. Bolstrum."

"Indeed," the clerk said. "If we can discover a link between Mrs. Harper's landlord and anyone else recently deceased under questionable circumstances, we might have our answer. Such a coincidence would be suspicious, to say the least."

Worry and hope appeared on Max's face. "Did you ask him about Madeline? Could it be that *she* boarded there?"

"Bolstrum *claims* he has never met her," Mr. Hawley said.

"But . . ." Max prodded.

Even sitting there in abject misery and shame, Abigail could tell by the clerk's inflection that he wasn't convinced of Bolstrum's verity in that regard any more than how Anna Harper had died.

"I got the impression he was lying."

"Mr. Bolstrum is a stranger to you, Hobbs."

Abigail hadn't heard Max call Mr. Hawley by his nickname before. But, seeing how they interacted, she got the impression they had known each other a long time, which only made all she had said worse.

"He seemed to grow nervous when I mentioned her, was suddenly far more eager to send me on my way," Hawley said.

Max rubbed his temples. "Maybe Jack hasn't killed anyone. Maybe it's someone else—Mr. Bolstrum—who's to blame for Madeline and the woman with the enamel eye."

Abby had promised herself she wouldn't say another word, but she couldn't let that go. "It has to be Jack," she argued. "We already know that he is capable of murder. What happened to Tom tells us so."

"We have no body for Tom, no proof," Max responded.

She folded her hands in her lap. "There's a chance I could get it. And if we can prove they killed Tom, chances are very good that they killed Mrs. Harper and Madeline, too."

He looked at her despite the enmity between them. "How can *you* get proof?"

"I could go college to college, searching for his corpse. Before Jack could stop him, Bill said they made up for what we lost when we were interrupted at St. George's last night. He mentioned fifteen guineas."

"That's a fairly high price for a corpse. It could be two, and they could be strangers to us—the results of information that gravedigger gave Jack."

"Or it could be Tom. Corpses with a deformity like Tom's harelip often sell for a premium."

"If they killed Tom, they would have to be fools to sell his body," Max said. "It would have been far wiser to simply dump it in the Thames."

"In the heat of passion, people don't always do what is wise," she said. Hadn't she just proven it? "Especially when there's money involved."

She could tell she was getting through to him, and yet Max still seemed reluctant to give her permission to do as she suggested.

"You know how careful the colleges have to be," he said. "They won't share any information."

"With *you*." Abigail felt confident *she* could persuade them—or most of them. "I might be associated with one of their competitors, but no one wants what Burke and Hare did repeated, least of all those in the medical community. Our reputation has suffered enough. Besides, I have met most of the surgeons in London at one time or another. They would rather let me in than you or the police. At least they know I will be as discreet as possible, that their interests are, to a large extent, *my* interests."

He folded his arms as he sat back to study her. "Word of your inquiries could get back to your father. Have you considered that?"

She had, of course. "He might not like my involvement, but at least then he will understand that I am involved in something bigger than running away with a resurrection gang." And falling in love with a man she could not have . . .

"We have to take *some* chances," she added. "If Madeline's alive, she could need help."

He sighed. "I fear she is not alive. She would have reached out to her son, if she could."

Feeling sheepish for letting her personal interest in him supersede the fact that he was trying to help his poor sister, Abby attempted a smile. No matter how hurt and disappointed she was, she couldn't hold what had happened against him. He had never promised her more than what he had delivered. "We'll find her. And we'll put a stop to Jack Hurtsill, too."

She put her hand over his to convince him, to apologize for her sharp tongue and encourage him at the same time, and felt his fingers slip through hers. She had thought he would give her a quick squeeze and let go—if she was forgiven. But she fell in love with him that much more when, in spite of his clerk's presence, he lifted her hand to his mouth and kissed it.

Chapter 21

Before he would let her start making the rounds at the colleges to search for Tom's body, Max took Abby to Cable Street, where Mrs. Harper's landlord lived. He wasn't satisfied with what they had learned from Mr. Hawley. He wanted her to pretend to be a friend of Madeline's, to ask after his sister as if she were under the belief that Madeline had once resided there.

Abigail smoothed her hair as she waited on the stoop. Maybe some other woman would have Max when this was over—oh how she hated the thought of that—but Abby at least wanted to know she had done everything she could to help him. Finding Madeline meant so much to him.

Cable Street was known for its brothels and cheap lodgings, but this house wasn't as dilapidated as some of the others. She expected to confront Mr. Bolstrum, as Mr. Hawley had, but a short, stout woman with gray hair responded to her knock.

"Good morning." Abigail used her dimples to appear as young and appealing as possible.

The woman held the door with an ample hip while drying her hands on an apron—all business. "What can I do for you?"

"I've come all the way from Bristol to see Madeline." She stepped back and looked at the house with a critical eye. "I do hope I've come to the right place."

"I'm afraid you haven't," she said in no uncertain terms and started to go back in.

"Wait!" Abby caught the door before it could slam shut. "Madeline Alcott? You don't know her? She has red hair and . . . and some freckles on her nose?"

"I can't help you," the woman replied, but this time there was something that rang false in her words. She recognized Madeline's name; Abby could see it in her eyes. So she tried again, adding more distress to her performance, as if she might burst into tears.

"But this is the address she sent me. And I *have* to find her. I know no one else here in London."

The woman glanced behind her as if she was afraid she might be overheard. Then she stepped out and closed the door. "I don't know what she promised you, Miss, but there's nothing she can do for you now."

Abby was tempted to twist around and wave at Max. This woman knew Madeline; she had just admitted as much! But he was down the street, staying out of sight, and she dared not draw attention to him.

Suddenly far more anxious than before, lest she unknowingly give herself away now that she was making progress, she cleared her throat. "I'm a friend of a friend—new to the area, like I said. She wrote me, said if I came to her, she might be able to help me find lodgings."

"That would be like her," the woman said. "There wasn't anyone with a softer heart than Madeline's."

Wasn't? Past tense? "So you *do* know her? Are you Mrs. Bolstrum then?"

"No, I'm just a charwoman who comes in to clean one day a week. My help eases some of the pressure on Mrs. Bolstrum, who's ill more often than not."

"But you met Madeline here?"

She lowered her voice. "Aye, she was a boarder, for a short time. But not anymore."

Abby pressed a hand to her chest as if this was harsh news indeed. "Where did she go?"

The charwoman's eyes grew troubled and, with a frown that suggested she was contemplating how she would respond, she stared off into space.

"Mum?"

Blinking, she focused. "She left a month or so ago when she lost her job at the textile mill. Went to live with Jack Hurtsill. He claims to be a ratter, but from what I've heard, he's a bloody resurrectionist. She met him through Jack's brother, who lives just down the street." She indicated the direction where Abby could find Bill, then shook her head. "Unfortunately, Jack isn't the kind of man I ever wanted to see her with."

"Because he's a resurrectionist?"

"Because he's *dangerous*. Has a mean temper, that one. And he can be vengeful when crossed." She waved a hand. "But he made her a lot of promises. And she was desperate to be able to raise her child."

"So she has her boy with her?"

"Who can say? Last I heard her boy was living with a family in Whitechapel. I don't know which family. But she sure talked of Byron a lot—and dreamed of being a proper mother to him."

Abigail added fresh concern to her voice. "You haven't seen her since she left?"

"No, and that makes me sad. Of all the boarders I've met here through the years, she was my favorite. I was quite fond of her."

Again, Abigail resisted the urge to look where Max was watching. "Have there been other boarders who have left unexpectedly and not returned? Or . . . or who have suddenly grown ill and maybe even . . . died?"

The charwoman gave her a piercing look. "Why do you want to know?"

"Madeline mentioned that something odd was going on. In her letter. She was worried—that's all. I thought that might have something to do with her leaving."

"If so, she had no reason to be fearful. Only Anna Harper has died here, and she was ailing for some time, the poor thing."

That didn't seem to attach the Bolstrums to any other unexplained deaths . . . "I really must find her. Have you seen Jack or his brother since she left?"

"Aye. Several times. They come here often, mostly to drink. They're friends with Mr. Bolstrum."

"Have you asked them about her?"

"I have. I expected her to come back and see me now and then and started to worry when she didn't."

"And?"

"They told me she ran off, but I don't believe that for a second."

"Why not?"

Her eyes took on that faraway look again. "Maybe she took Byron and headed to the country," she relented as if that was what she preferred to believe, even if it wasn't true.

Someone called out from inside the house.

"I've got to go," she said.

"Wait, can you tell me where I might be able to find her? Where I could at least look?"

"She had a good friend, a . . . a prostitute she once lived with, before she got her job at the factory. Her name is Gertrude. She lives over on Flower Street—205 Flower Street. I went by there a week ago myself. Gertrude hadn't heard anything. But maybe that has changed." She started to go again but turned back. "And I would ask Bill, of course. He's a bit friendlier than his brother."

"Thank you," Abby said. "Thank you for your help."

"I'm afraid I've been scant help. I wish I could do more," the woman said and was gone.

Abby was flushed when she met up with Max again. The expression on her face gave him hope, but it also reminded him of just how pretty she was—as if he needed a reminder.

"You were right!" she said, breathless with excitement. "Your sister was there!"

The concern he felt for Madeline pressed in on him again. If only she were *still* there.

He pulled Abigail out of the street when he saw a horse and buggy coming—then found it difficult to let go of her. Given the cool autumn temperatures, she was covered head to toe in fabric. But he could feel the way her flesh gave ever so slightly beneath his grip and remembered all too clearly how soft she was.

He wished he found his fiancée even half as appealing . . .

"Mrs. Bolstrum told you?" he asked.

"No, a charwoman who helps out there once a week. I got the impression she's privy to a lot that goes on—not that she always approves of it."

With the horse and buggy well past, he stepped back. He was afraid of what he might do if he didn't put some space between them. The temptation to kiss her intruded on his thoughts more and more often. He could understand having such a compulsion when they were in bed together. Just about any man would be tempted by Abby. But they were standing in the street!

"What, exactly, did she say?" he asked.

Once Abby explained, he ransacked his brain for any memory of Gertrude. "Madeline never mentioned her," he said, but she hadn't confided in him much. He hadn't been deserving of her secrets. He had been too busy trying to avoid her, to pretend she didn't exist.

Abby gazed down the street, toward Bill's house. "Should we visit Bill first? Since we are here?"

Max hadn't mentioned Madeline's name to any of the London Supply Company. It had seemed like the quickest route to giving himself away. "Asking about her could make him suspicious. And, if Jack did harm her, that would only put my life, and yours, in greater danger."

"We could pretend to be on an innocent errand . . ."

"What reason would we have to visit Bill's house when we see him almost every night?"

"We are worried about Emmett! We are out looking for him and want to know if he has heard anything."

Max *was* concerned about young Emmett, so that wouldn't be fabricated. He didn't particularly admire *any* member of the resurrection gang, but Emmett was the last one he would ever want to see hurt.

Besides, maybe Bill would be gone, and they would have the opportunity to speak to his wife—a brash, loud woman who liked to talk and might provide details Bill would know to hide.

"Good idea," he said. "Let's see what we can find out."

Taking Abby's elbow, he guided her down the street to Bill's residence. He should have been too nervous to think of anything other than the task at hand. But once they were standing on the stoop, and Abby smiled up at him, he couldn't seem to quit looking at her.

"What?" she said. "Aren't you going to knock?"

Dragging his focus to the door, he pounded on the wooden panel. What was happening to him? He could hardly believe that someone who had been cloistered away from regular society for most of her life and knew nothing of the usual flirtations could hold such power over him.

"Max, what are you doing here?"

It was Bill who answered.

Max quickly hid his disappointment that it wasn't Agnes, Bill's wife, as he had hoped. "Looking for Emmett."

"Again?"

"He must be somewhere. You haven't seen him yet, have you?"

"No." He yawned as if he had just rolled out of bed, and adjusted the bandage that covered his gunshot wound. "What makes you think he would come here?"

"I thought he might check in, let one of us know if he made it through. He hasn't shown up at Farmer's Landing. We went by the cemetery again, too."

"He'll turn up."

"It's been more than twenty-four hours."

"So he's nursing a few injuries somewhere. He's young. He'll survive."

"Maybe not," Max said. "Maybe he'll be like that woman who used to be with Jack. She's never reappeared, has she?"

Bill seemed mildly surprised. It wasn't as smooth of a transition as Max had wished, but he couldn't think of a better one. "*What* woman?"

"I don't know her name. I think she was Jack's wife."

"Jack's never been married."

"A sexton at St. James's mentioned her a couple of weeks ago, remember?"

"That woman's gone," he mumbled.

"What woman?" Someone—Bill's wife?—asked this from behind Bill, but he didn't answer.

Max inadvertently spoke at the same time. "Where did she go?"

"What does it matter to you?"

Growing more frustrated and desperate than ever, Max nearly grabbed him by the throat and threw him up against the door. Maybe force would bring him what diplomacy and subterfuge, so far, had not. "It seems that people are disappearing right and left."

"She didn't disappear." This came from Bill's wife, who suddenly grabbed the door. "She left."

"Agnes!" he complained when she squished into the opening, but she ignored him.

"You're talking about Madeline, aren't you?" she said. "I don't know her last name, but she lived over at Farmer's Landing before you did. Jack was crazy about her." Her lips curved into a self-satisfied smile, one that suggested she wasn't particularly unhappy her brother-in-law's love affair had ended badly. "Might have married her. He wanted to. But she ran off."

Max didn't have to pretend to be amazed. "*With another man?*"

"No." Agnes shook her head. "Emmett was the only other man in her life. That boy followed her around like a whipped puppy."

Emmett? "Did she like him?" Max asked.

"No. She once told me that he frightened her."

"More than Jack?" Abby asked.

Bill sent his wife a sullen look for being so forthcoming. Then relented with a shrug, as if he couldn't see what harm talking could do, anyway—not if Jack wasn't around to disapprove of the way they bandied about the details of his personal life. "Emmett had a thing for her. But she obviously didn't go anywhere with him. She could've gone back to her family, though."

"Gone back to her family," his wife repeated with a skeptical laugh. "Sure she did. They wouldn't have her, and you know it."

"Why would you say that?" Abby asked.

Max could hear the defensiveness in her voice, knew she felt the need to stand up for him. But he didn't deserve it. He didn't appreciate the question, either—didn't want to hear Bill's take on the family's shortcomings, or anyone else's. He already knew he was largely to blame and felt badly about it. He was also afraid that some tidbit Madeline had shared might give away his identity.

But there was no stopping Agnes. She lowered her voice as if she was about to impart the most delicious gossip.

"She wouldn't say who her family was, wouldn't name them. I think she was afraid Jack would approach them for money. She admitted that they were rich. Told me they took her in at one point, even hired her a governess who taught her to read and write. Then, for some reason, they tossed her out."

Fresh talons of regret sunk, deep and sharp, into Max's heart. What had happened hadn't been *that* arbitrary. But, in hindsight, he could see where his mother had been anxious for any excuse to get rid of the reminder of his father's infidelity—especially because his father had cared more for Madeline's mother than he had for Elizabeth. That was also the reason Max had been so defensive of Elizabeth. No man wanted to believe his own mother was receiving less than her due.

Still, none of that should have cost Madeline the safety and security she had so briefly enjoyed. She was an innocent party.

"See this locket?" Agnes pulled a gold locket out from under her shawl. "She sold me this, she did. Needed the money to help her son."

Max felt sick at the sight of his sister's mourning locket. He knew it contained some of their father's hair. It had been Madeline's most treasured possession.

"It's beautiful," Abby breathed.

Max couldn't seem to say anything.

"I got it for two shillings," Agnes bragged.

Even setting aside the sentimental value, it was worth much more than two shillings. Was that the extent to which this woman was willing to help a child? Max wondered.

The way Agnes had taken advantage of Madeline's desperation disgusted him. But he was upset with no one more than himself. Madeline had come to him for help, too. He had given her money and sent her on her way. But he should have done more, should have kept in contact with her and made himself more approachable, so she would feel free to come back when she encountered such need. Only now did he understand how dire her circumstances had been—that she had done everything she could before she ever approached him.

"I love it," Abby said.

"We were friends," Agnes responded. "She and I talked often about her son and how she missed him. Being a mother myself, I could relate to her. And no one knows Jack better than—"

"Enough about Madeline and my brother." Bill lifted a hand to cut her off, but his wife was having too much fun as the center of attention.

"She knew people," Agnes volunteered, ignoring him, "*important* people."

"Why doesn't Jack ever talk about her?" Max jumped in, hoping to direct the conversation away from those *important* people. "If she meant so much to him," he added, to justify the question.

Bill pulled on the loose skin beneath his neck. "What's the point? She's gone now."

"He thinks she stole his money, reclaimed her son and ran away," Agnes explained.

This answer wasn't one Max had expected—but it helped ease his anger and upset, gave him hope that maybe what he had assumed had happened to Madeline was wrong. "Some money went missing, too?"

"Quite a bit," she confirmed.

"It's not like Jack to let that go," Max said. "Why hasn't he tried to find her?"

"He has." This time it was Bill who spoke. "We fairly tore Wapping apart looking for her, and every town around it."

"But she was nowhere to be found," Agnes said.

Could he be wrong about Jack? Max wondered. Why would Jack bother looking for Madeline if he had killed her—or knew she was dead?

"You said she talked about her son often. Where was he?" Abby stepped in again, trying to keep the conversation going. "Did you check there?"

"We would have, if we could," Agnes confided. "But she never said exactly where he was staying. And it's a good thing. Angry as Jack was, who knows what he might have done."

The way Jack had ogled Abigail the first night they met didn't make him appear too distraught over Madeline. Something didn't add up—but maybe Jack was only capable of caring so much. As the days went by, he was probably angrier about the money than anything else. If Madeline had indeed stolen from him. But that didn't seem like her.

"How much did she get away with?" Max asked.

"I've never had the bollocks to ask," Bill said. "You know how Jack is. Anyone who gets him riled up is a fool."

"Things were bad there for a while," Agnes agreed. "Jack was fairly mad with rage and anything could set him off."

Did that mean that Madeline was alive? Had she taken Jack's money and abandoned her child, as Bill and Agnes seemed to believe? Set off to make a better life for herself?

She wouldn't be the first unmarried mother to do so. There were stories circulating all the time of destitute women abandoning illegitimate children—or worse.

But Madeline had planned to marry a man she didn't love, or even respect, for the sake of her child. If she robbed Jack, it was to be able to help Byron. She wouldn't leave him in dire straits and flee town.

"Hopefully she'll turn up," Max said.

"If she does, she'd better have that money with her," Bill responded and shut the door.

Chapter 22

Max sent Abby to the lodging house corresponding to 205 Flower Street—and again waited for her a block away. She was to use the same story that had worked so well with the charwoman at the Bolstrum's. If that didn't bring the results they were hoping to achieve, he would pay Gertrude a visit himself. That gave them two chances.

While she waited for someone to answer her knock, Abby prayed Gertrude would be at home. Max had done so much, and risked so much, to find his sister. He deserved to have the answers he craved.

It was just after noon, so the chances of catching a "working girl" where she resided should be fairly favorable. But there were no guarantees. The poorer prostitutes typically had to take whatever business they could get. If Gertrude had regulars, she could be up and on her way to a midday rendezvous.

An older woman with smudged face paint and a dress that revealed almost all of her bosom answered the door. She held a blanket to one side that had been hung across the entrance to stop any draft the warped panel let in.

By the irritation in her expression, she wasn't pleased to be disturbed. She had obviously been asleep. Once she saw Abigail, however, she glanced up and down the street as if checking to be sure Abby was alone. Then her expression cleared. "You're a pretty thing," she said. "If you're looking for work, I can see that you get it."

Abigail smiled at the compliment but was chilled, at the same time, by what that work would entail. "I'm afraid that . . . that's not why I'm here," she said. "I'm looking for a woman by the name of Gertrude. I was told she lives at this address?"

Her former impatience returned. "Gertie's asleep. Come back later," she said and closed the door.

For Max's sake, Abigail summoned her nerve and knocked again.

The woman didn't reappear, but someone—it sounded like the same person—called out, "Oh, bugger off!"

Since she had just learned that "Gertie" was inside, Abigail began calling out. "Gertrude?" She banged on the flimsy wooden panel, which was nearly enough to break it. "Are you there? Gertrude, please! I would like to speak with you about Madeline."

After the mention of Madeline's name, it took only a few seconds to bring Gertrude to the door. She peered out, her long hair tangled from sleep, her large, dark eyes filled with a mixture of hope and concern. "Who are you?"

"A friend of a friend of Madeline's. She . . . she wrote me several months ago, said I could come to her, that she would help me find lodgings here in London."

A hint of skepticism shadowed her pale face. "And your name?"

"Abigail. Abigail Hale." Abby saw no reason not to use her real identity. There was no way this woman would ever recognize it. They had no knowledge of each other—and would very likely never meet again.

"I don't remember her ever mentioning you."

"Have you talked to her recently? The charwoman at the Bolstrums' said she hasn't been seen in some time."

"That's true," she said. "I fear . . . I fear something terrible has happened."

"So you have no idea where she could have gone? Where she might be?"

"None. The last time she visited me, she was so excited to tell me that she would finally get to raise her son. I thought she had found a way to be happy. Byron means everything to her. But when I went to check on her not long ago—at the address she gave me on Farmer's Landing—she wasn't there. The man she was supposed to marry told me she ran off." She ran her fingers absently through her hair in an effort to work out the worst of the tangles. "But I don't believe it for a second. She would never leave Byron."

"Of course she wouldn't."

"I've been out searching since then," Gertrude said. "But no one has seen or heard from her. She's just . . . gone." She choked up and had to wipe the tears that rolled down her face.

"You don't think . . . that the Bolstrums did anything to her, do you?" Abby asked.

"No, they would never harm her."

"Anna Harper recently died in their house."

"Did Margaret tell you that?"

"Margaret?"

"The charwoman."

"Oh, yes," Abby said, because how else could she have learned? She didn't want to make Gertrude suspicious of *her.*

"I hadn't heard. I'm sorry about that. I met Anna once and liked her—but she was ill for some time. I'm not surprised she has passed."

"So there's no one else who has died there."

"No."

Again, Abby got the feeling if anyone had harmed Anna Harper or Madeline, it had to be Jack. "That's good to hear. I was, of course, fearing the worse for Madeline."

"She left. Margaret would say if it was otherwise. If she was harmed, it had to be at that house on Farmer's Landing. Even if she's alive somewhere, for some reason she's not able to help her son. So I've been trying to save enough money to . . . to give to his caretakers," Gertrude said. "I can't stand the thought of him being turned out, of what might become of him. But in my current situation"—the tears came faster now—"I barely earn enough to survive. I-I haven't had anything to offer the poor tyke. I haven't even dared to inquire after him since I first learned she left for fear . . ."

When emotion choked off her words, Abby changed her mind about continuing to pretend she was a "friend of a friend from out of town." Gertrude was so distressed over Madeline's disappearance she deserved the truth and whatever solace that truth might bring. "Don't despair. I can assure you her son is fine."

She sniffed and dried her face again. "He is? Because I have been so worried. Madeline was like a sister to me. I miss her every day."

Abby reached out to squeeze her arm. "Don't give up hope. We'll find her."

"Who? You and me?" she scoffed. "What can *we* do? We have nothing. If only her family cared enough to get involved. Yesterday I spent what little coin I had to take a cab to her brother's town house in Mayfair. I wanted to plead with him to . . . to at least take in her son! She might be a bastard, and the boy, too—but, to a certain extent, they all share the same blood. That has to count for something! How can one live so high and the other so low?"

"It doesn't seem fair," Abby murmured in an attempt to comfort her. "What did they tell you when you went to Mayfair?"

"I was turned away at the door. The butler stared down his nose at me and claimed the master was 'not currently in residence.'"

If Max lived in Mayfair, he was as affluent as Abby had guessed. That came as no surprise. But it bothered her that Gertrude would think so poorly of him when he was doing all he could. "What the butler told you is true," she said. "Her brother is not in Mayfair—he is right here in Wapping. And he *does* care. He has been risking life and limb searching for her."

Gertrude's eyes narrowed in skepticism. "How do you know this?"

"Because I have been helping him."

Shocked, she overcame her tears and spoke clearly, stridently. "You're saying the Duke of Rowenberry is here? In *Wapping*?"

"Did you say *duke*?" Abby shook her head. "No, that can't be true."

"Exactly. He has never been receptive to Madeline."

"Then I must be helping a different brother."

This seemed to surprise her more than anything. "Or no brother at all. She has only one. His name is Lucien Cavendish and, when the old duke died a few years ago, he inherited the lands and title."

Abby gaped at the girl. She started to reject what Gertrude said . . . but Max had mentioned that his sister was illegitimate. So were Lucien and Max the same person? If so, he wasn't just a merchant. He was a member of the bloody aristocracy!

No wonder he had been so reticent about his real life. All of London would be agog if they knew the great Duke of Rowenberry was posing as a body snatcher. How could he have risked his safety and his reputation like this?

Suddenly intense and desperate again, Gertrude leaned closer. "But if it's true, if you do have his ear, will you tell him about little Byron? *Please* . . . plead with him to rescue Madeline's child."

"He has already done that," Abby responded, but she was speaking mechanically, merely keeping up her end of the conversation while her mind raced down other avenues—and her heart broke. In some secret corner of her soul, she had been holding out hope that maybe, by some miracle, Max would become enamored with her and break off his engagement. He readily admitted that it wasn't a love match.

But now she knew that would never happen. What could she, a virgin with aspirations of becoming a medical student, possibly have to offer a duke? Maybe her father was being considered for knighthood, but he had no lands, no proud heritage, no special bloodline or anything else to recommend her. She would be nothing but an embarrassment to someone of Max's ranking.

No wonder Mr. Hawley had been so shocked by their exchange at the warehouse. *I wouldn't want you anyway.* She had said that to the Duke of Rowenberry!

"Is something wrong?" Gertrude peered at her in concern.

"Excuse me, what?"

"You look as if you've seen a ghost. Would you like to come in and sit down while we sort this out? I don't have much space, but—"

The smell of the doss-house alone would have been enough to discourage her. "No, I'm fine. Truly."

"You're sure?"

Madeline liked this woman, wished she had an easier life. "I'm sure. And I will tell Madeline's brother . . . er . . . His Grace that you have been very helpful."

"I'm so pleased for Byron. I pray they will treat him well, better than they treated Madeline."

"He's a child. Of course they will."

"The duke might. But not his mother."

Abby didn't know how to respond to that. Max hadn't told her much about the family dynamic. She just knew he suffered great regret. "I'm sure he will protect the boy." The man she knew certainly would. "And we haven't given up on Madeline."

"Good."

After that, Abby promised Gertrude that she and Max would let her know what they found out, and she told Gertrude to deliver a message to Mr. Hawley at the warehouse if she heard anything that might help. Then, feeling as if they were already friends themselves, she embraced the woman and hurried away.

But her footsteps slowed as soon as she reached the corner. Max, who'd been watching for her, stepped out of a chandler's shop.

"How did it go?" he asked, his expression anxious. "Has she seen Madeline?"

He was truly concerned for his sister. Deeply. *Look at all he has done.* "No."

His face fell. "This woman, Gertrude, had *no* information? No place for us to look?"

"I'm afraid not. She's as worried as we are, has been searching everywhere, all to no avail."

With a sigh, he rubbed his forehead. Abigail watched him, wondering if this Max she had come to care about could really be such an important man. So out of reach. He seemed the opposite of how she had always pictured a duke—a person almost equal in importance to a prince. Not only was Max accessible and human and warm, he seemed to share the same concerns everyone else had.

"Then this has been a waste of time," he said, clearly disappointed.

"Not completely," she said. "At least it has taught *me* a few things."

"Like . . . ?"

"Is it true—what she told me?"

His eyebrows slammed together. He could tell by her tone that she was no longer talking about Madeline. "Is *what* true?"

"Are you the Duke of Rowenberry?"

He muttered a curse as if she had just asked him the hardest question in the world.

"Are you?" she pressed.

"Would you believe me if I said no?" he asked.

She shook her head.

"I'm sorry, Abby. I'm sure you feel . . . misled. But you understand why I would keep such a secret."

Of course she understood. It was just that she had indulged in so many hopeful imaginings where he was concerned, felt such . . . infatuation. She had fancied herself *in love* with him, although she dared not call it love now. "I'm sure if word of your identity were to get out, it would cause quite a stir," she said stiffly.

"Indeed." He seemed relieved and eager to leave it at that, but she wasn't done with him yet.

"And you included me in the ruse because you, apparently, couldn't trust me—while I trusted you with my *life*." Although she tried to walk off, he caught her.

"Abby, stop. Trust has nothing to do with it."

"Then why wouldn't you tell me? You told me that you weren't really a body snatcher, that you were a man of business, that you were engaged. Why not *all* of the truth?"

He seemed to grapple for the right words. "I was simply trying to keep that identity, my *real* identity, separate from this one so that . . . so that—"

"So that what?" she demanded. "Were you afraid I might be so bold as to count you among my friends? That I might embarrass you by my familiarity if I encountered you later or . . . or be presumptuous enough to impose upon you?"

"Impose on me how?" he asked, incredulous.

"I don't know! By asking a favor! Isn't that what most people do? Certainly it must be true of those, like myself, who are far less fortunate than you."

"That isn't it," he snapped. "I know you have far too much pride to ask anything of me. And I already plan to see if I can't do something to get a medical college to admit you—even if I have to buy one and admit you myself, damn it. I want you to be happy, Abby."

"Happy without you."

"Yes, of course. Happy at all costs."

It just wouldn't be possible. Didn't he understand that? "You must be dying to get back to the bowing and scraping you are more accustomed to. And to your educated, elegant fiancée, whoever she is."

"Believe it or not, there are elements of *this* existence, as simple as it is, that I will be loath to lose."

She lifted her chin. "You will miss digging up putrefying bodies?"

He caught her chin in his hand and forced her to look at him. "I will miss *you*."

"So much that you weren't even going to tell me who you are." She tried to jerk away, but he held her fast.

"Because I knew, if I saw you through the eyes of Lucien Cavendish and not Max Wilder, you would become part of that life, too, and maybe . . . maybe I wouldn't be able to let you go despite my engagement."

That last part sounded torn from him and so sincere it made Abigail's heart leap into her throat. "Is that also why you wouldn't make love to me?" she asked. "Why you wouldn't give me that much?"

"*Give* you that much. I was trying not to *take* that much." A tortured expression claimed his face. "I went too far as it was, Abby. You didn't even know that I was unavailable, until recently. And then you wisely wouldn't listen to my desperate entreaties."

Only because she'd been hurt. She was still hurt. But now that she knew who he was, that their time here in Wapping was all she would ever get and there was no chance for more . . . "What if I have changed my mind?"

His eyes lowered to her mouth. "Just tell me you still want me."

"I've wanted you from almost the first moment I laid eyes on you," she admitted.

The relief that crossed his face surprised her. "Holding back . . . it's been torture," he admitted and, pulling her to him right there in the street, kissed her.

She closed her eyes as she met his tongue with her own and the rest of the world ceased to exist. It wasn't until someone in the passing crowd whistled that he broke off the kiss.

"See what you do to me?" he said with a breathy chuckle. "But you deserve better than a public spectacle."

After hailing a cab, he told the driver to take them to an address in Mayfair.

"Mayfair?" Abby echoed numbly. It was difficult to concentrate when she missed Max's arms around her as acutely as she did.

"I'm taking you home," he said.

Home to his town house?

"No." She shook her head. "Take me to Farmer's Landing. That's how I want to remember you. You, as"—conscious of the cabby listening in, she avoided saying *a duke*—"as that man from Mayfair, would be a stranger to me."

He cocked his head as he looked down at her. Then he nodded.

Chapter 23

Max feared he was making a terrible mistake. He had been trying so hard not to let Abby become too important to him—and to make sure he didn't become too important to her. The thought of causing her unhappiness upset him far more than the idea of his own needs going unmet. He had duties, responsibilities. He had to act in accordance with his station, and that often required sacrifice. Honor dictated that he fulfill his commitment to marry Lady Hortense Brimble. If he pulled out, especially for a poor surgeon's daughter, he would damage his reputation and his family's good name. His own mother would probably never speak to him again. So he had done all he could to resist the temptation to reach for Abby in the night. It was the only reason he hadn't taken her maidenhead.

But all his good intentions were coming to naught. Now that she knew who he was, now that there were no more secrets between them, he couldn't continue to deny himself. He wanted her too badly.

The drive to No. 8 Farmer's Landing seemed to take forever. He hated the thought that they might run into Jack when they arrived. Jack was the last person he wanted to see. But he could understand why Abby would find their room more comfortable than a strange place in an unfamiliar part of the city. Besides, it was wise that he not leave the area. He had purposely refrained from returning to Mayfair over the past three weeks lest he be seen coming or going. He didn't want the cabby questioned.

Fortunately, Jack wasn't home. Late afternoon the leader of the London Supply Company was almost always at one of the various taverns he frequented, buying dinner and drinking. Bill was probably with him—or would join him shortly. If Tom and Emmett were around, they would be there, too. They met gravediggers, sextons and the like, paid bribes and plotted out the cemeteries to be visited. Until Abby came to live with them, Max had almost always joined the group, unless he needed to meet with his clerk, and then he offered some excuse.

But a lot had changed in a short time. Tom was likely dead, Emmett was missing and Max was desperately hoping that something he had learned today would prove to be the string that would unravel the mystery of Madeline's disappearance. Gertrude, despite her willingness to help, had proved to be a great disappointment. She knew nothing. But something Agnes had said stuck with him. Something about Emmett trailing Madeline around . . . Emmett had done the same with Max—had followed him on more than one occasion. And although he claimed that Jack put him up to it, perhaps that wasn't true.

Perhaps he knew something the others did not.

If only Max could ask him . . .

"He's not here," Abby breathed as soon as they walked into the house. She didn't mention who *he* was, but she didn't have to. She had obviously been as worried as he was about confronting Jack.

As soon as they reached the bedroom, Max built a fire, then locked the door. He didn't want anything interrupting them.

"Let down your hair and take off your clothes," he said.

Abby turned to face him but backed away. "Shouldn't we wait until we are under the covers? It's . . . it's full daylight."

"That's the point—I want to see you." He smiled, hoping to reassure her. "Don't tell me a woman who uses the word *cock* as readily as a man and speaks of spermatozoa is suddenly shy."

"I'm afraid I've had too much time to think about it. I'm nervous," she admitted.

He sobered. "You haven't changed your mind . . ."

She didn't refuse him as he feared. She lifted her skirt and began to roll down her stockings.

Max's breath caught as he sat on the stool and watched her undress. He was afraid if he touched her right away it would all go too fast— and this deserved a moment. "You are so beautiful, Abby, so unique. You fill my mind, dominate my thoughts. Even when I tell myself not to think of you, I can't help it."

He already knew he would never forget her; she was nothing like the women he had known so far, not even the ones he had taken to his bed.

Maybe that was what frightened him, he decided. He felt something deeper for her, something protective and powerful. He felt . . . *possessive,* he realized as he lifted his eyes to hers—and that was a first.

"Then what are you waiting for?" She sounded as breathless as he was.

"I could look at you forever," he admitted.

"It requires a great deal of nerve to stand here naked, when you're fully clothed and not saying or doing *anything.*"

"It requires a bit of faith and trust, too. But you trust me enough to let me look, don't you, Abby? I would never hurt you, not if I could possibly avoid it."

She smiled even though they both knew he would hurt her the very moment it was time to return to regular life. He wished there was another way, wished he wouldn't have to give her up. He could ask her to be his mistress. Many men of his rank kept mistresses. But the jealousy that incurred—it was no kind of life for his wife, especially after they started having children. Max had seen what his father's dalliances had done to his own mother. He couldn't be selfish enough to cheat Abby like that, either. She deserved a man who could live with her and openly love her.

"What happens after today doesn't matter," she said. "I ask only for this."

He would make sure she was admitted to a medical college somewhere, he promised himself, and drew her into his arms.

Max's absolute focus made Abby feel oddly powerful. He was engaged to someone else, but *she* was the object of his desire. As hard as he had been fighting to resist the temptation she posed, he couldn't.

"You could cause a saint to fall, Abby," he muttered.

She didn't respond. She felt no inclination to talk. As his mouth closed over her breast, he made a throaty, animal-like sound that let her know this was exactly what he had craved all along. He was taking it now, and this time he wouldn't stop. She could tell he was well beyond that.

"Are you sure you want this?" he asked as he led her to the bed. "I hate the thought that you might regret it."

She combed her fingers through his hair, reveling in the fact that she had the freedom to do so. "I'm nearly an old maid. Don't you think it's time?"

"I've never seen an old maid who looks quite like you do." He stared down at her. Then he kissed her as his hand found that sensitive region between her legs.

When he slid a finger inside her, Abby gasped at the pleasure it provided and arched her hips for more. She felt as if she had waited an eternity for Max, that nothing had mattered until he came into her life.

The way he touched her was every bit as erotic as what he had done before. But the intent behind it, the promise of where their lovemaking was going, made it that much better.

"You're making me tremble," she told him.

His teeth flashed as he smiled. But that smile was gone by the time he removed his finger and used it to lubricate himself.

"What are you doing?" she asked as she watched.

"I'm hoping this will make my entrance a little easier on you," he said, and then he angled her hips up to receive him, and began to press inside her.

He watched her so intently she could tell he was taking guidance from the expression on her face.

She bit her lip, slightly nervous, but she wasn't going to let a little bit of pain stop her.

The muscles of his arms bunched as he let go of her hips and held himself above her. Admiring the beautiful sight he made, she tried to relax but couldn't help flinching when that moment arrived.

He hesitated as soon as he felt the change. "I'll give you . . . time to adjust," he muttered, but his breathing was ragged, and she could tell it wasn't easy for him to hold back.

"Don't stop." Eager to get this part over with, so she could enjoy what she had been looking forward to, she closed her eyes and gripped his buttocks to encourage him to press the rest of the way inside her. When he did, it was almost as if she had no idea where her body stopped and his began: they were one.

"How does it feel?" he murmured.

"Are you soliciting compliments?" she teased. "Because the pain is already gone."

He paused to kiss her, as if he didn't believe her and wanted to be sure. "This is heaven for me, Abby."

She had dreamed of this moment. But the reality was far better than any imagining. He found her mouth again, and she felt his tongue slide against hers as he began to thrust. She loved the full sensation she experienced when they were joined, the rhythm of his movements, the desperation that gripped them both as the cadence quickened.

She moaned to let him know she had nearly reached that special peak, and his muscles grew tauter. "Are you close, Abby?"

She closed her eyes and gripped him tight. "Almost there . . ."

"I'm trying to last," he told her. "But you make me feel like an over-eager schoolboy, someone who's never been with a woman before."

As she hovered on the cusp of the same tremendous pleasure he had given her before, he suddenly muttered that it was too late, that he had to withdraw. But when she gasped and clung to him, he groaned and thrust again. Then she shuddered and he shuddered and it felt as if their bodies melted and fused together.

When Jack came home, he banged on the door, dragging Abby out of a blissful sleep. Max seemed to be sleeping even more deeply. He tightened his arms around her but didn't answer, so she did.

"Yes?"

"Tell Max to get his arse out of bed and come to work," Jack barked.

She tensed, lest he say more. She didn't want to fully engage him. But when she heard the hall creak as he walked past, she let her breath go.

Max would be leaving, heading out to gather up more dead bodies with Jack and Bill. Given the dwindling numbers of the gang, they would need him tonight more than ever. She hated to let him go, because she would not be waiting for him when he came back. She had known, from the moment she confronted him about his true identity, that this would be the last memory she would have of him.

At least they had made the most of it. They had made love three times. He hadn't managed to withdraw the first time, which left her a little uneasy, but they had been more careful after. And now, for better or worse, it was over, in almost every aspect.

She was glad she no longer had to help procure bodies, no longer had to deceive people by pretending to be part of their mourning party. But she wasn't even going to try to convince herself that she wouldn't miss Max. She—a woman who never planned to marry, never planned to give a man that much control over her life—would do anything to have *this* man. But this man wasn't available. Socially, he was so far above her, she couldn't have him, regardless—so she told herself there was no use feeling sad.

It was time to go home, face her father, and try to rebuild her life. Staying would only break her heart. If there was no way to be with Max, really be with him, she was foolish to risk her life living among body snatchers. He was already doing all he could to find Madeline and had so many resources to pull from—time, money and contacts. She was foolish to think she could assist someone like him. In reality, she was just giving him someone else to protect, and she was taking something that belonged to another woman. She wouldn't be able to live with herself if she continued as she was.

Jack wouldn't like her leaving. He might even try to exact some type
of retribution. But she couldn't stay forever. And she planned to offer
him a contract at the school. Hopefully, that would mollify him until
Max turned him in to the police.

"You coming?" When Jack passed their door to go back downstairs,
he banged on it again.

"Max." She used his assumed name even though she knew it wasn't
the correct one. That was who he was to her—even if it wasn't who he
could continue to be. "Are you awake?"

"I don't want to be." He kissed her shoulder. "Then I'll have to leave
you."

Although she hadn't told him she wouldn't be waiting when he
returned, he knew, as she did, that their time was limited.

"But maybe Emmett will show up for work tonight," he said.
"Maybe I will have a chance to ask him about Madeline."

"I hope so." When she returned home, she planned to keep searching the colleges for Tom's body. She could still help in that regard.

He dragged himself out of bed and began pulling on his clothes.
"Even with that possibility, I can't wait to get back to you. I'll bring you
a gift, if not by morning, later in the day."

She pulled up the sheet. "What kind of gift?"

"One that will make you happy, better than that mirror and brush
you prize so highly." He motioned as if his previous offering, though
expensive to her, was nothing to him.

"Don't get me anything, Max." She didn't want him to waste the
money, no matter how rich he was, not if she wasn't going to be there
to receive it. "There's no need."

At the honest insistence in her voice, he scowled. "That, my dear, is
my choice, not yours. Although our relationship may have certain . . .
restrictions, I can bestow on you whatever appeals to me—and I plan
to do just that."

No matter how expensive his gifts, they would always be a poor
substitute for what she dearly wanted. Besides, he was talking as if he

expected to have an ongoing relationship with her. "What do you mean by that?" she asked.

"I may not be able to marry you, but that doesn't mean we can't be together . . . in some way," he replied.

He wasn't looking at her. It was almost as if he knew, in his heart, that this wouldn't please her. "You mean . . . I could become your mistress?"

"It isn't what I would've wished for you. I realize it's not as much as you deserve. But . . . it's better than nothing, isn't it?"

"If it is, please tell me in what way," she said.

"Think of what I could give you, Abby."

"How can I think of that when all I can think about is the opposite—what you would never be able to give me. I fear, if I were to accept such an offer, I would obsess about the part of you that was missing for the rest of my life."

"I would do everything I could to make you happy. I swear it."

"It would be futile. We could only be happy if we ignore what our involvement will do to the other people in our lives—your wife, your future children, any children we might have, my father, your mother. How can either of us feel justified in our love if we're constantly hurting and embarrassing our loved ones?"

The look of defeat and resignation that appeared on his face told her that, in his heart of hearts, he agreed. He didn't really want to be that kind of man—and she didn't want to push him into it. "You didn't even take a minute to consider it."

She didn't need to. It was obvious to her. But she knew how terribly easy it would be to wake up one day and, against all intention to the contrary, find that she had indeed succumbed to the desire to be with Max in any capacity, which was why she had to break away now, while she had the strength.

"Just make sure you get back safely," she said.

He paused to kiss her. "I'll bring you some sandwiches before I go so you can keep the door locked while you're here alone."

When he delivered the food, she told herself she should eat. But she had no appetite. She felt sick at the thought of walking away from him. The only thing that kept her firm in her purpose was the knowledge that it would be easier now than later.

After he left, she got up and dressed in her gypsy rags—then hesitated at the last second. She was afraid of the threats Jack had launched. Her father, Max, anyone could be at risk. But with Tom and Emmett gone, Jack had never been weaker than he was right now. And the fear of falling into the kind of relationship that awaited her if she remained with Max frightened her more than anything, because then *she* would be the cause of heartache.

Max had taught her what love was all about. Perhaps she would find it again someday, with someone who could be hers.

She considered leaving the dress she had made and her brush and mirror set for Jack to sell. She hoped, by doing so, she would mitigate some of his anger. It was all she had to give him. But she doubted sacrificing these items would change his reaction, and she had a better use for them.

Carefully wrapping the brush and mirror in the dress, she carried it all out of the house, along with her mother's elephant.

Chapter 24

Abby didn't think Agnes would answer. She felt strange, banging on her door in the middle of the night. But if she was going to do this, it had to be before she returned to Aldersgate. Once she got home, she wasn't sure what would happen.

"Who is it?" Agnes called out.

Hugging her treasures a little tighter, as if in farewell, Abby glanced around the dark, foggy street. Smoke from the many coal fires of London had mixed with the mist coming off the Thames to create a thick blanket that was, at times, almost impenetrable. She could barely see the gaslight ten feet away. It was dangerous to be out in such conditions, especially in this area, but Abby didn't plan on staying long.

"It's Abigail, the woman who was with Max earlier," she said.

"Aye. I know who you are." She opened up but stood in her mob-cap and robe, frowning at Abby over the dim light of a candle. "What is it? Somethin' wrong?"

"No, nothing. I just . . . I couldn't quit thinking about the beautiful locket you showed me earlier."

She seemed confused, and it was no wonder. "Madeline's locket?"

"That's the one."

"You dragged me out of bed because you like that locket?"

"I was hoping to purchase it for . . . for my mother. She lost one similar to it. I would love to surprise her by replacing it as it held a great deal of sentimental value."

She shielded her candle from the draft. "Well, this one holds a great deal of sentimental value to me. Reminds me of my good friend, Madeline, it does. So . . . how much are you prepared to offer?"

"I don't have any money," Abby admitted. "But I thought perhaps you might be interested in a trade."

She gestured as if Abby couldn't possibly have anything to entice her. "I'd rather keep the locket if you don't have any coin," she said and closed the door.

Abby knocked again. "But you haven't seen what I have brought. Agnes? I think you'll like it. It's worth more than that locket."

She wasn't sure Agnes would care—until the door cracked open. "Fine. As long as you have me out of bed, what is it?"

Abby said a quick prayer that what she held would be enough. She so desperately wanted to acquire Madeline's locket for Max. "It's a . . . a sterling silver brush and mirror set. Very nice." She handed both over so Agnes could admire them. "And this dress"—she held it up—"made of fine fabric."

Ignoring the dress, Agnes turned the mirror and brush set over in her hands.

"That set was purchased by a duke, no less," Abby added, hoping to increase the value.

"How do you know?" she asked, obviously skeptical.

"My mother was a . . . a servant to the upper class. Her locket was a gift to her."

"Expensive gift for a servant."

"Not for a lady's maid who was retiring after many, many years of faithful service." Abby had never told more lies in her life. It was ironic that the statement that should have been most unbelievable—that the set had been purchased by a duke—was actually true.

"Hmm . . ." Turning her attention to the dress, she fingered the sleeve. "I saw you in this earlier. I doubt it will fit me."

Doubt? There was no question. Agnes easily outweighed Abby by five stone. "But you could sell it," she pointed out.

"True . . ."

"New as it is and well made, it should bring in a fair bit—certainly more than you paid for the locket."

"I got a bargain on the locket."

"This is also a bargain. So what do you say? Would you like to trade?"

When Agnes's eyes narrowed, Abby knew she had allowed herself to sound too eager—a mistake that was confirmed a moment later, when Agnes shook her head.

"No. You run along back to Farmer's Landing before something happens to you out here. I like my locket. I think I'll keep it."

With a silent curse, Abby turned to go, but stopped when Agnes called out, "Unless you have something else to include?"

Abby had nothing—except her elephant. Pulling it from the pocket of her old cloak, she stared down at it.

"What's that?" Agnes asked.

Abby held it up. "A rare and expensive ivory elephant." She was lying about the rare and expensive part, but she had to say *something* to get that locket.

"From where?"

"India, of course."

"I've always dreamed of going to India," she said, clearly tempted. "So . . . is that elephant part of the deal?"

Abby had risked so much to retrieve her mother's last gift. But now she craved that locket almost as much as she had craved the elephant. In case Max wasn't able to find Madeline, she wanted to leave him his sister's locket to remind him of how hard he had tried. She thought that might help him forgive himself for whatever their past relationship had been. And if he did find Madeline, he could give it to her. Abby knew what it was like to have only a small token to represent someone who was irreplaceable.

"The mirror and brush set are already worth more than the locket," she said. "And you have the dress."

"But I'm not interested in trading, not unless you include the elephant."

Abby sighed. Apparently, it was her reluctance that gave the elephant its value. She almost said no and walked away. It was partly the elephant that had brought her to Wapping, brought her together with Max. She thought it might provide some comfort to her in the future. Depending on how her reunion with her father went, she could soon be living on her own and doing all she could to survive.

"I don't have all night," Agnes said, growing impatient.

Again, Abby nearly turned on her heel and hurried away. Agnes wasn't someone she liked, no more than Jack or even Bill, who wasn't as mean as his brother but was just as eager to make a pound any way he could. His greedy, selfish wife wasn't much better. But just thinking of the way Max had kissed her before he left proved Abby's undoing. She wanted to leave him the locket. And she loved him enough to sacrifice almost anything, even her elephant.

"Fine." She handed everything over—and Agnes pivoted so she could unlatch the clasp.

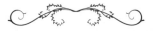

When Abby let herself in, the college seemed strangely unfamiliar. Nothing had changed since she left, not that she could see, and yet it felt as if *everything* was different. For one, the rooms came off as rather sterile in their spartan cleanliness. It was overly warm, too, given that she had been living in a house with little or no heat.

She considered alerting her father to the fact that she was home, but with the whole place dark and quiet, she decided not to disturb him. She didn't want to cause an uproar that would leave everyone exhausted come morning. There would be plenty of time to discuss what kind of punishment she deserved when her father was already up. Then perhaps Mrs. Fitzgerald would be preoccupied with her tasks and not able to listen in quite so carefully.

As she made her way to her bedroom, Abby wondered if her father would be happy to have her back, or merely relieved that she was safe . . .

Her bed felt lonely without Max. She was going to miss him even more than she had imagined. Although they hadn't been together for long, the minutes and hours of the days they had shared had been spent in very close and intimate circumstances. That made a week feel like a lifetime.

She pictured Max returning to find the locket she had left on his pillow—and hoped that it would bring him solace.

As soon as Max returned to Farmer's Landing, he hurried up the stairs to see Abby but found the room dark, cold and empty. In his heart, he had been afraid she would disappear. The suspicion had nagged him all night—and yet he knew he should be grateful. She had no place in his life, not the kind of life he wanted to lead. The look on his face when they were discussing it had made that clear. So removing herself from the situation, even if it meant leaving without a good-bye, made things easier on both of them. They no longer had to dread splitting up—because it had already happened. But if the sick feeling in the pit of his stomach was how it felt to go the *easy* route, he would hate to see how he would have felt had she stayed longer.

"Damn," he muttered.

Jack hit Max's door as he passed by. "Don't wake me up in the morning," he said. "I might just sleep for a week."

Max made no reply. Jack didn't demand one. The older man was so tired he could hardly talk, was fairly stumbling to his bed. As much as the London Supply Company's leader had been up the past few days, maybe he *would* sleep for a week. He had to recover at some point, didn't he? And if that happened, who could say how long it would be before he noticed Abby was gone? With any luck it would be so far after the fact that he wouldn't even raise a fuss.

Max certainly didn't plan on telling him. Jack would figure it out when he figured it out.

With a sigh—he was already missing Abby—Max put his candle on the dresser and began to remove his clothes. As he did so, he thought of his fiancée, Lady Hortense Brimble, a second cousin to his mother and the daughter of an earl. He wasn't due to be married for another year—he had bought himself that much freedom—but he would feel better going into marriage knowing he and Abby had already cut ties. Then he *couldn't* wind up loving Abby more than his wife, to the detriment of his family.

He felt robbed, though. He couldn't escape that sense of loss.

Although he had promised Abby a gift, he hadn't had the chance to buy anything—not while he was in Jack's company and not so early. At least she had taken the brush and mirror she liked so well. He smiled to himself when he realized that she had also taken the dress made out of his coat. Would she ever wear it at the school? And, if she did, would she think of him?

Then he saw the glitter of something gold on his pillow.

What the devil could that be? he wondered. But the second he went over and picked it up, he recognized the locket Agnes Hurtsill had purchased from Madeline. It had to be the same one: inside, he found the lock of his father's hair.

How, in the name of heaven, had this turned up in his room?

It could only have come from Abby. Somehow she had procured it—and left it as her parting gift.

Sinking onto the bed, he dropped his head in his hands.

The noise of the college didn't wake Abby as it usually did. Since she had been living at Farmer's Landing, she had been staying up most of the night—and the night before had been no different. That didn't make for an early riser. So when she did open her eyes, she guessed it was after noon, and yet she stayed in bed, listening to the familiar sounds and

wondering what would become of her. It wasn't hard to believe she was back. It was harder to believe she had ever been gone. Her time with Max felt like a dream. Only in dreams did a simple surgeon's daughter fall in love with a duke. But when she shoved up onto her elbows, she could see the gypsy clothes she had worn to Wapping there on the floor, and knew that Jack and Max really existed—and that Madeline was really gone.

When she gathered the resolve to slip out from under her covers, she pulled on her robe to combat the chill and rang for Jessamine, the housemaid who cleaned her room and the others, blackened the grates and hauled up the hot water. She needed a bath—and preferred to take one before she confronted her father. She thought it might help if she was calm, composed, prepared. But Bransby, Mrs. Fitzgerald and her father all appeared at her door instead of the servant she had been expecting.

"It's true! You're back!" Mrs. Fitzgerald exclaimed.

Bran looked her up and down, then nodded as if he was satisfied to see she wasn't any worse for her adventure. Of course, they couldn't see all the things that had changed—and so quickly—on the inside. Perhaps she had been on the brink of establishing her independence before she left. She had taken to it easily enough.

Her father said nothing. He waited for her to greet the servants. Then he told the others they should get back to their duties, came in and shut the door.

Abby drew a deep breath. "Hello, Father," she said. "I'm sorry if I . . . if I frightened you."

Edwin Hale frowned as he pulled the letter she had sent him out of his pocket. "You *did* frighten me, which is why I was so grateful to receive your letter. Thanks for sending that, at least."

She clasped her hands in front of her. "Of course."

He walked over and sat on the chair to her boudoir. "So . . . are you going to tell me why you left and just where you have been? I have nearly driven myself crazy trying to figure out why you would suddenly disappear, especially to go with a band of resurrection men. Men like Jack Hurtsill can't be trusted. He—" Suddenly at a loss for words, he glanced at the letter and lifted it to her attention yet again. "And to think you *wanted* to be there with him. I admit I can't quite fathom it."

Where did she start? So much had occurred. And so much of it wasn't the type of thing she could tell her father. She doubted he would want to hear that she had lost her virginity to a man who could never marry her, even if he was a duke. She could only hope—and pray— that she wasn't pregnant.

"It's not what you think," she said.

"I'm certainly glad to hear *that*."

"Are you familiar with the Duke of Rowenberry?"

She had succeeded in surprising him. "Did you say *duke*?"

"Yes."

"Although I don't know him personally, I know of him."

"That will help," she said and told him about Lucien posing as Max to search for his missing sister. She also told him about Tom and Emmett and Bill and Agnes and the others who figured into the story—and how she had tried to help "Max."

"So you didn't find her," he said when she finished.

Was he angry at the decisions she'd made? Surprisingly, it didn't seem like it. She got the impression he was relieved that he could understand her logic, that she hadn't really joined the London Supply Company. "Not yet. Unless Emmett turns up, and happens to know something about her, I think we may never know what happened."

"Is that why you returned?" he asked.

She went to the window so she wouldn't have to look at him when she replied. "For the most part. I didn't see what more I could do there. But here, I could possibly see to it that Jack faces justice."

He stood and came toward her. "How?"

"By finding Tom's body. If he's dead, we know that Jack must have killed him. His brother spoke to someone who saw Jack and Bill drag Tom into an alley the night he was likely murdered."

"Murdered," he repeated as if that word hadn't previously existed in his lexicon. "What you are doing is so dangerous, Abby. You realize that."

"Of course. But Big Jack has to be stopped before he hurts someone else."

"Surely the duke can see to it."

"Max—His Grace—has had his clerk asking about Madeline at the colleges. It has gotten him nowhere."

"That doesn't mean anyone is lying or withholding information, Abby. It could be that she isn't dead."

"Maybe not, but I'm rather certain Tom is. The way Bill and Jack were talking leads me to believe they sold his corpse. If so, we should be able to find it."

"There is so much at stake here—for everyone."

"Matters of life and death should outweigh all other factors."

"And they do," he assured her. "But . . . I don't want you involved in this any longer."

She opened her mouth to argue, to say that she didn't care one whit about her reputation, but he lifted a hand to stop her before she could even get started. "I don't want it to be *your* life that swings in the balance. So let *me* do it."

"*You'll* inquire about Tom?"

"Considering the reason for such inquiries, it would be far better coming from me."

She couldn't argue with that. "But you must let me go with you. That's the only way I will be able to put my mind at rest—and between us, I am the only one who will recognize Tom."

He hesitated as if he would deny her in spite of that. She knew he thought she would be better off to distance herself from the whole nasty business, let him take it from there. But she rushed on.

"And we have to act quickly, while he is still recognizable."

"Of course. But . . ."

"Father, no doubt everyone has heard that I went missing. Let this be our way of establishing why." She watched him expectantly.

"That means you don't want to pay a visit to Aunt Emily in Herefordshire," he said dryly.

"No, not now."

"Just until whatever happens with Jack Hurtsill happens? I don't like the idea that he might come back here, that he might try to achieve some sort of revenge."

Abby had been so prepared to argue against going to the country—at any point. She definitely wasn't going to go now, to be left waiting and wondering as to the outcome of all that had happened in Wapping. But perhaps it was a bit ironic given her heated opposition until now that she wasn't so sure she would remain as steadfast against it in the future. In London, all she could think about was Max. Perhaps, when all was said and done, a change of scenery—about the time he was to marry—would help her recover.

"I can't go now, Father. But . . . I'll consider it," she said.

Surprisingly, he didn't push her. He stood there, looking rather large and out of place in her room, and she realized how few times he had actually visited it. "I'm glad you're back, my dear."

Abby smiled. "I missed you, too."

He started to leave but turned at the door. "You seem different somehow."

"I *feel* different," she admitted.

"But it isn't because . . . I mean, you haven't been compromised in any way . . ."

She could tell how difficult it was for him to ask. "No. The duke kept me with him at all times and protected me from the others."

He studied her carefully. "It sounds as if I owe him a great deal. He's a good man, then?"

Carefully hiding the true nature of her feelings, she lifted her chin. "He is."

Relief replaced the concern on his face. "I'm pleased to hear it."

Chapter 25

Max sat in the corner, alone, at Forrester's Arms, a tavern not far from Farmer's Landing. He had slept the whole day. Now that it was getting dark, he finally felt rested, but when he had left the house, Jack was still in bed, snoring loudly.

Max couldn't imagine they would be going out to work that night and was glad for the reprieve. He'd had about all he could take of body snatching—and Jack, too. Or maybe it was just that his current circumstances were made all the worse because Abby was gone and wouldn't be coming back. He wasn't sure he had ever been in a darker mood. He could only hope that no one crossed him; he was spoiling for a fight.

Almost as soon as the barmaid put the pigeon pie he had ordered in front of him, a small street urchin hurried into the tavern, paused to study each of the patrons and finally approached him. "Excuse me, sir."

Max put down the fork he had just lifted. "Yes?"

"Are you the one called Max? Max Wilder?"

"I am."

"With the London Supply Company?"

Max bit back a sigh. "For the moment."

The boy adjusted his cap, which covered a mop of unruly brown hair, checked as if to be sure they couldn't be overheard and lowered his voice. "I've got a message for you."

Max accepted the folded paper the boy held out in one dirty hand. Then he gave him a few coins and watched him scurry off before leaning closer to the candle on the table, so he could read.

The note was from Mr. Hawley. Although it wasn't signed, Max easily recognized his clerk's handwriting:

Emmett showed up here, asking questions.

That was all it said. No doubt Mr. Hawley was trying to be discreet lest his missive fall into the wrong hands. But that single cryptic line evoked a million questions. If Emmett was alive and well, why hadn't he shown up at Jack's or Bill's? What was he up to? And where was *here*—the warehouse?

Probably, Max decided. It made sense. Emmett had likely followed him there, just as he had followed him other places. But what kind of information was Emmett after? Did Jack know Emmett was safe? Could it be *Jack* who was really behind these inquiries?

Then there was the biggest question of all: Did either Jack or Emmett suspect Max's true identity and purpose?

Max's mind reverted to the conversation he'd had at the door with Bill and Agnes. Perhaps they mentioned to Jack that he had been interested in learning more about Madeline and that had heightened Jack's suspicion.

To answer as many of these questions as he could, he had to speak to his clerk—preferably before Jack woke up. And this time he had to be sure Emmett, if he was around, wasn't following him.

When Mr. Holthouse, one of the other surgeons at the college, pulled her aside, Abby braced herself for the worst. She thought he was going to scold her for comprising her reputation, ruining her father's chance of a knighthood or further damaging the public's opinion of the medical community. Like her father, he was a very conservative man—one who, no doubt, found what she had done quite shocking. But as they stepped into the operating theatre, he surprised her by saying, "I just want to tell you how grateful I am."

At first, she thought he was being sarcastic. But he didn't *sound* sarcastic . . . "For . . . ?"

He motioned to the table at the center of the room, which bore the cadaver she had delivered, currently covered with a sheet. "For providing the specimen under dissection, of course. The situation here was becoming quite intolerable. You are the only one who stepped up to solve the problem—and it occurs to me that this wasn't the first time. You must have been responsible for the specimens we dissected last year, too. Am I correct?"

Abby acknowledged that with a nod. "I couldn't stand to see the college suffer—not to mention your work, my father's and the other the doctors' and surgeons'."

"You are a brave soul, Miss Hale. I would never have expected a woman, especially such a young woman, to have the temerity to act as you did. We all owe you a great debt for your bravery and willingness to take such a risk. If not for you, perhaps Aldersgate would have been forced to close its doors."

Abby had been prepared to defend herself, not accept praise. "Thank you, sir. I-I appreciate what you have said."

He gave her arm a slight squeeze. "Perhaps you can persuade your father to let you stay in your current position. I, for one, would not be opposed to it."

Meaning he wouldn't mind if she continued to do his dirty work? She wasn't all that flattered, especially because she would no longer be satisfied with her current situation. She wanted more out of life. If she couldn't have the man she loved, she at least wanted to plot a course that would be more mentally challenging—and rewarding—than her current day-to-day routine.

"Actually, I was hoping to be admitted to the college next term or . . . perhaps the term after," she said. She figured if she was ever going to gain his support, it would be now. And if she could get him to stand behind her, perhaps she could get others.

But his eyebrows shot up almost to his hairline. "As a *student*?"

"Yes. I would dearly love to become a surgeon," she admitted. Why was that so out of the realm of possibility? Was her mind not as quick or agile as those of the male students who attended Aldersgate?

From what *she* could tell, it was.

"My, you are modern in your ideas," he said and pulled out his watch as if he was suddenly too busy to continue the conversation. "I have my last class of the day coming up. If you will excuse me."

Abby frowned as she watched him hurry down the steps to the cadaver she had helped deliver. He was grateful to her for enabling *his* career, but he wasn't about to throw any support behind allowing her to embrace the same work. Although *she* had changed a great deal in the past week, not much else had.

"There you are." Mrs. Fitzgerald came upon her from behind. "Did Bransby find you?"

Abby hadn't seen him since he had welcomed her home that morning, but she hadn't been around. She had spent much of the day visiting the other colleges with her father. Her father was still out. He said he wanted to speak with some of his anatomist friends in private, that he thought it might help them gain more information—if there was more information out there. But no one at the six places they had visited admitted to accepting a cadaver with a harelip like Tom's.

"No. Has he been looking for me?"

"He was when I bumped into him a few minutes ago. As soon as he realized your father wasn't back, he asked if I had seen you."

"Where can I find him?"

"He was just coming out of your father's office. I told him you might be in the pantry, going over supplies."

That was something she needed to do. But she had been too preoccupied with the search for Tom's body. She didn't like the idea of Max staying in Wapping, in danger, any longer than absolutely necessary. "I'll see if I can find him."

Mrs. Fitzgerald offered her a smile, but it was rather stiff. The housekeeper didn't know the whole story behind her sudden disappearance and hadn't completely forgiven her for worrying her father.

All the nights when the housekeeper had waited up for Edwin, brought him his tea, asked after his health, tried to help him keep his daughter in line, suddenly seemed to make more sense. Maybe Mrs. Fitzgerald loved her father the way she loved Max, she thought, and felt far warmer toward the woman.

"What is it?" Mrs. Fitzgerald asked.

"Love is a funny thing, isn't it?" she said.

Mrs. Fitzgerald's face went red and she ducked her head to attach the massive ring of keys she carried to its place on her belt. "Excuse me?"

Abigail threw her arms around her and gave her a hug, which made the poor woman stumble and blush but ultimately smile. "Never mind." She headed to the pantry, but ran into Bransby before she even reached the kitchen.

"There you are," he said.

"Mrs. Fitzgerald told me you were looking for me?"

He glanced over his shoulder, as if he didn't want the kitchen help to hear what he had to say. "May I have a moment?"

"Of course." She led him back to her father's study. In the theatre next door, they could hear Mr. Holthouse welcoming his students and beginning his class.

"I'm sure you're upset with me, Bran," she said before he could get started. "I put you in a difficult situation when I decided to buy another corpse without my father's knowledge. It must have frightened you a great deal when I went missing."

"I wouldn't presume to find fault with you, Miss," he said. "I'm just glad you're home safe."

"Thank you." Supposing he had merely wanted to let her know he had no hard feelings, she stood up. She had to dress for dinner. But he didn't leave.

"This is regarding something else," he said.

Mildly surprised, she sat down again. "And that is . . ."

"The porter at Pembroke College is a Mr. Whitehill. He is a friend of mine—and came to see me a few minutes ago."

Pembroke was one of the colleges they had visited earlier that day. Mr. Bowden, the lead anatomist, had met with them and claimed to be in desperate need of a cadaver. Perhaps he thought, given her recent association with resurrection men, that she could provide him with one. She could easily imagine him sending his porter over to inquire— he wouldn't want to ask such a thing of her in front of her father— but she wasn't going to get involved in *that*. Only her love for her father, and *this* college, had caused her to take such matters into her own hands. "Don't tell me he's looking for me to supply him with a cadaver!"

"No, Miss. They currently have a large male."

This surprised her. She specifically remembered Mr. Bowden saying they *didn't* have a specimen. He had spent most of the time they were there lamenting the college's *difficult situation* as if they had been a long time without the ability to dissect. "Are you sure?"

"I trust Mr. Whitehill's word."

"But my father and I spoke to the head surgeon there not three hours ago and inquired after their status in that regard. You're not suggesting that Mr. Bowden lied to us . . ."

Abby had been trying to tuck a stray piece of hair back up in her chignon, but when he didn't answer, she dropped her hand. "Well?"

"If he told you they don't have a specimen, then I suppose I am, Miss. But . . . perhaps he felt forced into it."

"Because . . ."

"Mr. Whitehill believes he bought their new cadaver from Big Jack."

Heart pounding, Abby swallowed hard. She had a feeling she knew what was coming next. "He said that?"

"And more. According to Mr. Whitehill, there is some . . . imperfection in the lip."

"The *lip*?" A chill ran through Abigail, causing her pulse to race even faster. That had to be Tom's corpse. What were the chances that there would be some other recently deceased person with the same congenital defect currently in a college's dissection room?

"But . . . why would they tell us otherwise?" she asked. "No one could find fault with them, least of all us. Any college could have made the mistake of buying that corpse from Jack and Bill."

"Perhaps. Perhaps not," he said. "I can only guess that Mr. Bowden didn't want the notoriety—or feared he would be brought up on charges."

"That's exactly what I'm saying. He wouldn't be charged," she said. "No one asks questions when purchasing a cadaver—including me. Unless . . ." She jumped to her feet. "Was there something obvious about this cadaver? Something that should have made the situation apparent?"

It was one thing not to ask questions when confronted with a stiff corpse dug up from a cemetery and quite another to remain silent when confronted with a fresh body that had clearly not been disinterred. The difference between those two scenarios was the chief argument against Robert Knox—the doctor who had purchased those bodies from Burke and Hare two years ago—wasn't it? Many suspected that he was complicit. There were *still* newspaper articles that made various derogatory plays on his name—"Dr. Noxious" and "Dr. Obnoxious" and the like. Although no one had been able to prove that he knew any of the sixteen murder victims he bought from Burke and Hare had been killed— and it was possible that some of his assistants had actually dealt with the resurrection men instead of him—he couldn't escape the stigma of it. His reputation would likely never recover.

But even then . . . as with the female corpse that had the artificial eye, murder wasn't the only possibility.

"The cadaver's throat was slit before it ever went under a surgeon's knife."

So there *was* more than receiving a fresh body to indicate foul play. *That* was why Dr. Bowden hadn't been honest. He, or whoever on his staff actually purchased the body, had overlooked this not-so-minor detail—and he feared there would be repercussions because of it.

"I'm so glad you told me, Bran," she said. "We have to get the police over there right away, before they destroy the evidence, if they haven't already."

"Yes, Miss."

She also had to get some word to Max that Jack was indeed the murderer they suspected him of being.

Emmett was back. That was the first thing that registered. Jack heard his voice, knew he was standing in the bedroom before he could come fully awake and was instantly relieved. If he cared about anyone, it was Emmett. The young man was cunning and ruthless—someone Jack fancied to be a bit like himself. "Where the hell have you been these past few days?" he mumbled, trying to gather his senses.

"At a friend's. Recovering."

"That mob at the cemetery—they beat you?"

"Good enough to put me in bed for a few days. I'm only now able to move around, damn them to hell. We'll get their bodies and sell them, too, when they die."

"Aye." Reluctant to be dragged completely out of the sleep that was finally giving him the rest he needed, Jack pulled the covers higher. "We've been lookin' for you. Went to your house several times, the cemetery, asked around."

"Why would I go to my house? There's no one to look after me there."

"You could've come here."

"I'm not *that* stupid. You're no nursemaid. I had a lady friend tend to my needs."

Jack chuckled. "She take good care of you?"

"Aye. Especially where it matters most," he joked. "What she did for me there didn't help my injuries but it definitely made the recovery more enjoyable. I'm nearly good as new."

Managing to open his heavy eyelids, Jack first focused on the lamp Emmett carried. His interest in seeing the damage that was done to Emmett had at last overcome the lure of sleep. But they weren't alone, as he'd assumed. Emmett held a small boy by the collar—a young pickpocket or beggar, from the looks of him.

"What have you got there?" he muttered, shoving himself into a sitting position.

"From what I can tell, he's a messenger."

This didn't make sense. Jack thought perhaps his mind was still a bit muddled. "What kind of messenger?"

"He just delivered a note to our good friend Max."

Jack wondered if he was supposed to be alarmed by this. "What'd it say?"

"How should I know? I watched the boy go into the Forrester's Arms, deliver it, and hurry out. That's when I caught up with him."

Jack blinked at the ragamuffin, who kept twisting and turning in an effort to escape.

"Let me go!" he cried, but there wasn't as much fear in his voice as there should have been. This was a child who was accustomed to facing danger on a daily basis, and was ready and willing to fight back when necessary.

"What'd the note say?" Jack asked the boy.

"How should I know? I can't read—can you?"

Jack didn't want to answer that question. He'd never had the chance to go to school, but he prided himself on his intelligence so he found his inability to read and write embarrassing. That was one of the reasons he hated Max so much. He didn't like how he stacked up by comparison.

"It was just a bunch of scribbling to me," the boy added. "So let me go, you blimey bastards!"

Emmett gave him a hard shake, but that didn't stop him from swinging his fists wildly in an effort to connect with something in return.

"Who gave it to you?" Jack asked.

The boy was tiring himself out. At this, he dropped his fists and sighed aloud. "Some man at St. Catherine's."

"I saw the exchange and followed the boy," Emmett volunteered.

Jack covered a yawn. "What were you doing there?"

"Asking some questions. I've seen Max visit a particular warehouse on at least two different occasions. I wanted to know why."

"You've never mentioned that."

"I wasn't sure it was of any importance until now."

"And how do you know the man who gave you the note?" Jack asked the boy.

"Don't. Just seen him 'round the docks. He works there."

"You don't know his name?"

"Why would I? He's nothin' to me. He stopped me, gave me a shilling to find his friend, and promised me another shilling—if I came back to let him know whether the message got through. That's all I can tell you."

Jack rubbed the beard growth on his chin. From the way Emmett was acting, he expected this to be revealing. But now Jack was asking himself why. They didn't know enough to be alarmed. "So . . . what?" he asked Emmett.

"You're not concerned?" Emmett asked. "I show up at the docks, asking questions, and this man immediately sends a note to Max, to warn him. That's what it looked like to me."

"But warn him about *what*? Max probably has a lot of friends we don't know. What do we care if they send him a message?"

"He joined up with us for a reason, Jack—and it's not to pay off his gambling debts."

"I've wondered about that before. I've even said it. But the fact that some man from St. Catherine's sent a messenger to Max doesn't prove anything. We don't even know who the note was from or what it said. Maybe it's from one of the men Max owes. Maybe the bloke's growing impatient."

"No. Max has been asking about Madeline. I think he's connected to her. Maybe he's the one who put her up to stealing from you—and then she ran out on him, too."

The mere mention of Madeline's name brought the hackles up on Jack's neck. "How do you know he's been asking about Madeline?"

"Because I've followed him, talked to the people he's talked to."

This surprised Jack more than anything. "Why? I didn't ask you to do that."

"I haven't trusted him, not from the start. And for good reason. He's been to every tavern and brothel in the area, searching for Madeline."

"Why didn't you come to me before now?"

"It didn't mean anything until Ebenezer Holmes told me Max even spoke to him. That's when I realized that he suspects us of doing something to her, and I'm not about to let him drag me to meet the hangman."

A chill ran up Jack's spine. "When did you see Ebenezer?"

"This morning. It's his daughter who's been takin' care of me."

The anger inside of Jack began to build. "You think Madeline cuckolded me with Max?"

"Don't know about that, but Ebenezer claims Max is trying to take your place as leader of this gang. And Madeline is attached to him in some way. No matter what he's *really* doing, he hasn't been honest with us. *She's* the reason he's here, not money."

"Where is he now?"

"Having dinner at the Forrester's Arms."

"And Abby?"

"From what I can tell, she's gone. She's not in the room, and she wasn't with him at the tavern."

"Is she helping him?"

Emmett shrugged. "She's certainly not doing *us* any favors."

"That's for damn sure." After climbing out of bed, Jack bent over and grabbed a fistful of the gamin's hair, holding his head at an angle. "Do you know where the lady is?"

"What lady?" he asked—and Jack finally saw the fear that should have been there from the start.

"Never mind. You're going to take us to the man who gave you that shilling, and you're going to do it now," Jack said.

When Max emerged from the Forrester's Arms, it was raining, and he felt the damp weather down to his bones. He wished he could send a note ahead of himself to have Mr. Hawley wait and meet him after nightfall. The thick fog that often rolled in from the Thames, especially this time of year, made it easier to move around undetected, and since he was fairly certain Jack wasn't planning on having them work, he thought that might be safer.

But he didn't dare wait. He had to learn the details of Emmett's inquiry to know if it was still safe to remain in his current situation—and that meant he had to fall in with those who crowded the narrow streets on this wet, autumn afternoon and hope to go unnoticed by anyone who might suspect his returning to the docks so often.

Huddling deeper into his coat, he hurried past the alleys of Wapping—alleys with such unappealing names as Cats Hole, Shovel Alley, The Rookery and Dark Entry—to reach Ratcliffe Highway with its many taverns and shops and lodging houses.

Once he arrived at the wharf, the scent of damp wood and hemp overcame the cinnabar, ginger, tea and sandalwood of the various cargos, but the rain hadn't slowed the frenetic activity. All the usual watermen rowed men back and forth. There were lightermen, too, with their twenty-foot oars, ferrying cargo and what seemed like an endless array of barges bobbing in the current. Farther out, he saw the forest of masts that never ceased to amaze him—where hundreds of massive seagoing vessels were lashed side by side.

He had always loved the docks, even as a boy, which was why he took a special interest in his shipping enterprise. He didn't care that other members of the aristocracy chose not to "sully their hands" by getting involved in the daily running of their various businesses; he thrived on the constant challenge. But St. Catherine's wasn't always the safest place in the world. There was more theft at St. Catherine's than anywhere else in London, so he had to be aware of his surroundings even when he wasn't worried about being followed by the gang of resurrection men he had joined.

Before ducking into his own warehouse, he turned, once again, to look behind him, but could see nothing that raised any suspicion. He was fairly certain he hadn't been followed. With Bill at home and Jack asleep, he wasn't sure who would follow him. But there was something odd going on—not only odd but dangerous. That became apparent when he called out for Mr. Hawley and, instead of receiving an answer, someone rushed up from behind and hit him over the head.

Chapter 26

Abby spent the early evening pacing in the parlor. Her father had missed dinner and was still not at home, which was unusual. She wanted to tell him what Bran had learned, but she had no idea where Edwin had gone after their last stop together. So she'd acted on her own and sent Bransby to Wapping, hoping that he would be able to find Madeline's friend, Gertrude, and that Gertrude would pay Max a visit. Having a prostitute show up at Farmer's Landing would be far less remarkable from Jack's point of view than a servant, or Mr. Hawley. She could never risk giving Max away like that. But when Bran returned, she could tell by the expression on his face that he had not met with success.

"What happened?" she asked.

"I'm sorry, Miss. I managed to find the woman you sent me to find. And she went to Farmer's Landing as you requested. But when she met up with me again, to tell me what happened, she said no one was home."

It was early yet to be out harvesting corpses. Were Jack and Max at a public house, then? If so, which one?

"Did she look anywhere else?"

"She poked her head into a few of the closest taverns, but didn't see him. She didn't dare go to any greater lengths. She said if she drew too much attention to the fact that she was looking for Mr. Wilder, it would not serve His Grace well, and I had to agree."

So did Abby. But she was nervous about Max's well-being. Suspecting Jack was a murderer had been one thing; knowing was something else entirely. If Jack could so easily kill Tom, and sell his corpse to anatomists as if he were any stranger, he probably did the same to Madeline—and could do it to Max.

Max needed to get out while he could.

"Do you think we should notify his family? Or the police?"

"And risk giving him away when he hasn't sanctioned it?"

Abby wrung her hands. "But what if he needs our help?"

"From what I overheard the night he came here with Big Jack, he is a very capable man. I say we have to trust him to make his own way, lest we be the cause of his downfall."

"Of course, you're right," Abby said.

"Miss, er, Gertrude"—he seemed at a loss that they didn't have a last name for her—"promised she would try again later."

Abby moved closer to the fire. The damp and the cold chilled her from the outside; her concern for Max chilled her from within. "Thank you. That will be all for tonight, Bran."

"You're going to leave it at that, aren't you?" he asked.

She could hear the suspicion in his voice.

"I mean . . . you wouldn't go back there," he went on, "knowing it's even more dangerous than you believed before."

She would if she thought it would save Max, but she wasn't sure that was the case. The last thing she wanted was to make his situation worse by giving him someone he had to protect.

Max wiped the blood from his face and squinted in an attempt to correct his fuzzy vision. There was a lantern burning, but it was in the office in the corner of the building and couldn't do much to illuminate the narrow walkways between the caddies, or barrels, of his latest tobacco shipment from Virginia. Still, he was able to identify the four men surrounding him: Jack, Bill, Emmett—who had a black eye but looked fairly fit after encountering that angry mob in the cemetery at

St. George's—and Ebenezer Holmes. Of the four, the undertaker seemed the most pleased with the situation.

"*Now* are you going to try to tell me how to run my business?" Ebenezer asked, his voice an octave higher than usual, charged with the rush of victory.

Max tried to think through the pain. His arm throbbed where he'd been stabbed, his hands had sustained some damage, since he had fought like the devil to preserve his own life, and his head ached. He'd also been kneed, kicked or slugged several times in the struggle. "If I remember right, I wouldn't let you take your business from Jack." He chuckled. "So isn't this ironic."

"That's not true," Ebenezer insisted to the rest of them. "When he came to me, he tried to set up a side agreement. He said he was going to join forces with Madeline and take over the London Supply Company."

"Now that's where your story loses all credibility." Max didn't try to convince them that that had actually been Ebenezer's suggestion; he pointed out what they couldn't refute. "How can I join forces with a woman who's been missing for over a month?"

Ebenezer looked to the others. "That's what he said; that was his plan."

Jack stepped closer. "What are you to Madeline? Why have you been searching for her?"

Even in the dark, Max could tell that Jack was holding his knife at the ready—the same knife that had cut him once. "Who says I've been searching for her?"

"*I* do." Emmett spoke up. "You've been all over Wapping, asking about her. Why?"

Max didn't answer. "Where's Mr. Hawley?" The blood from the wound in his arm had already soaked through the fabric of his coat—but at least he'd had the protection that coat provided. His injury would have been much worse otherwise. He was more worried about his clerk than himself. Max was younger and stronger and could probably withstand greater injury. Hobbs wasn't a fighter. Was he lying dead behind his desk?

That thought turned Max's stomach. He'd merely been hoping to find Madeline; he hadn't wanted anyone else to get hurt.

"You should be a little more worried about yourself," Jack said. "In case you haven't noticed, you're in a bit of a . . . what an educated bloke such as yourself might call a—"

"Precarious situation?" Ebenezer broke in.

"That's it," Jack said with a laugh. "You're in a precarious situation, Max."

Bill glanced toward the heavy sliding door, obviously afraid someone would come through it and catch them unawares. "Jack, whatever you're going to do, get it done."

Jack waved him off, seemingly unconcerned, while Max prayed his arrogance would be his undoing. "First, I want to know where Abby is. She's not at home, and she's not with you. Did you send her to the police? Or is she back at the college?"

Abby . . . Max tried to clear his head. After they finished with him, would they go for her?

He couldn't bear the thought of her being frightened, let alone hurt. "I don't know where she is. She ran away while we were gone last night. Ran away like Madeline."

Jack's voice took on a steel edge. "What do *you* know about Madeline?"

Had they figured out his true identity? According to Agnes, Madeline had never revealed the name of her family. And, so far, no one had mentioned his title. He was confident that would have come up immediately. So he could only suppose that they thought he was the gambler he had made himself out to be, but a gambler who'd been hoping to see them hang for the death of his sister. "That she went missing."

"Where is she?"

Jack seemed intent on learning the answers—which meant he didn't kill her. He spoke as if he thought she was still alive and out there, somewhere. Because he didn't speak the same way about Tom, that seemed more significant than it would have been otherwise.

"If I could tell you that, I wouldn't be here," Max said wryly.

Jack pressed closer still, making Max nervous about that knife. He could have taken Jack but not with three others holding him back. And he was far less capable of defending himself now than he'd been a few minutes earlier.

"What interest do you have in her?" Jack demanded. "If you plan to take your next breath, you'd better speak up!"

Whatever Max said had to be believable. He knew that. So he went for the truth—or the part of it he dared to divulge. "I'm her brother."

"I told you," Jack said to the others. "I told you when you came to me at the house, Emmett. I know the other men she's been with. Ain't none of 'em have a Cambridge education."

"But how could that be?" Bill asked. "She told us again and again that her family doesn't care about her."

Max felt that familiar twisting in his gut. "She was wrong about that. *I* care, even if I haven't shown it as well as I should have."

"You wouldn't prance around Wapping, not with the likes of common body snatchers, using your real name," Ebenezer said. "So who is this great family she's associated with?"

"The Greensmiths."

"And you are?"

"Winton." Winton Greensmith was a good friend of Max's. He owned the warehouse next door, but it was the only credible lie Max could come up with on the spot and amid the pain and the dizziness that were slowly getting the best of him.

"I've never heard of anyone by that name," Jack said.

"My name isn't important. I'm a merchant—that's all."

Ebenezer sniffed as if he wasn't impressed. "And you think that makes you better than all of us?"

"He makes a hell of a lot more money," Emmett piped up. "Madeline once told me her family could buy anything they wanted."

Max lifted his good hand. The other was dripping blood onto the floor. "Don't forget I'm the profligate son, always in debt. That aspect of my story is true." He hoped he was playing his part well enough to be believed. He had nothing of any value on his person, so he had no worries of being robbed now. But he certainly didn't want them to get it in their heads to find out where Winton lived and rob *him*.

"Jack, let's go," Bill said. "Max just wants his sister. That's all. And he can't find her any more than we could. He's not out to bother us."

"That true?" Jack demanded. "Is that all you want?"

Max leaned against the caddies behind him for support. "It is. Besides having a good use for the money, Madeline is the reason I joined up with you."

Jack grabbed him by the shirtfront. "Then why didn't you ask me where she was instead of making me so bloody nervous with your fine clothes and your fancy talk?"

"I thought maybe you would lead me to her."

"No . . . you thought I murdered her and you were planning to see me swing for it."

"If you had murdered her, I would be a fool to announce my true purpose. I did nothing more than you would have done in the same situation."

"That doesn't mean I have to like it."

"Something has happened to her—and someone is responsible," Max said.

Jack barked out a laugh. "But for once, it's not me. I have no idea where she went. She took all my money and left me without a word."

"No." When Max shook his head, he had to grip the caddies to keep from falling. "That's not like her. It *can't* be true."

"How do *you* know?" Jack asked. "You don't know her as well as we do!"

"I know her well enough to be able to assure you that if she took any money, it would be for her son."

"You'll get no argument from me." Jack's voice and expression oozed bitterness. "She probably grabbed her boy from wherever he was staying right after she left my place and took off for Manchester or . . . or Liverpool. Used me the whole time."

"That wasn't her intention. She told me she was going to marry you. And she *didn't* take her son."

"How do you know?" Jack still sounded angry, but he lowered the hand with the knife.

"Because *I've* got him."

"You're lying . . ." He lifted the knife again as if he might try to finish what he had started simply to appease the emotion that had welled up.

"Jack, if you're going to kill him, do it and let's get out of here," Bill cried. "Do you want to hang for this?"

Max ignored him. Fortunately, so did Jack. "It's true."

"Then where in the bloody hell did she go?"

He sounded desperate enough that, for the first time, Max *almost* liked him. He was obviously in love with Madeline. "That's what I've been trying to find out." Max stripped off his coat so he could wrap it around his wound. "But she didn't take your money."

"Then who did?" Jack asked.

"Who else knew where you kept it?"

"No one!"

Max concentrated on the pungent scent of the tobacco, doing all he could to hang on to consciousness. "Someone *had* to know."

"Who'd dare?"

Unable to staunch the bleeding, Max gave up on that. "Anyone—if they thought they had a handy scapegoat."

There was a moment of stunned silence. "You think someone else took the money and killed Madeline so I'd think she did it?" Jack asked.

Before Max could reply, Emmett entered the conversation again. "If that's the case, it had to be Tom. He was living there, too."

"Then we'll never know," Bill jumped in, "because Tom ain't comin' back. Jack already made sure of that."

"Shut the bloody hell up," Jack snapped. "It couldn't have been Tom. Tom wasn't half that clever. Besides, he adored Madeline. He would never have hurt her."

The argument that ensued between them caused Max's ears to ring: "Of course it was Tom . . . But we would've seen evidence of the money . . . Maybe he gave it to his brother . . . Then why would he steal it in the first place? And his brother doesn't seem to be any better off than he was before."

Max wanted to control the conversation as much as possible, to employ the diplomacy it would require to get out of the warehouse alive. He also had to find his clerk and send for help, if Hobbs needed it. The poor man had to be lying hurt somewhere, if they hadn't killed him . . .

But specific words wouldn't come. The moment he tried to speak, tried to straighten, the floor came rushing up to meet him.

Chapter 27

"What do we do now?" Bill asked.

Jack glanced at his brother, who was as pale as he had been the night they caught Tom. Bill didn't want any more killing, but Bill was weak. Jack didn't see where they had any choice. If Max lived to see that his clerk was dead, he would go straight to the police.

Max deserved what he was getting, anyway. It wasn't as if he was any kind of friend. He had hoped to catch them in a crime from the beginning, had admitted as much. It was one thing to lose Madeline; Jack wasn't going to be blamed for whatever happened to her.

Deciding to get it over with quick, he shoved his knife into Max's inert body. Then he rolled him over to steal his watch. That watch was a beauty. Jack had always admired it—but what he hadn't expected was to find Madeline's necklace in the same pocket.

"Look at this! Madeline prized this above everything—claimed it contained her father's hair," he said as he opened it.

Bill's mouth dropped open. Then he said, "Agnes would never part with that. So how did Max get it?"

Jack made a clicking sound with his tongue as he pocketed both the watch and the locket. "It's too late to ask him now."

"What about that other guy?" Emmett jerked his head toward the office. They'd left Mr. Hawley, who'd refused to say a single word from the moment they confronted him, slumped over his desk. "He might have a watch worth taking."

Jack wanted to check. But there were noises beyond the warehouse—two men walking past. He lifted a hand, indicating silence. He didn't want to draw outside attention. Madeline had said her brother was an important man and, if he owned this much cargo, she hadn't been exaggerating his wealth. Tangling with a powerful family would not work in their favor. If they were caught by the police, they'd all hang.

When those he heard were gone, Jack pulled his knife out of Max's body, wiped off the blood and put it back in his boot. "We leave them both for others to discover; no one will ever be the wiser if we do."

"Good," Bill said. "Let's go."

Ebenezer pulled him back. "Wait a second. What about all this tobacco?" He gestured to the vast stores surrounding them. "This cargo is worth a fortune."

"But we don't have a wagon with us, and these hogsheads are much too heavy to haul away without one," Emmett said. "Do you have any idea how much they weigh?"

"We could come back later," Ebenezer suggested. He was already prying off the lid of the closest one and taking as many of the leaves as he could shove into his pockets.

Jack stopped him. "Are you mad? There are two dead men in here, and you want to walk out with leaves of tobacco stuffing your clothes? Why don't you just ring a bell and announce what you've been doing?"

He didn't take any more but didn't give up what he had. He merely squished it down, where it couldn't be seen.

"So we're leaving their bodies here for someone else, too?" Emmett asked. "Max is an impressive specimen. He would bring in a fair amount."

Jack considered his options. It was dangerous to return—but too tempting to resist. They had made fifteen whole guineas off Tom. "We'll come back later with a cart, when it will be easier to haul both bodies off without being seen."

"And what about Abby?" Bill asked.

"We won't be stupid enough to sell either one to Aldersgate."

"I mean, she might come back and wonder what happened to Max."

"So? We leave her be. If we do anything else, they could tie this back to us. Besides, we won't see her. She's scared to death of me." He shoved a few of the tobacco leaves into his own pockets. "Maybe when we return, we'll even be able to get some of this tobacco."

"This is our lucky night," Ebenezer said. Then they slipped out, one by one, and each took a different route to Farmer's Landing.

Abby was still in the parlor, waiting for her father, when Bransby notified her that Gertrude was at the door. Hoping Madeline's friend had more information than she'd been able to glean earlier, Abby asked Bran to show her in right away.

"Come, warm yourself by the fire," Abby told her. Apparently, Bran had already taken whatever bonnet and cloak Gertie had worn but, thanks to the weather, she was drenched to the bone.

"It's so wet out," she complained, shivering.

"That makes it all the more impressive that you would venture all the way to Smithfield," Abby said. "I will, of course, reimburse you for the cab ride."

"I had to come," Gertie said. "I think something terrible might have happened to His Grace."

To *Max?* Fear clutched at Abby's chest. She'd been so uneasy all night. Was this the reason? Was Max in trouble? "Why?"

"I went back later, as promised, and visited several more taverns, looking for him. I had to be discreet, which took time, but I discovered that he had dinner at the Forrester's Arms. I spoke to the barmaid who served him. She said that a small boy delivered a message at almost the same time she brought his meal and he left shortly after."

"What did the message say? Did she have any idea?"

"No. But she recognized the boy who delivered it and told me where I could find him. It took me all evening, but I managed to track him down."

"And?"

"He didn't know what the message said, either. But he could tell me that he was hired by a man who works in a warehouse at St. Catherine's docks."

"Mr. Hawley." Relief swept over Abby. "That's nothing to be concerned about. Mr. Hawley is Max—er, His Grace's—clerk." She would never get used to Max's true identity. "He is also helping to find Madeline. So . . . perhaps Max is with him, safe and sound." She still wanted to get word to Max about Tom, but as long as he wasn't in imminent danger, she supposed that news could wait another day.

But then she saw the grim expression on Gertie's face.

"What is it?"

"The boy told me about someone else who took an interest in that message."

Abby's nails curved into her palms. "Who?"

"A big man with a pockmarked face."

"Jack!"

"It had to be him. The boy couldn't remember his name but told me a younger fellow with a black eye dragged him to No. 8 Farmer's Landing and they got the man with the pockmarked face out of bed."

Abby recognized the address. But who was the younger fellow? Could it be Emmett? Was that black eye a result of what happened at St. George's? She couldn't come up with any other explanation.

"At Farmer's Landing, he was questioned about what he had delivered and who it was from," Gertrude was saying.

"Did he tell them?"

"He did. It was the only way they would let him go. He said they were angry, that they thought a man named Max had lied to them. The boy was fairly certain they were on their way to St. Catherine's."

No longer possessing sufficient strength to stand, Abby sank into the closest chair. "When was this?"

"It's been some hours."

"And there's been no sign of Max?"

"Not since he left the tavern."

Abby's mind whirled with images she didn't want to see—Jack with that knife of his at the table, Jack showing no regret or sympathy when Tom's brother showed up, Tom lying on a dissection table with his throat slit.

What was Big Jack doing now? Was Mr. Hawley or Max in danger? After what she had just learned, she could only assume they were, and that meant she had to act. "Gertie, stay here by the fire, and get warm before you catch your death," she said. "I'll order tea and cakes after I send Bransby for the police."

"Even the police don't like to go down to the docks after dark," Gertie said with a wince for their predicament.

Did that mean Peel's bobbies wouldn't search in earnest? Abby couldn't take that chance. So she left Gertie to eat alone, donned her finest dress and bonnet and took a cab to Mayfair.

She would get help, even if she had to appeal to Max's mother.

When Max came to, his mind was so muddled he couldn't figure out what had happened. He lay on the hard floor, staring up into darkness, trying to remember where he was and how he had gotten there. He may never have found those answers, if not for the smell.

Tobacco. It was such a familiar scent. *Why?*

Then, a little late and rather lethargically, the answer crystalized in his mind. This had to be his warehouse. And with that memory came a surfeit of others: the boy with the message, finishing his dinner and trying to look unhurried as he made his way to the docks, being attacked as soon as he threw open the door and called out Hobbs's name.

But it was the memory of Jack with that knife that really got his heart pumping. He had been stabbed! Or was that a dream? He felt no pain, just a pervading numbness and an inability to move . . .

"Hobbs?" he croaked, but he didn't think anyone as far away as the office could hear him. He didn't possess enough energy to project his voice.

Putting more effort into it, he tried again. *"Hobbs?"*

When he received no answer, he nearly closed his eyes and went back to sleep. It was too daunting to move. Just opening his eyes proved a difficult task. But the fear that his clerk might need him goaded him into fighting the temptation to slip away.

He felt around to make sure he was alone and quickly determined that he was lying in a puddle. He could hear the rain outside. At first, he believed the roof was leaking. That explained why he was so wet and cold. But the consistency of this liquid—it was too viscous, not like water. Then he found that his shirt was sticking to him and began to feel pain—a burning sensation that overtook him, suddenly radiating out from his chest, his arm, his head.

Obviously, he was hurt—and the puddle wasn't water. He tasted it to be sure: blood. Not only had Jack stabbed him, Jack—and the others—had left him for dead!

That realization gave him the jolt he needed to get to his feet. Using the caddies on either side of him to support most of his weight, he staggered to the end of the row. He needed to reach the office, but he was so damn disoriented in the darkness.

"Hobbs?" he croaked again.

This time there was a rustle. Had that noise come from inside or outside the warehouse? It was tough to tell. Like always, there was a lot of shouting and movement on the wharf, the usual din. Max wasn't even sure he was truly awake—until someone lit a lamp.

Max's town house was every bit as well appointed as Abby had imagined it would be. And the dowager duchess was just as austere and frightening. It wasn't until Abby insisted she had news of His Grace that Max's mother would even agree to see her, and then she made it clear that she was skeptical of the visit and not pleased to have her evening so rudely interrupted.

"You are not friends with Madeline, are you, come here to beg for money?" This was the first question she asked, as soon as she stalked into the drawing room where the butler had Abby wait. The glance she gave Abby's dress acted as a second slap. It made Abby well aware that her apparel was far behind the latest fashions and beneath the duchess's standards. But surely she didn't look quite as desperate as one might expect a friend of Madeline's to look. That Max's mother would treat her this way was further proof that he was miles above her humble, middle-class station.

"No, Your Grace. I'm here about your son, as I told your butler at the door."

She waved her hand dismissively. "Lucien is visiting a friend in the country. He isn't even in town."

"In the country?" she repeated, surprised by this statement.

"Yes. He has been gone for several weeks."

Apparently, his mother didn't know, didn't even suspect, what Max was doing. But of course, given how she felt about Madeline, he wouldn't be foolish enough to tell her. Otherwise, she would have done all she could to stop him.

Now Abby was about to divulge the big secret. If he didn't need help, he would probably never speak to her again. But they had no reason to remain in touch, anyway. And the possibility—the strong possibility—that he was in danger forced her hand.

"I'm afraid that isn't true, Your Grace."

The dowager's eyes nearly popped out of her head. "*Excuse me?*"

Abby cleared her throat and stood. "I regret to inform you that your son is actually in Wapping and has been there some time."

"How do you know that?" she asked. "How is it that you know Lucien at all? Don't tell me you're from there—that you're one of his little . . . diversions—and you dare come here, to this house!"

Abby wasn't sure whether she could honestly answer that she wasn't one of Max's diversions. Given the difference in their social status, she was no one who could expect him to take her seriously. But she had not been working as a prostitute. And she had given her heart as well as her body.

As she explained how they met, the dowager stepped closer. "He went after that . . . that trollop?" she cried.

"Because he feared for her safety, Your Grace. I'm sure he felt he had no choice."

"But to risk his own life in the process? A life worth infinitely more than the one he is trying to save?"

Abby said nothing. She valued Max's life more than any other, too, but she couldn't approve of how careless his mother seemed to be of Madeline's safety. Madeline was her husband's bastard child, which would rankle—Abby had to admit it—but Madeline had no culpability in her conception. She deserved to live as much as anyone, even a member of the aristocracy.

"What I am here to convey is that . . . I believe Jack Hurtsill has figured out your son is there under false pretenses," Abby said, "and Jack is a very dangerous man."

As soon as Madeline explained why she was so concerned, the color drained from the dowager's face, but she flew into action—calling for her brougham to be prepared, for her coachmen and footmen to be armed, for someone to send a message to the home secretary to get some of his bobbies over to St. Catherine's as soon as possible.

"I have also sent for the police," Abby said. "I just thought . . . I thought you might like to be notified as well." She had paid the dowager a visit for her own peace of mind—because she knew, if anyone would provide the help Max, or Lucien, needed, it would be his powerful family.

"Indeed. I will not let that bastard cost me my only son."

Abby said nothing to that—but she winced, for Madeline's sake. Then the butler reappeared.

"All is ready," he informed the dowager. "Shall I send them off?"

"Not without me," she replied.

Although the butler tried, as diplomatically as possible, to talk her out of going—by telling her how dangerous it was and that His Grace would not want her to put herself at risk—she would have none of it.

"That's my son!" she shouted and barely gave the maid who brought her cloak time to put it around her shoulders before she marched out of the house.

Abby dared not presume that she—a mere messenger as far as Max's mother was concerned—would be included in this rescue party. And she wasn't. The dowager duchess didn't so much as turn back to thank her. Completely devoted to her task, she climbed into her coach and, the moment the door closed, they started off.

Abby stood at the entrance and watched them go, feeling a strange mixture of emotions. Had she done enough?

Or was it already too late?

The butler stood next to her. "I'll have someone take you home," he said after they had gone.

For this welcome kindness, she managed a polite smile.

Max staggered toward the light. Every few minutes, his vision would dim and he would almost black out. But, with effort, he was able to continue on. Although he had never traveled a distance that felt even half as long as the fifty feet to the warehouse office, that light acted as a beacon. Hobbs was there; he could hear the poor man moaning.

"I'm . . . coming," Max gasped. Although he was tempted, he couldn't simply launch himself out onto the wharf and shout for help. There was no telling what might happen if he did. With so much valuable inventory tempting the desperate individuals who frequented the docks after dark to rob him, chances were they wouldn't survive. First, he had to arm himself with the pistol Hobbs kept in his desk. At least then he would have some way to defend himself and his clerk when they sallied forth, hopefully together.

Once Max finally reached the office and saw Hobbs's reaction to the way he looked, he knew he wasn't in any better shape than his poor clerk. Hobbs had managed to light the lamp but couldn't do much else. Briefly closing his eyes, he muttered a curse and shook his head.

"Your Grace . . ." he started, but Max cut him off before he could put any more effort into speaking. At this point, only one thing mattered—and that was the one thing he could use to protect them until they could get help.

"Where's the . . . where's the pistol?" he asked.

"I tried to . . . to get it out . . . when they came. But . . . there were too many of them. I knew . . . it would wind up costing me my life instead, so—"

"Where?" Max couldn't wait for a long explanation, and he couldn't string a whole sentence together, not again.

A bloodied Hobbs motioned to the desk drawer. From what Max could see, Hobbs had been stabbed in the throat. He kept gripping it as if he could staunch the blood. Max was doing the same with his chest.

As Max reached for the drawer, he swayed on his feet. He feared he would not be able to retain consciousness this time—that he would crumble to the ground and that would be the end of them both.

But the sound of the doors sliding open kept him fighting, kept him pushing himself beyond what he thought he could do, especially when he heard Jack's voice.

Chapter 28

Abby knew her father would want her to stay well away from St. Catherine's. He would tell her she had done all she could by sending for the police and getting the dowager, that whatever was going to happen would happen. But Abby wasn't willing to accept that. Although it took some convincing, she managed to talk the stable hand, who the butler had employed to drive her home, into taking her halfway to St. Catherine's. Then she paid a cabby to take her the rest of the way.

What if the dowager's coachman had never been to the docks and didn't know quite where to find the warehouse? Or Sir Robert Peel's bobbies couldn't locate Jack to arrest him for Tom's murder?

Jack needed to be in custody. Until he was, Max wouldn't be safe. At the least, Abby felt she could guide whoever needed help to the warehouse, if she came upon them before arriving herself. Or she could show the police Bill's house or even Emmett's garret, should that be necessary.

By the time she arrived, however, she realized that she couldn't affect the outcome of what had just transpired. Fortunately, the police had found the warehouse. So had the dowager. But it appeared as if they were too late to help Max. Abby heard a gaggle of onlookers talking about the shots that had rung out only moments before several bobbies came rushing onto the scene. She could even smell the gunpowder—and when she went inside, she could see Max lying on the ground at the entrance to the office, covered in blood. His mother was leaning over him, weeping.

"God, no," the dowager wailed. "No, not him!"

Was Max dead? He couldn't be . . .

Tears sprang to Abby's eyes. Max's clerk, Mr. Hawley, didn't look much better. He was also in the office, but he was groaning and moving and attempting to tell them what happened. Several men were in a hurry to carry him out and load him into a wagon so they could take him to the closest hospital, but the way they shifted Max to one side suggested that they thought he was beyond help—and the dowager assumed they were right, because she did nothing to stop them.

Unable to hold back, Abby pressed through the tight knot of people surrounding Max to see him for herself. She couldn't accept what had happened, couldn't conceive of the fact that the man she loved, a man so full of life, was really gone.

The dowager glanced up at the disruption Abby caused, but her eyes were so glazed with pain she didn't react.

Praying that Max's pale, inert body was not as lifeless as it seemed, Abby pressed her fingers to his carotid artery to search for a pulse. She knew exactly where she would find it; she had sat in on enough anatomy lectures to be able to locate it with her eyes closed.

At first she thought she had to be imagining what she felt—that her heart just wouldn't accept the truth. Max *looked* dead. Everyone thought he *was* dead. But, to her surprise, she found a faint heartbeat.

"He's alive!" she announced. "Get out of the way. Hurry, we need to get help—he doesn't have much time."

The dowager reared back and gaped at her. The look in her eye was so fierce Abby thought she might fly into hysterics. But she didn't. She scrambled to get out of the way. "Yes, take him to the hospital!" she ordered. "Take him now!"

Abby willed Max to be strong as she watched four men carry him to the wagon outside and lay him inside next to Mr. Hawley.

Be strong, my love. Be strong, she prayed. Then she was again forgotten as everyone rushed off, except the bobbies that remained. It was only then that she realized Max and Mr. Hawley weren't the only ones who were hurt. Jack had been shot. Bill, Emmett and some tall, bony man she didn't recognize, were in custody.

"What happened?" she asked Bill.

He seemed dazed as he stared at his brother—too shocked to react with the appropriate anger or sadness. "Somehow he dragged himself into the office and got a pistol."

"*Who?*" Abby pressed.

"Max! The bastard shot Jack dead just before the police arrived."

Abby bent to feel Jack's carotid artery. If Max could survive what he had been through, Jack could, too, she thought. But she didn't feel so much as a slight flutter. "He's dead."

Wiping his blood on her dress, she backed away and eyed each of the other members of the London Supply Company.

"Who ever thought it would come to this," Emmett mumbled.

"The night doesn't have to be a complete loss," Abby said.

They seemed surprised at her words.

"What do you mean?" Emmett asked.

"He'll make a nice dissection specimen. I'll pay you fifteen guineas for his corpse."

"*You're* not going to dissect him!" Bill cried. "Nobody's going to dissect him!"

Abby managed a small smile for her joke. "You don't have to worry about us doing it at Aldersgate. They'll take care of him at the College of Surgeons—make a public spectacle out of it, just like they did with William Burke. And they won't pay you a farthing for the pleasure."

"The rest of us haven't done anything!" the tall man cried. "They should let us go."

"Jack and Bill murdered Tom. I would say that's something."

"I wasn't even there," the same man said.

"And you know I wasn't," Emmett added.

Abby turned to the man she didn't recognize. "Who are you?"

"No one," one of the bobbies supplied. "Just a lowly undertaker who will be standing trial for trying to kill a duke."

"We didn't know who he was!" the man cried.

"Did *you* know?" Emmett asked her.

"Not until recently. Where's Madeline?" she asked Bill. "Did Jack kill her? Is she dead?"

"Madeline left," he said.

So he was sticking to the usual story. She focused on Emmett. "I thought maybe you were rethinking the course of your life."

He scowled at her. "*What?*"

"If you had stayed away, maybe you wouldn't have been involved."

She had always sort of liked Emmett, but he didn't seem to return the sentiment.

"You're just another stupid woman," he snapped, and a police officer led him away.

Abby let them go without further comment. The bobbie who had spoken to her was starting to remove Jack's possessions from his body, which caught her attention. She saw him show a fellow officer the knife he took from Jack's boot.

"That's all he's got?" the other man responded.

"Not quite." The first bobbie drew Madeline's locket from Jack's pocket. "There's this, too."

Abby interrupted. "That's mine," she said and believed it was true. She had traded her brush, comb, dress and elephant for that necklace. She wasn't about to let it get lost—or taken home to someone's wife.

The second constable raised his eyebrows in question, but there was no one to refute her claim—and it obviously didn't belong to Jack. "Go ahead and give it to her," he said.

"What if she's not telling the truth?" the first constable asked.

"Who's going to say anything about it?" he replied. "If the duke lives, it'll be because of her."

He *had* to live, Abby thought. She couldn't bear the thought that only a few minutes could have made the difference.

For the next two weeks, Lucien faded in and out of consciousness. He didn't think he was going to live. He had never felt so weak in his life. But every time he slipped away, he came back again and grew more determined to keep fighting. He may have failed in what he had set out to do by becoming Max Wilder and going to Wapping. He hadn't been able to find Madeline, let alone help her. But he would not let Big Jack take his life. Although he had been told, at various points in his recovery, that Jack was dead and the others arrested, Lucien felt as if "Max" still had something to prove.

During those times when he was lucid, he found his mother at his side. She hovered and worried and employed a nurse, who fed him soup whenever she could rouse him. The clinical atmosphere he had noted upon first opening his eyes, however, had been replaced by his own bedroom. So he knew he had been moved. He was more comfortable in his bed, but he wasn't pleased by the change. He was pretty sure that, at the hospital, Abby had come to visit him at least once. He even feared that it was the fact that he had begun calling for her that his mother had closeted him away. Since those foggy, early memories of Abby holding his hand, right after what had occurred at the warehouse, he had found his fiancée at his side instead.

"Lucien?" His mother had noticed him stirring. "Can you eat? Are you feeling stronger?"

He was, for a change. It was no longer such a struggle just to open his eyes. And his stomach felt empty. "A meal would be welcome. Preferably something besides broth."

"Thank God," she responded, and he smelled her lavender perfume as she bent to kiss his forehead. "You've given me quite a scare, you know that, don't you? I won't quite forgive you for it, either. You didn't have to go to Wapping. You nearly lost your life for nothing."

She had to start on this already? "Not for nothing, Mother. For Madeline."

Straightening, she propped her hands on her hips and glared down at him—those old familiar sparks in her eyes. "And did you find her?"

Leave it to his mother to strike at the heart of the matter—*his* heart, in hopes of finally beating it into submission. But he didn't have the strength to argue, especially with someone as headstrong as she was. He didn't regret what he had done. At least he had tried. He only wished he had befriended Madeline while he could have saved her.

"It's time to quit blaming her for what Father did," he said but moved right on, hoping she would let that subject go. "How's Hobbs?"

"Recovering far quicker than you, I'm afraid. He's actually on his feet, although not quite back at work." They had told him before that Hobbs survived. It was one of the things that had kept him clinging tenaciously to life—that and the knowledge that Abby was somehow close.

"I'm glad to hear it." He shifted to ease the ache in his back. "Where's Hortense? She must be staying here with us."

His mother frowned. "Don't talk like that."

"Like what?" he asked with a slight chuckle. "I can barely talk at all."

"As if having her here is such an . . . imposition."

"I'm supposed to awake eager for my coming nuptials?"

"Why not? And of course she's staying here. Being the dutiful fiancée that she is, she came as soon as she learned you were hurt."

"You mean she came as soon as you sent for her because I was calling for another woman," he said dryly.

"You were delirious and obviously didn't know who you really wanted."

No. He definitely knew who he wanted. Duty didn't change that. But he wouldn't argue with her about Hortense. What was the point? He had made the commitment to marry his mother's cousin many years ago—and he couldn't go back on it now, not without compromising his honor and good name, and having it reflect poorly on his entire family.

"Food," he reminded her. "And then I need to sleep."

Although Abby periodically considered going to Herefordshire to visit her aunt, where she could lay low and, hopefully, mend her broken heart, she couldn't bring herself to leave London, not while Lucien was in such a compromised state. She felt as if he might die if she did. She knew that didn't make a lot of sense. She wasn't even able to see him. But the fact that she wanted to be close, that she was thinking of him and praying for him constantly, just in case there was a God, held her in London all the same.

So she threw herself back into her old routine and waited for some word, to hopefully learn that he was fine and would go on with his life. Then she could, too, she told herself. But even though he had acted pleased to see her when he roused, briefly, during her hospital visits, she heard nothing from him. She was reduced to watching the obituaries, and breathing sigh after sigh of relief when she saw nothing in there about his passing.

After six weeks of waiting and wondering, she began to consider paying him a visit. She didn't want to disrupt his life; she merely craved proof that he yet lived and was going to be as close to the man she had known as possible. And she wanted to deliver Madeline's locket. That was the last of any business between them. One final meeting, the good-bye they had never received—that was all she asked.

But the dowager wouldn't be happy to see her. Lucien's mother had been chilly enough when they bumped into each other at the hospital. And, as December advanced, Abby had a very serious concern of her own, one that was quickly invading her every thought, every action, and holding her hostage by a growing fear.

She hadn't received her monthly flow since before her stint in Wapping nearly two months earlier. Perhaps it was normal for a woman to miss her menses one month and start the next. Abby didn't know, and she had no one she could ask, especially without raising the specter of pregnancy. But according to her father's medical journals and the lectures she had overheard, since she wasn't allowed to attend legitimately, what she was experiencing did suggest that a baby might be involved—and with that came the inevitable question: What would she do?

She was staring down at her stomach, trying to see if it was bulging in any way, when Mrs. Fitzgerald came upon her in the pantry.

"Did you get the new candles in?"

Startled, Abby nearly fell off the stool she was using to straighten the top shelves. "Yes. We should have plenty now."

"Good." The housekeeper started to go but turned back. "Are you feeling unwell, dear?"

Dear? Mrs. Fitzgerald had been far kinder to her recently than ever before. "No. No, not at all."

"You look a little peaked. And you've grown quiet these days. It worries your father, you know, to see you so changed since . . . since you were gone."

"I'm fine," Abby insisted. "Truly."

"You're not pining away, are you? Your father would admit you, you know, if he could."

"To Aldersgate?" Thank God her thoughts had gone in that direction and not any other. "He hasn't ever said anything like that to me."

"He doesn't want to get your hopes up. But he doesn't see the sense in denying you. He thinks you would make a very capable surgeon."

Abby smiled. If anyone would know what her father was doing and feeling, it was Mrs. Fitzgerald, who paid strict attention to his every whim and fancy. "Thanks for telling me," she said.

"Perhaps it will happen someday."

"But that day isn't now. We're not even anywhere close." He would be ostracized if he ever even tried, so ostracized that there probably wouldn't be another male student who would sign up for classes at Aldersgate ever again. It would probably even cause a riot. "I . . . I think I shall retire to the country for a few months." Maybe a few years—if she was facing the humiliation and ostracism of becoming an unwed mother. Fear of the backlash she would face made her weak in the knees, which was one of the reasons she'd been so quiet, as Mrs. Fitzgerald had noted. She felt like she was constantly holding her breath against the day that she would know for sure. But, with the recent tenderness in her breasts, her body was changing, and she feared she knew why.

"You . . . *want* to move to Herefordshire?"

And leave everything she knew and loved? Not necessarily. The very thought frightened her—especially because she knew what she would contend with. If she was expecting, Aunt Emily would be mortified. *She* would be mortified, too—except for one small but very important piece of her heart, which would be glad to have the child of the man she loved, to retain such an intimate connection to him despite all his fiancée would receive in her place. Although she didn't want to spend the next five or ten years—maybe longer—with Aunt Emily, having a baby out of wedlock would necessitate it. Where else did she have to go?

Maybe it was just as well, she decided. She would never get into medical school. She had to face that and plot some other path for her life. "The change of scenery and the fresh air might do me some good."

"Indeed, but . . . you have always been so opposed to leaving the college."

Obviously, Mrs. Fitzgerald knew as much about Abby's resistance to that as she did everything else at Aldersgate. But pregnancy would make it impossible for Abby to remain in London. "As I said, I need a change."

Mrs. Fitzgerald didn't look as pleased as Abby had expected her to be. "When will you go?" she asked.

"I think . . . just after the holidays." If she didn't get her monthly flow, she would have no choice but to go *somewhere*. There was no way she would further embarrass her father by making her situation obvious, or run the risk of Lucien finding out that he had left her with child. He had warned her beforehand that she could not be part of his life. He would be marrying his fiancée, and she would not stand in the way of his happiness.

Chapter 29

As Christmas approached, Max felt well enough to be restless. Although his doctor pleaded with him to remain in bed, he had been cooped up so long that he would have risked just about anything to get out on a horse, and that included bad weather. He wanted to visit Hobbs, which he did one day. Later that same week, he attended Bill, Emmett and Ebenezer Holmes's hanging. He didn't enjoy the gory spectacle as much as the other spectators who crowded around and cheered, but he felt it was only right that he see it through. Maybe they hadn't hurt Madeline, but they had killed Tom and had attempted to kill him and Hobbs as well. His mother had received word from Abby's father that they had located Tom's body. According to the law, they deserved what they were getting but, as Lucien led his horse away, he felt unsettled. He still didn't know where Madeline was. He hadn't brought his nephew's mother home to him, as he had set out to do . . .

He wondered if he would ever find peace. He wanted to see Abby, to thank her for all she had done and assure himself that she was happy being back in her regular life. He thought it might be easier for him to go on without her if she seemed content, but he veered away from Aldersgate and toward Mayfair in spite of that. At the same time he thought a visit might help, he feared where it might lead. She was all he thought about. It wasn't fair to Hortense, who was trying so hard to be the perfect companion whenever they were together. She had even come to his bed recently to let him know she would "allow him to expend his lust upon her" if he wanted.

The sad thing was that he hadn't even been tempted. He had turned her away with the flimsy excuse that he would not take what wasn't yet his and prayed she wouldn't recognize his response for the lack of desire it signified.

He had almost reached home when he suddenly wheeled his horse around. He was feeling much stronger than he had after visiting Hobbs. The past three days had made a noticeable difference. He liked being out, away from the house, his mother and Hortense, and the constant reminder of his nephew who trailed him everywhere. He couldn't go back quite yet. Whether it was wise or not, he had to see Abby. He had already held off as long as he could.

Once the decision was made, he encouraged his mount to hurry the pace and felt his heart lift the closer he came to Smithfield. He even stopped to buy her a gift. He couldn't help himself. Since he wanted to be able to give her so much more, a small trinket seemed insignificant in the bigger picture.

Surely, he could indulge himself that much.

When Mrs. Fitzgerald came to get Abby, she seemed flustered.

"What is it?" Abby asked before the other woman could even say a word.

"His Grace, the Duke of Rowenberry, is here to see you," she gasped.

Abby's heart nearly stopped in her chest. She had been *dying* to see Lucien. Every day since they had been together in Wapping had felt like a month or longer. But now . . . now that she feared she was pregnant, she was afraid. Was there something about her that would give her condition away?

She smoothed a hand over her stomach, just to be sure she was still as slender as she had been that morning, when she had checked the mirror—which was something she was quickly becoming obsessed with doing. She didn't want anyone to guess, didn't want to ruin the holidays.

Once she was well away, and living in Herefordshire, she would send a letter to her father. He was the only one in London who needed to know—who *could* know. And a letter would cause him the least amount of embarrassment. She had it all planned out, knew how difficult it would be, for both of them, to have any kind of discussion.

"Abby?" Mrs. Fitzgerald prompted. "Did you hear me?"

Clearing her throat, Abby turned to the housekeeper in appeal. "Do I . . . do I look presentable?"

"You look fine. Regardless, he's a duke. You can't keep him waiting."

He had kept *her* waiting for weeks. She supposed it was human nature to grow hurt and angry over that, even though she understood exactly why he had.

After smoothing her dress and her hair, she threw back her shoulders. "He's in the parlor?"

"Yes."

"Of course." God in heaven, what would she say to him? How would she keep from throwing herself into his arms?

No matter what happened, she couldn't do that, she reminded herself. She was very likely carrying his baby, and that meant she had to be sure this was good-bye, or he would find out.

She stopped at the door, and caught the arm of Mrs. Fitzgerald. "I have to get something that belongs to him. Tell him I will be right there."

The housekeeper hesitated. She thought every second was a breach in etiquette. But she marched down the hall as Abby turned the other way and ran to her room for Madeline's locket.

When she finally entered the parlor, Abby saw Lucien standing at the fireplace, staring into the flames.

"Hello, Your Grace."

At the sound of her voice, he whipped around and his eyes devoured her instantly. "Abby . . ."

She took several steps toward him, and he took several steps toward her, but she forced herself to stop before they could actually meet. "It's good to see you looking so fit."

"And you. You are beautiful, as always." He lifted a small box. "I brought you something."

As she accepted it, he ran a hand along the inside of her arm, and she closed her eyes. His touch caused such yearning, such exquisite anguish.

"You shouldn't have," she said.

"I wanted to."

With a nod, she opened it and found a diamond necklace that was far more expensive than anything she could ever keep.

"Do you like it?" he asked, sounding anxious.

"It's . . . gorgeous. Stunning. But . . . nothing I can accept."

"Of course it is," he said, suddenly the imperious duke. "I won't hear of you returning it."

She chose not to argue. Maybe she could keep it, as a memento. A necklace such as this could provide a great many necessities for their child, if ever she grew desperate enough to sell it. "I have something for you, too," she said.

His eyebrows lifted as she unhooked Madeline's necklace from around her neck and handed it to him.

"How did you get this?" he asked. "It was in my pocket when Jack and the others attacked me at the warehouse. I thought . . . I thought it was gone for good."

"They found it on Jack's body after you shot him. I told the police that it was mine so that I could return it to you."

A tender smile curved his lips as he held it up. "Thank you."

She nodded. "I hope . . . it brings you some peace."

Lines appeared in his normally smooth forehead. "I don't know if I will ever find peace without you in my life."

Those words gave her so much hope that she almost told him about the baby. She felt he would want to know. But then she remembered that his father had gotten involved in a similar situation, and that he had sworn not to do the same. If she loved him, she would support him in what would make him the happiest, and she knew what that was.

"Of course you will," she said. "I am going to Herefordshire in January. That might make things easier on both of us."

He didn't seem pleased. "What's in Herefordshire?"

"My aunt."

"And you want to go there?"

"I think it's best."

Silence fell, during which he seemed to be struggling to know what to do with his hands. "You heard they hung Emmett and Bill today?" he said at length.

"I did."

"You didn't go?"

"No. I couldn't watch. Were Agnes and the children there?" Bill's wife had Abby's brush and mirror, and her elephant. Abby hadn't been pleased about that. But she couldn't begrudge them to a widow, even a rather unlikeable widow—not after all Agnes had lost. "How will she get by?"

"I sent some money to help her. But I'm sure it won't be easy."

Abby nodded. "That was nice."

He paused as his eyes met and locked with hers. "I'm dying to touch you."

Abby felt the same. Her chest was so tight she could scarcely draw breath. "I've missed you," she admitted, her words the softest of whispers and all the more revealing for that.

"Let me at least put on the necklace I bought you."

She would have to hide it under her dress. There was no way she could walk around flaunting such an expensive piece of jewelry. Everyone would remark on it and wonder where it had come from. But she didn't point out the obvious. She knew it would only disappoint him that he couldn't even give her this.

So she turned, and he came up behind her and fastened the necklace. But he didn't stop there. His mouth found her neck and began moving up toward her ear.

"I think of you every day, every night," he breathed.

"We can't give in to this . . . this wanton desire," she said, but she was convinced that she was carrying his child. That had to count for something, didn't it? Give her some claim on him?

She didn't move out of reach. She leaned back, and felt her bones melt as his hands came up to cup her breasts.

"What happened to us in Wapping?" he asked.

It seemed an unlikely place to find happiness, to find *home*, but she felt as if she had found exactly that. "I fell in love with you," she told him.

"Abby . . ." Turning her in his arms, he kissed her mouth and she was so lost in the taste of him, the solid feel of him in her arms, that she couldn't even bring herself to care that anyone could walk in on them, including her father. This put a stop to the endless yearning; this was everything she craved.

It wasn't until she heard a noise out in the hall that the threat of discovery became real enough she could bring herself to break off the kiss. "We can't do this, can't act like this," she said.

He didn't seem to be listening. That kiss had only inflamed his desire. She could see it in his eyes. "Come to me tonight at the town house," he said. "Let me hold you one more time."

"Max—"

"Call me Lucien," he said.

"Lucien. Don't you remember what you said? How hard you were trying to keep me out of your real life?"

He waved her words away. "That's impossible. Come to me. I'm only asking for one more night."

She could feel the weight of the diamond pendant he had bought her resting between her breasts. She loved it, loved knowing she would have at least a token of his regard. But was she making a mistake in accepting his gift? In accepting his invitation, too?

"What time?" she asked.

"Whatever time you say."

"It would have to be late or my father or Mrs. Fitzgerald might notice that I'm gone."

"I'll send someone for you after everyone is asleep. Eleven?"

"I'll be waiting at the door in my father's office. Have your man come down the alley."

"I wish it were eleven now," he said.

Abby stood in the room long after he was gone, staring into the fire. She hadn't told him about the baby, and she wouldn't, couldn't. She would allow herself tonight, would make love with him one last time. That would be good-bye. Then she would pack up and go to Herefordshire regardless of the holidays.

Lucien paced in his bedroom while he waited for his most trusted footman to return with Abby. Hortense had left earlier in the afternoon, at his request. He had met with her and suggested, now that he was healed, that they return to their regular lives until the date of their wedding. It hardly seemed fair that he had to endure her constant presence ten months earlier than expected. He didn't dislike her in any way, but it was difficult not to resent her when she stood between him and the woman he really wanted. It was difficult not to resent his mother, too, who seemed so eager to thrust Hortense upon him.

In reality, he knew it was his own sense of duty, more than anything else, that hemmed him in, but he couldn't avoid who he was, who he had to be, and that rankled, too, because it cost him Abby.

He felt cross as he waited, angry for no particular reason. But then Abby was there, wearing only the diamond pendant he had given her, and the rest of the world simply fell away.

Abby had never known such opulence. The duke's bedroom was a world apart from Wapping, from the college, even from all she had imagined. She might have felt strange, swallowed up in the unfamiliar, but he was there and that was all that mattered. The moment he touched her, she forgot the many reasons she shouldn't be in his arms and let him carry her to greater and greater heights of pleasure.

He withdrew every time they made love. She would have preferred that not happen, knew it was a pointless exercise since she was already with child. But she couldn't let on. She didn't want him to change what he was going to do because she was carrying his child, didn't want to feel as if she had tried to trap him or force him to take care of her—and she knew that was what everyone would believe.

"It'll be dawn soon," she murmured.

He had just pulled her to him as if they would sleep, the way they had slept after making love at Farmer's Landing. "Don't go," he said. "Not yet."

Abby leaned up on one elbow to look down at him. They had left a lamp burning all night, had both wanted to enjoy the sight of each other as well as the touch. "I can't be driving off as your mother watches from the window, Lucien."

He didn't answer. With his hands, he pressed her to lie on him and ran his fingers lightly down the valley of her spine to her behind. "Come back tonight."

"Lucien, no. We talked about this."

"I have only ten months before I marry. I don't want to throw them away."

"If we spend those ten months in your bed, you will only be that much more entrenched."

"I won't give you up before I have to!"

"And now you sound like a spoiled child."

He sighed. "How dare you speak to a duke that way," he grumbled.

She would have taken offense, would have called him on his arrogance, but he had spoken with enough irony to let her know he wasn't taking himself seriously.

"Even a duke doesn't always get what he wants."

He pulled her down to kiss him again. "One more night. I can have that, can't I?"

"That's what you said yesterday at the college," she reminded him.

"So? What will it take?" He buried his face in her neck. "I'll buy you anything you want."

"You can't give me what I want, and we both know it."

"Abby . . ." he started but then fell silent.

"What?"

"Nothing."

She didn't press him. She could guess what he was thinking. Every now and then the same thought went through her mind: Why *couldn't* she become his mistress? Seeing him some of the time was better than giving him up for good, wasn't it? A great number of the aristocracy took lovers. How else could they compensate for marriages that were more about social standing or money or power?

But then she thought of Madeline and how terrible Lucien felt about how she had been treated; the dowager duchess and the crippling jealousy that had caused her to act as she had; how torn his father must have been, knowing he had hurt so many of those he loved. Lucien could never be happy playing his father's role in a similar situation.

"I love you enough to want you to be proud of yourself," she told him. "To be everything you can be—and you could never become that man if I was always tucked away somewhere, waiting for you, dividing your loyalties and your heart."

He kissed her softly, meaningfully. "I'm afraid I will never get over you."

Abby had her own fears. She was afraid they wouldn't actually give each other up, which was why, after spending the next five nights in his bed, she packed her clothes and, without telling him for fear he would talk her out of it, left London.

Chapter 30

"What do you mean 'she wasn't there'?"

Rufus, the footman who had been escorting Abby back and forth from the college, shifted on his feet. "I'm sorry, Your Grace. She . . . she wasn't waiting when I arrived. But . . . I found this envelope under a rock where she normally stands. And, although your name isn't on it, I presume I was meant to find it and deliver it to you."

Lucien felt sick as he accepted what the footman handed him. Each night he had anticipated Abby's arrival even more than the one before. With Hortense gone and his health back, he could almost pretend they had forever. He had been so happy—except that he had been getting the itch to take Abby out to enjoy the many things he could show her and had begun to feel stifled by the secrecy.

Rufus bowed slightly. "Will that be all, Your Grace?"

"Yes. Thank you."

Lucien didn't open Abby's note even after he was alone. If it was good-bye he wasn't sure he could bear to read it. Instead, he stood drinking a glass of brandy and staring out at the moon. It was going to be a long night.

Without Abby, his whole life might feel like this night, he realized.

Finally, in the wee hours of the morning, he sat on his bed and unsealed what his footman had brought him. Abby had sent him only five words: *I will always love you.*

Except for her aunt, who was every bit as prying and intrusive and bossy as Abby feared she would be, Ewyas Harold turned out to be a respite. She missed the college and how productive she had always felt there. She missed the dream she had once held of becoming a surgeon. And she missed Lucien a million times more than all of that. But at least she was safe from her weaker self. There was little question she would have given in and continued to see him if she had remained in London. How did a woman go about giving up a man she loved that much?

She could only put physical distance between them and hope that, when her pregnancy became obvious to her aunt, Emily wouldn't toss her out in the street. Abby hadn't yet told her father about the baby, either. Doing so was going to be the hardest thing she had ever done, especially now that he was so happy she had quit pressing him to admit her to the college and had taken up more *womanly* pursuits.

"*Abby?*"

At her aunt's sharp tone, she glanced up to find Emily holding a tea tray.

"Could you move that book from the table so I can set this down, *please?*"

"Of course." Setting aside her needlepoint, Abby did as she was asked. She really should have noticed that her aunt needed help. She would have, if not for how dreadful she was feeling. Since Christmas, she had been so nauseous she could scarcely swallow a bite of food; it took all of her willpower and focus just to keep herself from being sick on the rug. Although there was no other evidence of the baby yet, besides the soreness in her breasts, she feared her inability to eat normally—and how difficult it was to keep what she did consume down—would give her away.

"I swear, sometimes I wonder if that father of yours ever taught you anything," her aunt grumbled.

Abby had been treated to other such comments, but because she had nowhere else to go, she smiled politely and ignored them. Her aunt had never approved of her. Now Emily was getting the chance to express that—and to try to remake her into a better version, something far more similar to what a young Englishwoman *should* be.

"We have been invited over to the Nesbitts' for a gathering come Saturday," Emily announced once she had poured them both some tea.

With effort, Abby managed to keep a pleasant expression on her face, but she couldn't have had less interest in social gatherings. That included this one. The Nesbitts had two unmarried sons, and Emily had made no secret that she hoped one of them would take a liking to her "odd" niece. "How nice."

Her aunt leaned forward to peer into her face. "You are pleased, then?"

Abby placed a crumpet, the very sight of which turned her stomach, on her plate. "The Nesbitts are a very nice family."

"Yes, they are, but I have told you of their sons."

"Indeed." *Countless* times.

"Wait until you meet them. I think either would be the perfect match for you."

Either. As if it were that easy. One could replace the other. Abby had mentioned that she didn't want any suitors, had indicated that she had no intention of marrying. But her aunt wouldn't acknowledge those statements. It was her goal to see Abby with a husband and a family, and she wouldn't rest until that happened.

"You don't want to wind up alone like me, do you?" she always said. Emily had lost her husband to a carriage accident shortly after the birth of their only son, who had joined the navy and died, at nineteen, in the battle of Trafalgar. "At least *I* didn't ask for this kind of life," she would often add, as if Abby would sorely regret her choices.

Fortunately, Emily didn't take the conversation in that direction today. Battling nausea was bad enough; Abby didn't want to fight tears at the same time, and she had no doubt she would break down at the mere mention of having a family.

"So what will you wear?" Emily asked.

"My best dress, of course." Abby provided what she knew to be the appropriate answer and pretended to sip her tea but dared not actually swallow. When her aunt wasn't looking, she would slip her crumpet into the folds of her dress or her needlepoint and feed it to the pigs outside. They had consumed her food on several other occasions already.

"I wish we could afford the fabric for a new one," Emily lamented. "Maybe I will write your father and see if he will send the funds."

"Please, don't bother him about that!"

Emily blinked in surprise that Abby would be so forcefully opposed. But Abby would not fit into anything Emily sewed for very much longer and couldn't bear the thought of Edwin sacrificing while she was keeping something so important from him. She needed to figure out a way to tell him, but she couldn't bring herself to do it quite yet. She needed some more time to cope with her heartache and sickness before tackling that obstacle. "There's no need to put any more pressure on him," she added in a far less strident tone.

"Pressure!" Emily echoed. "Your concern for him does you credit, my dear. You can be very sweet when it comes to Edwin. But he *is* your father, and he should provide for you a bit better than he does, I dare say. How will you ever catch a husband otherwise?"

She could have said she didn't want to catch a husband. No one else could compare to the man she loved. But she had stated her position on marriage before, and Emily wouldn't accept it. So what was the point? "The dress I have is fine," she said instead.

"We'll see how this first outing goes." Emily gestured toward her plate. "You're scarcely eating a thing. Are you not hungry?"

"Not particularly."

"You're never hungry," she complained. "You eat like a bird—and are far too thin. That won't be a good thing when you start bearing children, let me tell you. You'll need your strength then. So many women die in childbirth. It's tragic."

Abby pretended to knock her needlepoint to the floor to create a diversion so that her aunt wouldn't see the tears that welled up. Her predicament frightened her enough without hearing about the physical danger, which, like everything else with this child, she would face on her own. But when she bent over, matters only grew worse when the necklace Lucien had given her slipped out from under her dress, because Emily spotted it right away.

"Where did you get *that*?" her aunt asked, jumping up to take a closer look. "It looks very expensive."

Abby's breath stuck in her throat as she searched for an acceptable response.

"*Abby?*"

"It was a . . . a thank-you gift," she said.

"From whom? Who can afford such a fancy bauble? I dare say that must have cost fifty pounds."

"It came from the Duke of Rowenberry."

"A *duke*? No!"

"Yes, Aunt, it's true."

Emily studied it skeptically. "And how would *you* come to associate with such a powerful man?"

"Quite by accident." She pressed a hand to her stomach as she fought off a fresh wave of nausea and told her aunt a far more innocent version of how she and Lucien had become acquainted.

"He was pretending to be a resurrection man?" Emily finally let go of her pendant, but she remained where she was, standing over Abby, only inches away. "And you bought a . . . a *corpse* from him? How terribly *sordid*!"

Abby could understand her horror and distress. But the parts of the story she held back would have shocked her aunt far more. "For the sake of the college, yes."

"Lord in heaven, child!" she cried. "No wonder your father sent you to me."

"Coming was my decision, Aunt Emily," she responded. "I am one and twenty, after all."

Her aunt ignored that. As long as she was financially dependent on her father, it didn't matter how old she was. "You really *must* remember to leave such issues to the men who should be taking care of them in the first place."

It was so tempting to argue, to tell Emily that she would have done exactly that—providing someone else had stepped forward to save Aldersgate. But she bit her tongue. She would be far wiser to do all she could to smooth this over. Then maybe she could come up with an excuse to return to her room.

"I have learned my lesson," she said, choosing to appease her aunt.

Fortunately, that had the desired—and calculated—effect. "I wager you did!" Emily said. "How frightening it must have been, coming into direct contact with . . . with body snatchers!"

Abby took a tiny sip of her tea, but held her breath as she did so. The smell alone could be her undoing. "My father didn't tell you, then?" she asked when she had managed—successfully—to swallow.

"No. But you know how reticent he can be. When he does write, I get barely a few lines and it's months between letters."

"Perhaps he thought my little adventure was of no consequence—since there was no harm done. It was kind of His Grace to keep me safe."

"Indeed! But the duke is obviously very grateful to you, as well—if he would give you such a gift. Perhaps I should write to him and express my concern for your future. With his patronage and connections, he could see to it that you strike a far better match than any I could arrange."

Abby nearly choked on another sip of her tea. "He is barely a . . . a distant acquaintance. And he has compensated me with this gift, Aunt Emily. That is the end of it. I would never impose on him further."

"Of course you wouldn't, dear. But, after an experience like that, he has to understand how it could hurt a young woman's prospects. One must do what one must do."

"Please! Do not contact him," she pleaded. "I am . . . I am excited to meet the Nesbitts."

Slightly mollified that Abby was at last showing some enthusiasm for her matchmaking efforts, her aunt patted her hand. "Perhaps one of them will strike your fancy."

"What has been wrong with you these past few weeks?"

Lucien scowled at his mother, who was sitting across from him at breakfast. "I have no idea what you are talking about."

"I have never seen you in such a foul mood. You were so happy to be recovered. Then the holidays arrived and you couldn't seem to say a civil word to anyone."

Because he was miserable. Since Christmas he had been spending a great deal of time with Madeline's son. He was becoming quite enamored of the boy, but he felt terrible that he was the reason Byron didn't have his mother. He had failed Byron *and* Madeline. He had failed his fiancée, too—by giving his heart to someone else. Maybe he had even failed himself, because he had destroyed his own chance at happiness by falling in love with the wrong woman. "I'm fine."

He hoped that would be the end of it. He had nothing to say to his mother or anyone else. But, of course, she wouldn't let it go.

"You tell me that every time I ask, but you are obviously not fine."

"Mother, I will take my breakfast elsewhere, if you insist on badgering me."

She opened her mouth to respond, but he waved her off. "Enough! I am trying to eat!"

Her eyebrows lifted at his imperious tone, but he was so angry he didn't regret how he had acted. Indeed, he was tempted to go much further. It was all too easy to blame his mother for his predicament, since she was so eager for him to wed Hortense—and had, indeed, been the one to arrange it.

"It has nothing to do with that little strumpet you were having Rufus bring to your bed right after you sent your fiancée away, does it?" she asked.

When his eyes flew to her face, she put down her fork. "What? You think I didn't know?"

"Rufus told you?"

"No, he is far too loyal to you for that. But there are other servants who see him coming and going—maids who smell the perfume on your linens as well as . . . other scents."

"And they come and tell *you*? Then perhaps I will sack the entire staff, except Rufus, and protect my privacy by sending you to the country before I hire more."

She stiffened. He had never threatened her with anything, let alone banishment from London.

"Perhaps you believe yourself to be in love with her," she started, but he cut her off immediately.

"Do not presume to tell me how I feel. And if you ever call her a strumpet again, you can pack your bags and leave for good." With that he got up and strode from the room.

"Lucien, stop," his mother called after him. "You are overreacting. You will get over her, with time."

He ignored her. He had to get out of the house, away from her, away from the staff, away from every reminder of his duties. But Maurice, the butler, caught him on his way out.

"Your Grace, there is a woman in the parlor who claims she has information you would like to receive."

Lucien couldn't imagine what information that would be. "Who is she?" he snapped.

Hearing his tone, the butler stood taller but, unflappable as always, he allowed no change in his expression. "Mrs. Agnes Hurtsill, the wife of the body snatcher who was hanged recently, I believe."

What could Agnes want from him? "If she needs more money, give it to her," he said and brushed past, but when Maurice spoke, he stopped again.

"Your Grace, she says it's about Madeline."

The anger that had been pumping through his blood was suddenly replaced by curiosity—and maybe even hope. "Have someone bring tea," he said and switched direction.

He found Agnes standing in his drawing room, looking nervous and pensive and out of place. She smoothed her dress when he walked in and managed an awkward curtsy.

"Your Grace, I-I wanted to thank you for the money you sent. You didn't have to . . . to take pity on me, but I don't know how I would have survived these weeks without it."

"I don't blame you for the mistakes of your husband, Agnes. You or the children."

"I've made my own mistakes. I admit that. I knew Jack and Bill weren't doing right. And to think they almost killed you . . . I miss Bill, but I feel bad for everything. I do."

"Thank you. We can agree that they have had a destructive influence on us both."

"When I learned who you really are, I couldn't believe it, couldn't believe I know a *duke*."

He hoped she hadn't merely used what she had told Maurice as an excuse to gain an audience with him. "My butler tells me that you have information on Madeline."

"It's true. I . . . I should have told you before, but . . . I didn't, and my conscience has been troublin' me a great deal since, what with you being so kind to me and all, despite . . . despite the fact that I don't deserve it."

He had helped her mostly because of the children, but he didn't say so. "What do you know of my half sister? What can you tell me?"

"She's alive, Your Grace. Or she was last I saw her."

Lucien couldn't believe his ears. He'd finally convinced his stubborn heart that his half sister was lost to him—and to Byron—forever. "Where?"

She stared down at the rug. "Jack was so unkind to me and Bill, to everyone. We all hated him."

Lucien stepped toward her. He didn't care about that. He knew how difficult Jack had been. "*Where is she?*"

"Probably in Australia."

He stared at her, searching her face for any sign that she might not be telling the truth. "What could she be doing there? She would never leave her son. I can't believe she would take Jack's money and run away, if that's what you are about to tell me."

"No, Your Grace. It was Bill and Emmett what took the money— and they sold her to a ship's captain bound for Australia so Jack would think it was Madeline who'd robbed him."

"*Sold* her?" Lucien cried. "As a slave or a servant or—"

She wrung her hands. "Anything he wanted her to be, I suppose. He said he needed a woman to keep his house in Brisbane."

Lucien was so overcome by this information, he could scarcely catch his breath. "And Jack believed what Emmett and Bill wanted him to believe."

"As much as Jack loved Madeline, I was a little surprised. But he couldn't trust anyone, even her. He thought everyone was out to get him."

"Apparently he had good reason to doubt those around him, if his own brother would betray him."

"Jack always humiliated Bill," she said, instantly defensive. "He was the one who led my husband wrong to begin with. He killed Tom, he did. Right in front of Bill. Bill had nightmares about it after. And Jack always took the lion's share of whatever they earned. Bill and Emmett didn't think that was fair, since they did the same amount of work."

Lucien didn't care to argue about who was right and who was wrong, or who deserved what. As far as he was concerned, they had all gotten what they deserved in the end. "So Madeline didn't sell you her locket. You took it from her."

Agnes hung her head. "I did. I'd give it back but Abby's got it now."

Lucien pinched the bridge of his nose. "And what did you take from Abby before you would give it to her?"

"A . . . a brush and mirror that . . . that I sold."

The one he had given Abby. As much as Abby had loved it, she had parted with it for the sake of Madeline's locket.

"I needed the money," Agnes said plaintively. "But I still have this."

When she pulled out Abby's elephant, Lucien felt his jaw drop. Abby had given this woman *everything* she had. "I will take that myself."

"Yes, Your Grace." She flinched as if he might strike her when he reached out. For the first time in his life, he was tempted to harm a woman. Not only had she stolen Madeline's prized possession, and allowed Madeline to be sold into slavery, which could have caused her son to be turned out into the street, but she had taken Abby's most precious things, too.

"Can you give me the name of this captain?" he asked, forcing himself to step away.

He prayed she would remember it. With Emmett hanged, it wasn't as if he could get the answers he needed there, and he had to have some way of tracing Madeline.

Perhaps his half sister was still alive.

Perhaps he could find her.

"It was Captain Alfson," she said. "He sailed a merchant vessel, a bark called the *Dromahair*. I remember 'cause it was such an odd name."

Lucien rang for Maurice. "Give Mrs. Hurtsill ten pounds for her trouble and see that she gets a ride back to Wapping," he said when the butler arrived.

"Yes, Your Grace."

Without bothering to say good-bye, Lucien headed for the door. He expected Maurice to step out of his way when he reached it, but the butler didn't do so immediately.

"Your mother has requested that I let you know she would like to speak to you in the small parlor," he said.

Hell, no. Lucien wasn't about to pay his mother a visit. He had heard all he wanted to hear from her and couldn't bear for her to extoll the virtues of Hortense—and how strategically perfect his marriage was. He was leaving for St. Catherine's in search of information on the *Dromahair* and its captain. Then, if necessary, he was going all the way to Australia.

Chapter 31

Abigail was beginning to show. She could see the slight swell of her stomach in the mirror when she turned sideways, which was something she did before getting dressed every morning. And every morning, she would sit down to write her father about the baby—and then put it off again when she couldn't think of any way to confess without throwing him into the depths of despair. Not only did she have his feelings to consider, she knew as soon as she told her father, she had to tell her aunt, and she and Emily were struggling to get along as it was. The more suitors Abby rejected, the angrier Emily became. Abby could hardly imagine the strain it would put on their relationship when Emily learned she was carrying a bastard child.

Bastard. *Such* an ugly word. Abby cringed when she thought of how that word had been attached to Madeline—and how she had been treated in consequence. There was little doubt in Abby's mind that Madeline's son had been treated any better.

How would she protect her own child? How would she support herself and the baby if Aunt Emily turned her out?

Instinctively, her hand went to the necklace Lucien had given her. If she could find the right buyer, that would help. It might even support her long enough that she could get a job in service or working at another college.

One day at a time, she reminded herself. Fortunately, the morning sickness that had plagued her for nearly two months was beginning to ease. Much to the pigs' chagrin—both of which had gotten much fatter since she came to visit—she could now hold down her food. She hoped that would help her put on some of the weight she had lost.

As she began to dress, her thoughts turned to Lucien and how much she missed him—but she steered her mind clear of that right away. She could not continue to suffer such longing. It was too imperative that she prepare herself for the difficult future ahead.

"Abby? Abby, are you ready?" her aunt called up.

Emily was insisting they go over to the Nesbitts' for a visit. It was the last place Abby wanted to go. It was awkward with both brothers eager to court her even though she wasn't interested in either one of them.

"Coming," she called back. Then she put on her dress and prayed she could get through another day without anyone noticing her pregnancy.

It took Lucien nearly two months to track Madeline to Brisbane, but the sea voyage was to blame for most of that time. He endured those days on the ocean impatiently, which made the passage of each day feel even longer. He had thought he might lose his mind before they arrived. But at last he was back on dry ground and looking at a small shack supposedly owned by Captain Alfson.

According to everything he had learned, *this* was where Madeline had to be—if she was still with the captain. There was nothing to say she had to be, but several people along the docks and at the taverns in town had pointed him to the same place. They said the captain resided here when he was in town. Although no one remembered him with a woman, Lucien wasn't convinced Alfson would parade Madeline around town, not when he had a wife and family in England. If he was the type to take her as a slave to begin with, it was likely something he kept secret and far distant from his regular life at home.

Or she wasn't there.

Surely he hadn't come all this way for nothing . . .

As he approached the door, anxiety caused him to stop and draw a deep breath before continuing. *Please, God—for Byron's sake,* he prayed and knocked.

There was no answer, no sound coming from inside. Was this place as deserted as it appeared? The captain wasn't in port. Lucien knew that much. Alfson was on a voyage to America. But Lucien had actually believed a rescue might work out better if he didn't run into the captain—since he wasn't confident he would be able to stop himself from ripping the bastard's heart out.

"Madeline?" he called.

Nothing.

Maybe the captain had taken her with him. Or he had passed her to someone else along the way. It was even possible she had come down with something and died.

Fighting the discouragement that edged closer with each passing second, he walked around to the back. There was a garden there—and it was wet, as if someone had watered it. That meant someone was tending to matters at the shack. Who?

Lucien approached the back door and knocked again. "Madeline? It's Lucien. Please, open up."

He was about to force his way inside, to search for any sign of her, when he heard his name.

"Lucien? Is it really you?"

"Madeline? Let me in!" he called. "I'm here to take you home."

"I can't."

He could tell she was weeping.

"Why?"

"I'm chained to the floor."

Lucien broke the door and charged inside to see his half sister huddled on a mattress. She was wearing a threadbare dress and no shoes and there was a leg iron around one ankle that chained her to a metal post in the middle of the floor. The windows were covered; there was a chamber pot in the corner, and a partially eaten crust of bread on a metal plate.

"My God, what is this?"

She didn't answer. "My son!" she said. "Please tell me he's alive and well."

He could see the sores around her ankle, how hard she had tried to free herself. "Byron is fine," he assured her. "I have him at the town house in Mayfair. He is learning a great deal from his new tutor and will be so excited to see you."

"Thank God." She wiped at the tears streaming down her cheeks, which smudged the dirt that covered her face as well. "How did you find me?"

Lucien thought about the London Supply Company, the corpses he had had to dig up and sell as part of his cover, his own monthlong recovery after Jack stabbed him. "It wasn't easy," he admitted. "But I'm here now, and no one is ever going to hurt you again."

As he came toward her, she tilted her head to see around him. "You must be careful," she said. "I never know when Alfson is going to return, or—or when Joseph will show up."

He cast a glance over his shoulder to make sure they were still alone. "Who's Joseph?"

"Alfson pays him to take care of me when he is gone." She motioned at her plate. "What little I get comes from him. But"—her eyes took on a faraway look—"he is even more vile."

"He will pay for what he's done," Lucien promised her. "So will the captain."

Lucien fought his own tears as they stared at each other. "I'm sorry, Madeline. I'm so sorry I allowed this to happen."

She didn't seem to trust him. "Why?" she said. "Why do you even care?"

He offered her a crooked smile. "Because you're my sister."

"What about your mother?"

"She'll have to make the adjustment."

"I don't want to come between you. I have never wanted that."

"You deserve more out of life than you have received," he said and bent down to embrace her.

It took some time to get the saw he needed to cut off Madeline's anklet. If Joseph came by and realized she was no longer alone and defenseless, he didn't make his presence known. Lucien figured there would be time to deal with him and Alfson later. He just wanted to get Madeline somewhere she could bathe, put on some decent clothes and begin to put this part of her life behind her.

"You shouldn't be touching me, Your Grace," she said as he carried her out. "I'm too dirty."

"Lucien, Madeline. I'm your brother. And I'm not concerned about the dirt," he said. "I'm just glad I got you and that you are safe at last."

"What are you thinking about?"

Lucien glanced up to see Madeline watching him carefully. She looked so beautiful standing at the railing of the ship that was carrying them home, the wind blowing her hair back from her face. It was hard to believe that it had only been two weeks since he had rescued her. He'd thought they should stay in Brisbane longer, allow her more time to recover, but she was as anxious to get back to London as he was.

"You must have driven Alfson crazy, always talking about your son," he teased.

She managed a smile despite the subject matter. "It was the fact that I kept trying to escape that he put me on a chain. Our relationship definitely took a turn for the worse, at that point."

"I'll hunt him to the ends of the earth, if I have to."

She covered his hand with her small, cool one. "If you are half as dedicated about that as you were to finding me, I have no doubt you will see him punished. Fortunately, I believe he won't be difficult to trace."

The man she had called Joseph was already in gaol. Lucien had seen to it while he was in Brisbane. He promised himself that Alfson would soon follow.

"But you didn't answer my question," she said.

"About . . . ?"

"A moment ago you looked so . . . pensive. You often look that way, as if . . . as if you are hiding a bit of sadness yourself."

Lucien had been thinking about Abby. He had thought it would get easier to forget her with time, but that definitely wasn't the case. She came to him in his dreams even when he wasn't consciously thinking of her. It didn't help that he carried her elephant with him everywhere. He meant to return it but hadn't yet figured out how.

"I was considering my coming marriage," he admitted. "It's only six or seven months away now."

"To Lady Brimble."

"Yes."

"Are you looking forward to it?"

He affected a shrug. "She seems eager enough to please."

She laughed.

"What?"

"Again, you didn't answer my question."

"If you are you asking if I'm in love with her, no."

"That you would even mention love leads me to believe you might fancy someone else."

Surprised by how intuitive she could be—or was he that transparent?—he quirked an eyebrow at her but said nothing.

"You are!" she accused. "You're in love! With whom?"

He had kept Abby and everything about her to himself. It had been a constant battle to suppress the desire he felt for her, the concern that she might be as miserable as he was, the natural inclination to provide her with a better life. But that afternoon, and several others afterward as they passed the days on the voyage home, he found himself telling Madeline about her.

They had almost arrived in London when she came up behind him, again at the railing, and said, "You have that look on your face."

"Fortunately, you are the only one who knows what it means," he joked. "Once we are home, you can't let my secrets out, you know."

She slid her arm through his. They had grown quite fond of each other in these past weeks. "Can I tell you a secret of my own?"

"Of course."

"I'm worried about you."

"*Me?* But I'm a duke," he teased. "I have everything, remember?"

She could be so somber, so serious. He had merely been trying to make light of the situation, to get her to smile, but she shook her head instead. "Everything but what really matters, and you are *willingly* giving it up."

"I can't break my engagement, Madeline," he said.

"Normally, I wouldn't presume to correct you, Your Grace."

He slanted her a wry look for addressing him so formally. "But . . ."

"But I believe you are making a terrible mistake, trading your happiness for . . . for what you will gain in your marriage."

"I'm not worried about gaining anything. I'm worried about losing something—my dignity, my honor, my reputation."

She briefly rested her head on his shoulder in a loving gesture. "I admire you for caring about those things. But surely the Cavendish dynasty will survive without one more arranged marriage. Could having Abby in your life, by your side as your wife and the mother of your children, really hurt anyone?"

He wished he didn't want to hear what she was telling him quite so much. He knew it was undermining his resolve. But he was so desperate for some way to reunite with Abby. "Hortense would be hurt, for one."

"I doubt you will be doing her any favors by marrying her when your heart is so committed to someone else."

"My love for her could grow."

"It would have to grow quite a bit to keep pace with your resentment—and resentment engenders hate, not love. No one deserves to be hated simply because they unwittingly stood in the way of what should have been."

What should have been . . . Could she be right about that? "I can't think only of myself," he told her.

That earned him a kiss on the cheek and a small, sad little frown. "I may be a common bastard, brother, but I pray you will listen to me before it's too late."

He slid an arm around her, helping her brace against the wind. "If only I could."

Abby had finally penned the letter to her father and planned to drop it in the post that afternoon. She had designated this day to tell her aunt, too. She did what she could to hide her stomach, always wore a loose-fitting dress, even if she had to alter it—and donned an apron or tied something else around her waist. But after what she had seen in the mirror this morning, it was a miracle her aunt hadn't already guessed. She could only credit Emily's continued ignorance to her poor eyesight and that the change had been so gradual. Surely a stranger would spot her condition in an instant.

Abby worked in the garden as she tried to gather the nerve she would need to sit her aunt down and have the discussion that had been weighing on her mind for so long. She had come to like working outdoors in the morning hours, before it grew too warm. It wasn't something Emily particularly enjoyed, so it gave Abby a respite from her aunt's company and provided a refuge of sorts. The garden had become a thing of tremendous beauty as a result of her devotion and love. Sometimes she dragged her time there out for several hours, until her aunt came to chastise her, claiming the sun would ruin her skin despite all she did to cover it.

Abby stayed in the garden that day even longer than normal. So when her aunt didn't come get her, she began to grow curious as to what had stolen Emily's attention. Nothing had ever held her up this long.

After clipping some roses for the dinner table, Abby removed her gloves and her wide-brimmed hat and went inside. She was about to call out to her aunt that the peach rosebush had produced its first bloom—and also that they needed to talk about something very important. But she heard voices in the drawing room and realized her aunt hadn't come to summon her from outdoors because they had company.

"Yes, Your Grace. Thank you for responding to my letter."

Abby froze. Aunt Emily had written Lucien, after all? Even after Abby had pleaded with her not to?

Blind rage might have hit her. Emily was such a busybody; she had no right to get involved! But Abby couldn't feel anything except the rush of anticipation that welled up at the prospect of seeing Lucien again—and fear. Surely, he would notice her condition right away.

"I was hoping you would take an interest, of course," her aunt was saying, "but I can hardly believe that you have troubled yourself to come so far."

"I am eager to see Abby."

"Indeed, and you shall."

"Then she is still here."

"Indeed. She spends her mornings in the garden. I will get her straightaway. But before I do, I just want to . . . er . . . warn you that she can be quite stubborn. And by that I mean she doesn't always know what's best for her. It goes that way with young people sometimes. If she tells you she doesn't wish to marry, you mustn't believe it. You and I both know she would never be happy spending her life as a spinster."

"What a waste that would be," he agreed and sounded surprisingly sincere, although Abby didn't know how he could keep a straight face. He knew her—the real her and not the polite façade she had been forced to create to get along at her aunt's—far better than Emily.

"Yes. Yes, I am glad you see my point." Her aunt clapped her hands but then lowered her voice. "So . . . we must be . . . delicate with her."

"Can I see her?"

Abby almost slipped out the back. She had to run away, go missing until after Lucien left, but Emily came puffing around the corner and caught her before she could slip out the door.

"Abby, you are never going to believe this!" she cried. "His Grace, the Duke of Rowenberry, is here! He must be very interested in helping me arrange a good marriage for you, because he has come clear from London! Who could ask for anything more personal than that? I am now sure everything I have been so worried about will be taken care of. I just hope . . . I hope you will cooperate." She gave Abby a pleading expression. "He will know what is best for you. Please, let him advise you."

He would know what is best because of his title? Abby couldn't believe some of the absurd things Emily said. She considered telling her aunt right then—just to watch her face after thinking so highly of a duke simply for being a duke—that Lucien had fathered a child with her and she was carrying it right now. But, with him waiting, that was a conversation best reserved for later. Thank goodness she hadn't told Aunt Emily about the baby quite yet. Somehow she needed to get through the next few minutes without giving away her condition.

"Go. Talk to him," Emily said and gave her a little push.

Briefly closing her eyes, Abby fought the tears that threatened. She couldn't break down the moment she saw him. That would only humiliate her and embarrass him. But the lump that was growing in her throat threatened to choke her—and her heart was beating so terribly hard.

She might have argued that she needed time to change, but she knew her other dresses wouldn't conceal her condition half as well, so she threw her shoulders back and entered the drawing room.

He stood at the window with his back to her, seemingly deep in thought, and she stopped behind a high-backed chair for the cover it could give her. "Your Grace," she said softly.

He pivoted immediately, and his eyes swept over what he could see of her. "Abby . . ."

"You look well." She managed a smile to go with that understatement. He looked even better than normal.

She got the impression he wanted to come to her, to take her in his arms but held off. Emily had entered the room behind her and was looking on, which made it imperative that they be cautious of both their words and actions.

"So do you, thank God," he said. "I've been so worried."

"I'm fine," she insisted.

"You've been happy?"

"As happy as can be expected."

"Let's all sit down," Emily suggested, but Abby wasn't about to come out from behind the chair and Lucien was too wrapped up in what he wanted to say to respond to her aunt.

"I found Madeline, Abby."

Abby gripped the chair in front of her. "Where? When?"

"Emmett and Bill are the ones who stole Jack's money. They sold Madeline to a ship's captain, who took her to Australia and used her as a slave, so that Jack would think it was her."

"No!"

"Yes."

"And you've seen her?"

"I have indeed."

"She's . . . well then, I hope?"

"Alive and well and living with me in Mayfair."

She clasped her hands together. "But . . . what about your mother? Surely, she wasn't happy to see Madeline return."

"She didn't say much. I didn't give her the opportunity. She merely packed up and retired to the country, and I have to admit I have not missed her company."

"I see." Her smile felt natural for the first time in ages. "Little Byron must be so happy."

"He is. We all are."

She felt a moment of confusion as certain details came to mind. "But Emmett and Bill are . . . are dead, hanged. How did you find out?"

"Agnes came forward." He went to the coat rack, where Aunt Emily had hung his coat, and retrieved her elephant from the pocket, which he held out to her. "And, just recently, she brought me this."

Abby covered her mouth. "My mother's gift . . ." Now she understood why he had made the trip. He knew how important the ivory elephant was to her.

Fortunately, Emily was standing closer to him than Abby was and took the elephant, so Abby was able to continue concealing the shape of her body.

"Elizabeth, God rest her soul," Emily said. "She gave you this?"

Abby nodded. "Not long before she died." She focused on Lucien again. "And what of Anna Harper? Did you ever determine if she died a natural death?"

"I believe so. According to what Bill said before he went to the gallows, she died of illness, as we have already been told."

"That's a relief. I'm glad the Bolstrums didn't harm her."

"Yes. Three hanged is enough."

She swallowed hard. "Indeed. Thank you for coming—and for letting me know."

He didn't take his leave, as she expected. He stepped forward and cleared his throat. "Your aunt has been concerned about you."

"My aunt has always been concerned about me," she said. "Please, don't allow anything she has conveyed unsettle you in any way. When she mentioned soliciting your help, I pleaded with her to leave you in peace."

"I believe that. But she thinks you need to marry, and I have to say I agree with her wholeheartedly. I would see you safe and well taken care of, if I could."

Abby held up a hand. "Don't involve yourself, Your Grace. I can make my own decisions and . . . selections, especially when it comes to a husband, thank you."

"But I have the ideal candidate in mind."

Abby couldn't help being hurt that he would not only marry someone else but presume to pawn her off on a friend or associate. Did he think they would be able to continue their affair if they both had a spouse? Was this an attempt to bring her back to London, where they would once again be able to see each other? "Ideal in what regard, Your Grace?"

His eyes, when they riveted on hers, were filled with . . . hope? He certainly didn't seem to think he was doing anything she might find offensive. "Ideal in that he loves you, Abby, and only you. And he will do everything in his power to make you happy. I think you should accept a man like that."

Abby felt her eyebrows slide up. "Truly. If there was such a man."

"But there is." A smile curved his lips. "That man is me."

Aunt Emily gasped and sank into a chair as if she might faint, but Abby and Lucien couldn't concentrate on anything except each other.

"Lucien, no," Abby said. "You could never be happy feeling as if you have let your mother, your entire family, down. Don't let Aunt Emily's letter force you into something you don't really want."

"I didn't get your aunt's letter until *after* I had made my decision, Abby. I have had several months to think about it. And Madeline managed to talk some sense into me along the way."

"Sense . . . ?"

"She told me the greatest tragedy would be to deny a love like ours." He came to her then, and went down on one knee. "Will you marry me, Abby? Will you be my wife?"

Abby could scarcely breathe, scarcely think. Surely, she was dreaming. "And your fiancée?"

"Hortense comes from a very powerful family. She will make an advantageous match . . . eventually."

"What about your mother? Without question, she will disapprove."

"That may be true, but there are several things she will have to learn to live with. Having you in my life will be one of them." He caught her hand. "Well? What do you say?"

It wouldn't be easy to be despised by his mother as Madeline had been. There would be other difficulties as well. She would very likely be spurned by his entire social class. But how could she deny him? "Yes! I say yes. You are the only man I could ever marry, because you are the only man I will ever love."

Abby was so happy she forgot about her pregnancy long enough to let him sweep her into his arms. Then he froze, and his hands sought the swell she had been hiding.

"Abby?" He pulled back to look at what he had felt.

"Perhaps we will have a son shortly after the wedding," she said.

He looked stunned. "When?"

"I have four months more."

He came to his feet. "And you weren't going to tell me?"

She gave him a look that pleaded with him to understand. "I didn't want to put you in the same position your father was in, Lucien. If you came back to me, it had to be because you loved me, not because you felt a sense of obligation. I didn't want to live the rest of my life feeling like I had forced you or created a burden you didn't want to carry."

His mouth opened and shut twice before he could find words. He seemed completely overcome. "Thank God I came to my senses. I almost lost even more than you," he said at length, as if the mere thought frightened him, and buried his face in her neck.

"*You're with child, too?*" Emily cried, but they were kissing and couldn't answer.

Epilogue

Lucien paced in the drawing room where he awaited news of the birth of his baby along with Abby's father, who had just received his knighthood; Mrs. Fitzgerald, who seemed to be a bit more than a housekeeper to Edwin these days; and Madeline; Byron and two cousins Lucien had grown up with. He wasn't sure he had ever been quite so nervous or concerned about anything in his life. He and Abby had only been married a short while, but he had grown to love her more than ever in that time. He couldn't bear the thought of losing her if something went wrong.

"Have another glass of brandy," Edwin suggested. "It might calm your nerves."

It might also get him roaring drunk, and Lucien didn't want that. As useless as he felt, as unable to defend Abby against the threat she faced, he couldn't abandon her by becoming intoxicated. "No, thank you."

"They will both be fine," Edwin assured him. "Dr. Bartello is the best baby doctor there is. He has taught at Aldersgate for years."

Mrs. Fitzgerald beamed at him as if what he had said had to be God's own truth—completely trusting and adoring—and he acknowledged that by patting her hand.

"I appreciate that," Lucien responded, but nothing could ease his anxiety, not until he heard some word that Abby was fine and the baby, too.

"You will soon have an heir," one of his cousins said. They had been speculating on the gender of the baby all day, in an effort to distract him and help pass the time. But even that wouldn't work any longer.

No one mentioned the dowager duchess. His mother had declined to attend this gathering, and that bothered Lucien. She wouldn't accept Abby, as he had feared. But he didn't, for a moment, regret the decision he had made to marry her. Abby changed everything, made his world better and brighter and happier. He would give up *anything* before he would give her up.

"Uncle Lucien?"

Lucien focused on his nephew. "Aunt Abby told me to tell you, when you were at your most worried, that she is a strong woman and will make it through."

Leave it to Abby to think of how he would feel ahead of time. "Your aunt means a great deal to me."

"I know," he responded, sounding much older than his years.

Madeline lovingly mussed her son's hair. "It shouldn't be much longer, Lucien."

It had already been twelve hours! Lucien wasn't sure how much more he could endure—and he wasn't even the one going through the pain!

"It seems like it should have happened already," he said.

With Mrs. Fitzgerald always only a few feet away, Edwin perched on the arm of the sofa. He acted as if he had no doubt that all was well, but Lucien could discern the worry that had crept into his eyes as the hours passed. That was what frightened him the most. If even Edwin was growing concerned . . . "First babies sometimes take their time."

Suddenly, Lucien realized that he couldn't wait another second. "I have to see her."

Edwin scowled at him. "Have faith, man. Let Dr. Bartello do his job."

"I can't," he responded. "I must reassure myself. I must—go to her." With that, he strode out of the room and took the stairs two at a time. What had he been thinking, waiting in some drawing room in Abby's moment of need? He didn't care how unseemly it was for him to attend the birth, he would not be denied. He could not believe he had allowed convention to trap him thus far.

But as he approached the bedroom they shared, he heard Abby cry out in pain and froze. Could he really stand by and watch her suffer?

He hovered in indecision for several minutes—until another cry rang out.

Only this time it was a baby's squall.

That got him moving again. His child had been born. It was obviously alive. Was it a boy or a girl? And what of Abby?

Saying yet another silent prayer for her safety, he threw open the doors. The doctor had the baby in his arms, but Lucien couldn't focus on that. First, he had to know Abby had survived.

"Get out of my way," he snapped as the servants who were helping the doctor came toward him as if they would stop him. "I want to see my wife!"

They parted immediately. No doubt they could tell by the tone of his voice that he would brook no interference. There was blood everywhere, so much that the sight of it nearly brought him to his knees. How could a woman survive that?

Then he saw her. She was pale and exhausted as she lay on the bed, propped up by several pillows, but when she looked up she offered him a wan smile. "Hello, Your Grace."

"Abby . . ." He crossed to her immediately, took her hand and raised it to his lips. Tears welled up at the same time and, as much as that weakness embarrassed him, he was powerless to stop them. "I have been so worried."

"I'm fine," she said and even managed to give his hand a squeeze. "I'm going to be fine."

He looked to the doctor for confirmation, and was relieved when Bartello gave him a confident nod. "She came through it wonderfully," he said. "She is a determined young woman."

"But all the blood . . ."

"Is normal," the doctor said. "We would have cleaned it up before inviting you in had you waited just a little longer."

He couldn't have waited any longer. He had nearly gone mad as it was. "And my baby?"

One of the servants stepped forward and put a squirming bundle into his arms. "Congratulations, Your Grace. You have a son—and he's a big boy with a powerful set of lungs."

"Look what you gave me," he told Abby in absolute awe.

She focused on him briefly, but then her eyes closed in apparent exhaustion. "He's beautiful."

Lucien pressed his lips to her forehead. "Not as beautiful as you, my love," he said. "There is no one as beautiful as you."

ABOUT THE AUTHOR

MICAH KANDROS, 2011

When Brenda Novak caught her daycare provider drugging her young children with cough medicine to get them to sleep all day while she was away at work, she quit her job as a loan officer to stay home with them. She felt she could no longer trust others with their care. But she still had to find some way to make a living. That was when she picked up one of her favorite books. She was looking for a brief escape from the stress and worry—and found the inspiration to become a novelist.

Since her first sale to HarperCollins in 1998 (*Of Noble Birth*), Brenda has written fifty books in a variety of genres. Now a *New York Times* and *USA Today* bestselling author, she still juggles her writing career with the demands of her large family and interests such as cycling, traveling and reading. A three-time Rita nominee, Brenda has won many awards for her books, including The National Readers' Choice, The Bookseller's Best, The Book Buyer's Best and The Holt Medallion. She also runs an annual online auction for diabetes research every May at www.brendanovak.com (her youngest son suffers from this disease). To date, she's raised nearly $2.4 million.